ZODIAC RISING

ZODIAC RISING

KATIE ZHAO

Random House ⌂ New York

Text copyright © 2024 by Katherine Zhao
Jacket art copyright © 2024 by Deb JJ Lee
Interior illustrations copyright © 2024 by Cathy Kwan

Visit us on the Web! GetUnderlined.com

Educators and librarians, for a variety of teaching tools, visit us at RHTeachersLibrarians.com

Library of Congress Cataloging-in-Publication Data
Name: Zhao, Katie, author.
Title: Zodiac rising / Katie Zhao.
Description: First edition. | New York: Random House Children's Books, 2024. |
Series: Descendants of the zodiac; 1 | Summary: "When a student is killed over priceless treasure,
the Descendants of Chinese zodiac magic assemble a crew to avenge the murder and heist
back what is rightfully theirs"—Provided by publisher.
Identifiers: LCCN 2023044366 (print) | LCCN 2023044367 (ebook) |
ISBN 978-0-593-64641-0 (trade) | ISBN 978-0-593-64642-7 (lib. bdg.) |
ISBN 978-0-593-64643-4 (ebook)
Subjects: CYAC: Mythology, Chinese—Fiction. | Zodiac—Fiction. |
Lost and found possessions—Fiction. | Friends—Fiction. | Fantasy. | LCGFT: Fantasy fiction. | Novels.
Classification: LCC PZ7.1.Z513 Zo 2024 (print) | LCC PZ7.1.Z513 (ebook) | DDC [Fic]—dc23

The text of this book is set in 11.25-point Adobe Garamond Pro.

Editor: Tricia Lin
Cover Designers: Liz Dresner and Casey Moses
Interior Designer: Jen Valero
Copy Editor: Barbara Bakowski
Managing Editor: Rebecca Vitkus
Production Manager: Tim Terhune

Printed in the United States of America
10 9 8 7 6 5 4 3 2 1
First Edition

Random House Children's Books supports the First Amendment and celebrates the right to read.

For my family—near, far, and found

龙的传人

They came in pursuit of a better life.
They got much more than they bargained for.

EVANGELINE LONG

"I'm going to rob them, and then I'm going to kill them."

CHINESE NAME:

龙依诺 (Lóng Yīnuò)

HOUSE:

Dragon

SUPERNATURAL DESIGNATION:

Vampire

ROLE IN HEIST:

Mastermind

TRISTAN SHE

"We've been on the run nonstop, so forgive me
if my body requires more sustenance than just fumes and vibes."

CHINESE NAME:

蛇健强 (Shé Jiànqiáng)

HOUSE:

Snake

SUPERNATURAL DESIGNATION:

Werewolf

ROLE IN HEIST:

Master of thieving

NICHOLAS HU

"I've had decades of experience over you in fighting others for the bill."

CHINESE NAME:

虎俊文 (Hǔ Jùnwén)

HOUSE:

Tiger

SUPERNATURAL DESIGNATION:

Fox spirit

ROLE IN HEIST:

Master of disguise

ALICE JIANG

"Can you tell me more about my father?"

CHINESE NAME:

江爱玲 (Jiāng Àilíng)

HOUSE:

Boar

SUPERNATURAL DESIGNATION:

?

ROLE IN HEIST:

Master of mind reading

PROLOGUE

It is a tale as old as time: the destructive hubris of a man bringing about catastrophic consequences. Throughout history, wars have been fought to stroke men's egos. Kingdoms have fallen to prop up a man's pride. Heroes in epics have met such grisly, tragic ends—all because mankind dared to defy nature, dared to defy the gods themselves.

This particular story of hubris, however, is not an ending, but a beginning.

Doomsday began like this: with a single monster spawning on the shores of the Middle Kingdom. It was a foul thing stitched from nightmares, an abomination crafted by the hands of vengeful gods. A large, slimy creature that at once had gills and lungs; a four-legged, winged beast that could travel by land or sea or air. The monster opened its mouth to release a roar, a terrible sound that struck fear into the hearts of even the bravest men, and with one foul breath, it parted the sand all the way down the shore.

The monster's appearance was not a warning, nor was it an omen. It was a reckoning. It was damnation.

In the same manner as an infestation of cockroaches, first there was only one; then, before the alarm was even raised, there were many. The monsters terrorized the people of the Middle Kingdom. They razed villages. They devoured men, women, and children. Destruction trailed in their wake, and in no time at all, they brought the kingdom—and its Emperor—to its knees.

Nobody knew for certain where these monsters had come from, nor why, but a village prophet spread the rumor, and the rumor traveled far and wide. The monsters, which the people named Wrathlings, had been born from the first Emperor's greed. The Emperor, who had drained the land's bountiful resources to build a vast and rich empire, had never stopped to consider the nature he conquered; the animals whose homes he razed; the gods whose dominion he claimed as *his*.

And so the Wrathlings burst forth, woven from greed and nightmares, making the gods' displeasure known.

When all that was good and precious about the land was nearly gone, when at last he understood the costly price of his hubris, the Emperor, who had exhausted all his options, held a meeting with his advisors. They agreed that there was only one chance for the salvation of the kingdom; the Emperor needed to pay the ultimate price. Only with great sacrifice could great miracles happen, they said. The gods would settle for nothing less.

On a cold, stormy night, it happened thus: the Emperor sacrificed his newborn son to make a prayer to the gods.

"Help my subjects!" cried the Emperor. "Banish the Wrathlings. My people, oh, my people—they are dying."

Miraculously, the Jade Emperor, ruler of all the Heavens, answered the plea, his disembodied voice filling the whole room with a sense of despair. "It is too late to undo what has been done. However, given that you've learned your lesson, I will provide you with twelve warriors to protect the Middle Kingdom from the Wrathlings. Should you ever revert to your old ways, your warriors will disappear, and your kingdom will fall to complete ruin."

The Emperor, terrified beyond belief, babbled that he would spend the rest of his days in service of the gods. In a blink, a group of robed warriors surrounded the Emperor.

"We pledge our services, and those of our descendants, to the protection of the Middle Kingdom, now and evermore," they said, each bent on one knee.

The warriors formed the Circle of Twelve, a fountain surrounded by twelve bronze zodiac fountainheads in Beijing's Old Summer Palace, the source of their power. As long as the Summer Palace stood resilient against any enemies, so would the warriors.

And thus a new day dawned upon the Middle Kingdom. The Emperor took great care to ensure that the twelve warriors—and their descendants—would be treated with the utmost care and respect. In record time, the twelve zodiac warriors slew the Wrathlings that had threatened the kingdom. Stories of their greatness traveled far and wide, and soon the entire kingdom knew their names.

The Shus, descended from the rat bloodline, quick-witted and charming.

The Nius, descended from the ox bloodline, strong and stubborn.

The Hus, descended from the tiger bloodline, courageous and competitive.

The Tus, descended from the rabbit bloodline, elegant and kind.

The Longs, descended from the dragon bloodline, intelligent and charismatic.

The Shes, descended from the snake bloodline, sharp-sighted and adventurous.

The Mas, descended from the horse bloodline, lively and independent.

The Yangs, descended from the sheep bloodline, gentle and empathetic.

The Hous, descended from the monkey bloodline, sharp and curious.

The Jis, descended from the rooster bloodline, hardworking and observant.

The Gous, descended from the dog bloodline, honest and loyal.

The Zhus, descended from the boar bloodline, generous and smart.

With the guidance of the twelve warriors and their descendants, peace at last fell upon the land. But peace is a fickle thing, and humans in particular are a species prone to violence.

Long after the first Emperor had withered to ashes, many generations after the original twelve Descendants were assigned to protect the Middle Kingdom, when the land became known around the world as China, the greatest threat to the Descendants arrived at last, the most horrifying of monsters.

They were foreigners, looking to strip lands of their precious treasures and resources for their own gain.

War was an inevitable consequence of the arrival of greedy men with monumental egos and loose morals. It was the fall of 1860, in the midst of the Second Opium War, and China took a bloody beating. British soldiers pillaged the Old Summer Palace, which crumbled under sheer brute force. And the beautiful city of Beijing fell at the feet of the plunderers.

Ancient techniques clashed with modern warfare, and even the Descendants could not fully prevail against the onslaught of evil. The Circle of Twelve was smashed wide open; the foreign devils carried off five of the bronze zodiac fountainheads and other precious art.

And a curse fell upon the Descendants, such that they turned into supernatural creatures, such that they lost their magic and might. It is a terribly gutting experience, to lose everything and everyone dear in one fell swoop.

The Descendants never forgot, and they never forgave. Year after year, decade after decade, their yearning and aching festered and grew, and oh—should the thieves ever fall into their hands, not even the gods themselves could save them from the wrath of the Descendants.

PART
ONE

1

JULIUS

Julius Long was no stranger to being thrust into unexpected, poten-tially dangerous situations. In fact, he was something of an expert on navigating—and evading—danger. For decades now, Julius had guarded the legacy of the wealthy Long family, one of Manhattan's most powerful players, which had primed his abilities to improvise and survive perilous plights by the skin of his teeth.

It was shortly after sunset on a school night, and Julius had cut class to come out to the glittering Brooklyn Bridge to wait for someone who might not show up—or, worse, someone who might show up to put an end to him once and for all.

Julius had told no one about his plans for the night. Not his com-bat teacher, Elder Hou, who was doubtless already worried by Julius's unexplained absence. Not his Talons, his eight-member gang, who were at his beck and call and who controlled the streets of Chinatown. Not even his younger sister, Evangeline. Oh, he'd left a note behind for Evangeline—he couldn't shake off the thought that this dangerous de-cision might be his last. Strolling into what was almost certainly a trap was a rash and irresponsible gamble on his part—a move that was most unlike him, the levelheaded Chancellor who headed the High Council at Earthly Branches Academy.

Julius hadn't slept or fed on blood in days. He didn't really need the sleep, as vampires could operate fine without rest, but he found himself regretting not downing one last blood bag before heading out tonight. Well, it was too late for regrets now. No matter what, Julius would see through his duty to his people, the Descendants.

"Gou, Ji, Yang, She, Long," Julius said into the shadows, as he had been instructed. Dog, rooster, sheep, snake, dragon.

For a long moment, only silence answered. Then the quiet was broken by the sound of chatter. A pair of people, a homeless man and woman by the looks of their disheveled clothing, walked by. They threw Julius a curious look.

"What're you looking at?" Julius grumbled, and the pair hurried off.

Annoyance welled within Julius as he gazed upon the abandoned building in front of him. It was once the site of the Fulton Fish Market, but now the old building stood silent, left to crumble and rot. It was also the site of Julius's appointment, except it was past 8 p.m. now, and the appointer was nowhere in sight. If there was one thing Julius despised, it was having his time wasted.

The only reason Julius had come tonight was the magical stationery that had appeared on his desk the day before. It was a sign, he'd thought, the sign he had been waiting for. At long last, the five missing bronze zodiac statues—dog, rooster, sheep, snake, dragon—had surely been found. Whoever had sent the note was no doubt a powerful being capable of great magic. A shaman, perhaps. More likely, the note had come from a faerie. It would explain why the note had been covered in glimmering magical dust. But the dust could very well be a red herring.

Well, no matter. In moments, Julius would have his answer.

Come alone to the building where the Fulton Fish Market used to be, near the Brooklyn Bridge on South Street between Beekman and Fulton Streets,

4

at 8 p.m. sharp tomorrow. I have information about the five missing zodiac heads. Announce your presence to me by naming the heads, and I will give you that which you desire—for a price.

The note had burst into fire and burned into nothingness shortly after Julius read it, but thankfully his sharp memory retained the contents of the message. It was a risk coming out here, but it was a risk Julius was willing to take. The fae hadn't communicated with the Descendants in decades. He needed to see for himself why that had changed. Why now, of all times, they'd decided to come forward with information regarding the missing fountainheads.

After receiving the note, Julius had rushed about the estate, taking care of as many affairs as possible, tying up loose ends. He did his best to behave as though it were business as usual, especially in front of Evangeline. Julius's darling little sister mustn't know that he was swimming through dangerous waters. Not until it was necessary for her to know. He would do anything to protect and help her—even when he knew she wouldn't agree with his actions. That was why, against his every instinct, Julius had traipsed out here tonight.

A hoarse whisper floated on the wind, entering Julius's ear.

"My, how obedient you are, Descendant."

That voice. He could've *sworn* he recognized that voice, though he couldn't quite place it. Was it one of the fae he'd clashed with during and after the Opium Wars? Julius's memory was exceptional, yet even he could not recall specific details from the battles he'd fought over a century ago. Back then, the shamans were waging a turf war with the fae in Chinatown, which ended in neutrality in the 1930s. Both had kept to themselves afterward, with the shamans disappearing into the Underground and the fae taking up residence north of Fifty-Ninth Street. As immortals who were proud of their magic and legacy, the shamans and fae particularly detested supernatural beings who had once been human, like the Descendants. In fact, following the turf war, the shamans and fae agreed, for once, that it was in each of their best interests never to align with the Descendants, to do whatever they could to keep the Descendants from growing too powerful.

In this manner, the supernaturals reached an uneasy truce. The difficult thing about an uneasy truce, however, is that any single incident can upset the balance.

Tonight, Julius thought, could be that upsetting event.

Julius clenched his hands into fists, whirling around. This being, whoever they were, brimmed with ancient magic. He sensed the energy humming in the air, subtle but sharp. He felt it deep in his bones. And he knew instinctively, too, that on this night—an otherwise innocuous summer night, a night like any other—he had arrived, at last, at the point of no return. He had delivered himself to Death's doorstep, in fact. The knowledge didn't frighten Julius. It electrified him.

Twelve powerful families—no, all of China and its diaspora—had waited decades for an answer, for justice, for anything at all to be done in the wake of the ruination of the Old Summer Palace. Now Julius sensed that he was finally on the brink of uncovering something revolutionary. The question was—would he survive to carry the message back to his people?

For once in his life, Julius did not have the answer.

The messenger emerged out of thin air, wearing emerald robes that shimmered with golden light at the ends of his sleeves. His long white-blond hair floated around him. His skin was the palest snow, glowing with an ethereal light, and his eyes were the black of eternal night. A faerie, indeed.

Julius had to force himself to glance away from the faerie, lest his beauty blind him or drive him mad. He knew the tricks of the fae—knew that their glamour made them appear even more beautiful than they were—and yet, for all his decades of knowledge, he still found himself vulnerable to faerie beauty. Perhaps the immortals were right. Perhaps those who were once mortal would always bear their mortal weaknesses.

"You are the one who sent the note?" asked Julius, his voice hoarse. He cleared his throat and straightened his shoulders, drawing himself to his full height. He felt tiny next to the faerie, and hideous compared with his beauty. But Julius had to at least *appear* to be in control of the situation, and he quite excelled at this after more than a hundred years of practice. "You told me you had information about the missing zodiac fountainheads."

"I do. In fact, I know exactly where they are." The Mandarin rolled off the faerie's tongue as smoothly as though it were his native language, but Julius knew the truth: the fae were extremely intelligent and worldly creatures who needed only to overhear one foreign conversation in order to smoothly incorporate it into their linguistic repertoire. The faerie's voice was high and wispy, and it had a lyrical quality, like a song—an enticing melody that could easily ensnare Julius, if he wasn't careful.

"The fountainheads are together? All five of them? In *Faerieland*?" For a moment, Julius's disbelief overcame the power of the faerie's aura. He hadn't expected all five missing fountainheads to be together; he thought, coming here tonight, that he'd learn information about one or two at best.

The faerie nodded. "Do not accuse the Folk of being thieves," he continued as though he'd read Julius's mind, his words adopting a sharp, biting quality. "We merely intercepted the British soldiers—the true culprits."

Still, you did not come forward until now, Julius thought spitefully, but he managed to restrain himself from retorting aloud. Instead he smoothed over his features. The first trick to successfully doing business, which his own father had taught him over a century ago, was mastering the poker face. Showing emotion was as good as giving the other party the upper hand.

"Well," Julius said, a bit of snark oozing into his voice despite his best efforts, "I am unsurprised that the fae have secretly had possession of Descendant property, given how your kind is . . . mischief-prone."

The faerie covered his mouth with a slender hand, and he began to laugh. That, too, sounded like music, which both pleased and irritated Julius no end.

"Why are you coming forward now?" Julius asked, eyes narrowed in suspicion. "Why are you helping me?"

"The fae do not all think alike. We are not a monolith. We do not all believe that pillaging and thieving are proper conduct."

"Could have fooled me," Julius muttered. From what he'd seen, the fae never cared about anyone besides themselves, but they *did* enjoy the opportunity to make fools out of the shamans. "So how can I find the fountainheads?"

The faerie scoffed. "*You* can't find them. Or rather, I should say, you aren't the one meant to bring them back to your people."

"What's that supposed to mean?" Julius asked sharply.

"A faerie Seer delivered a prophecy to the High Council of the Descendants one day and one night after the Circle of Twelve was broken." The faerie's voice grew lower and more ethereal, and he closed his eyes as he recited the words that Julius had heard so long ago: "*The key to restoring glory rests with Midsummer's sprout; but if greed sows discord, harmony will be in doubt.*"

"I know, I know. I was already Chancellor of the High Council by then. I heard that prophecy in person." Every Descendant knew about this prophecy, so Julius wasn't sure why the faerie was rambling on about such matters of common knowledge. He tried to bite back his impatience, but this proved very difficult, as it had been well over a century since the Circle of Twelve had been cruelly broken, and now, at last, he stood a chance of reclaiming the might that rightfully belonged to his people—if only this creature would *stop talking in riddles.*

Now the faerie's eyes fluttered open, and they had, alarmingly, changed color from black to white, like two glowing orbs against the dark of night. Ignoring Julius's frustration, he continued. "The Seer then stated that he would make a reappearance when the time was nigh, when the full moon coincided with the summer solstice during the Midsummer Celebration. He would claim the soul of a worthy Descendant in exchange for the successful completion of the prophecy."

This, too, Julius recalled the Seer predicting those many years ago; only now, a small pit of dread began to form in his stomach. There was a hungry glint in the faerie's eye that he did not like. The full moon . . . He glanced upward, and his stomach did a flip. The moon was a swollen, almost fully circular orb in the sky.

Slowly, ever so slowly, Julius began to back away. His instinct was screaming for him to run, to put as much space between him and this faerie as he possibly could. It had been a very long time since he was that young, adjusting to his new role as Chancellor, and the sands of time had blurred that memory, had dulled every sharp edge of the faerie Seer's appearance, so he had not put the pieces together at first. The longer he stared at the faerie, however, the more puzzle pieces clicked into place. "You . . ."

"Did you really forget my face, Long Yineng?" asked the faerie, his lips curling into a smile that did not reach his eyes.

"It's Julius now." This he said in English, as a reminder that he had spent most of his life in the States and was as much American now as he was Chinese.

"Julius? An American name." The faerie shifted just as easily from Mandarin to English.

Julius spoke with a calm and pleasant air even as he continued to inch backward. "Indeed. Nobody has called me Yineng in a long, long time."

"Shedding your identity and shunning your old ways in a drab attempt at assimilation. What could possibly be more American?"

Julius might have taken offense under different circumstances, but at the moment, he didn't care if the faerie pelted him with every insult under the sun; he just had to keep him talking while he planned his escape. The fingers of his left hand curled into a fist, and then unfurled. In his palm, there was an emptiness where once there had been blazing power, the ghost of a magic long lost. If only he still held that power—then Julius would bring this infernal faerie to his knees by Paralyzing him with a single flick of his wrist, as he had done to many unfortunate opponents back in the glory days of the Descendants. Yet Julius had made peace with this *new* life of his, this immortal life—and he would not give it up without a fight.

The faerie did not follow as Julius continued to back away, and this was even more frightening than if he had. The only reason the faerie Seer would not come after him was that he had absolute confidence Julius could not escape.

"I must confess I am a little disappointed in you, *Julius,* but that is neither here nor there. It is time now. The full moon and summer solstice will converge in a little over three days, and I have come to collect my payment from the Descendants."

"You cannot," Julius stated with as much authority as he could force into his voice—a considerable amount. He had led the Descendants for decades, had built them up once more after the pillaging of the Old Summer Palace wiped out their numbers and might and morale. Julius was accustomed to bending others to his will, and a faerie Seer would be no different. "How dare you try to take *my* soul? You must be out of your mind."

The faerie's eyes flashed a brilliant red, and the air around him crackled with magic. "A true leader would willingly sacrifice himself for the good of his people, Julius."

"A true *fool* would do such a thing."

The Seer blinked, unfazed. Perhaps he often encountered resistance from those who heard his prophecies. "When your kind summoned me all those years ago, I named the hefty price of the prophecy, and you agreed to pay it, did you not?"

"I didn't realize you would come for *my* soul," Julius growled. "You can have almost any other soul except mine. The Descendants would not be here without my leadership, and they cannot hope to endure without me."

"But the soul of any other Descendant would be lesser, and thus worth the sacrifice?" Contempt dripped from the faerie's words.

"You can drop that high-and-mighty tone with me, Seer. I'm not here to debate moralities with you. My soul is not up for bargaining."

"Oh, rest assured—there will be no bargaining tonight," said the faerie coldly. "I delivered the prophecy, and now I am here to collect my payment. You cannot stop fate, so do not try, Julius Long."

Quick as a flash, the faerie flung out his sleeve toward Julius's chest—the place where a heart would have been beating if he had still been human. A vampire's reflexes were superbly fast, and Julius was able to duck the attack. A sharp weapon went sailing over his head.

"A wooden stake," Julius sneered, backflipping high up into the air and landing in a nearby tree. "You came prepared."

The Seer licked his lips as he gazed up at Julius. "You really ought not to prolong the inevitable, Descendant. You are only drawing out your own excruciating ending."

"We'll see which of us meets an excruciating ending tonight." With that, Julius leapt down and grabbed the wooden stake. There was a struggle to gain control of the weapon, during which Julius judged that he'd vastly underestimated the strength of the faerie Seer. His grip was like iron, his eyes returned to their bottomless black.

"Give it up," Julius snarled. He and the Seer were so close to each other now that they were practically nose to nose. They were the same height, yet the faerie still dared to look down upon him.

"What you are doing now will cost your people greatly. Do not be stupid."

Julius's muscles were aching. Even his superhuman strength was slowly being sapped by the faerie Seer.

"You grow weak," hissed the faerie.

"I do nothing of the sort."

"Oh, do not lie to me, Descendant. I am sorry for this—truly I am— but there is no other way. Such a grand prophecy requires steep payment. Trading five priceless artifacts for just one—rather a nice bargain for you, don't you think?"

Cold sweat beaded on Julius's forehead, dripping down his nose. Despite the fact that the odds of survival were stacked against him, Julius maintained a cool, calm facade. If he had learned one lesson over decades of navigating life-threatening situations, it was this: There was always a way out. One only needed to be clever and resourceful enough to pave the path of escape.

"What does a faerie Seer want with a soul, anyway?" Julius asked. It was imperative that he keep the faerie talking for as long as possible.

"A soul, even a mortal human one, is worth so much more than you could even fathom, Descendant. And the soul of the leader of the Descendants—the amount of *power* one could harness from it . . ." The faerie Seer closed his eyes dreamily and shuddered. "These souls are wasted in your bodies."

Gritting his teeth, Julius glanced up into the faerie's face, and the face shifted, and he saw him. Truly saw him, in all his great and terrible beauty. He did not know whether he wanted to fall at the Seer's feet and kiss the ground or sprint away screaming.

"You—" Julius let go of the wooden stake, almost without thinking. It finally, finally dawned on him that he wasn't going to make it back to the estate. And Evangeline—he would be leaving his mèi mei all alone, just as their parents had left them all those long years ago. He'd known that this outcome was a possibility, but faced with the imminent reality of it, Julius was filled with a piercing sensation of fear and regret.

Was he truly ready? For parting with Evangeline forever? For the end of everything he'd ever known?

"Struggling is pointless. It will only prolong your suffering." A note of sadness entered the Seer's voice as he aimed the wooden stake at Julius's chest. Perhaps he regretted what he was doing.

Faced with his mortality after so long, Julius thought only of his sister. She was going to be upset when he didn't bring her a fresh bag of blood tomorrow, as he did every evening before classes. He croaked, "Is Evangeline . . . Midsummer's sprout . . ."

"Farewell, Descendant."

When the faerie pressed the tip of the wooden stake into Julius's chest, fire burst forth out of nowhere, surrounding them. The Seer's eyes widened in surprise. But it was too late to choke out any last words, for the smoke had already entered the lungs of both Descendant and faerie.

Sirens sounded from the distance, the macabre tune to which the city thrummed. In fact, the song of sirens was so commonplace that it would scarcely turn the heads of the Manhattanites, who were focused on rushing to their next destination.

By the time the fire trucks at last reached the bottom of the Brooklyn Bridge, it was too late. Julius Long, beloved son of the late Muchen and Jiaqi Long, Chancellor of the High Council of the Descendants, the last remaining male heir to the House of Dragon . . . was gone.

2
EVANGELINE

Evangeline Long was certain that these painfully dull council meetings would be the death of her. That is, *if* she were still able to die. She hadn't known the fear of death for over one hundred and fifty years now, not since the day she was cursed to eternity as a vampire.

And what a *curse* it was. Although some supernaturals thought of immortality as a blessing, as they were all very hard to kill, the prospect of living on a deteriorating planet with no end in sight was horribly depressing to Evangeline—especially given that the trade-off for immortality was losing almost all her magical abilities as a Descendant. Once, Evangeline had possessed the power to Compel others with her words, but that had been stripped from her. There was an ache in her body where her magic had once been, like a missing limb, and every day, that ache throbbed and grew.

Over the decades, Evangeline had, out of a combination of desperation and boredom, attempted to end her existence in a number of ways. It turned out that she lacked the necessary willpower to end herself with the only surefire method—by stabbing a wooden stake through her cold,

dead heart. One of her fellow Descendants had gone out this way a few decades back, and the whole ordeal was unnecessarily nasty and messy. So Evangeline had, for a while, been set on discovering another way to kill a vampire, by treating her own monstrous body as a test subject.

Throwing herself off the school roof had only led to her discovering that vampires, much like cats, landed on their feet—even from dizzying heights. Setting fire to her body merely resulted in a warm, tingling sensation, much like a hot bath, and she'd nearly burned down an entire forest in the process. Starving herself of blood for too long had driven her sanity to its limits, until her parched throat and skin turned her into a feral creature, wild and unthinking. When she'd finally given in to her primal cravings, it had led to a gruesome slaughter. To this day, the NYPD was still on the lookout for the mass murderer who had seemingly bled out ten people on the A train and then vanished. After that incident, Evangeline never again tried to starve her body of its needs, even if its primal cravings were gruesome. The heavy guilt of killing innocent humans in a frenzied fit of hunger weighed on her conscience; she couldn't and wouldn't bear any more of it.

The Descendants had dedicated their lives to fighting Wrathlings. Now, depending on who you asked, it seemed that *they* were the monsters.

Evangeline blinked, forcing her mind away from the unpleasant train of thought and back to the present—the High Council meeting in progress. The High Council consisted of thirteen of the eldest active members of the twelve Descendant families, who oversaw operations at Earthly Branches, in addition to supernatural relations across the country. Because House of Dragon led the other houses, it was allowed two members on the High Council—Julius and Evangeline.

It was a few hours after sunset, which, for the supernaturals, marked the day's beginning. Evangeline had been the first to arrive at the meeting room, and she'd watched the eleven other Descendants trickle in one by one. The weekly meetings were held in the library at Earthly Branches Academy, the largest room in the main building, an impressive, grand space with the widest selection of reading Evangeline had ever seen—books published from the Xia dynasty all the way up to books published last week.

While everyone else took their seats around the rectangular mahogany table, Evangeline remained standing. The seat to her left—Julius's—remained empty. The previous morning, her older brother had let her know that he wouldn't be able to make tonight's meeting, which meant the responsibility fell to Evangeline to lead. She had no choice but to assume that Julius was taking care of an emergency that had cropped up and, in his overly protective manner, refused to let Evangeline know the details or worry about him. It must have been a serious issue, too, as Julius had never missed a meeting since he'd been appointed Chancellor of the High Council.

However, Evangeline's brother had still left her a few buns filled with animal blood last night, even in the midst of handling his top-secret business. The Descendants drank animal blood in place of human blood, for it was much more ethical, if not as satisfying—after all, they were meant to protect humans, not devour them. The buns had warmed her in Julius's absence. Julius trusted Evangeline to run things smoothly in his stead; she would not disappoint her brother.

"Where is Julius?" demanded Marcus Niu, a bulky, thick-necked Descendant from the House of Ox with a thick skull to match. He ran a hand lazily through his buzz cut and kicked his feet up on the table, lounging back in his chair.

Evangeline closed her eyes. How had Julius run the High Council so smoothly for decades? She prayed for the patience to deal with Marcus today. Normally he wouldn't dare act so boldly when Julius was in charge, but Marcus made it no secret that he had much less respect for Evangeline than he did for her older brother—and Evangeline had no doubt that this was because she, unlike Julius, was a girl. To her knowledge, the Descendants had always had a male leader, and Marcus wouldn't be the only one who thought that tradition ought to stick.

Evangeline clamped down her frustration. There was nothing she could do about that now, except prove that she *was* capable. If she was to command the respect of every Descendant in this room, even if only for the duration of the meeting, then she needed to make it known that she wouldn't tolerate his blatant disrespect. "Marcus, get your feet off the table, please." Adding that "please" at the end almost killed her, but Evangeline was doing her best to avoid an all-out war before classes started.

Marcus sneered at her for a long moment. Silence blanketed the library as the ten other Descendants stared from Evangeline to Marcus, and the whole place seemed to hold its breath. Ever so slowly, as though mocking her, Marcus removed his feet from the table one after the other.

"Julius has an important matter that requires his attention," Evangeline explained, yanking her gaze away from Marcus. Staring at his irksome face any longer was likely to make her say something she'd regret. "Sorry for the disappointment, but I'm stepping in for my brother today." She nodded at the short-haired, well-muscled girl sitting to her right, a werewolf from the House of Rabbit who was the appointed note-taker for all High Council meetings. "Sylvia. Please refresh everyone as to where we left off at last week's meeting."

Sylvia Tu glanced down at the black notebook sitting open in front of her. "We were discussing the topic of . . . um, extinction."

Shudders rippled among the Descendants. It took everything within Evangeline not to show how uncomfortable she was with that word. *Extinction.* Extinction was what had happened to the dinosaurs and other prehistoric creatures. Extinction was never supposed to happen to the Descendants. Unfortunately, when they all became immortal supernatural creatures, they also became infertile—and since there were still ways to kill them off, the Descendants had slowly dwindled in number over the decades.

But stepping into Julius's shoes meant behaving as he would, so Evangeline cleared her face of any emotion and simply said, "Who would like to pick up where we left off?" She cast her gaze around the table, but the only Descendant to raise a hand was Marcus. Inwardly, Evangeline cursed. Protocol dictated that the High Council members got to speak in order of hands raised, and she had no choice but to call on him. "Yes, Marcus?"

He leapt in immediately. "I stand by what I said last time. The last line of mortal Descendants who are capable of reproducing—the House of Boar—should step up to create as many new Descendants as possible. It's the most realistic solution."

"You mean barbaric," Evangeline snapped before she could stop herself. She regretted the words as soon as they left her mouth. Julius had always done his best to stay neutral in any heated discussions among the High Council members, acting more as a moderator, and Evangeline had immediately let Marcus rile her up.

Marcus sneered. "Oh, I know you and your brother would rather we Descendants enact some miracle scenario in which we bumble around the world like a merry little gang searching for the five lost fountainheads, restore the Circle of Twelve, and return to our mortal selves. That's called a fantasy, Evangeline. It. Won't. Happen."

At this point, Evangeline was certain she couldn't be her brother. Julius would have responded to Marcus's insulting tone in a cold, calm manner, which would have been a sign of impending doom for anybody who knew him, as Julius was quite the expert at maintaining a collected facade while secretly concocting an elaborate plan for revenge. Evangeline, however, could not contain her outburst. She slammed her open palms against the table, and her full and considerable strength shook it, making a few Descendants gasp. "Know your place, Marcus Niu. While Julius is absent, *I* am the Chancellor. And you will not speak to me in a tone of disrespect."

Marcus stood up, too, his eyes alight with malice. He licked his lips, goading her. He wanted Evangeline to throw a punch at him, and she was *sorely* tempted. Which was more important: teaching Marcus a lesson and sending a message about how she ought to be treated in front of the High Council, or staying calm and mediating as Julius would?

She shut her eyes. In the end, if she was ever to take over for Julius as Chancellor, then she needed to make a statement here. She needed everyone at Earthly Branches Academy, including Marcus Niu, to view her with utmost respect.

But before either of them could make a move, the silver-haired boy seated between Marcus and Sylvia got up, positioning himself so that he was nose to nose with Marcus. Although Nicholas had almost half a foot of height over Marcus, the latter didn't back down at all; in fact, his lips twisted into a cruel smirk.

"What is it you have to say to me, pretty boy?" Marcus taunted.

"You'll treat the Chancellor with respect, Marcus, even if she's only filling in temporarily," snarled Nicholas Hu, curling his hands into fists. Evangeline's best friend was soft-spoken, and rarely did he raise his voice—which meant that Marcus must have *really* pissed him off.

"Or else? You'll take me on, princess?" Marcus let out a mirthless laugh, eyeing Nicholas's fists. "The way you took on those soldiers during the Second Opium War?"

Evangeline winced. That was a sore spot for Nicholas—the memory of his failure, as one of the Descendants closest to the scene at the time, to stop the British soldiers from seizing the fountainheads by force. Marcus was swinging low to bring that up now. Though Marcus had never been a classy fellow.

"That's neither here nor there," Evangeline said. She fixed Marcus with her coldest glare.

"Ah, and here comes your knight in shining armor to swoop in and save you in the nick of time. Predictable," Marcus scoffed.

An ugly flush crept up Nicholas's neck, coloring his cheeks. "I dare you to say that again." He clenched his fingers into fists at his sides, and his fingertips began to flame. A telltale sign that Nicholas, who had been cursed into a fox spirit, was feeling a very strong emotion—anger. Another sign: the barest shadow of nine tails had formed behind him. Although Nicholas appeared completely human most of the time, whenever he got emotional, his fox spirit side flared up.

"Oh, don't egg Nicholas on," Evangeline said to Marcus. This was as much for his own good as everyone else's, for fox spirits, the rarest kind among the supernatural Descendants, could also be the most powerful—and the most destructive. "Final warning, Marcus. If you don't sit down, Julius will hear every last detail of what happened at this meeting, and he won't take kindly to your behavior."

Marcus clenched his teeth and looked around at the other Descendants, as though hoping they would back him up. When he was met only with blank stares or disaffected looks, he finally sat back down, though not before giving Evangeline an ugly glance. Nicholas, too, had calmed, and his nine tails had vanished.

Evangeline tried not to let her relief show on her face. Even if somebody still ought to put Marcus in his place, she'd already done and said enough; the last thing she needed was for this meeting, the first one she'd ever led, to erupt into chaos.

Another hand shot up into the air. "Travis," Evangeline called, relieved that somebody else had entered the discussion.

Travis Shu of the House of Rat, a vampire with impeccably gelled black hair, cleared his throat. "I'd like to vocalize what some of us are thinking. We don't necessarily agree with either plan, but given that time is running out, the more practical solution is the more realistic one, no?"

Evangeline's stomach dropped as she caught the whispers and nods from the other High Council members, not to mention the reappearance of Marcus's satisfied smirk.

Someone coughed loudly, and all heads turned to the source of the noise. Kate Zhu of the House of Boar, the lone human Descendant sitting on the High Council, folded her arms across her chest. "You'll all have to forgive me if I don't leap at the idea of my brothers and sisters being turned into guinea pigs for some half-baked breeding experiment," she said in a voice full of forced calm.

"It wouldn't be just any human Descendant," Marcus scoffed. "As if we'd want to pass on weak genetics."

Kate grew red in the face and stood up quickly. "I'm sorry? *Weak?*"

It was no secret that some of the supernatural Descendants looked down on the human Descendants, but they were usually tactful enough not to say that part out loud. This meeting was going completely off the rails, and if Evangeline didn't intervene soon, it was going to end in a physical altercation. But then a diversion arrived just in time, in the form of the library door swinging wide open with a muffled *bang*.

"B-Breaking news!" Brian Ji of the House of Rooster shouted breathlessly. "A dead body was found at the Brooklyn Bridge—and it . . . it . . . wasn't a human body."

3
ALICE

Alice Jiang awoke in the morning to rumors that a supernatural had been found dead. Though nobody knew the source of the rumors, the gossip spread throughout the House of Boar like wildfire. Everywhere Alice turned, she was met by a curiously morbid mixture of excitement and fear that permeated the walls of the building and the student body. Someone had even started a rumor that the body was that of Julius Long. Nothing so terrible had happened to the supernatural Descendants still at school, Alice gathered, and the entire student body was shell-shocked by this unexpected turn of events.

Alice couldn't fathom the thought if the body did end up being Julius. She didn't know Julius personally, but she knew *of* him. She was a new human Descendant who'd only been in school for a few months; he was a vampire, the leader of the High Council, and by all accounts the king of Earthly Branches Academy. The other students whispered tales about Julius, legends that seemed almost too exaggerated to be true—and yet were just within the realm of believability. Julius Long had single-handedly fought off one hundred British soldiers during the Opium War.

Julius Long had an underground torture chamber that he used to deal with his enemies.

Alice had never spoken a single word to Julius. Actually, she hadn't interacted much with the supernaturals at all, given that their classes didn't overlap and the supernaturals were clearly superior to the humans in social ranking. From what Alice could tell, the High Council members were considered the cream of the crop, with the House of Dragon regarded as the leader of the other houses. Besides that, there were no clear distinctions of status among the different houses or types of supernaturals. However, it *was* clear that aside from them all being Descendants, the humans and supernaturals belonged to two different worlds. This didn't bother Alice too much, as the supernaturals were quite intimidating, and she thought it was perhaps better for their circles not to intersect.

"You think Julius is really dead?" Alice's human roommate, Madison, spoke in a hushed, conspiratorial tone. "What a waste. He was *so* cute."

Alice made a face. Of course, Julius had been striking, but so were all the supernatural Descendants. They were so beautiful that it was almost painful to look at them. "He was so much older than us, Madison."

"Maybe in mind, but not in body, and that's what counts."

"Madison!"

"What? I'm just telling it like it is. Guys take too long to mature, anyway. He was probably the same age as us mentally." Madison peeled her banana and ate it in a few bites. "You'd think it would be really, really tough to kill a vampire Descendant, though. Doesn't Julius have a gang to protect him, too? Who would've gone after him? Do you think it was someone at this school who did it?"

Madison was firing off questions at the speed of light, and Alice didn't have a response for a single one. Moreover, she wasn't particularly invested in the conversation. Madison was nice enough, but she had a big mouth for gossip, and Alice had never been the type to involve herself in other people's business. Drama was the last thing she wanted at school.

"Have you finished your homework for Elder Yang's class yet?" Madison asked. Evidently, the topic of their Chancellor's rumored demise had already lost her interest.

"Yeah, I did."

"Mind if I see it? I just need a bit of inspiration."

Alice sighed. She dug into her backpack, fished out her laptop, and opened it up to her just-finished essay on Chinese weaponry in the Song dynasty. She handed it over to Madison. "Knock yourself out."

"Thanks. You're a lifesaver."

The room filled with the sounds of Madison clacking away at her keyboard. Alice kept holding her breath, waiting for Kate or another authority figure to come by and tell the human Descendants they needed to evacuate the premises. But nobody came. That did nothing to quell Alice's anxiety, though.

After a while, Alice couldn't stand being in her room for a moment longer. "I'm gonna go get breakfast. You coming?"

Madison shook her head without even looking up from her laptop. "Go without me."

At Earthly Branches Academy, there were twelve houses in twelve different buildings, each representing an animal of the Chinese zodiac. Alice had been placed in the House of Boar, and though she wasn't sure why, she liked to think it was because she shared the same traits as the zodiac sign: ambition, compassion, diligence. The House of Boar had a large red plaque hanging above the door proclaiming its name, as well as two pillars carved into the shape of large, fearsome-looking boars.

The commons was large and spacious. There were several chairs and couches and a fireplace. On the walls hung artwork of fantasy creatures, and every time she passed them, Alice had the creeping sensation of having seen them before somewhere else, but she could not for the life of her remember where. A large white stone statue of a boar stood in the center of the room, the couches arranged around it. There were also two stone guardian lion statues at opposite ends of the room, reminding Alice of the statues placed in palaces in Chinese dramas.

As she headed into the commons, Alice happened upon a few familiar faces. There was Darla Tang, a short girl with glossy black hair that hung past her waist. Jimmy Cheng, a tall boy who had thick, round glasses and greased back his short hair. Rebecca Wu, a tall, slim girl. They'd put their heads together and were whispering—about Julius, Alice guessed. In her short time at Earthly Branches Academy, Alice had figured out that whatever gossip was going around the school, Darla Tang more than likely had a hand in spreading it.

"Oh, hey, Alice," said Darla. Jimmy and Rebecca smiled at her, and then they all put their heads together and went right back to whispering.

Even though they'd all only been at Earthly Branches for a few months, the three of them had already formed a tight-knit trio. Though they were friendly enough with Alice and sometimes got together with her to do homework, Alice was aware that she was on the outskirts of the House of Boar students. For the most part, this didn't bother her too much—as an only child raised by a busy single mother, she had learned to love solitude. But sometimes, when she watched Darla, Rebecca, and Jimmy taking their lunches out to the courtyard together, or when they stopped their conversation as she walked into the room, Alice couldn't help but feel the sting of loneliness—the feeling that though everyone else had found where they belonged, she was . . . lost.

Maybe fresh air would do her some good. She started toward the exit, passing by one of the stone guardian lions. She pressed her fingertips against the stone to get around it.

And then something very strange happened. A swooping feeling stirred her stomach, and she had the distinct sensation that she was no longer quite anchored to reality as she knew it. She whirled around, but before she could get her bearings, she was walloped in the stomach by an invisible force. She reeled back, gasping. Before she could piece together what had just transpired, new voices whispered in her ear—voices speaking a different language, speaking Mandarin.

"Quickly! The soldiers are coming! Protect the Emperor."

"We don't have much time—take only the most valuable art with you—"

"The Old Summer Palace is about to fall—"

The voices sounded far away, as if coming through with static interference. If Alice had to guess, these voices were decades, if not centuries, old. But she couldn't even begin to guess at how she was hearing them now, at this school, in the present.

And then a roaring filled her ears, and then screams of agony, as though the disembodied voices had experienced a great and terrible loss and their suffering was becoming Alice's suffering. She did not know for how long this endless screaming rang in her head, until finally she registered that somebody was shaking her shoulder.

"Alice—*Alice!*"

Alice was jerked out of the reverie, or whatever it was, by someone literally shaking her. Darla was gripping her arm and staring at her with wide eyes. Some other students were gathered around her, a few of them pressing their hands to their mouths in shock, confusion, and even horror.

"Are you all right?" Darla, Alice knew, had a big mouth and an even bigger Instagram following, and she was currently gazing upon Alice not with shock or horror but with the sharp, hungry stare of a predator eyeing its prey. Alice's stomach sank as she recognized that she might shortly become the source of the latest gossip at Earthly Branches Academy.

"You were screaming and doubling over," said Rebecca. She, at least, sounded genuinely concerned. "We thought you were having a seizure."

"I . . ." Alice's throat hurt, and a pounding headache was developing over her right eye. She was trying to think about too many things at once, but she needed to focus on the most important thread—that she had somehow channeled the voices of long ago.

"Do you need to go to the infirmary?" Darla pressed.

"N-No, I— I'm fine," Alice mumbled, her cheeks heating as she grew more and more aware of the other girls' stares. She wished more than anything that there hadn't been an audience to witness her undergoing . . . whatever that was.

"It's probably a panic attack or something similar," Darla said with a knowing nod. "Not an unusual reaction to learning that a student just died."

"Yeah, that's probably it." Alice agreed quickly, hoping to move past the topic of her strange episode as soon as possible. But she was certain it hadn't been a panic attack at all. Nothing about her life had been certain or ordinary since she'd turned sixteen.

Ever since Alice's sixteenth birthday, almost a year ago to the day, Mama had been constantly reminding her that she wasn't a child anymore, warning her that life would be different. Of course, this in itself had been nothing out of the ordinary. Alice knew that her life, like her peers', was changing in many aspects—schoolwork was harder, extracurriculars were more important, and everyone's stress levels were rising because college applications were just over the horizon. However, Alice suspected that Mama didn't only mean that Alice's life was changing in an academic way. Her mother had become jumpier and stricter than usual, locking windows and doors with a newfound vigilance. She'd even taken to calling Alice at random intervals throughout the day to check in, as though frightened that Alice might get kidnapped at any moment.

Mama's warnings hadn't been for nothing after all. She'd sent Alice to this strange school, seeming to believe it would be better for her than staying in public school, and now Alice's life had grown stranger than ever.

Seventeen was mere days away. Alice wondered what chaos her next birthday might bring her, given how much sixteen had wrought.

Despite her embarrassment over her episode in the commons, Alice's day was just beginning. No matter how daunting it seemed, she had to scrape together what little dignity remained to her and attend her classes for the day. Forgetting the idea of breakfast in the dining hall, she headed back to her room and allowed herself two seconds to close her eyes and breathe. When she opened her eyes again, she studied the schedule she'd pinned above her desk.

Monday
8 a.m.—Human Nutrition
9 a.m.—Supernatural Beings 101
10 a.m.—Study Hall

12 p.m.—Lunch

1 p.m.—Extracurriculars

6 p.m.—Dinner

Tuesday

8 a.m.—Mandarin 101

9 a.m.—The Basics of Combat

10 a.m.—Study Hall

12 p.m.—Lunch

1 p.m.—Extracurriculars

6 p.m.—Dinner

Wednesday

8 a.m.—Biology

9 a.m.—All About Assignment

10 a.m.—Study Hall

12 p.m.—Lunch

1 p.m.—Extracurriculars

6 p.m.—Dinner

Thursday

8 a.m.—So You're a Descendant, So What?

9 a.m.—History of Art Magic

10 a.m.—Study Hall

12 p.m.—Lunch

1 p.m.—Extracurriculars

6 p.m.—Dinner

Today was Tuesday, which meant Alice had Mandarin first. Luckily, the students got Fridays and weekends completely off, and Alice had taken to using her free time to explore the campus and Manhattan, trying to find out more about Baba. While she was at Earthly Branches

Academy, she was determined to dig up as much information as possible about the half of her family that she'd never known.

Alice often wondered what the supernaturals did during their time off. Scare humans, maybe? Or play baseball?

"You ready for class?"

Madison's voice startled Alice out of her thoughts. She turned to find her roommate running a comb through her curly shoulder-length black hair, her book bag slung over one shoulder.

Alice quickly stuffed her schedule into her backpack and swung it over her shoulders. "Yeah. Let's go."

The girls headed down to the commons, where Darla, Jimmy, and Rebecca were still gathered. Thankfully, nobody mentioned what had happened to Alice earlier, though Darla did study Alice for a little longer than seemed natural. Alice turned away from Darla's gaze and pretended to be fascinated by the wall. To make up for earlier, she was going to act *extra* normal in classes today.

"Do you think Elder Niu's going to give us as much homework as he did last week?" asked Jimmy nervously as they headed out of the dorm together, making a beeline for the main building. "I barely finished my essay an hour ago."

"Maybe you should start on your homework earlier than the night before," Rebecca snickered.

Leaves and branches crunched underfoot as the students rushed over the stone pavement. Like everything else at Earthly Branches Academy, the paths seemed to have been constructed decades ago and were overgrown with greenery.

"I can't wait for class to be over," said Darla. She stifled a yawn. "This school is more boring than I thought it'd be."

"Boring? But we're learning about supernaturals, and magic, and stuff," Alice pointed out. She'd been far from bored since entering Earthly Branches Academy. Antsy, nervous, fearful, and excited, maybe. But definitely not bored.

"Studying is boring. I wanted to go to my family's vacation home in Greece for the year," Darla sighed, twirling her long hair around her finger. "And . . ." She suddenly stopped walking, causing Alice to accidentally step on her heel.

"Sorry!" Alice quickly backtracked, but Darla gave no indication that she'd noticed. Madison didn't seem to notice or care, either. Nor did Rebecca or Jimmy. They were focused on a group of extremely attractive supernaturals who'd congregated in front of the main building and drawn the attention of every student rushing off to morning classes.

"Is that the High Council?" Madison gasped. "Why are they still hanging around school?"

Alice blinked. This *was* a very strange occurrence. Since the supernaturals took night classes and the human students took their lessons during the day, the supernaturals rarely mingled with the humans, and vice versa. Alice could count on one hand the number of times she'd spotted a supernatural Descendant on campus, not to mention a High Council member. Something about these students made them stand out from the others, even among the other supernatural Descendants.

The High Council members were striking in appearance, tall and almost shining. They carried themselves with the confident air of folks who'd been told their whole lives that they were important. If they hadn't been moving, Alice would have thought the High Council members were the most expertly crafted statues. If she tried to paint them, she knew she could never do their beauty justice.

"Okay, *now* I'm not bored," Darla said in a high, breathy voice. She fanned her face. "Do you think they're here because of Julius's death?"

"There's no confirmation on the identity of the body yet," Alice reminded her. "A lot of people are saying it *can't* be Julius, actually."

Darla ignored her.

"Let's keep walking," said Jimmy, though his voice sounded far away, as though he, too, was having trouble dragging his attention from the High Council members. "We're . . . we're gonna be late for class."

They kept moving. Alice forced her feet forward, though she couldn't tear her eyes away from the High Council. As she watched, awestruck, the girl who stood at the front of the group turned around. Dark brown eyes met Alice's. Her skin was the color of fresh snow. Alice drew closer, like a moth to a flame; she couldn't have been more than a few feet away from them now, close enough to eavesdrop on their conversation.

"Aren't there fewer human recruits than usual this year?" asked one of the boys.

"Well, seeing as how the human Descendants keep dying off on their Assignments, perhaps some of them are learning to stay away," answered the pale girl.

The girl kept speaking, but Alice had stopped listening after she'd heard that apparently the humans were *dying at this place.*

"Wait, Alice, watch where you're—"

But Alice didn't process Madison's words until it was too late. She hadn't been paying attention at all to where she was walking, too engrossed in the conversation among the High Council members. She tripped over something underfoot and went flying, landing on all fours on the hard concrete. Pain shot through her palms and knees.

Laughter floated to Alice's ears, and her cheeks burned with mortification. Great. The first lesson of the day hadn't even started yet, and she'd already managed to embarrass herself in front of many onlookers—twice. That was a new record.

She hastily got to her feet and rushed back to Madison and the others, but not before glancing toward the High Council members. And immediately wishing she hadn't.

Those High Council members were laughing and staring—at Alice. The blindingly beautiful girl standing at the front was licking her lips while she gave Alice the once-over, like a huntress sighting her new prey. Her glossy black hair flowed in the wind, moving almost like water; Alice had never seen hair move like that before.

The girl smiled, baring fangs, and Alice's heart thudded in her chest.

A vampire. She'd never seen one in real life—as far as she was aware—but she'd watched plenty of vampire movies and TV shows, and there was no mistaking the real thing.

"What kind of riffraff are they letting into the Academy now? Does any human with a drop of Descendant blood get put into the House of Boar these days? I swear the mortals get clumsier every year," grumbled one of the guys. His skin tone was closer to yellow than white, and he had long, curly black hair, bushy eyebrows, and rather hairy legs. A werewolf.

Alice's cheeks burned. Although she'd always been a bit of a loner, she generally flew so far below the radar that bullies never targeted her in school. Here, though, there was already a target on her back. She wanted nothing more than to sink through the ground.

"Clumsiness is cute," answered another High Council member, a pale, beautiful guy. Another vampire. He winked at her.

Now Alice blushed for a different reason. *Cute?*

"You call *that* cute?" the beautiful vampire girl huffed. "You have terrible taste, Travis."

"Don't be jealous, Evangeline. It's unsightly," Travis retorted.

"Oh, let it go," urged another girl next to Travis. She was neither pale nor hairy, and her beauty was on a level that was ethereal. This was a dangerous type of beauty with an alluring quality to it, such that Alice suspected if the girl asked her to do just about anything, she would obey. A fox spirit.

Evangeline turned back toward Alice, her eyes flashing red. "What's your name?"

Alice struggled for a couple of seconds to remember. "Alice . . . Alice Jiang."

The name seemed to cause a ripple effect among the High Council. A few of the members stiffened, and some did a double take. The interest in their eyes reminded Alice of Kate's when she'd told her name.

"Jiang—like *that* Jiang?" asked Travis, his eyes glittering.

"Doubt it," sniffed Evangeline, though she flicked her eyes toward Alice again with renewed interest. "Jiang's not that uncommon a surname."

32

"There's only one known human Descendant family with that name, though," pointed out the fox spirit girl.

"Lily," Evangeline said in a voice full of skepticism, "are you really implying what I think you're implying?"

"She *smells* just like him. Don't you smell his scent in her blood?" Lily raised her nose in the air and gave an exaggerated sniff in Alice's direction, which made Alice stumble back in horror.

What were they all talking about? They'd referenced a "him"—could it possibly be Alice's father? She'd never known him, or even much about him; at home, Mama had scarcely spoken about Baba. Alice had learned long ago not to bring him up, because Mama batted away any mention of Baba without even a moment of consideration. Mama had raised her as a single mother, and Alice had never even met the man; she knew him only from a few pictures that Mama kept in her wallet: light brown eyes and a kind, dimpled smile, which he'd passed on to Alice.

How was it possible that these strangers would know anything about Baba?

"Yes, she *does* smell like him, but . . ." Evangeline's perfectly shaped mouth opened and closed as she evidently struggled to process some unwelcome bit of information. "But how could she possibly be descended from *those* Jiangs? She's so . . . small and pathetic-looking."

"I'm *not* small and pathetic," Alice snapped before she could stop herself. Then she immediately slapped a hand over her mouth. Had she just challenged the High Council members? Even if they'd been rude to her, Alice couldn't afford to make waves when she was so new to the Academy.

Evangeline's eyes narrowed. Her mouth parted slightly, revealing her surprise at Alice's remark. "I beg your pardon?"

Perhaps she should have run away at that moment and prayed that Evangeline would forget her face. However, right now, with all of the High Council's attention on her, this was Alice's best chance to dig up more information about her father. And somehow her normal shyness and anxiety melted away. She couldn't let this lead slip through her fingers.

All that mattered was the task at hand. And Alice would stop at nothing to see it through.

"Did you all know my father?" she asked. Though it was hard, she tried to scale back her excitement and fear so that the others couldn't hear it in her voice. She almost couldn't believe what she was doing, speaking so boldly in front of the High Council, as though they were all on the same level. If she paused to think it over now, she'd definitely lose her nerve, so she had no choice but to plow onward.

"We did. Ruiting was briefly part of the High Council as the House of Boar representative." Lily slowly walked toward Alice as though approaching a small animal that she thought might flee. "He had . . . special abilities that set him apart from the other human Descendants."

They were getting somewhere, finally. Alice swallowed. "Can you tell me more about that?" She couldn't help it; a note of desperation entered her voice.

Instead of Lily, though, it was Evangeline who spoke up. "What he had was unnatural, and it's doubtless the reason why he went the way he did."

"Wh-What?" Alice spluttered, alarmed. "Why he went the way he did?"

Now it was Evangeline's turn to look taken aback. For a moment, she simply stared at Alice as though she hadn't looked at her clearly before. "I didn't say that part out loud. Did you just . . ." She cocked her head to the side, studying Alice with greater interest.

"Did she just read your mind?" Travis said, perking up. "So it seems there is *one* interesting human Descendant among the group."

Reading minds? No, Alice had heard the girl speak, loud and clear. Or—hadn't she? Now she couldn't be quite sure. Either the girl had spoken out loud, or she'd somehow spoken in Alice's *mind*. But that wasn't possible. Alice couldn't read minds . . . or at least, she couldn't do that before coming to Earthly Branches Academy. But perhaps something about this supernatural school was activating some dormant part of her that she hadn't even known existed.

Alice shook her head, hardly able to believe that she was seriously contemplating something as impossible as mind-reading powers. She had no idea what was going on. The line between what could and couldn't be real was beginning to blur, and she had the distinct sense that instead of feeling more assured about herself, she was more lost than ever. All she knew was that the entire High Council was staring at her as though she'd done something outrageous.

There was no way she was going to be able to fish any more information out of them about Baba. She needed to get away, and fast. She nearly tripped again in her effort to head back toward her dorm mates.

Madison, Darla, Rebecca, and Jimmy stared at her like she'd sprouted a third head. They'd watched this entire exchange wordlessly and probably had a slew of questions to ask Alice. But for now, Alice didn't want to answer any of them. Even *she* didn't know where she'd summoned such courage moments ago, for that bout of bravery had already abandoned her.

Tucking a lock of hair behind her ear self-consciously, she muttered, "Let's get to class." She didn't want to attract more unwanted attention to herself than she already had; it had been the roughest of mornings, and all she longed for was to be out of the spotlight.

The human Descendants hurried off, but the voices of the High Council members continued to loop in Alice's mind—especially what they'd said about dying on Assignments. She hoped they'd only said that to intimidate the human students, but she couldn't be sure.

Alice could really only be certain of one thing: that the truth of Baba's fate was at her fingertips, and she would pay any price to learn what it was.

4

EVANGELINE

Evangeline had remained distinctly unsatisfied in the aftermath of the abruptly ended High Council meeting the night before, which had, despite her best efforts to prevent it, consummated in chaos anyway. So much for proving that she'd be as capable a leader as her older brother. She rubbed her temple, where a slight headache had begun to develop. Julius, she decided, was the saint of the century for keeping the High Council together for so long.

The other factor contributing to her restlessness was the fact that Julius hadn't responded to any of her calls or messages. This was most unlike him, for even if he went away on unexpected, last-minute missions, he'd at least give Evangeline a heads-up.

Besides, there was still an undercurrent of fear running throughout the student body. Rumors about the unidentified and likely supernatural corpse were swirling during Evangeline's first class that evening, History of Art Magic. She fixed her eyes on tiny, flighty Elder Yang, who was enthusiastically gesturing toward her notes on the board while lecturing about the Second Opium War and its link to the looting of Chinese art and destruction of magic in the 1860s.

". . . when the soldiers destroyed the fountain and broke the Circle of Twelve by carrying off five of the zodiac fountainheads, the Descendants, led by the High Council, escaped to the United States," the Elder explained. "As you all know, shortly after, Earthly Branches Academy was founded, with twelve houses to represent each of the twelve powerful Descendant bloodlines, and the oldest surviving Descendants turning into Elders."

Elder Yang's words were met by a few unenthusiastic nods and glazed eyes from the students in the classroom. By now this history was as familiar to Evangeline as the lines in her own palm. The High Council had officially founded Earthly Branches Academy as a Mandarin immersion school in 1904. Since then, the school had been glamoured from the human world. It was a cover for the Descendants, a safe haven where they could exist away from the prying eyes of mortals and the potential disturbance from other immortals. The supernaturals took night classes, taught by their elders who were no longer active Descendants either in training or Assigned, and learned how to best protect the mortals. Long had the Descendants protected the defenseless mortals, and long would they continue their duties. They were to learn how to blend in with society and take on temporary Assignments, like stopping a rogue Wrathling, until they were tasked with a permanent Assignment, like watching over a prominent family. On that day, called the Assignment Day, the chosen Descendant would leave the school to fulfill their mission.

Some of the students sitting in the back of the room were even bold enough to have started up a game of mah-jongg behind the Elder's back. As Evangeline looked on, the ringleader—Marcus, of course—pocketed cash greedily from poor Delilah Hou of the House of Monkey. Evangeline hoped Elder Yang would turn around and catch Marcus in the act, but Marcus had always been far too slick to get caught—a trait that was at once annoying and, she begrudgingly admitted, admirable. When the

Elder did turn to face the class, Marcus had already kicked a scroll of paper over the board and pieces to cover up the evidence.

From across the room, Marcus caught Evangeline's eye and flashed a nasty grin, as though he knew exactly what she'd been thinking and hoping for. Evangeline did her best to suppress her fury; she'd never forgive him for the disrespect he'd shown her at the High Council meeting. One of these days, Marcus was going to get what was coming to him—and oh, Evangeline so wished for the pleasure of being the one to deliver his karma.

Evangeline had been at the Academy ever since its creation. She'd taken on various temporary Assignments, but she hadn't yet been called up to take on a permanent Assignment, which was just fine in her book; she didn't relish the thought of being bossed around by self-important assholes day in and day out. Sometimes the idea of staying put in the Academy for an unpredictable period of time made her anxious, but it was for the best; the Descendants had spent most of their long lives adhering to the school system, and they were strongest together, after all. Leaving the Academy prematurely was akin to turning one's back on the other Descendants, which could mean the complete loss of one's powers. Besides, the curriculum at Earthly Branches Academy was at least more interesting than that of a normal high school.

For example, on Monday nights, Evangeline attended a combat class with Elder Gou, where she learned how to knock out men thrice her size and shoot a target from hundreds of feet away.

On Tuesdays—like today—there was History of Art Magic, where their instructor, Elder Yang, taught them all about their unique history as Descendants.

On Wednesdays, Evangeline got to attend Vampire Nutrition class—which was all about blood, and what sources of blood were most nourishing to vampires (humans, naturally; though, as the punishment for drinking the blood of their occasional human classmates was quite severe, no vampires dared to do so).

Evangeline slid her fingers through her long, silky black hair, which was always in pristine condition, every strand perfectly in place. She leaned back in her chair and allowed her mind to drown out the teacher's lecture. Grades *did* matter in the sense that better grades led to better Assignments, but Evangeline wasn't too worried about her scores—she'd never received anything lower than an A minus. And in any case, she was certain she'd pass this particular class with flying colors. History had always been her strongest subject.

It seemed she wasn't the only student having trouble concentrating on the lesson. All around Evangeline, her classmates were passing notes when they thought Elder Yang wasn't looking.

"If I see one more note being passed around about unrelated topics," Elder Yang threatened, making half the class jump, "I'll be handing out detentions."

"Idiots," Nicholas muttered from the seat to Evangeline's right. He rolled his black eyes at her, his short, spiky silver hair glinting in the classroom light. As always, no fewer than five classmates were either sneakily or openly checking Nicholas out. While all the supernatural Descendants were beautiful in the way that humans could only achieve through beauty filters and plastic surgery, the fox spirits were undoubtedly the *most* striking—and Nicholas one of the most alluring of them all.

Nicholas's expression turned downright sour as he appeared to spot something distasteful on their right. Evangeline followed his gaze, and immediately wished she hadn't when she locked stares with an intense pair of gold-flecked brown eyes. Tristan She, a werewolf from the House of Snake, was staring right at *her*. Evangeline quickly turned away to face the front of the class. Her heart would have been racing madly, if she'd still had a heartbeat. For how long had Tristan had his eyes glued to her like that? And why did she still care so much that her ex-boyfriend clearly had her so squarely on his radar?

"Is he making you uncomfortable?" Nicholas murmured, low enough so that only Evangeline could hear. "I can talk to him after class." Besides Cecil, he was the only other Descendant who knew about her secret relationship with Tristan, as the Descendants were forbidden to marry one another, in order to avoid the issue of inbreeding and keep their bloodlines healthy for generations. Of course, that didn't stop Descendants from getting involved with one another, either secretly or not so secretly—but with the caveat that they could never marry, unless they chose to leave behind the Descendants entirely.

"Don't worry about it, Nicholas. I'm fine." Evangeline had more or less accepted the notion that she'd have to deal with Tristan's presence for the foreseeable future. Nicholas, though, seemed to have taken it upon himself to glower at Tristan every chance he got—and Evangeline didn't exactly feel the urge to stop him.

"Ahem," coughed the Elder, and Evangeline nearly jolted out of her seat, certain that the teacher was about to scold them for carrying on a conversation during her lecture. However, Elder Yang's eyes were fixed on something behind Evangeline and Nicholas. "Just because you're in the back of the room doesn't mean you're out of my field of vision," she snapped.

Now everyone turned toward the back of the class, where the students were guiltily stowing away their notes.

As Elder Yang settled back into the lecture, Evangeline's mind began drifting off again. Her throat was parched, and her stomach panged with hunger; but she had grown used to her vampire body after so long, a body that was never fully satisfied subsisting on animal blood. She thought longingly of the blood-filled red bean buns she'd left back in her dorm. There were only thirty minutes until the end of class—she hoped she'd make it. She had trained herself to control her appetite, as even the thought of feasting on animal blood still bothered her to some degree. She could subsist on little blood for long increments of time at this point, but the ever-present hunger and thirst were not pleasant sensations by any means.

"Ms. Long."

Evangeline jolted out of her reverie. She'd only been partially paying attention, but enough that she had the gist of the lesson. Something about art as a source of power. Surely it would be enough to cobble together a satisfactory answer to the Elder's forthcoming question.

But after a moment, it dawned on her that Elder Yang wasn't the one who'd spoken. The Elder's eyes were on the doorway, where Elder Shu stood, a somber expression on her face. Elder Shu was a tall, slim vampire who appeared to be about sixty years old. There had been a timeless quality to her beauty even when she had been mortal. She was the eldest of the Elders and therefore their natural leader, though no such formal discussion had ever been held regarding the matter; none was required.

"Ms. Long," Elder Shu repeated. "Please follow me. I need to speak with you about an urgent matter."

The murmurs and stares of her classmates didn't bother Evangeline as much as the look on Shu's face, which suggested that something ghastly had happened. Evangeline stood up.

"You'll need your belongings," said Elder Shu, looking pointedly at the open textbook and notebook on the desk. "You won't be coming back."

The volume of the curious muttering rose around Evangeline. Marcus Niu, in particular, didn't bother to lower his voice as he speculated about the likelihood that Evangeline was in trouble.

Normally Evangeline wouldn't have taken Marcus's slander without retaliation, but right now he was the least of her concerns. It was, indeed, very strange for Elder Shu to call her down like this—and to say that Evangeline wouldn't be coming back? That sounded like expulsion, only such a word didn't even exist within her realm of possibilities. Evangeline racked her mind for something, anything, she might have done to get in trouble. No, summer classes had only started two weeks ago, and she'd been on her best behavior.

Evangeline shoved her books into her backpack. Without meeting her classmates' prying eyes, she quickly followed Elder Shu out the door.

Evangeline had never been in trouble before—not the kind that she couldn't wriggle out of with sweet talk, anyway—but she couldn't shake off the bone-deep dread that this time, something horrific had happened.

The Elder's office was plainly decorated. A huge wooden bookshelf was positioned behind her mahogany desk. A simple clock hung on the wall above the bookshelf.

Evangeline could imagine any number of scenarios that might take place in the Elder's office. None of them were pleasant.

"Sit, please," said Shu. Her face was carefully arranged into an impassive mask, but Evangeline recognized the brief emotion that flitted across her eyes—something that resembled pity.

After a moment of hesitation, Evangeline sat down gingerly in the cushioned armchair in front of the desk.

"This isn't easy news for me to deliver to you," said the Elder in cold, stilted tones. "I wish the circumstances were different, truly I do."

Evangeline's eyebrows stitched together. Why was Shu speaking like she was about to tell Evangeline that her house had burned down or that she had a disease or something? Evangeline was a vampire. It wasn't possible for her to contract mortal illnesses, and no matters could be considered life-or-death, since she couldn't die from anything besides a wooden stake to the heart.

"What's wrong?" Evangeline asked.

Shu's hands shook as she clasped them into fists in front of her. Then the stoic mask shattered. Her lips trembled, and her eyes misted over. Evangeline had never seen the Elder as emotional as this, and the knot of nerves in her stomach grew. "I'm afraid . . . I'm afraid your brother—Julius—is dead. His remains were officially identified at the Brooklyn Bridge just an hour ago."

For a long moment, the words didn't register in Evangeline's mind. There had to be a mistake. Or maybe Evangeline had simply misheard Elder Shu. Julius couldn't possibly be dead.

"Ms. Long?"

Evangeline blinked. The Elder was waving a hand in her face. For how long had she been staring into space, trying to let these terrible words fully register? "That's not possible," Evangeline said flatly. Less than two days ago, Julius had rushed out of the Long estate after instructing her to lead the upcoming High Council meeting. Sure, that behavior was out of the ordinary for him, and sure, Julius hadn't been seen since then . . . but that didn't mean her brother was *dead*. Even if her brain knew that the timeline matched up—the dead body appearing at the bottom of the Brooklyn Bridge shortly after Julius vanished—Evangeline hadn't considered this as even a possibility. A Descendant of Julius Long's caliber didn't simply *die*. Because he was as much cursed with immortality as she, Julius literally couldn't die—not unless he was staked through the heart, and that could only be the work of somebody or something supernatural.

"I understand this news is hard for you to process. It's . . . difficult for me as well." Shu's normally stern features had turned to concern, and her reddening eyes suggested she was on the verge of bloody tears. "But I swear to you that this is the truth, and Julius would want you to face reality head-on."

Evangeline opened her mouth to snap back at the Elder, but she caught herself just in time. What would she say? Even if her heart was screaming that Julius must still be alive, her head was telling her the exact opposite, and she would look a fool if she threw an emotional fit in this office.

"You should leave the school for the evening. Attend to your estate. I imagine you'll have many new responsibilities to shoulder now." The Elder paused. "There is also the matter of the High Council and the now-vacant position of Chancellor. Traditionally, the Longs have led the Descendants, but there have been recent stirrings of dissatisfaction among some. . . . The position isn't guaranteed to you, Evangeline. There is talk of new blood in the Chancellor seat, and ultimately the majority will decide the best course of action for the Descendants."

The Elder's words were like a punch to the gut, even though on some level Evangeline had feared that this might be the sentiment. However, she couldn't worry about the position of Chancellor right now, not when there were more important matters to attend to first.

"Who . . . did that to Julius?" she managed to ask. She couldn't bring herself to say the word *killed*. "Are the Wrathlings back?"

Shu said cryptically, "We know very little right now, but as there have been no known Wrathling attacks in the vicinity for years, we've no reason to panic."

The Wrathlings wouldn't have been sophisticated enough to pull off such an assassination, anyway, Evangeline realized. "The shamans? The fae?"

"We don't know yet, and we can't point fingers without evidence," said the Elder. "There is a chance you may be in danger, since you're Julius's only remaining blood relative. We can Assign a couple of Descendants to you for your protection."

"No need. The aid of Cecil Long should be enough." Cecil was not only a fellow student at Earthly Branches but also a longtime servant of Evangeline and the Long family. Evangeline entered autopilot mode. She hadn't quite accepted the truth yet, but she knew that at this critical moment, she needed to be able to display magnificent leadership skills. She could not break down. "Besides," she continued, more to herself than to the Elder, "the Long estate is guarded by countless enchantments. I'd like to see any outsiders *try* to intrude."

The estate wasn't far—only a mile from school. With her vampire speed, Evangeline could travel there in seconds. But if someone had gone after her brother and managed to kill him, then they could very well be lying in wait for her. Though, truthfully, *they* needed to fear *her*. Evangeline's insides twisted with a mixture of grief and rage. Her hands curled into fists. There was no question about it. Whenever she found out who was behind this, they would suffer the full extent of her wrath, and then even Hell would be a blessing.

The Elder's eyebrows rose, but she didn't push the matter. Cecil alone was worth more than all of Julius's Talons combined. She was one of the most accomplished combat students at the school, and consistently received top grades in all her studies. Evangeline pitied the fool who decided to go against Cecil. Yet Julius had been an accomplished Descendant, too. She tried not to dwell on that fact. The murderer had lured

Julius out of the estate rather than try to penetrate its magical defenses. As long as Evangeline didn't make any rash moves, she would be fine.

If anything, the perpetrator behind Julius's death ought to be the one fearing for their life. For Evangeline didn't plan to waste a moment before she began to plot their demise.

Vaguely, she registered the sensation of her phone vibrating in her pants pocket. Of course, by now everybody would be speculating about her absence, and the school would be abuzz with gossip. Evangeline couldn't care less what was being said about her, though. There was a single thought on her mind: revenge.

The culprit was not to be underestimated, however. Evangeline's older brother was dead—not *un*dead, but *dead* dead, as in erased from this planet. It was a fate she had never imagined for her brother. Because if he was dead at someone else's hands, that meant some beast stronger and more fearsome than Julius Long had just made its move on the Longs—on *her*—and on Earthly Branches Academy.

Something that could pose a danger to all of Manhattan.

5
NICHOLAS

All hell broke loose, it seemed to Nicholas Hu, once Evangeline was pulled out of their lessons. The students barely paid attention to Elder Yang as she ended the lecture, so focused were they on speculating about what had just happened. The Elder must have been fed up, and there were far too many of them to send everyone to detention, so she simply ended class twenty minutes early. No doubt Elder Yang would want to gossip about this latest development with the other members of the staff, too.

Nicholas, who was normally one of the first to rush out of the classroom to get to the next one, hung back this time. "Dylan," he called toward the departing back of a short, brown-haired boy. As soon as the name left his lips, Nicholas kicked himself, wondering why he had called for his younger brother, when it had been decades since they had a conversation of any depth.

Dylan Hu turned around with a sullen look on his face. Unlike Nicholas, Dylan had been cursed into a werewolf, and he had filled out with a much stockier build. "What?" he asked, his eyes staring at a spot over Nicholas's shoulder.

"I . . . Have you heard from Evangeline?"

"Why would I have heard anything from her? She's *your* friend, not mine." Without waiting for Nicholas's reply, Dylan turned and rejoined his group of friends, who'd hung around the entrance waiting for him. None of them so much as acknowledged Nicholas before traipsing off.

Anger spiked through Nicholas. Who did Dylan think he was, ignoring him like that? His pulse quickened, and a familiar heat surged through his body, and—*no.* Nicholas stopped himself before his body could betray him and do something he'd later regret.

Instead, Nicholas closed his eyes. What else had he expected from his estranged little brother, really? That was the most they'd interacted in recent memory, and it would be the most they would interact in a long time more. Nicholas and Dylan had once been as tight-knit as brothers could be—but that was before that fateful October day in 1860 when their lives had been utterly destroyed. Before he and Dylan said and did unforgivable things to each other.

Nicholas did his best to ignore the heaviness in his heart. He waited for the other students to depart the classroom, the last of whom were a pair of girls who wouldn't stop stealing glances at him and giggling. They weren't being nearly as discreet as they thought they were.

A blessing—or curse, depending on how you looked at it—in being turned into a fox spirit was that Nicholas's strikingly good looks drew attention to him no matter what. Though he would never do so without an extremely compelling reason, many a fox spirit had used their spell-binding beauty to bend others to their whims. Even before the curse, Nicholas had always been extraordinarily good-looking, as was the case for the Descendants who'd turned into fox spirits, which gave him reason to theorize that there *was* a method to the madness after all. The Descendants had each been cursed into the supernatural being that most resembled their mortal selves; Evangeline and Julius, for example, were cut from the same cold, ruthless cloth, and turning into vampires only accentuated those traits. Werewolves like Tristan She and Marcus Niu were brash and impulsive, always leaping at the chance to fight. Finally, fox spirits like Nicholas were calm and cool thinkers, intelligent almost to the point of being geniuses, but often let their decisions be swayed by matters of the heart; it was this genius quality that made them the rarest among the Descendants.

It was hard for others to believe that anything else about Nicholas was as remarkable as his looks—but his intelligence, in *his* opinion, had always been the most interesting part of him. Of course, in this world, beauty mattered most. Beauty was an advantage afforded only to the genetically lucky ones; beauty was social currency, and this was the case even among the Descendants.

When at last the classroom had emptied, Nicholas whipped out his phone and called Evangeline once, twice, three times, only to be sent to voicemail.

"Where are you, Evangeline?" he muttered under his breath as he composed a couple of texts instead.

NICHOLAS:

Are you okay? What happened??

Evangeline??

Nicholas closed his eyes and did his best to keep his mind from running through worst-case scenarios, but it was very difficult to focus on any positive thoughts. Why was he so *useless*? Perhaps Marcus's words during the meeting had gotten under his skin more than he cared to admit. He'd been so furious in the moment that he'd nearly lost control of his emotions. That would only have led to a fiery disaster, as fox spirits harnessed fire with often destructive consequences.

Nicholas couldn't help but beat himself up over once again failing to help Evangeline. She'd bailed him out more times than he could count, ever since they were kids, given that he grew up a frail, shy child who'd been an easy target for bullies.

But there was nothing he could do if Evangeline wasn't even answering her phone, and he had no clue where she was. It was still the middle of the school night, too. Frustrated, he followed the other students out of the classroom and into the hall.

In their second class, Advanced Mandarin, nobody was even pretending to pay attention, causing Elder Ma to practically froth at the mouth with anger (which was effectively threatening, given that he was a werewolf).

By lunchtime, the rumors about Evangeline's being called out of class had only grown wilder. In the halls as they headed for the dining hall, they whispered among themselves.

"Did you hear about Julius? . . ."

"They found a body at that place where the Fulton Fish Market used to be. . . ."

"Was it the Wrathlings?"

"But the Wrathlings haven't directly attacked us for decades. . . ."

Nicholas had never been one to rely on rumors to draw his own conclusions, but this time the rumors seemed to have a drop of truth in them. He, too, had read the news about the charred body that had been found at the Brooklyn Bridge. Putting together the pieces—Julius's unexplained absence from school today, his younger sister being pulled out of classes—well, it didn't take a genius to deduce the likeliest explanation. Still, rumors were only rumors. Until he saw an official statement, he wasn't inclined to put stock in his classmates' wild conjectures.

Nicholas strode to his locker, carving a path through the gaggle of students. He was used to crowds parting for him; he stood out, quite literally. Not only was he a fox spirit of the House of Tiger who possessed an extraordinary talent for makeup and fashion; at six foot five, he was one of the tallest students at Earthly Branches.

The dining hall was buzzing as Nicholas entered. There were clear divisions in the various social circles that the Descendants ran in, though the divisions weren't necessarily by house, nor by type of supernatural being.

There was Julius's gang of Talons, the toughest, burliest-looking students, who typically claimed the tables near the entrance. A smaller but less pleasant-looking group sat on the opposite side of the entrance: the die-hard supporters of Marcus and Max Niu. The artsy students camped out in the middle of the group. Dylan and his punk rock–obsessed friends sat not too far from the artsy Descendants. The high table, at the far end of the dining hall, was reserved for the thirteen High Council members.

Nicholas made a beeline for the high table, nodding at the other members. Sylvia nodded back at him before biting into her meatball sub. Beside her, Travis took a swig out of his blood pouch and then saluted Nicholas. Both looked puzzled, as though stuck on solving a particularly complex problem. Sylvia's fingers tensed around the sub, and conversation died down among the other High Council members as they registered Nicholas's approach. They'd been waiting for him to sit down and tell them what was going on, he gathered. He tended to have the answers—especially in regard to Evangeline. This time, however, he was as clueless as the rest of them.

"What's good, Nicky?" asked Travis, his fangs glistening with blood.

"I told you not to call me that," Nicholas grumbled, but that only made Travis laugh.

Nicholas took his usual spot on the left, and then he glanced over at the vacant middle seat. Julius's seat. His throat tightened at the sight. Nicholas was a big believer in following his intuition, and right now his intuition was screaming that the rumors were true. He couldn't imagine attending classes in the future with only one of the Long siblings present. Julius Long's absence was already being felt all around the dining hall, from the curious glances at his empty seat to the Talons' somber expressions. Overnight, the social atmosphere of Earthly Branches Academy had shifted forevermore.

"I heard Evangeline got pulled out of class earlier," Travis drawled, lounging in his chair with an air of forced casualness. The tightened cords of muscle in his arms and neck gave away his anxiety. "Did you hear anything, Nicky—Nicholas? Julius, they think he's—"

"Dead," Nicholas supplied without emotion. "So I've heard."

"Murdered, more like," interjected Sylvia darkly. "There's no way Julius Long was burned to death on accident." Her eyes flicked to Nicholas, squinting slightly. Nicholas supposed this was the question Sylvia and the others had been hoping he'd answer for them. Could it be true? Could the fearless and invincible Julius Long actually have been *murdered*?

"We don't even know that Julius is dead," Nicholas pointed out. "Everything we've heard so far is just speculation." But for all the good it did, he might as well have been talking to the wall. The others seemed to consider Julius's death a foregone conclusion. Perhaps Nicholas was the one foolishly clinging to false hope, against his own intuition.

"Who do you think did it?" Travis asked in hushed tones, as though he was afraid someone—or something—would overhear them. It was obvious he'd been dying to discuss his theories about Julius's murder. "Marcus has been saying something about Wrathlings . . ."

"Couldn't have been any Wrathlings." Nicholas jumped in. "They're not smart enough to take down someone as clever as Julius. All they can do is mindlessly swarm and attack."

"Mmmm." Travis looked unconvinced, but he didn't press. "Or it could have been the fae, those sneaky bastards. They haven't made an appearance in—what—almost a century?"

"Not since the end of the turf war in Chinatown," Sylvia said grimly.

"Bet they've been biding their time, pretending they've disappeared for good, just to strike at us all. Julius's death was a warning."

"This is our Chancellor you're talking about," Nicholas said. "You could speak with more respect."

Travis rolled his eyes, but Sylvia had the sense to drop her gaze. "Does it matter anymore? Julius isn't here. He's . . ." She bit her lip and swallowed the rest of her words.

As Travis and Sylvia continued discussing their theories, Nicholas cast a glance around the room. His gaze fell upon the table of outcasts, primarily werewolves, in the opposite corner. His hands clenched into fists at the sight of one in particular—Tristan She, Evangeline's ex-boyfriend. Tristan had once been Nicholas's closest thing to a best friend. That had been so long in the past, and the sands of time had eroded any lingering affection between the two of them.

Nicholas swallowed back the stab of anger that rose within him. Mid-laugh, Tristan stretched lazily, and then his gaze met Nicholas's. The laughter left his expression, and his eyes narrowed.

Although werewolves were decidedly beautiful, it was in a more rugged way than the fox spirits. Tristan, Nicholas thought, was certainly rough around the edges, and it irked him no end. Tristan's lank brown hair was always rumpled, as though he'd rolled out of bed right before going to class, which in all likelihood was the case.

Though he couldn't read minds, Nicholas could sense the wavelengths of moods in the air—and those wavelengths were telling him that Tristan had an *intense* dislike for him. Even without that sense, though, Nicholas would've been able to tell that Tristan was annoyed at the sight of him.

Well, Nicholas was more than annoyed at the sight of Tristan. Normally, he could stomach it, but not today. Evangeline had disappeared, rumors were flying about the Chancellor's death, and Tristan looked as though he didn't have a care in the world. Perhaps Tristan knew something the others didn't, or perhaps he was just being an insensitive ass, as usual.

Besides, Tristan had damn near broken Evangeline's heart, and anyone who hurt Evangeline would have to answer to Nicholas. He would never forgive the werewolf for that.

Nicholas was halfway across the dining hall before he realized what he was doing, and then he was a couple of inches from Tristan's face. The eyes of the other students were now on him, but he didn't care that he had an audience for this exchange. In fact, perhaps it was better that Nicholas call out Tristan right here, right now, while he commanded the attention of the students. Somebody needed to put Tristan in his place, and now was as good as ever.

"What's the joke, Tristan?" Nicholas asked, injecting into his voice a forced calm he didn't feel. The smiles of Tristan's friends had slipped off their faces. Good. "Please do share with the rest of us."

Tristan sneered. "I don't think I will, given that you lack the sense of humor to properly appreciate it. What's so important that the High Council came over here to grace us with their presence, anyway?" At that, Tristan's group snickered around him, though Nicholas couldn't help but notice that the girls of the group, Meredith and Bethany Yang, were too busy gawking at him to laugh at Tristan's quips.

Nicholas ran a hand through his hair to smooth it down, focusing his attention on the girls. He might as well use his good looks to his advantage. "Hope you all don't mind if I steal Tristan away for a word in private."

"Steal away," giggled Meredith.

Even the other guys didn't seem immune to Nicholas's charm, because they shrugged at one another and nodded.

Tristan scowled. "Whatever you'd like to say to me, Nicholas, you can say in front of everyone."

It was taking every ounce of Nicholas's self-control not to smack that cocky grin off Tristan's face. Nicholas dropped the suave act and slammed his fists down onto the table, making Meredith and Bethany jump. "Believe me, I wouldn't be over here if it weren't serious."

After a long moment, Tristan finally got up from the table. Nicholas led them toward the nearest wall and turned his back to it, facing Tristan. Tristan walked toward Nicholas until the two were mere inches apart. "This had better be good, Hu."

Brusquely, Nicholas asked, "Do you know where Evangeline's vanished to? She hasn't responded to my texts."

53

Tristan's scowl deepened at the mention of Evangeline. "Why would *I* know? I haven't spoken to her in years." His eyes flashed, a warning that Nicholas was swimming in dangerous waters.

"I see the way you look at her in class. I don't believe that you aren't still in contact with Evangeline." A pang of something—protectiveness and maybe even jealousy—shot through Nicholas, but he didn't allow himself time to think about that emotion. Right now, it was far more important that he squeeze any information he could out of Tristan.

Tristan glowered, the tips of his ears turning red. "Look, just because you're obsessed with her doesn't mean the rest of us are—"

"Obsessed?" Nicholas's temper was getting the better of him, causing a familiar, dangerous rise in his temperature. He knew he ought to get it under control lest his powers flare up once more, but at the moment he didn't care enough. He'd put up with Tristan for too long. Heat traveled to the tips of his fingers, begging for release. Nicholas knew this feeling too well. It was a warning that if he didn't calm down, and soon, the fire within would erupt. "I'm not obsessed. I'm looking out for her, not that *you* would know what that entails."

Tristan bared his unnaturally sharp front teeth, and his golden eyes grew brighter. Nicholas's words had clearly struck a nerve. "I'm amazed you managed to lose her, Nicholas, given how you're practically up her ass at all hours. Did it ever occur to you that perhaps Evangeline disappeared to get away from *you*?"

Blood thundered in Nicholas's ears. He couldn't believe it. At this hour, when Tristan should have been worried about Evangeline's absence, as the other students were, he was still mocking Nicholas and glowering as though he'd like nothing better than to pound Nicholas into the pavement.

Yeah, well, the feeling's mutual, Nicholas thought. The bad blood between Nicholas and Tristan was bound to erupt into violence one of these days. Of the two of them, Tristan was undoubtedly better at combat, but Nicholas had more to prove. As if his body meant to prove it right at this moment, flames burst forth at Nicholas's fingertips. Oh, he could easily threaten Tristan—no, *hurt* Tristan—with a single, swift movement—

No. The rational, calm part of Nicholas broke through the swirling chaos. He had to stay in control of his body or face potentially disastrous consequences.

Tristan glanced down at the motion and then slowly raised his gaze back to Nicholas's. There was a steely glint in his eyes that made Nicholas feel like Tristan had surely seen through him, seen his internal war. "Finally, you're growing a backbone, rather than letting Evangeline or Julius fight your battles for you. It's too bad you're over a hundred years too late."

That stung. Tristan hadn't come right out and said it, but Nicholas could guess at what his words implied, and the worst part of it all was that Nicholas couldn't say definitively that Tristan was wrong.

"Speak to me clearly," Nicholas said coldly. "I despise riddles."

Tristan licked his lip. "I don't think your ego could handle it if I did."

The pain was reaching a crescendo within Nicholas. Oh, how he *longed* to lunge at Tristan and unleash the full force of his powers. He was losing his grip on his own mind—a dangerous warning sign. He opened his mouth, unsure if a snarl or a cry of pain would emerge, but then his eyes landed on Dylan. His younger brother had been watching their argument. Although he was all the way across the dining hall, Nicholas could clearly see the alarm in Dylan's expression.

Dylan.

All the fight went out of Nicholas's body, just like that. The fiery heat fled his system. Instead, he was overcome by guilt. He needed to rein in his temper better. Once, years ago, Nicholas had lost his temper in an argument with Dylan. He had nearly killed his brother that day, though Dylan had managed to escape with only minimal burns. Dylan had never forgiven him, and Nicholas had never forgiven himself.

The intercom crackled overhead, jolting Nicholas back to the present.

"Attention, students. Lessons have been canceled for the rest of the day. It has been confirmed that a student, Julius Long, has been found dead. Please return to your dorms at once."

The announcement had a ripple effect on the students in the dining hall. As everyone put their heads together to discuss what this could mean, not bothering to whisper or lower their voices, Nicholas could think of only one thing—Evangeline. He had to get to her.

"Gods," Tristan breathed in shock.

Forgetting everything that had just happened with Tristan, Nicholas turned on his heel and fled the dining hall in the direction of the House of Dragon. Evangeline split her time between the dorms and the Long estate; there was a good chance she was still on campus. He sprinted so quickly he was practically flying across the grass in the courtyard. In the center of the yard was a broken fountain, which had once been a dazzling centerpiece of the Old Summer Palace. There were seven fountainheads, each slightly larger than a human head, placed in a circle in the same positions as when they'd been part of the Old Summer Palace. There were five gaps, one for each missing fountainhead.

Wherever the Descendants went, the source of their power couldn't be too far; thus, when the Academy had been built in the States, the Descendants had painstakingly brought over each piece that remained of the Circle of Twelve. Every time he passed by the broken circle, Nicholas found himself having to quickly look away. The sight of the ruins brought back terrible memories that he'd rather not relive.

The House of Dragon building was notable because of the two golden dragon pillars that held up the red roof. In moments, Nicholas reached the building and flung open the door. He startled a freshman girl rounding the corner, who screamed at the sight of him.

Nicholas hardly noticed; he was laser-focused on his mission as he barreled down the hallway. *Third door on the left, and—*

The door to Evangeline's room was open, but there was no Evangeline in sight. Her bed appeared perfectly tidy, as though nobody had used it for some time.

Nicholas swore under his breath. If only he'd moved a little faster, if only he hadn't wasted so much time on that moron Tristan She. With both of the Long siblings gone, he predicted that the power balance among the Descendants would be thrown off more than it had in a long, long time. He just hoped Evangeline would come back soon.

6
ALICE

For the human students who hadn't fallen asleep yet, there was terrible news to give them even more trouble sleeping: the death of Julius Long.

That evening, Alice had a strange dream. This was not out of the ordinary for her. When she was younger, she'd often had these dreams, which were terrifying and yet beautiful. Dreams that were so real she was surprised when she awoke from them.

This time, Alice dreamed of creatures that were human-like, but not quite. Sharp pointed ears, dark green hair, and a mesmerizing beauty that could put the most stunning models to shame.

Even in a different place far, far away from her home, the same dreams haunted her.

Sometimes these creatures entered Alice's dreams; sometimes they were disguised as humans in real life. They moved freely in society, which was the confusing part. When she was little, she used to point them out to her mother. ("Mama, do you see that man over there with those fangs?" "Have you ever noticed that the head librarian has fox ears?") But it became quite clear after a while that her mother couldn't see these

creatures, and she would grow agitated and sometimes even burst into tears whenever Alice spoke about them.

Eventually, Alice learned to stop bringing up her ability to see these creatures. But that didn't mean she'd stopped seeing them. It was never anything covert, but Alice, who possessed unusually sharp senses, could perceive what other humans could not. Like the neighbor across the street whose eyes flashed red and whose teeth lengthened into fangs before he headed back into his house. Or the peculiar grandmother who'd been Alice's babysitter for all of twenty-four hours when she was very little, almost too little to remember anything, but she recalled abnormally gnarled fingers that gripped her wrists tight enough to cause bruises. When Alice showed the marks to Mama, she fired the babysitter the very next day.

Mama grew so paranoid that she scarcely let Alice around any strangers, and Alice found that her real-life encounters with these odd people became less frequent as she grew older. However, this was directly proportionate to the increased rate at which Alice had these bizarre dreams. They came to her often now, more and more frequently in the past few months—and especially since she'd enrolled at Earthly Branches Academy.

And tonight, the creatures in her dreams were much more fully formed. She glimpsed dazzling details in their appearances: from the dresses woven of flower petals to the shiny golden rings they wore on their fingers, the sparkling jewelry that dangled from their necks and earlobes.

One stepped up in front of the others, a male with long black hair and piercing eyes. On his head perched a golden crown, to match the gold and silver jewelry that decorated his body. At the sight of him, Alice was hit with a dizzying sense of déjà vu, that perhaps they had known each other in this lifetime or another, but such a thing couldn't be possible, and anyhow, weren't dreams always bizarre and irrational?

"Stolen child," he whispered. "Come back to us."

The male creature reached out and grabbed Alice's wrist, gripping it so hard that she cried out with the pain, and she did not know whether it was dream Alice or real Alice experiencing this pain.

59

"Alice. *Alice!*"

The creatures disappeared, and Alice awoke groggily to the sound of someone yelling her name. Someone was still gripping her wrist painfully hard. After blinking the sleep out of her eyes, Alice realized that her roommate, Madison, was standing over her, her eyes wild and fearful.

"Ow! You're hurting me." Alice shook her wrist free from Madison's grasp and rubbed it. It was already starting to turn red.

"You were having a nightmare," Madison said. "You kept tossing and turning."

The details of Alice's dream were slipping away, but she didn't remember being all that frightened in her sleep. Maybe just a little. She hadn't minded. She hadn't noticed, really. Such was the beauty of the creatures in her imagination—they could lull her into a false sense of security. How could these beautiful creatures be capable of harming Alice?

"It's natural to have nightmares. I had one, too, once we found out what happened to Julius," Madison continued.

Julius. Right. Reality slowly returned to Alice. "Do you think they'll send the whole school home because of this?" she asked.

"I don't know. Probably not. Like, those of us who are normal—well, I mean, human—we can go back to society, no problem," Madison said, waving a hand to accentuate her points. "But the vampires, werewolves, foxes? Forget it. There's a reason they're staying at Earthly Branches Academy. It would be disastrous if they all tried to blend in with the humans."

Alice nodded. Her roommate was right. The school likely wasn't going to shut down unless it was literally burned down, or something equally damaging and permanent.

"My mother will definitely make me come home if she finds out what happened." Alice sighed.

"My parents knew as soon as we did," Madison said. "They're nosy like that."

Like parents, like daughter, Alice thought. "What do you think's going to happen next?" she asked. "The High Council will have to select a new Chancellor, I imagine."

"It'll be Julius's younger sister, of course," Madison said swiftly, "unless Marcus Niu puts up a good fight. He's the only High Council member with enough pull to dethrone the Longs. One thing's for sure—it'll be chaos for the next few weeks as the High Council scrambles to figure out their next move." Her smile revealed teeth, as though the thought of the oncoming drama delighted her. "I'm just sad I won't be around to see it."

"What? Why not?" Alice sat up, confused. Then, for the first time, she registered that Madison's side of the room had been stripped bare. Though they hadn't had much time to decorate yet, what few decorations Madison had put up—some green vines and fairy lights—had been haphazardly yanked down. "Are you . . . going somewhere?"

There was a loud rustling as Madison wrestled with the zipper of her Vera Wang duffel bag. "Yeah. Home. I told my parents what happened to Julius, and they insisted I leave the school. They were a bit hesitant sending me here in the first place—my father is a former Descendant, and he never wanted his children or grandchildren to go down the same path, but I insisted. Now, though, my parents really want me to come back home. They're terrified, you know. I'm their only child. And if someone or something is really after the students at this school, who do you think is the easiest target?"

That went without saying. Alice's pulse quickened at the thought. The human Descendants were vulnerable. The other students could defend themselves, but the regular mortal students had barely begun to learn self-defense. Combat was probably Alice's worst subject so far, and Madison hadn't been faring better than her.

Alice pictured herself returning home. Mama would be thrilled to have her back in time to celebrate her seventeenth birthday, and more than that, she would undoubtedly be relieved that Alice had made the safe choice. Alice *always* made the safe choice. This time, though, despite knowing the dangers of staying at Earthly Branches Academy, she couldn't imagine leaving. She couldn't imagine leaving behind all this—this totally new world that had just opened up before her, this part of herself that she'd never known, this place where she felt closer to *Baba* than ever before.

And how could Alice explain all this to Madison? Madison wouldn't get it. She had both of her parents eagerly awaiting her return. For Madison, there was no mystery about an absent family member to solve here at the Academy.

Madison raised her eyebrow. "You should really tell your family, too. Ask them to come pick you up before it's too late. Staying at Earthly Branches isn't worth risking your life." She shrugged. "That's just my opinion."

"But . . ." Although Madison's logic sounded correct, the situation didn't sit right with Alice. After all, if every Descendant up and fled at the first sign of danger, how would there be any left? "But what happened to Julius occurred *off* school grounds. The school . . . it's supposed to be safe."

Madison rolled her eyes. Swinging her duffel bag over one shoulder, she grabbed the handle of her oversized suitcase. "Well, I'm out of here. You've got my number, so call me if you ever need anything. If not—it was nice knowing you." And with that, she strode through the doorway and down the hall.

Alice stood there for a beat, shocked. Madison had just *left*, and so boldly at that. Alice wasn't sure whether to think her roommate—*former* roommate—very brave, or very stupid. The abrupt, cold departure was almost too sudden to register. Though she and Madison had been more acquaintances than friends—academic friends at best—they had both existed on the outskirts at the House of Boar; and now, with Madison gone, Alice would be the only one. Alice felt as though she'd lost something she hadn't even realized she'd had.

After a moment, she dashed into the hall, only to find Kate Zhu standing in front of the elevator as it closed.

Slowly, Kate turned to face Alice. The expression on her face suggested mild curiosity. "What are you doing out here?"

"Did you see Madison just now?"

No change in Kate's expression. "Yes. She's left Earthly Branches Academy. We said our goodbyes."

"You—you let her go just like that?"

"I can't stop those who have decided to turn their backs on the Descendants," said Kate with a shrug. "No one can. We can warn them of the dangers, of course, but ultimately you're all old enough to make your own decisions and live with the consequences."

Alice turned away from Kate long enough to glance out the window. The sun had barely started to rise, and the streetlamps were still lit, casting the grounds in a misty glow. Three stories below, among the magnificent oak trees that lined the school entrance, Alice glimpsed a black van sitting out front. Madison walked in front of it, dragging her luggage behind her, and an older man got out of the driver's seat to help her. Her father, Alice presumed. Then, after a few moments, Madison got into the van. They drove off, and that was the last Alice saw of her roommate.

"You have good timing, Alice," Kate was saying. Her face was drawn, and a bit gaunt. There were dark circles under her eyes. Alice wondered if Kate had been sleeping poorly, too. "I was about to come get you. I've summoned the House of Boar for an emergency meeting. I'm sure you have a lot of questions about what's going on."

That was an understatement.

With that, Kate stepped down the empty hall toward the staircase. After a moment's hesitation, Alice followed.

Kate led her to a meeting room, where the other human students had already congregated at a round table lit by candlelight. Perhaps it was the dim lighting, but the confusion and fear Alice was feeling appeared to be magnified in the others' expressions. Jimmy was biting his nails. Rebecca stared down at the table as though she'd like nothing better than to sink through it. Even Darla was uncharacteristically quiet. Alice sat down in one of the two empty chairs, between Darla and Rebecca. Neither of them so much as glanced at her.

Kate sat down and folded her hands in front of her. "I don't believe in beating around the bush, so I'll cut right to the chase. Recent events have thrown the safety of Earthly Branches Academy into question. As you've just witnessed, a fellow House of Boar Descendant—Madison—has left the Academy and, in doing so, lost her birthright to her powers forevermore. Her offspring can be part of the line of Descendants, but Madison herself will live and die an ordinary human being."

Alice startled. She hadn't realized that in leaving the Academy, Madison had given up her powers and severed her ties to all the Descendants. That she couldn't go back on that decision. A sweeping glance around the table showed that the other humans were equally pale-faced and shocked.

Kate steamrollered on. "As I explained to you on your first day of classes, you are each either directly or distantly related to the only mortal bloodline that remained among the twelve Descendant families—the Zhus, who mysteriously evaded the supernatural curse, for reasons we still don't understand to this day." Kate pointed toward the back wall, and everyone turned around at once to stare at the portrait of a beautiful, curvy woman posed in an armchair, and a handsome, well-muscled man standing behind her. "Although the original Zhus have long since passed—bless their souls—their legacy and power live on in you. Now that you're all sixteen, your powers will be growing stronger than ever, which will make you targets for shamans, fae, and monstrous beings."

"Was it a Wrathling that killed Julius?" Jimmy blurted out. He was trembling from head to foot now. "Is there likely to be a Wrathling attack?"

Kate shook her head and emphatically said, "No. The Descendants have slowly been able to wipe out the Wrathlings over the years, and in any case, Wrathlings aren't smart enough to coordinate such a precise assassination. Nevertheless, Earthly Branches offers protection from those beings. The school was established to promote what the Descendants have always found most crucial to progress: constant learning and

64

consistent structure, as best provided in a school environment." Kate was speaking so quickly that Alice could barely keep up.

"The point I am making—the point I need to stress the most—is that you are *safe* here. In fact, you're safer here than anywhere else in the world, given your abilities, which would attract the attention of horrible creatures out there. Believe me, if anyone else at this school intended to hurt you, you would already be dead." Kate smiled grimly. "If, after hearing me out, you still decide to leave Earthly Branches Academy, then I have no choice but to hold the door open for you and wish you all the best." As she said this, Kate fixed each of them with a cold, hard stare. When those determined eyes looked into Alice's, she found it difficult not to avert her gaze. "But I plan to lay my life down to protect those who can't protect themselves, as my ancestors did. I hope you'll join me in doing the same."

The candlelight flickered when Kate finished speaking, as though to emphasize the gravity of her words.

School had just gone from fun to deadly in the blink of an eye, leaving Alice's head spinning. She almost wanted to laugh at how naive she'd been just a handful of months ago, how little she'd known about the world around her—about herself. And now here she was, unearthing powers that she'd never been aware of, pledging her life to protect all humans alongside her fellow Descendants.

Though Alice didn't *have* to pledge her life. Kate had just given them all an out. But that would mean leaving behind any possibility of getting the answers to all the questions about her father that she'd harbored for years, and the new questions that had emerged after she'd arrived at the Academy. That would mean turning her back on the life Baba had lived. That would mean never grasping the full extent of her own magic, her own destiny. Never knowing herself, fully and truly.

Alice stayed in her seat. So did all the others.

"I'm with you, Kate," Alice said quietly, surprising even herself by being the first to break the silence. There was fear in her heart, yes, but above all else, there was excitement. Determination, and a hunger to prove herself.

Kate flashed Alice a wan, relieved smile.

"And me," said Rebecca, her fists clenched on the table in determination.

"And me," added Jimmy in a shaky voice.

Darla sighed as all eyes turned to her. If anyone were to up and leave now, it would be Darla, Alice thought. But she surprised Alice by saying, with just a hint of regret, "I guess I won't be going to Greece for a while."

"Well." Kate sat back, grinning widely. "I didn't expect all of you to stay. I'm grateful."

In this room, Alice sensed that something huge had shifted. A gentle breeze lifted her hair from her nape, though there shouldn't have been any wind in the enclosed room. The candle flame flickered and then grew brighter and stronger. A shiver ran up Alice's spine. Even though nobody else was in the room, it was as though somebody or something greater—possibly even the spirits of their ancestors themselves—had overseen their vows to the Descendants.

No longer were they all merely classmates, getting accustomed to Earthly Branches Academy life together. They would train with a greater purpose now—to carry out the legacy of their ancestors and to protect the people of Earth, even at the risk of their own lives.

Now that she had committed to staying with the Descendants, Alice was certain of one thing: this would either be the best decision or the biggest mistake of her life.

7
EVANGELINE

Evangeline was certain she could never, ever go back to Earthly Branches Academy. Not now that her brother was dead. She couldn't even *think* about school without pain stabbing her chest. No, she didn't have a beating heart any longer, but that didn't make this news any less devastating. Her cheeks were streaked with tears of blood, the only tears her vampire body could produce.

For decades, it had just been Evangeline and Julius, Julius and Evangeline. She had assumed that if they ever met their ends, it would be together—because how could there be Evangeline without Julius? How could Earth continue to spin in its orbit, as though the world could simply go *on* in Julius's absence, when Evangeline's heart was shattering into a million pieces? Now that she had found herself in this predicament, she didn't know how to continue.

It hadn't always been like this. Once, the dragon bloodline had boasted formidable numbers. When the Circle of Twelve had broken, the dragon fountainhead carried off, their powers had weakened, and every last member of the dragon bloodline had died defending their magic, their country. Everyone except Julius and Evangeline. Although all of the Descendants had suffered, no other bloodline had dealt with such a tremendous loss.

So for decades now, Julius had been all that Evangeline had left, the only family that had been chained to this cursed existence as she was. Now he had gone, leaving her behind. She wasn't sure if what she was feeling was grief or fury.

All Evangeline knew for certain was that with her older brother gone, the responsibilities of running the Long estate, leading the Descendants as the Chancellor of the High Council, had fallen to her. It was a weight almost too sudden and heavy to bear. Yet bear it she would, for the House of Dragon had led the Descendants since the beginning of everything, and as she was a Long—the *only* Long remaining, as far as she knew—she would claim her rightful place among the Descendants. She would not let their legacy die.

Evangeline walked into Julius's study. Everything was in the exact same position as the last time she'd seen her brother there. The large mahogany bookshelf that housed Julius's hundreds of books. The coaster Julius had used for his morning coffee and nightly tea. The file cabinets—locked, of course—that contained the secret portfolios of the family's wealth, mostly real estate investments, the details of which had never been privy even to Evangeline. If she just turned around, Evangeline thought, she still might see her brother's tall figure framed in the doorway. He would place a steaming mug of coffee on the coaster, lounge in his leather desk chair, and greet her with his trademark mischievous grin.

But that was no more. Julius was no more.

Reaching out with shaking hands, Evangeline ran her fingertips along the edges of the desk—and winced as they found the sharp edge of a yellowed piece of paper, sitting next to her brother's computer. She picked it up and looked more closely, and her eyes widened in surprise at the words inscribed in Julius's familiar loopy script.

My dearest Evangeline—

I leave tonight in what may well be my final attempt to right the terrible injustice that was done to our people in the looting of the Old Summer Palace. The five lost bronze statues—rooster, dog, snake, dragon, and sheep—have recently resurfaced, and the opportunity to restore them to the Old Summer Palace is at my fingertips. But, as with any deal that is almost too good to be true, there is a catch. I must go alone to meet the informant, on their orders. The informant has not revealed their identity, but my best guess is that they're fae.

I won't lie. There is a very good chance that I will never return. If I don't, it means that negotiations have gone awry and that the enemy we face is more powerful than I feared. It also means that you must be the one to take back the magical artifacts that rightfully belong to our people. If my suspicions are correct, it's the fae who stole our magic and have been hiding it within Faerieland. I wish I could give you a clear plan to accomplish this monumental task, but there are so many unknown variables that I fear my guidance would only hinder you, not help.

On the flip side of this paper is a map of the Underground—the shamans don't know it exists and is in my possession, else they'd have sent in someone ages ago to have it destroyed. You might find it handy to consult the Scarlet Spy for help—if you can first navigate your way into the deepest cell of the Underground prison.

I leave in your care the Long family wealth and the reins to take over as Chancellor of the High Council, though it will be up to you to prove yourself worthy of the title.

Most importantly, remember the prophecy that the faerie Seer delivered to us in the aftermath of the looting:

69

THE KEY TO RESTORING GLORY RESTS WITH MIDSUMMER'S SPROUT; BUT IF GREED
SOWS DISCORD, HARMONY WILL BE IN DOUBT.

I have long suspected that you, the only known Descendant born on Midsummer's Day, are "Midsummer's sprout"—the one capable of restoring glory to the Descendants. As for what the second half of the prophecy entails . . . I, for one, don't believe we've beaten the Wrathlings back indefinitely, even if I have no concrete evidence to prove my theory. I caution you to move forward with your wits about you. I trust that you will do all of us Descendants proud.

Be well, sister. For everyone's sake, I hope my instincts are very, very wrong.

—J.L.

Her fingers still trembling, Evangeline flipped over the note. Just as Julius had described it, the back side showed a weathered map of a perplexing arrangement of tunnels that led to a large central point. The prison sector lay in one of the tunnels to the left.

Julius was always careful and concise with his words. He did not say anything he did not mean, which meant he wrote this letter knowing full well that what he feared might come to pass. Given how long he'd kept this secret map of the Underground, he had been planning to make this move for a long, long time, without Evangeline being any the wiser.

"Dammit, Julius," she hissed under her breath. She didn't know whether it was appropriate to curse him or not, now that he was already dead, but it had never even crossed her mind that Julius could be moving in secret without letting her in on his plans. If only she had known that he had gone to this dangerous meeting. What if she had secretly followed him? Could she have protected and saved her brother—or would she have ended up dead as well?

Evangeline took a deep, shaky breath. Her brother's hands had once held this piece of paper. It was one of the last things he'd done. She blinked back tears. Now wasn't the time to cry. Now was the time to process what she needed to do, to ensure that *she* would lead the Descendants into their next chapter of glory.

Shamans. Fae. Stolen fountainheads. A prophecy—about *her*. The Descendants had been split half and half on the matter of the faerie Seer's prophecy; some believed the events prophesized would come to pass, and some merely chalked up the prophecy as myth. Julius had always firmly believed the faerie Seer's words, though, and Evangeline would be wise to lean into her brother's intuition. She wasn't sure yet how she felt about Julius's hypothesis that she was the subject of the prophecy; he'd never shared that with her before, and she'd certainly never thought of herself as such. She felt dazed, perhaps. Shocked. With this revelation, even more pressure sat on her shoulders.

And then, at the end of his letter, Julius had slipped in that ominous warning about the Wrathlings. Elder Shu had seemed unconvinced about the threat of Wrathlings returning. But Julius was so rarely wrong. Perhaps there was more to the situation than met the eye.

The information in Julius's parting letter was a lot to process at once, almost too much. Evangeline couldn't even think about tackling everything she needed to without giving her brain and body a boost of energy. She didn't want to deal with a hungry stomach and parched throat on top of all this.

"Cecil, where's my coffee? With blood?"

"Coming." The vampire servant girl hurried into the room, carrying a tray with a pot of coffee, a small white cup, and a box of tissues. She placed it on Julius's desk. Cecil took one look at Evangeline's face and ducked her head, her long, straight black hair hanging over her face like a curtain, as though she'd witnessed something unsightly.

Feeling self-conscious, Evangeline wiped at her cheeks. She'd been crying on and off since hearing the awful news, and it was time she got her emotions under control. Over the years she'd gotten very good at hiding her weaknesses—it was the only way to conduct herself as a Long.

Deep down, Evangeline had known this day would come. She'd never dreamed it would be this soon, but a vampire like Julius Long, who brashly made both alliances and enemies among Manhattan's most powerful players, was bound to meet an untimely fate. She had always known she would make an excellent leader, and now she would prove it with all the watchful eyes of the Descendants upon her.

Evangeline was many things, but she was not a thief. Oh, she was certain she had the *makings* of a great thief. She didn't want to stoop so low, however, and she'd never had to—her life, up until now, had been fairly cushy. Partnering with criminals was her brother's line of business. But if it came down to it, Evangeline wasn't above playing dirty to preserve her family fortune.

Little by little, she warmed to the idea of being the subject of prophecy. It had never sat well with her that the thieves who broke apart the Circle of Twelve had gotten away scot-free, while the Descendants had to suffer the consequences for so long; it wasn't right, and now that she might have the power to turn the situation around, she wouldn't let the chance slip through her fingers.

Sometimes, when she was alone, Evangeline heard the voices of the dying Descendants shrieking in her head over and over again, as clear as though she were back in 1860. Those screams of pain would haunt her for an eternity. Julius had never let her see her parents' bodies in the aftermath of that day; he had seen them, and they were so mangled that he couldn't bear to let her witness her parents in their state of disgrace.

And who was to answer for these crimes? Who would pay for taking so many Descendant lives that fateful day? Evangeline had long since learned to bury her rage and grief deep down, else she'd do nothing but simmer all day and night. Yet now that there was an opportunity to move forward, to finally grasp justice for their dead loved ones, for the glory of what had once been, she let the emotions rise and fuel her.

Whoever had killed and cursed the Descendants—they might be long dead themselves, as far as she knew. But the zodiac fountainheads must still be out there, and she would get them back at any cost.

"Are you all right?" Cecil asked in concern. "I know . . . Julius's death . . . all of it has to be overwhelming." Cecil let out a hiccup, sounding as though she was forcing back sobs. Her eyes were red and puffy. She must have cried a great deal upon hearing the news. It struck Evangeline that all of this had to be traumatic for Cecil, too.

"I'm fine," Evangeline said dully, although she had never been less fine, except during the fall of the Old Summer Palace. For a moment, she toyed with the idea of actually opening up to Cecil for once—dear Cecil, who gazed upon her with shining, worried eyes, and who extended a hand to comfort her. Evangeline's ironclad resolve crumbled just a bit. She reached out and took Cecil's hand in hers, and the two girls stood there with the comfort of knowing that they still had each other to weather the storm of grief.

"I think it would be a good idea for you to rest up," Cecil suggested gently after a moment. "And I'll bring you more blood, too. When was the last time you fed? You don't look well."

"Don't overreach," said Evangeline, snatching her hand back. She hadn't had enough blood for a few days now, which always made her irritable. She didn't know how to deal with all the rage and grief inside her, besides closing up and lashing out. "I know my parents took you in and gave you our family name, but don't forget that you are a servant to the family, Cecil. You don't tell me what to do."

Cecil stumbled back as though she'd been slapped, and regret immediately burned in the pit of Evangeline's stomach. Evangeline normally treated Cecil as though they were equals, and on the few emotional occasions when she reminded Cecil that they were in fact *not* on equal standing, it was always in a very harsh manner.

"I'm sorry, xiǎo jiě," Cecil mumbled. "I would never presume to tell you what to do."

Evangeline sighed and pressed her perfectly manicured fingertips to her temples. She was taking her anger out on her loyal servant, and it was wrong. Even in the midst of emotional turmoil, she knew that much. "No, *I'm* sorry. It's been . . . it's been a long day. And I have funeral arrangements to think about on top of everything. Please bring me a few of those blood buns, but otherwise I'd like to be left alone, Cecil."

"As you wish." With a bow, Cecil made to sweep out of the room.

And Evangeline immediately wanted to take back her order. Loath as she was to admit it, much as she wished she could take matters into her own hands, she needed help. If Evangeline was to take on this Assignment, if she was to exact vengeance for her people, she couldn't do it alone. She was good, but not good enough to execute the perfect heist on her first try on her own—and she would get no second chances. The words came out of Evangeline's mouth before she could stop them. "Actually, wait."

Cecil turned, her head tilted in confusion. "Yes?"

"I . . . Give me a moment to think." Evangeline's mind had cleared somewhat after she'd gotten blood into her system. Her brain ran a mile a minute as she broke down the task into manageable elements. She glanced over Julius's note again. He hadn't given her all that much to go on, just the bare bones of what needed to happen to pull off a successful heist. It was enough. It had to be.

Evangeline's eyes zeroed in on that name: *Scarlet Spy.* It had been years since she'd heard that name, and memories rushed back to her all at once. Evangeline had known the Scarlet Spy as an old friend and business partner of Julius's. Whatever the Scarlet Spy's real name was, that had never been revealed to Evangeline. From time to time when she was younger, Julius would invite the Scarlet Spy around for drinks at the estate. Evangeline remembered the day she'd found out that the Scarlet Spy had been caught and locked up in the Underground for betraying information about the shamans to the Descendants. Julius had spent the evening drinking alone in his office. Her brother had never held many close, not even the Talons, and the Scarlet Spy had been allowed closer than most.

How was Evangeline supposed to track down the Scarlet Spy and convince him to take on this impossible heist? If the faerie Seer's prophecy really referred to her, then she had no choice *but* to take on this Assignment. She was the key to uncovering the long-lost fountainheads.

As Evangeline probed her memories, she had a sudden realization. Julius hadn't been the only partner of the Scarlet Spy—the shaman had spent a curious amount of time with Tristan, too, though she had never known the nature of their interactions. Tristan, for all his flaws, had always been admirably good about creating and keeping connections in both high and low places. . . . The thought of swallowing her pride and going to him for help made her almost prefer a stake to her heart, but there were no better options as far as she could tell. She needed somebody to persuade the Scarlet Spy to their cause. And she needed the aid of an expert criminal. Someone who pickpocketed for fun. Someone who could probably steal the highest-security works out of the Louvre if he wanted to.

"I need you to drop a line to Elder Shu," Evangeline said briskly. "Ask her to grant me and a small group of students permission to leave the school for an extended period, in order to take on an Assignment."

"Do you think she'll allow it on such short notice?"

Evangeline didn't hesitate for even a moment. "Yes. This is an emergency, and I'm the last of the dragon bloodline—she'll respect my wishes." Cecil nodded, and Evangeline sighed and continued. "Next, summon Tristan to me." Evangeline spat out the name like one might spit out poison. As much as it pained her to go to him for help, she saw no other option. She would keep this matter strictly professional and go through Cecil for the messaging, even though she knew that if she wanted to, she could simply call Tristan herself. The history between Evangeline and Tristan was long and messy, and she didn't need to get into it now—or ever, really. "He's owed me a favor for a while—remind him of that fact, please—and now I require his services."

"Services? What . . . what kind of services?"

Cecil's tone was innocent enough, but there was a slight suggestion in that pause that caused Evangeline's cheeks to heat. Cecil knew what had happened between Evangeline and Tristan, but she wouldn't say a word. Evangeline had made it crystal clear that unless she brought up Tristan herself, nobody else was allowed to. Unless, of course, they wanted to invoke her wrath. "Much as I hate to admit it, Tristan's help will be invaluable for this Assignment. I need a thief—a good thief with powerful connections. It's not like he's good for anything else."

"Of course, xiǎo jiě." Cecil turned to leave.

"Where are you going? I'm not finished yet."

Slowly Cecil swiveled back.

Evangeline licked her lips. In her head, she visualized the plan as a chessboard, with chess pieces moving into place one by one, each piece invaluable to pulling off her vision for victory. In addition to a seasoned thief, she would need the aid of a supernatural with the ability to disguise them all as they navigated dangerous territories. Finally, the crew would best be rounded out by an individual who could give them a leg up over any adversary, and bonus points if that individual could secretly be of additional value to Evangeline.

"After you've fetched Tristan, I want you to summon two more Descendants." Evangeline spoke with as much conviction as she could muster. Adrenaline raced through her veins. This would be a huge gamble, but given the enormity of the possible payoff, she needed to grit her teeth and hedge her bets. "Nicholas Hu and . . . Alice Jiang."

Cecil's lips parted in surprise. "Alice Jiang? The human girl?"

"Yes, Cecil, the human girl. Do you know of another Alice Jiang?" Evangeline asked in a clipped tone. The dismissal was loud and clear. Evangeline had made up her mind, and she would not be changing it, no matter how confusing Cecil might find her orders. Cecil, of course, realized this quickly. She turned and ducked out of the room.

Evangeline watched Cecil go. The adrenaline fled her body all at once. Hatching this wild plan based on Julius's notes had been a brief distraction, and now that she was left alone again, the soul-crushing grief returned with a vengeance.

Evangeline was no longer the last Descendant of the House of Dragon; no longer the vampire ice queen; no longer a contender for the next Chancellor of the High Council.

She was just a girl who'd lost her only brother. She let her shoulders crumple, and she sobbed.

8
TRISTAN

Sirens blared through the streets of Koreatown, an eternal, seemingly unending warning of the debauchery that infected the city streets. High up in the sky, partially obscured by the numerous skyscrapers, the near-full moon hung like a crystal ball. To most citizens of the city, the moon was nothing particularly remarkable, and certainly nothing dangerous—but for Tristan, the approach of the full moon was when he was most in danger of losing control of himself to the beast within.

Tristan had found, over many years of experimentation and (often quite miserable) experiences, that he was best able to control the werewolf within when he was heavily distracted. Being drunk helped, too. Therefore, the only option for tonight, of course, was to find the best of both worlds—at a club. Conveniently, there was a matter of business he needed to handle at the very same place.

Tristan was a regular at the nightclub called the Nest. He didn't enjoy the stench of sweat and alcohol that permeated the air, nor was he particularly fond of the electronic dance music that blared from the speakers. But he found himself drawn to the scene anyway. Cabaret dancing had been a popular pastime in Shanghai over a century ago, and Tristan could be found frequenting those establishments whenever he was in town. Though much time and distance had passed for him between now and then, much remained quite the same. Humans still found astonishing enjoyment in gathering at places where the music was turned up so loud it ought to be illegal, yelling themselves hoarse trying to carry on a conversation.

Observing the K-town nightlife, watching the humans make fools of themselves, was a semi-entertaining way to pass the hours and most certainly a better use of time than attending classes at Earthly Branches. And tonight, it was helping to ease Tristan's racing pulse and gnawing hunger—the signs that unless he maintained total mental control, he'd soon find himself transforming into a werewolf. That hadn't happened in years, though—except for an incident four years ago that nearly resulted in a horrible disaster. Tristan had just about mastered the level of control necessary for prevention, so he had every reason to believe that this next full moon would pass without a hitch.

Tristan especially delighted in the fact that one of the cute bartenders at the Nest had an obvious crush on him. If she knew he was in some ways technically seventeen, she'd no doubt be horrified. Though the key word here was *technically,* because while Tristan was seventeen according to his legal papers, he was actually over a hundred years old—180, to be exact.

"You're back, Theodore," said the bartender, Lydia, batting her outrageously long eyelashes at Tristan. *Theodore* was the name Tristan had chosen for himself for when he wanted to escape from his real name and all the baggage that came with it. *Theodore* wasn't a troublemaker and a disappointment as a Descendant, cutting class at this very moment. *Theodore* wouldn't even dream of putting a toe out of line.

"I was hoping you'd be working tonight," Tristan said smoothly.

Lydia flushed. She tucked a strand of her short black hair behind her ear and gave him a flirtatious little smile. "Peach soju for you again?"

"You know me too well, Lydia." At Tristan's words, Lydia smiled. Tristan gave the barest trace of a grin in return.

The gag was that this was simply not true at all, and both knew it. Tristan and Lydia had no relationship outside of their insignificant little exchanges at the Nest. In fact, Lydia did not even know his real name. Yet Tristan took comfort in such surface-level relationships as this; his greatest fear was that if he let anyone get too close, they would come to hurt him, and he them. No such harm could come from casual flirting. Besides, who didn't enjoy feeling attractive every now and then?

Lydia beamed at Tristan and went to the back to grab a bottle of soju. Leaning against the counter, Tristan turned and examined his surroundings. It was only half past eleven, which, in the city that never slept, meant most people were still getting ready to go out for the night. There was one couple on the dance floor, and a few other people standing around the tables on the edge of the floor. They looked young, like college students, maybe fresh graduates at most. The Nest attracted the younger crowd, so Tristan blended right in.

Tonight, Tristan wasn't here to play around (though he still welcomed any and all flirting, of course). He actually had a mission this time. He surveyed the crowd again. Some faces were vaguely familiar, which was his sign that he really ought to cut down on his visits to this place. But still, he hadn't spotted his target.

Then—there. Out of the corner of his eye, Tristan watched the two of them wandering into the bar, slightly stumbling, clearly already half drunk. This came as no surprise; he knew they would be, as they often came to K-town to let off steam from the stress of school and other responsibilities. As the figures stepped closer in the dim lighting, Tristan recognized those inhumanly beautiful faces, and the nine tails that swooped in the shadows behind them. Mortals wouldn't notice the tails—their poor eyesight simply couldn't register the image—but Tristan did. Gina and Louis. Two House of Dog students, twin sister and brother, who were also part of Julius's exclusive inner circle, the Talons. Gina and Louis cut class and frequented the Nest, though not nearly as often as Tristan. He'd known they would be here tonight, though, as they wouldn't be able to resist coming to see their favorite DJ, Trip.

A gold watch glimmered on Louis's left wrist. A magical watch that could help its user travel up to twelve hours into the past or future. A few days ago, Louis had been bragging about it to anyone who would stay still long enough. The watch was a handy and priceless artifact, one that Tristan certainly could have used for himself.

This wasn't a mission he was completing for himself, though. It was a mission for the Collector, the shadowy lord of Manhattan's Underground activities who hired Tristan for shady jobs here and there, retrieving precious magical artifacts from their (usually rightful) owners. In return, Tristan received money and consistent access to aubrum, an illicit pill that altered his hormones so that he was far less likely to transform into a werewolf during a full moon.

Tristan melted into the shadows. Even untransformed, werewolves could move three times faster than humans and were twice as fast as fox spirits. Now he used his full speed to reach the twins. He brushed past without touching their bodies at all, except to unbuckle and lift Louis's watch from his wrist in less than a second. Then Tristan was back across the room, the gold watch now weighing down his pocket, with none around them any the wiser.

Job well done, he thought, because there was nobody around to compliment him. There never was, so Tristan had to pretend it no longer mattered to him.

A finger tapped Tristan's left shoulder. He startled, nearly jumping out of the way. His senses were a hundred times sharper than almost any creature's, so if it *were* a human next to him—no, that wouldn't be possible, because he would've sensed any human. Would've been able to smell a werewolf or fox spirit a mile off as well, and Louis and Gina were still all the way across the room, oblivious to his presence in the club. That left only one possibility.

"Vampire," he growled. "You shouldn't be here right now."

"Seeing as how we're both out late on a school night, I suppose this is a case of the pot calling the kettle black, isn't it?"

Tristan would know that infuriating, holier-than-thou voice anywhere.

Though normally he expected to hear it coming from beside the ice queen herself, Evangeline Long. He turned around, not bothering to disguise his disgust. Yet he was a bit nervous, too. Had Cecil seen what he'd done just now? "How did you find me here?"

Cecil Long was standing there with a haughty expression on her face, looking remarkably like Evangeline. Those two really did spend too much time together. "It wasn't hard. I followed the smell of wet dog."

"Impressive that you were able to smell that over the stench of vampire. Personally, I can't smell anything else."

That wiped the smirk right off Cecil's face. Well, the vampire shouldn't be dishing out anything she couldn't take.

"Be serious, Tristan. I wouldn't come bother you if it weren't for an important matter."

"What's so important it couldn't have waited until class tomorrow?" Tristan asked, annoyed. He eased up a little, though. It seemed Cecil hadn't noticed that he'd just stolen Louis's watch right off his wrist.

Cecil wrinkled her nose. "I figured you'd cut class." Without giving Tristan a chance to defend himself, she steamrollered on. "Evangeline has sent word that she requires your *services*."

What ran through Tristan's thoughts first was definitely not the type of services that Cecil had meant, he was sure.

As though she'd read his mind—maybe she had—Cecil's eyes narrowed, and she bared her fangs. "Get your head out of the gutter."

"You're testing my patience." If it weren't for the fact that they were in public, in full view of many mortals, Tristan wouldn't have let her talk to him like this. Cecil was clearly itching to fight; he wanted nothing more than to grant her wish, but not here, and not now. Cecil was being a fool, too, if she thought it a sound idea to provoke him near the full moon, when his emotions were already running high. "Give me one good reason to answer Evangeline's summons."

Cecil's lip curled. "If you *don't* answer her summons, I'll be forced to drag you kicking and screaming before her. She asked me to remind you that you've owed her a favor for some time, Tristan. Have you sunk so low that you don't repay your debts?"

Tristan clenched his jaw. The condescension in Cecil's voice was really grating on his nerves. Maybe some of his actions were questionable, but he made it a point to pay his debts—and to collect when others owed *him* debts. He racked his brains; off the top of his head, he couldn't recall owing anything to Evangeline. "I'm not sure what debt she's referring to . . ."

Then it hit him. Tristan groaned. Years ago, before they dated, Evangeline had found him in a tight spot, where Marcus and Max Niu had ganged up on him and started to beat him up pretty badly. When Evangeline entered the fight, the two brothers didn't have a chance—and she'd only let them go when they'd sworn up and down that they wouldn't lay a hand on Tristan. He hadn't realized until this moment that Evangeline would count that as a debt to be repaid, but it *did* make sense.

"Well? Do you remember now?" Cecil asked.

"Um, excuse me?"

They both turned at the sound of a woman's uncertain voice. Lydia the cute bartender was standing there, holding Tristan's soju, giving the two of them a confused look.

"You can put that drink down," Cecil said, flashing Lydia a cold smile.

"Oh, okay." Lydia obeyed, but her eyes were full of concern as they darted toward security and then toward Tristan. Clearly, Tristan and Cecil had been conversing with enough hostility that even the staff had caught on. "Is everything all right, Theodore?"

"Who?" Cecil squinted at Tristan and then let out a snort of incredulity as she seemed to realize who "Theodore" was. "Surely not—"

"Everything's *peachy*, Lydia." He raised the peach soju.

"Oh, ha ha," Cecil deadpanned. "You always were a clown."

"Here, have a shot, Cecil—it might improve that attitude of yours." Tristan moved the bottle under Cecil's nose.

The vampire glared down at it with a pinched expression as though it had personally offended her. "Oh, no thank you, *Theodore*." She shoved his hand away.

Tristan frowned. How did Cecil make the name Theodore sound like a disease? Perhaps he needed to rethink his alias for his next night out in K-town.

Just then, one of the other bartenders called for Lydia, and she hurried away, but not before casting a backward glance at the two of them. Tristan started to take a swig of soju, but Cecil snatched it out of his hand. With her other hand, she grabbed his wrist in an ice-cold grip.

"Oh, come on. I deserve to at least get drunk before I have to face your fire-breathing mistress."

"You'll have to do this sober, I'm afraid," Cecil said in a voice that indicated she'd break Tristan's hand if he didn't come.

"Get off me." He tried to twist out of her icy grasp, but he couldn't. It was like trying to remove a handcuff from his wrist. Normally he was strong enough to overpower any vampire, but he hadn't had dinner tonight, and—when was the last time he'd eaten anything of substance? He was so famished, it felt as though his stomach were tearing itself into pieces. "I'll call Evangeline later, all right? She's probably got enough shit to deal with right now." Besides, why would Evangeline want to see him, of all people? Her brother had been found dead, and Tristan was probably the Descendant she hated the most. If he were in her shoes, he'd be the *last* person he'd want to see. And he didn't want to see her, either. Or at least, he didn't want the sight of her to bring back everything he'd spent the past four years burying.

Cecil's eyes flashed. "Evangeline said for you to come immediately. In person. It's an urgent matter."

"And *I* said—"

"You don't get a say right now."

It was evident that Cecil had come with her full and considerable vampire strength, and meanwhile Tristan really should have thought twice before downing half a bottle of vodka earlier in the evening. Sure, as a werewolf his metabolism was fast—much faster than a human's—but he'd overestimated it. He was drunk enough now that there wasn't nearly enough strength left in his limbs to fight against Cecil's viselike grip.

"Um, I hope there's not a problem?" Lydia the bartender's voice came out trembly. She'd returned with a burly coworker at her shoulder. Tristan sensed that if he and Cecil didn't make themselves scarce now, they'd shortly be escorted out by security. These Koreatown establishments were quick to stamp out any potential drunken fistfights.

"Just sorting out some private affairs," Cecil said in a bright tone. "Have a good evening."

Cecil hauled Tristan out the door. Once he was across the threshold, he glanced up at the moon. Was it his imagination, or did it appear fuller than before? The moon was taunting him. It knew how hard he worked to keep the beast at bay, how much he hated losing control of his own body.

"Don't even think about transforming tonight," Cecil barked. She'd followed his gaze toward the moon and now turned toward him with cold eyes.

Tristan gritted his teeth. He could have snapped at her, but something stopped him from firing back with his usual bravado. Besides, he wasn't even granted the time to reply. No sooner had he stumbled down the back alley than two shadowy figures dropped from the rooftop and landed on all fours on the street, in what was decidedly not a human fashion.

Cecil cursed and leapt out of the way.

It was the twins, Louis and Gina. Their faces were contorted with fury, and Tristan couldn't blame them.

"Did you really think you'd get away with stealing my watch?" snarled Louis, his red eyes drilling holes into Tristan.

Tristan groaned. Of course, he'd thought he *had* gotten away with it. Damn Louis for being sharper than Tristan had realized. No, damn himself for getting too comfortable, too complacent. That was the greatest danger with Tristan's line of work—becoming complacent. And now he was about to pay the price for letting down his guard. He really shouldn't have had that vodka earlier.

"Oh, come on." Cecil pushed Tristan aside and stood between him and the advancing fox spirits. "Sorry, but you'll have to settle the score with this idiot later. Right now, Evangeline needs him."

"Cecil, he's a thief," spat Gina, her eyes flashing a murderous red warning. "He's a criminal, and a liar, and—"

"I don't disagree with any of that, but do you dare defy Evangeline Long?" Cecil cut in. "The two of you are Talons. You swore loyalty to Julius, and though he may be gone now, you should know that he would expect you to show Evangeline the same respect and obedience as you would him. I'm acting on Evangeline's orders right now, which means you also have to obey *me*."

While they bickered, Tristan turned ever so slightly to glance down the street, toward the massive billboards that marked Times Square. He could easily slip away while they were caught up in their argument. Blend into the crowd and be gone before any of them noticed. He started to back away.

Gina turned aside, looking slightly shamed, and said nothing. Clearly, Cecil's words had gotten to her. Louis, however, spat on the grimy concrete in front of Cecil's feet. "Evangeline can handle this piece of trash later. Besides, you and Evangeline should watch your backs."

Cecil paused and stared at Louis, as though giving his words careful consideration for the first time. "Why is that?"

"Haven't you heard? The Longs may not be in power much longer."

Tristan froze. This new development was too interesting to ignore. "What do you mean?"

"Yes, whatever *do* you mean?" Cecil demanded, a frosty edge in her voice.

"Brother," Gina hissed, shoving her twin's bulky, tattooed arm as though warning him against speaking further. But for all the good it did, she might as well have shoved the wall instead.

"You mean you haven't heard?" Louis sneered. "I guess you aren't considered important enough for anyone to communicate the news to you. The other High Council members don't hold Evangeline in high regard. They were willing to abide by Julius's rule, as legacy deemed appropriate, but with his passing, there is now a shift in the wind." He licked his lips. His eyes were lighting up, as though he delighted in being the one to break the news to Tristan. "For the first time, the Descendants may have a Chancellor from the House of Ox next."

Tristan narrowed his eyes. If there was one name that could put him in a foul mood instantly, it was Marcus Niu. House of Ox was currently led by the brutish werewolf who'd been immortalized in his early twenties. After the Longs, the Nius were largely considered the second-most-influential bloodline of the Descendants, with a small but loyal following that Julius had never successfully swayed to his side. Though from time to time there might be rumors of a challenge for power, never before had the Nius actually made any moves to usurp the Longs' rule.

Tristan's grudge with Marcus was more personal, though, with roots so far-reaching that it extended back generations, so deep ran their hate. An enmity that just *was,* as simple as fact, as sure as the sun rose and fell through the sky each day.

"Just how is Marcus planning to challenge the Longs when he can't even win the battle against his receding hairline?" Tristan drawled.

That earned a snort of appreciation from Cecil. For once, it seemed, the two were on the same side. "Anyone foolish enough to challenge the House of Dragon would fail," Cecil said without missing a beat. "Evangeline was second only to Julius in power, and he has been training her to be his successor for decades. Nobody else is fit to preside over the Descendants. And you had better watch what you say, Louis, for you are teetering dangerously on the edge of treachery against the Longs."

Louis glowered, but his sister stepped in before he could put his foot in his mouth again.

"What my dear brother is saying, in a terribly ineffective way, is that the Longs' rule is not a given any longer," Gina said. "If you care for

Evangeline, you should tell her to prepare herself. And we will prepare to defend the Longs as well. We remain loyal to Julius until the end of time."

"Or death." Louis ran his tongue over his teeth and grinned. "Whichever comes first."

Tristan's mind began racing. If rumors were already spreading about the possibility of the Nius fighting for power, that meant Descendants were already beginning to throw their weight behind their chosen alliances. Did Evangeline know this yet? And why did he care whether Evangeline was left in the dark?

". . . won't kill him," Louis was saying to a stone-faced Cecil. "Just mess him up so he can't walk properly for a while."

"That would be inconvenient for Evangeline, as she'll need him fully functional," Cecil snapped back.

Tristan frowned. Cecil was speaking of him as though he were a machine and his only merit was his usefulness to Evangeline.

Louis gnashed his teeth, and then, surprisingly, he turned away. "Fine. I'll wait. Watch your step, Tristan."

"Watch out for pickpockets," Tristan couldn't resist retorting.

Louis spat at his foot in response, and Tristan jumped out of the way. "Tell your darling Evangeline to watch her back, too," Louis snarled. Then he and Gina took off down the sidewalk.

Cecil watched them go with an unreadable expression, but her clenched fists gave her away. Then she turned her furious gaze on Tristan, who flinched. "Next time come quickly with me when I ask you to."

"Thanks for helping," Tristan muttered.

"Don't thank me." She whirled on him, her features pinched up in a threatening look. "Did you steal Louis's watch?"

"Uh . . ." The guilt in Tristan's face must have been enough answer, because Cecil rolled her eyes.

"Idiot. I hope Louis beats your ass at school."

Tristan wanted to argue but found that he couldn't. Before he knew it, Cecil had grabbed his hand and was practically flying through the air. He was going so fast, he couldn't speak.

The two of them arrived on the great stone steps of the Long mansion, right beside the stone lions that guarded the entrance to the magnificent building. The red doors opened, and his ex-girlfriend stood there in a purple power suit with golden cuffs on the sleeves.

Her beauty was startling even as her features scrunched in disgust. There were pink streaks on her face, the evidence of blood tears that she'd failed to wipe away. Tristan hated that the sight of them tugged on his heart. Hated that after their disastrous relationship, he still felt anything for Evangeline at all. That he was still so in tune with her that he knew the mask she wore right now was just to cover up whatever turmoil she felt inside.

This meeting would be equally difficult for them both. Tristan just hoped it wouldn't end in disaster.

"Hello," he said, and immediately regretted how pathetic he sounded.

"Hello, Tristan." Evangeline remained unsmiling. "Let's catch up, shall we?"

9
EVANGELINE

Evangeline had hoped, after her short-lived and disastrous relationship with Tristan that had blown up four years ago, that they'd never have to speak one-on-one again. That secret relationship had been a mistake—probably the worst judgment call she'd made in her entire long life thus far—and she'd suffered the consequences ever since. Earthly Branches Academy was one of those tiny private schools where everyone knew everyone, so of course Evangeline understood it would be impossible to avoid Tristan altogether. But given that they ran in separate circles, *and* that Tristan was a terrible student who hardly bothered to show up for class, she had hoped that their paths wouldn't cross much again.

Oh, how very, very wrong she had been.

When Tristan poked his head through the doorway of the Long mansion, Evangeline fought to keep her expression blank. Despite how hard she'd worked to squash down the memories in the past four years, now they emerged with an almost vindictive clarity. Running her hands through that messy dark brown hair. Brushing her finger against the small

mole next to his left ear. So strange that although Evangeline had grieved the relationship as though Tristan were dead, he was still very much a presence in her life.

Evangeline wondered if she was making a mistake in recruiting Tristan. There were some doors that ought to remain firmly shut.

"So what did you want to talk about that couldn't wait?" Tristan rubbed the back of his neck. His eyes darted from the door to the staircase to the living room, anywhere but at Evangeline, who'd taken a seat on the black leather couch. Likely, he was plotting an escape route. Well, there was no way Tristan would be getting past the levels of protection guarding the Long estate—in fact, he wouldn't even be able to slip around the first layer of security, which was Evangeline herself.

"Sit down," she commanded, pointing at the leather armchair across from her. She couldn't let Tristan get to her. Looking away from his sharp jaw, she resolved to focus only on the mission ahead of them.

Tristan didn't need to be told twice, at least. Evangeline took a dark delight in knowing that he had stared down hardened criminals and yet in the face of her wrath, he sat down obediently. He was so fast to obey that for a moment, Evangeline remembered what it had been like to be able to Compel others with mere words. Ah, those had been the days.

Cecil stood by Evangeline like her shadow, but her glare never left Tristan. It was clear she hadn't forgiven him for how things had ended between him and Evangeline.

Evangeline took a deep breath. It was best to state the facts of the situation, leaving emotion out of the equation. That was how the Longs had always dealt with difficult situations. "Julius was murdered." She was proud of how steady and even the statement came out.

Tristan blinked slowly, as though he couldn't believe her words. Evangeline couldn't blame him. Julius Long's name was legend, and his deeds were spoken about with reverence. The idea that her brother had been murdered was extremely hard to believe, especially for her. In her mind, Julius was an ever-present figure, commanding attention whenever he walked into a room.

After a beat of thick silence, Tristan said in a voice hardly above a whisper, "I heard they'd found his body, but murder . . . I . . . My condolences, Ev."

Evangeline startled at the old nickname. Nobody called her Ev any longer. Least of all *him*.

"Evangeline," Tristan corrected himself, lowering his gaze.

Evangeline's eyebrows rose, but she didn't say anything. She could barely hold back the tears, but it was imperative that she present herself as the picture of grace and strength, as always. This was the way she'd been taught to conduct herself even before immortality, and she'd sooner burn in Hell than let anyone—least of all Tristan—see her otherwise. "Thank you." Her voice caught, and she swallowed. *Be strong,* she willed herself. And when she spoke again, it was with her usual calm, cold authority.

"Earlier tonight, I heard something . . . something you should know." Tristan's voice was unusually serious. "The Nius are rallying support from the other Descendant families. It appears they're using Julius's death as an excuse to finally end the Long rule. They're planning to seize that power for themselves."

It took a moment for the gravity of Tristan's words to sink in, and when they did, Evangeline clenched her fingers into tight fists. Of *course.* In the back of her mind, she had had an inkling that this period of transition of power from Julius to her would be the moment for any ambitious Descendants to make their bid. If she were Marcus Niu, that was exactly what *she* would do—strike before the next Long had a chance to solidify the loyalty of the other Descendants. Marcus had always looked down on Evangeline. She just hadn't thought the cold-hearted bastard would sink so low as to strike before she could even attend to her older brother's funeral arrangements.

"That doesn't surprise me," Evangeline said in a voice of forced calm. "Nor does it change my plans."

"It doesn't?"

"No." She thought quickly. There was no choice but to assume that right at this very moment, Marcus was out rallying Descendants to his cause, getting them to pledge allegiance to *him* and the House of Ox. Tradition dictated that the House of Dragon led the other eleven houses, as the Chinese diaspora had always referred to themselves as lóng de chuán rén, or the descendants of the dragon. However, this didn't mean that things always needed to operate that way. If Marcus was already swaying others, then Evangeline needed to convince them with her *actions*. And what better way of convincing everyone that she was the best candidate to lead than by successfully completing this Assignment? By establishing dominance over the fae, fulfilling an old prophecy, and restoring power and glory to the Descendants, Evangeline would seal her fate as the next Chancellor. Julius must have known this threat to House of Dragon was likely to happen, must have been secretly preparing to help Evangeline for when he could no longer be by her side.

"We'll proceed as planned," she said. "I called you here, Tristan, because Julius left unfinished business that requires immediate attention. You'll even be excused from class if you aid me on an Assignment."

Tristan's golden eyes narrowed. Evangeline knew that the mention of getting out of classes alone would entice him, but the prospect of the two of them going on an Assignment, spending copious amounts of time together, might be a deal-breaker.

"What kind of Assignment?" Tristan asked slowly.

"Help me finish the task that Julius started—and then help me find my brother's murderer."

"What're you going to do once you find the culprit?" Tristan asked.

"I'm going to rob them," Evangeline said with a thin-lipped smile that promised blood, "and then I'm going to kill them."

If Tristan was at all surprised by her words, he didn't show it. A muscle worked in his jaw as he seemed to mull this over. If ever there was a time when being able to Compel others would truly come in handy, that would be now, Evangeline thought; still, she wasn't worried about Tristan rejecting her proposal. If she still knew Tristan as well as she used to, then his agreeing to the task was inevitable. Tristan couldn't resist a challenge any more than she could.

"What do you need me for? I'm not a killer."

"No, but you're a thief—probably the best in our school," Evangeline admitted grudgingly.

"Best in Manhattan."

Evangeline didn't bother to dignify that claim with a response. "Also, we're going to break the Scarlet Spy out of a prison deep in the Underground. I know you have some kind of relationship with him, Tristan, and I'll be counting on you to sway him to our cause."

Tristan raised an eyebrow. "What does the Scarlet Spy have to do with anything?"

"Julius hinted that he'll be useful for navigating Faerie, as none of us have been there," Evangeline explained.

"Hmm. That shaman *does* owe me a favor, but he got himself thrown into jail before he could fulfill it," Tristan muttered.

"We'll call in that favor as a last resort," Evangeline said. "This is no ordinary Assignment, so you'll have to take it a lot more seriously than you take most other things in life."

"I treat every situation with the seriousness it deserves," Tristan said.

"I'm going to need help, and *good* help. The kind of help that could, say, break into a hidden faerie dwelling, or perhaps one of the most secure, well-guarded museums in the world."

Tristan leaned back and closed his eyes. For a long moment, there was silence except for the sound of his steady breathing, and then he said slowly, "Evangeline . . . you are going to get us killed. Or worse, eternally imprisoned in Faerieland."

"No, I am going to make us—the Descendants—the most powerful force in the universe. I'm going to ensure that everything returns to the way it was before our Circle of Twelve was broken—no, *better*. We'll reproduce even stronger Descendants. And most importantly, I am going to make Marcus Niu wish he had never been born, much less challenged the Longs."

It was high time Evangeline stopped beating around the bush. She reached into her pocket, produced her brother's note, and tossed it onto the coffee table in front of Tristan. The words were already imprinted on the insides of her eyelids, carved into her very skin.

After he finished reading it, Tristan raised his gaze to Evangeline's. He licked his lips. Evangeline had always been capable of reading him like a book, and she could tell by his tensed shoulders and the tightened muscles in his jaw that he did not fear the danger of their Assignment. Rather, Tristan was excited.

"I found this note in Julius's study," Evangeline said. She looked away from Tristan, past Cecil. Her gaze fixed on the window, though in the darkness there was nothing to see but their own reflections staring back at them. "It seemed he knew he wouldn't return."

"Your brother . . . He'd been making these preparations for a long time."

"Yes."

"You're going to take on this Assignment, whether or not you can convince anyone else to come with you."

"Yes."

"Even if you never return from it."

"*Yes,* Tristan."

"You believe yourself to be the subject of this prophecy."

"Julius believed so, and he's never been wrong yet. Now, are you quite finished making these pointless statements?"

There was a long, heavy pause.

"Wrathlings, too. The Wrathlings haven't posed a real threat in ages. What does Julius think they have to do with the prophecy?"

"I don't know," Evangeline admitted. "But I intend to find out."

"So that's the plan, then? Go find the shamans and hope they'll care enough to help us find the lost fountainheads?" Tristan asked.

"That, and then kill whoever it was who murdered Julius. An eye for an eye."

"Sounds very simple. A very normal thing for two people to do."

"It won't just be you and me, of course. I'll be enlisting the help of two others who will be equally useful to the mission. Nicholas Hu—"

"The fox spirit," murmured Tristan, his expression suggesting he'd been forced to sniff something foul.

"Yes, Nicholas Hu the fox spirit," Evangeline said with just a small smile. Nicholas was Tristan's opposite in many ways—even-tempered, punctual, studious, perfect. What bothered Evangeline so much about Tristan was that in other ways, he was eerily similar to Nicholas. They were both clever, dangerously so, and ambitious. The two boys were like opposite sides of the same coin. Nicholas applied his intelligence and talents to schoolwork and aided Julius in running the High Council, whereas Tristan chose to squander his abilities by behaving like a common thief. *That* was one major reason why Evangeline could never accept Tristan fully as he was. Lacking talent was one matter. Using one's talent for inane, selfish reasons was an entirely different issue.

"You're sure he'll be a worthy addition?" Tristan asked, his voice full of doubt. "I can think of several more qualified Descendants who are stronger candidates—better fighters in every way—I can go get one of them right now if you want me to."

"No, Tristan." Evangeline spoke calmly but firmly. "I don't need a Descendant who's capable of brute force. I need somebody with Nicholas's specific skill set—the ability to change appearances. Besides, his brains will be much more valuable than brawn."

Tristan made a tsking noise and murmured something that sounded like, "Well, don't say I didn't warn you when that coward ends up being a burden." He was unconvinced, Evangeline could tell, but he also had to know there would be no swaying her now that she'd made up her mind.

There had always been bad blood between Tristan and Nicholas. Evangeline could only hope that Nicholas would agree to help her knowing that she'd gone to Tristan for help as well. Nicholas had never turned her down in the past, so she had good reason to believe he'd help this time as well.

"Who's the fourth member of the team, then?" Tristan asked.

Now it was Evangeline's turn to be disgusted. She'd thought this over and over since finding Julius's note, but she couldn't see a way out. She needed a team member who could read minds, and ultimately one who could be used for . . . alternative purposes. And the only student at Earthly Branches Academy who fit both descriptions was—"Alice Jiang," Evangeline bit out, as though the name had left a foul taste in her mouth.

Tristan grinned, which made her want to punch him in the face. "No way. Really? The human girl who can read minds—Ruiting's daughter? You chose her?"

"Problem?" Evangeline said haughtily.

"Of course *I* don't have a problem with that girl. I thought *you* had a problem with her."

"This isn't the time to bring up silly school matters," Evangeline sniffed. The mischievous grin on Tristan's face was irking her.

"Right. Alice Jiang . . . she'll be useful."

Evangeline didn't need to be able to read minds to know that she and Tristan were on the same wavelength, that he knew exactly what she was thinking when it came to Alice. However, she still had a trump card regarding Alice that even Tristan couldn't guess—and Evangeline intended to keep that information to herself. She thought of how Julius had kept secrets all to himself, too. Perhaps she and her brother were more alike than she'd realized.

Tristan's grin melted away. "Marcus Niu can't be allowed to rule over the Descendants, Evangeline." He spoke with a gravity that rarely entered his voice, each word weighing heavily in the air. "He's a bully through and through. Putting him in power would be the worst thing to ever happen to all of us."

"I know that. Of course I know that. That's why I need to do this. I'll be calling you all to a meeting shortly," Evangeline said.

"I can't wait," Tristan drawled. He stood up and stretched, his eyes darting toward the door. "Well, if that's everything, I'll be on my way—"

"On your way? What do you mean?" Evangeline let out a soft laugh.

Tristan froze, his smile wavering. "What do *you* mean?"

She closed the distance between them in two smooth strides. "You're not going anywhere. If I let you go now, you wouldn't come back. You didn't give me a definitive agreement, and in your mind, that gives you a loophole to wiggle out of the Assignment, right?"

Tristan was clever—clever enough to be able to mask the surprise on his face. But cleverness alone wasn't enough to outwit the decades-sharpened gaze of Evangeline. "I wouldn't—"

"Don't deny it. Tristan, I know you too well."

Tristan visibly flinched at the harsh words, but he offered nothing in defense, for once. Evangeline was right; they both knew it. Even when they'd dated, Tristan had always run from Evangeline in her most vulnerable moments, whenever she needed him most, whenever their relationship had gotten difficult. It had been taxing to try to love someone so emotionally distant, like chasing the shadow of something beautiful that was forever just out of reach.

Cecil coughed. The sound was disruptive enough to bring Evangeline back to the present, where both Cecil and Tristan were staring at her in concern. Evangeline blinked back tears, surprised at her visceral reaction to the memories of herself with Tristan.

Tristan's eyes narrowed. "I'm aware that I owe you a debt, Evangeline, but the scale of *this* request . . . don't you think it far outstrips you saving me from being beaten up a few years ago? You're asking me to put my life on the line. You're putting *everybody's* life on the line."

Evangeline straightened her shoulders. "I know. But with your help, the odds are higher that we'll all survive. I can't let you go, Tristan. Sorry."

Before Tristan could respond, Evangeline grabbed his fingers. His gold-flecked eyes widened with a deer-in-headlights look, and he froze on the spot. Despite the harshness of his words, perhaps Tristan still had a soft spot for her. And even Evangeline couldn't suppress her body's reaction to their touch. Shivers ran down her skin, and she gave an involuntary swallow. Her fingertips ached, remembering the grooves of Tristan's hands, the smoothness of his skin interrupted by rough calluses. The way their fingers interlocked as though made for one another. It took Evangeline every ounce of willpower to ignore her own reaction, to refocus on projecting that stone-cold image of herself.

Tristan didn't even have a chance to react when the golden cuffs glowed bright white, detached from Evangeline's wrists, and slid onto his. "Wh-What's—?"

"Don't try to resist," Evangeline warned. "These cuffs are magic, custom fashioned by the shamans centuries ago. The more you resist, the more the cuffs will cut into you."

Already red welts were rising from where Tristan struggled to free his wrists. Right now, he would be slowly feeling the full effects of the cuffs. He'd have lost all desire to get away from the mansion. He would also have the strange, overwhelming sense that he needed to obey Evangeline; that to disobey would be a heinous crime, and of course he couldn't do such a thing to her.

Tristan stopped struggling, his muscles relaxing beneath his black T-shirt. "I didn't know you still had a trick up your sleeve," he said calmly.

"We could fill a ten-book series with everything you don't know, Tristan," Evangeline said savagely. One of the lessons Julius had taught her long ago was this: one should never reveal all of one's tricks. Better to be underestimated than overestimated. Even if Evangeline could no longer Compel with her words, the golden cuffs helped her retain some of that ability. "You've owed me a favor for a long while," she said. "It's high time you repay it—and you'll start with a small but important task tonight."

Tristan glowered up at her, but all the fight had gone out of his body. "What do you need me to do?"

"I don't yet know the secret to accessing the Underground," Evangeline admitted. "I assume there's some special password, or ingredient, or something required to gain entrance. I know you have connections with rogue shamans, Tristan. You're going to find out for us how we can get into the Underground—and you're going to do so quickly."

"Fine," Tristan said with a weary sigh. "But can I please have dinner first?"

10
TRISTAN

Tristan was so famished that he could have inhaled the medium-rare steak
Cecil had prepared for him. However, he chose—strategically—to eat his
meal in careful, deliberate bites.

Evangeline sat at the other end of the dining room table, arms crossed
over her chest, glaring as she watched him eat. The dim light of the flickering candles on the table emphasized the harsh lines of her face, making
her glare appear more threatening than usual. Even when she was upset,
Evangeline was beautiful in a cold, mildly frightening way.

Tristan hated himself for even noticing that.

"I miss it," Evangeline said quietly after a while, so quietly that Tristan
wasn't sure she was talking to him at all. In fact, he was quite sure she
wasn't.

"You miss what?"

Evangeline went silent for long enough that Tristan thought she was
going to ignore his question entirely. Then she said: "I miss eating meals—
eating anything that isn't just blood, or completely slathered in blood.
Human foods taste like dirt to me." She made a face.

Beneath that expression, though, Tristan sensed a real sadness and frustration. Sympathy rose up within him. He could understand wanting this curse to be lifted, wanting to return to life as they had known it when they were mortals—a life that seemed to have happened many lifetimes ago. He wasn't sure what had motivated Evangeline, who normally had walls up as high as Manhattan's skyscrapers, to open up to him, even if just this much. He was on the verge of offering words of encouragement when her expression shifted back to the annoyance it had held before.

"You're eating slowly on purpose," she accused, the moment over.

"I am not," Tristan lied.

While he chewed ever so slightly faster, he passed the time by brainstorming a list of all the things he'd rather be doing than going on a heist with his ex-girlfriend. The list was long and comprehensive and included plucking out his nose hairs. And Tristan was very fond of his nose hairs.

However, it was true that if Evangeline didn't take drastic measures to rally support while Marcus was out gathering Descendants to *his* cause, then soon the bubbling tension was likely to erupt in violence. While Tristan had no objection to chaos, if Evangeline fell out of power and Marcus took her place, things would take a very unpleasant turn for Tristan. As much as Evangeline disliked Tristan, Marcus absolutely *loathed* him. So really, Tristan was better off with Evangeline taking over for Julius than the alternative. And that meant he'd have to cooperate with her demands. A necessary evil for a long-term gain.

It was a quarter to one by the time he finished his last bite of steak, and he could drag his feet no longer. Evangeline might bite his head off if he did.

"Get the answer to accessing the Underground, and then come back immediately," she said. She tucked a strand of loose hair behind her ear, an old habit of hers, and Tristan recalled very briefly the feeling of being the one to tuck her hair and—and *no*. He couldn't go there, even for a moment. It wasn't worth reopening old wounds. "There's no time to waste," Evangeline was saying. "If you pull this off, I'll remove the cuffs," she added, and then lazily leaned back in her chair, examining her cuticles. "Otherwise, have fun attending to my orders for the rest of eternity."

Now *that* sounded like torture. Tristan was at once annoyed and impressed by Evangeline's thoroughness. He didn't think of himself as a particularly open individual, but she had always possessed the uncanny ability to read him like a book.

He needed to be more careful with her. The solution, of course, was for him not to help with this Assignment at all, which was *definitely* preferable to him. However, Evangeline didn't seem as though she'd let up at all and was determined to get his help at any cost.

Well, perhaps she'd have to learn her lesson the hard way.

"Okay, okay," he grumbled. "Be back soon."

Or so he said, but he intended to take as much time as possible. He wasn't at all eager to return to Evangeline's side. It was taking everything within him to act calmly, but truthfully, his mind and heart were racing with the adrenaline of his conversation with her.

What he needed was another drink.

Evangeline hadn't been wrong. Tristan *was* well connected with rogue shamans, though she didn't know the exact reason why. It came with the territory, doing odd, sketchy jobs for the Collector.

The Collector remained a mystery to Tristan, despite the fact that he'd been doing contract jobs for the man for decades now. He rarely appeared in person; instead, messages would be sent to Tristan, usually pushed under his dorm room door, outlining his next task or providing payment for the last. The notes were addressed to Tristan's alias under the Collector—*Tao*. They were also enchanted so that if anyone but Tristan found them, they'd read like silly notes from a secret admirer, which had earned Tristan the reputation of being a heartbreaker at Earthly Branches Academy. He didn't really care what the Descendants said about him, but it did bother him that the rumors had gotten him in trouble with Evangeline when they'd been dating.

Well, not that it mattered anymore. That was all ancient history. These days Evangeline hardly deigned to look at him.

The point was, the few times Tristan had been summoned to visit the Collector in person, the man had remained cloaked in shadows. Even Tristan's extra-sharp vision couldn't see the man beyond the darkness—couldn't even tell what kind of creature he might be, but whatever he was, Tristan sensed an ancient power emanating from him.

It wasn't the Collector Tristan was going to see when he headed to Bushwick, though; he would drop off the watch as soon as he had a free moment. He walked briskly down the street, past loud clubs and bars and eateries, toward a back alley. It was fascinating how much this area had changed just in the past decade; Brooklyn, a borough of the city that had once been dangerous to maneuver, was now lively, trendy, and gentrified. Tristan remembered his days of being the least shady character on the streets, and now, in the blink of an eye, he had become the *most*. He wasn't sure whether this change could be considered good or bad.

The moon still hung high up in the sky, a constant reminder of what could go wrong for Tristan. Even though he took his aubrum religiously every morning, the pill wasn't a fail-safe means of controlling the beast within, which grew stronger as the moon neared fullness—and if he wasn't careful to up the dose just the tiniest amount every so often, it would be less and less effective. He had taken the last of his aubrum yesterday, and he prayed it would be enough to hold him over this upcoming full moon until he could receive a fresh supply from the Collector.

Tristan rounded the corner and tapped five times on a bloodstained brick in the wall. He stepped back, and a doorway formed in the wall, just tall and wide enough for him. He walked inside: a small studio apartment, occupied by one young woman.

Not just any woman. A shaman. She looked like an ordinary but very fit woman, with long, wavy black hair that cascaded down her back. Although she was dressed in red robes that covered every inch of her body,

Tristan knew that her arms and legs were corded with lean muscle. When she lifted her head, her eyes were a fiery red. The most remarkable part of Ying's appearance, however, was the blue light that danced at her fingertips. Shamans could command the power of spirits to summon pure energy at will, which meant Tristan was very glad that Ying was on his side. Though that might change after the conversation they were about to have.

"Tao." Ying, who partnered with Tristan occasionally under the Collector's command, nodded at him from her dining table. He didn't know if her real name was Ying—in fact, he highly doubted it—but that was the name by which he knew her. Ying was just finishing up her dinner, which appeared to have been a large slice of greasy pizza. She pointed the remaining half slice at him, raising an eyebrow. "You know, I've come to associate your presence with forthcoming chaos."

"I'm honored to hear that, truly I am."

The shaman rolled her eyes and took another bite of her pizza. After she'd swallowed, she said in a brisk, businesslike tone, "To what do I owe the pleasure of your company? We don't have a mission together tonight."

"I know that. But *I* have a mission."

"For the Collector?"

"Not . . . exactly. I need your help, Ying."

Ying narrowed her fiery eyes. "If you're in trouble with somebody important, I don't want to get involved."

"It's nothing like that." It was the truth. He wasn't in trouble with anybody important—yet. Tristan couldn't blame Ying for being suspicious, because getting into trouble with important people was a specialty of his. "You've surely heard the news about Julius Long."

Ying didn't bat an eye. "Of course. It's the talk of the town."

"Well, I'm helping his younger sister resolve some unfinished business."

"Helping? You?" The shaman snorted in disbelief.

"Indeed. I'm actually *helping* someone who's having a difficult time, out of the goodness of my heart."

Ying laughed mirthlessly. "I know you better than this. You don't do anything if there isn't something in it for you, Tao."

A muscle twitched in Tristan's jaw. "Isn't that the way the world works?" It wasn't as though Ying herself were a saint. They were both thieves, liars, criminals. Where did Ying get the gall now to act as though she had the moral high ground?

"Believe it or not, there are some who *actually* do enjoy helping others just for the sake of helping. I so wish you would use your talents for more noble causes, Tao. But I'm not here to pass judgment on you for only looking out for yourself." She ate the last of her pizza and pressed a napkin daintily to her mouth. "Bushwick is out of the way for you, so you must be out of options if you're coming to me."

"It is quite a trek from the Academy," Tristan agreed. "Why Bushwick, by the way?"

Ying shrugged. "I like Bushwick. I like Brooklyn; it has such character, more so than any other borough or even central Manhattan, I'd like to think. Also, the people of Bushwick are so eccentric that they wouldn't question any strange happenings they might accidentally witness, which makes it the perfect place for a rogue shaman to settle." She chuckled. "My neighbors believe I'm a stuntwoman with a side hustle as a martial arts instructor. Incredible what humans are willing to see instead of the truth. But I digress. You're stalling, Tao." Sharp as ever, Ying was. "What is it that you need from me?"

Tristan sighed. Here came the hard part. He was aware that he was about to ask quite a lot of Ying, most likely more than she was willing to give. He took a deep breath to prepare himself. "I need to know how to access the Underground."

Whatever Ying might have been expecting to hear, it certainly wasn't that. She dropped her crumpled napkin to the floor, gaping at Tristan in shock. "No," she said after hardly a beat. "That's out of the question. Absolutely not."

Tristan hated to beg, but he didn't have any other choice. "Please, Ying. There are others counting on me. You're the only shaman I know and trust to—"

"I can't. Glad as I am to hear you're learning to help others—truly I am—to give away such a secret would be against the law of the shamans. What you're asking me to do is a betrayal of my people." She shook her head. "No."

The situation was going nothing like what Tristan had hoped for, and he desperately tried to regain some control. He'd always considered himself a bit of a smooth talker; indeed, his quick tongue had gotten him out of many a mess. Surely he could use that talent to bring Ying around. "You don't even like the shamans, though," he reminded her. "You fled the Underground because you couldn't stand to live with them any longer."

Ying's nostrils flared. "I might have my moral disagreements with the other shamans, and I might have chosen to make my living on the Sur- face away from them. However, that doesn't mean I would betray them."

"This is for an important matter, Ying. I wouldn't ask you to do this if it weren't—"

"I'm sorry, but you're not going to sweet-talk me into changing my mind, so stop wasting your breath. That's my final answer."

Tristan's temper flared. He'd known that Ying was as stubborn as he was. That was what made them good partners in this business. They were comrades, not particularly close, but they'd always understood each other, he'd thought—until tonight. Now the furious look Ying was giving him told him she thought he was the lowest of scoundrels.

Well, he was a bit of a scoundrel. And he wasn't about to change now.

"You like to act as though you're so different from the other shamans, Ying, but you're cut from the exact same cloth," he said spitefully, because he knew his words would hurt Ying like a knife to the heart.

"*Excuse* me?"

"The shamans never step in to help anyone unless it directly benefits them," Tristan said savagely. The words, which had sat in his chest for so long, had been clamoring for release. He had never said this aloud before, but there had always been a tiny seed of resentment toward the shamans buried deep inside him. "The shamans ignored the mortal immigrants' cries for help throughout stretches of American history. Where were the shamans when the Chinese were abused while building the transcontinental railroad? When the Chinese Exclusion Act was passed?"

"That is neither here nor there," said Ying, her voice shaking with cold fury. "That has nothing to do with your selfish request today."

"Maybe I'm finally fed up with the shamans standing by and twiddling their thumbs, when they—*you*—have the power to change everything," Tristan growled. He took a step forward, and Ying stood up, her hands curled into fists at her sides.

"I knew you disliked the shamans, Tao, but I never knew how deep your hatred ran. Else I never would have agreed to partner with you." Ying's words were so cold that Tristan had to suppress a shiver. The air between them could have crackled.

Tristan's internal temperature began to rise, hot flashes crawling up and down his skin. The beast was raring to get out now, and if Tristan wasn't careful, he really might lose all control. Still, he needed to stand his ground. "I can't leave until I've gotten what I came for." Perhaps this was because of the magic in Evangeline's cuffs; perhaps this was due to his own stubborn nature; perhaps, deep down, he feared what repercussions might come to him and all the Descendants if Evangeline lost this chance to reclaim their fountainheads, lost power to the Nius.

Whatever the case, Tristan would not even allow himself to entertain the thought of turning around having failed to do what he'd set out to do. If it came down to using force against Ying, then so be it.

"There are people depending on me to succeed here, and there's an important Assignment that needs to be done. I'll ask you one more time—will you tell me how to access the Underground?" Hoping against hope, Tristan wished Ying would give up the secret willingly. But he knew her too well.

"You'll have to kill me to wrest that knowledge from me," Ying said.

Tristan's heart thudded in his chest. So it had come to this. Part of him wondered if he *should* just leave Ying's apartment right now, should tell Evangeline that he'd failed even before they'd gotten to the actual Assignment, and to hell with the consequences.

But oh, how he loathed Marcus Niu. The thought of Marcus taking leadership of the High Council was infinitely worse than the idea of Evangeline occupying that spot. Evangeline's best shot at earning the respect and loyalty of the Descendants was successfully fulfilling this Assignment, bringing back the long-lost fountainheads. Tristan shouldn't care what happened to Evangeline, but even the thought of her falling from grace among the Descendants . . . that insufferable Marcus leading them all instead down his own twisted path.

No, Tristan's gut had a bad feeling about what Marcus Niu might have in store for the Descendants. There was only one way to protect Evangeline. And so, in a split second, he made his decision.

He reached into his pocket and drew out a tiny pin. When he squeezed it, it elongated into a short sword. It was his favorite weapon, a double-edged straight sword that he'd affectionately named Wrathbringer, and he didn't go anywhere without it. Tristan's father had given the sword to him when he was a boy. That was a very long time ago now, when Tristan was still mortal, and his father had died over a century ago. But Wrathbringer had stayed as sharp as the day Tristan had received it.

Ying's eyes followed the flash of the blade under the light. She bared her teeth, pulling out her own, longer sword. He'd never fought Ying seriously, and while he was fairly certain he could take her in a fight without magic, he was sure it would be tougher trying to beat her when she had her added shaman ability.

"I'm sorry, Ying. I didn't want it to come to this," Tristan said, "but you leave me no choice."

He wouldn't kill her, of course. Even Tristan knew where to draw the line. But Ying didn't know him well enough to know where he drew that line. The best strategy was to pretend to go in for the kill, capture the shaman, and then force the answer out of her.

Tristan dashed toward her, slicing Wrathbringer in a wide arc. Ying sidestepped and parried with her blade, and their swords clashed in a clang of steel. Ying's eyes narrowed, and a red glow formed around her sword. But before she could pull whatever trick she was about to, Tristan kicked her in the stomach and sent her flying backward. He didn't give her a chance to recover before slamming his foot into her throat. Ying's head collided with the edge of the table with a crack, and blood trickled out of her mouth.

"Surrender," Tristan ordered. "Surrender, and I won't hurt you."

Ying's eyes tilted up toward his, filled with hatred. They flashed, and too late, Tristan noticed the glow of magic that had formed around her. In an instant, he was blasted off his feet with a force that shook the apartment from ceiling to floor. Tristan was flung backward and crashed into the doorway with a sickening pain that lanced through his backside.

He groaned as he tried to drag himself up, the pain from the fall pulsing through his body. That monstrous urge within was growing to a crescendo, pain and frustration and fury roaring inside. Panic shot through him. Had his dosage of aubrum not been enough?

There was another bang. Suddenly a murderous-looking Ying hovered above him. She raised her arms above her head, chanting something under her breath—a spell. She was going to do something awful to him—and he couldn't let her, no matter what. He couldn't fail Evangeline.

Tristan clenched his teeth. *No,* he tried to command himself, but it was no use. Or maybe he was finally willing to do whatever it took to ensure he attained his goal. It was like he had been delaying the inevitable, trying to hold back an impending disaster, and now the floodgates were blown wide open. Typically, the greatest risk of transforming was on the day of the full moon, but there was risk on the couple of days before and after it, too. Tristan's luck appeared to have run out.

No, he thought desperately. *No, no, no.* His body shuddered, turned white-hot, and began to grow. Fur sprang up along his arms and legs, and his nails elongated. As he straightened, a roar released from his mouth.

Ying stumbled back from Tristan, wide-eyed. She'd never seen him transform; she didn't know what he was, truly, in his heart of hearts—a beast. Now this much was clear as day. Ying's screams echoed throughout the room, but they only served to fuel the wolf's rampage.

Tristan watched the scene unfold before him with horror, a passenger in his own body. The sharp claws on his hands swung at Ying; she dove out of the way, her robe tearing as it got caught along Tristan's nails. Wrathbringer swung in the dim light, the hilt clutched firmly in one massive paw.

Ying turned to face the beast that was Tristan. Though there was fear on her face, there was determination, too. Unfortunately, determination alone couldn't save her.

Whatever reservations Tristan had about going all out, the beast shared no such feelings. In one large stride, Tristan closed the gap between him and the shaman; and in the next moment, he drove Wrathbringer upward into Ying's unprotected chest.

For a moment, it seemed as though all time stopped. Ying hung there, suspended in the air, her mouth rounded in shock. Red blossomed where the wound was. Shamans bled just as mortals did; Tristan knew this, and yet for some absurd reason he'd thought Ying wouldn't bleed before him, Ying wouldn't actually suffer such agony at his hands.

He had been wrong. Ying crumpled to the floor, gasping and heaving.

Almost as though all the fighting spirit had gone out of him, the fur on his body shrank, the beast within calmed. Tristan fell forward onto his hands and knees, gasping for breath. He was shaking, and he hadn't felt so weakened in a long time—not since the last time he'd transformed—but he couldn't allow himself to succumb to weakness now.

"Ying—Ying—" Tristan crawled toward her, even as his brain was scrambling to come to the conclusion that his eyes already had, even as he was struggling to comprehend the magnitude of what had just happened. What he had just done.

"You . . ." Ying coughed, and blood sprayed her chin. "You . . . won."

Tristan began to shake. "I'm sorry," he gasped. He'd seen more than enough of death in his many decades of living, and certainly he'd had to kill before, but he'd never murdered an ally in cold blood until now. Even though Ying's stubbornness had led to this moment, it was his fault. He'd been unable to control the beast within. He'd driven the blade into her body. "I'm—I'm so fucking sorry."

Ying was struggling to grasp something in her pocket. With blood-stained, unsteady fingers, she finally produced a small, clear vial in her left hand. Then she raised it to her wound, and blood trickled from her chest into the vial. Tristan could only watch, wide-eyed and stricken and uncomprehending.

"Take . . . it . . ." Ying's trembling fingers forced the vial into Tristan's palm. Her eyes were rolling, and the blood was still flowing, so much blood that Tristan could see and smell nothing else. He was certain he would never get Ying's blood off him. "You . . . need . . . shaman . . . blood . . ."

"Sh-Shaman blood? That's . . . that's the key?" It seemed unnecessarily brutal, and yet he supposed it was a clever rite of passage. Any intruders would be effectively barred from entering the Underground. But Tristan didn't allow himself to linger on the ingenuity. Ying was dying before him, and though they'd never been more than distant business partners, he'd never wanted her dead—and especially not by his hands.

Tristan's mind raced as he tried to piece together everything he knew about Ying. She didn't have family, not any that lived with her, and she didn't seem to have friends. Still, someone—like the Collector, or one of Ying's other business partners—was bound to come looking for her sooner or later, and what would happen when they discovered the body? What punishment would await Tristan if he was traced back to Ying's body?

"Why didn't you just *give* me the blood?" he groaned.

Ying's right lip curled up into an attempt at a smirk. "Use it . . . well. Help . . . your fellow Descendants . . . Tao."

"Tristan. My real name—it's Tristan." He wasn't sure why it was so important to him that this dying shaman finally know his name, know something *real* about him. Perhaps it was *because* they knew so little about each other despite being connected by their rare line of work that Tristan felt the need, in Ying's last moments, to finally make something real out of their comradery.

She smiled, and blood dribbled out of the corner of her mouth. "Tristan. My name . . . is . . ."

But at that moment, before she could finish what she was saying, Ying's eyes turned glassy and her head went limp.

For a moment, Tristan sat there in disbelief. He had not seriously considered that the situation would go south like this. Ying had died at his hands, and he would never know anything real about her. Perhaps he didn't deserve to know.

Tristan leapt back and yelled when her body was engulfed in a rush of blue energy. In moments, the flames had disappeared, and there was nothing left behind at all, not even a pile of ash, to indicate that the shaman had lived and died right here.

11
ALICE

Madison's abrupt departure quickly became a hot topic of discussion in the dorm, as their already tiny class size had shrunk twenty percent in the blink of an eye. But Alice didn't have much time to dwell on her sudden lack of a roommate. The members of the House of Boar stayed up into the early hours of the morning to gossip about the chaos happening inside and outside Earthly Branches Academy. Despite her exhaustion, Alice decided to stay up with the others. After all, even though she was physically tired, her mind was restless with questions about the fate of the Descendants; she was unlikely to fall asleep.

Then, just after one in the morning, a visitor arrived at the dorm.

The vampire Cecil Long was in Evangeline's circle, but Alice hadn't really crossed paths with her much. Cecil really was beautiful, with plump pink lips and long, silky black hair that seemed to shimmer when she moved. Such was her beauty that it took Alice a few moments to register the fact that Cecil was looking at and talking to *her*.

". . . Jiang? Hello? Are you hearing me?" Cecil snapped her fingers impatiently, and Alice startled out of her thoughts.

"Oh, um, yes. Hi. That's me. I'm Jiang, Alice—I mean, A-Alice Jiang." Inwardly, Alice groaned. Could she have made more of a fool of herself?

The others around Alice giggled, not even bothering to pretend they weren't eavesdropping, but Cecil paid them no mind. Her eyes were fixed upon Alice's. Alice fought the urge to look away.

"Please come with me. You don't need to bring anything with you," Cecil clarified as Alice glanced behind her toward her room. "You're excused from class for the duration of this Assignment. Anything you'll need, Evangeline will provide for you."

"An Assignment? With Evangeline?" Alice wondered if she'd heard wrong. She couldn't think of what the school's queen bee would want with her. Plus, Cecil and Evangeline were *both* vampires. This couldn't bode well for Alice. And she couldn't process the fact that she was being asked to leave the school for an Assignment already, when she'd just gotten here. How could she possibly be useful when she'd barely gotten the hang of doing a right hook in combat class? There had to be some mistake . . . except Alice was certain Evangeline was not the type to make mistakes, and as they'd gotten off on the wrong foot at the beginning of the semester, surely Evangeline would never seek Alice out except as a last resort.

Honestly, that made this entire situation even more peculiar and intriguing. Alice steeled her nerves. Just earlier, she'd told Kate that she would stay at Earthly Branches Academy to train with her fellow Descendants. To become strong enough to offer protection to others. Sure, Alice hadn't expected to take on an Assignment *immediately* after that discussion, but what better way to prove the seriousness of her vows to Kate—to herself?

Besides, she had little choice but to see what Evangeline wanted. Ignoring a summons from Evangeline seemed even more dangerous than following through with this request.

"Good luck," whispered Darla, who was sitting closest to Alice. "Don't get eaten."

It was a mark of how nervous Alice was that she couldn't think of a single retort. As far as she was aware, Evangeline very well could eat her.

Luckily, Cecil's tongue wasn't as tied. "I can assure you, Darla Tang, that if it were a meal Evangeline wanted, she could dine on the finest gourmet human blood—not the mediocrity this dorm has to offer."

Darla choked on her rice, her face turning bright red. The girls gasped at Cecil's boldness. Alice wasn't sure whether to feel relieved that someone had spoken up or offended that she'd been lumped in with "the mediocrity this dorm has to offer." Quickly, before something dangerous actually happened, she stood up and placed her tray of uneaten food on the conveyor belt. Then she hurried over to Cecil.

"Let's not dally," said Cecil. With one more glance back at the girls, she strode out of the dorm, Alice trailing behind her. As soon as the doors of the commons swung shut behind her, Cecil turned toward Alice with a scrutinizing look. "Have you ever traveled with a vampire before?"

"Um, no."

"Okay, the main rule to remember is to keep your eyes and mouth shut. There are numerous enchantments protecting the Long estate, but you'll be able to bypass those as long as you're with me."

For the umpteenth time since she'd arrived at this school, Alice wondered what she'd gotten herself into—and if she'd survive.

Cecil grabbed her hand. Alice yelped, shocked by how ice-cold her grip was. Then Cecil bent over slightly, which surprised Alice even more. "Get on my back," Cecil commanded.

"What?"

"Do as I say. Please."

Feeling as though this scenario had come out of a bizarre dream, Alice swung her leg over Cecil's back.

"Hang on tight," said Cecil.

Alice wrapped her arms around Cecil's neck, and not a moment too soon. She scarcely had time to close her eyes and mouth before she was aware of the sensation of moving at breakneck speed. A pressure built up in her ears. Her stomach lurched, the sensation similar to being tilted forward on a roller coaster. It wasn't a pleasant feeling, and Alice kept her eyes and mouth shut tight as she fought the urge to scream.

In what felt like forever and yet no time at all, the world came to a halt beneath her again. She would have pitched forward, but Cecil steadied her as she climbed off her back.

"You all right?" Cecil said, not unkindly. "The first time's always the hardest. Or so I've been told."

"Yeah, I—I'm great," Alice lied. "Can all the supernaturals do that?"

"Travel at that speed? Yes, but it's very taxing, so we can't do it too often," Cecil explained. "Even supernaturals have our limits." ·

As Alice struggled to orient herself in the world once more, she glanced upward and found herself standing before a formidable mansion. Quickly, she tried to calculate how much money it would cost to own so much land in Manhattan. She came to the conclusion that the Longs were *extravagantly* wealthy. "Wow," Alice breathed.

"Nice, isn't it?" Cecil said.

Nice was an understatement. Not only was the building a stunning work of architecture, a combination of Gothic-style construction with sleek modern touches, but the *view* of the city from where Alice stood was equally breathtaking.

Here the redness of the sky was eclipsed by the darkness of night. The stars were obscured, the sky instead illuminated by the glittering lights of the skyscrapers. New York City came into view like a fuzzy black-and-white picture slowly sharpening in focus and color. Dazzling skyscrapers and sparkling lights spread out like the shining veins of a metropolitan body, the flow of traffic pumping out the city's steady heartbeat.

"Hurry, now," said Cecil. "Let's not keep Evangeline waiting."

Alice had a feeling that she should have stayed behind at school.

Evangeline was waiting for them in the room beyond the massive foyer, standing still as a statue, her arms folded across her chest. She wasn't alone, either. With her was Nicholas Hu, whom Evangeline recognized from the High Council. In fact, the only one here who *wasn't* a high-profile Descendant was Alice herself. She was also, quite clearly, the only human amid the beautiful immortals. Now Alice had even more questions. She squirmed, forcing a smile to her face. Even if she was utterly intimidated by the others, she couldn't show it.

"Alice. Good of you to join us," Evangeline said, her tone cold. Alice flinched. She'd had the feeling that she was on Evangeline's bad side since day one, and that feeling only grew stronger now. She wasn't sure why Evangeline had invited her to her home, much less why she had done so right after her brother had been pronounced dead.

Alice tried to read the others' minds, like she'd done at the Academy, but she was greeted with blankness. It was like there was a wall surrounding their thoughts. Try as she did to push through it, she couldn't. Maybe there was something special about Earthly Branches Academy that allowed her access into others' thoughts and conversations. She still didn't know anything about her ability.

"If you're trying to read our minds, human, you can stop," said Evangeline abruptly. "Your powers are useless against the enchantments guarding the Long estate."

Alice's jaw dropped. How had Evangeline known that she'd been attempting to read their minds? Nicholas threw her a mistrustful look, and Alice immediately lowered her gaze to the carpeted floor. It was as though she had been caught in the act of something shameful, and her cheeks flamed with heat.

Evangeline rolled her eyes. "You humans are insufferably predictable. And you might want to be more careful how and when you use that ability, because that's what got your father killed."

Whatever Evangeline had wanted to talk about, Alice could never have predicted that she'd bring up her father. "What do you know about my father?" Her voice came out breathy, rushed, and demanding, and upon seeing Evangeline's lip curl, she wished she'd asked the question more tactfully. But she couldn't help it.

To her surprise, Evangeline turned away. "We can discuss your father in due time, though he was always a guarded person, so there isn't much *to* discuss. You might even find out more about Ruiting if you stick with me—the answers you seek are likely to be found where we are headed." She leaned forward, her eyes steady on Alice once more. "There's an urgent matter at hand. I've called you to my home today precisely because I need that mind-reading ability of yours. You'll get the information you desire—in exchange for assisting me."

Alice was too nervous to press Evangeline, though curiosity and hope rose like a flame in her chest. For now, it would have to do that she'd learn more about her father at a later date. And despite her reservations about being thrown into the deep end like this, she shivered with excitement. Evangeline might have answers to the questions about Baba, about Alice herself.

"And why do you need me?" Alice's voice came out with a sureness that she didn't quite feel, and it both pleased her and terrified her. Nobody took such a bold tone with Evangeline at Earthly Branches Academy.

Evangeline gave a grim smile. "The Elder granted me permission to take on an Assignment. We need to pull off the heist of the century, and you're going to help us do it."

12
NICHOLAS

Nicholas sensed Evangeline's mood souring as soon as Alice walked through the front door. She'd never been particularly good at concealing her emotions—at least, not from his sharp eyes—but he could tell that something about Alice especially irked her. It wasn't Nicholas's business, but he didn't relish the thought of spending extended periods of time in Evangeline's and Alice's company in the very near future. He had to do this, though. For Evangeline. If she was involving herself in dangerous matters—matters that had gotten Julius killed—then Nicholas needed to be by her side, to protect her. He wouldn't fail this time.

If Evangeline moved with an overpowering confidence, as though all the world were meant to make a path for her, then Alice walked in the exact opposite manner—like a timid lamb, afraid to take up space.

Yet there was still something about Alice Jiang that was so very intriguing. Nicholas had taken notice of her above all the new human Descendants as soon as she arrived at Earthly Branches. There was an aura about Alice. Even when she was doing her utmost not to draw attention to herself, Nicholas found himself noticing her on those rare occasions when they crossed paths on campus. He'd glimpsed it, briefly, that fire deep inside her, when she'd practically interrogated the High Council members about her father on the first day. Indeed, she was a most interesting human, and Nicholas was almost glad to see that Evangeline had brought her on board for the Assignment.

"A heist?" Alice was saying, her expression blank, as though she'd never heard the word before. Then horror and understanding flashed across her face. "What—you want to *steal things*? You know we could go to jail for that, right?" She spoke with the same shock as if Evangeline had suggested they go out and commit manslaughter.

"It's not really stealing if we're taking back what was stolen, what rightfully belongs to *us*," Evangeline said sharply. "I prefer to think of it as righting history's wrongs. And if there were any justice in this world, the original thieves would be the ones going to jail, not us."

Alice's face paled. "But . . . But we aren't thieves," she protested, though she gave Nicholas a suspicious look. "Well, *I'm* not a thief."

"Neither am I." Nicholas frowned. Did he somehow give the impression of being skilled in this area?

"Trust me, I know you two are as straightedge as they come. That's why I've enlisted the aid of Tristan She," Evangeline said casually. "In fact, I already have him on the job stealing precious information that we need to access the Underground."

Nicholas felt his own mood sour considerably. "Tristan?" he couldn't help but growl. Not Tristan. *Anyone* but him. Especially after they'd had that argument that nearly ended with a violent fight, Nicholas didn't even want to see Tristan's face. He was surprised, too. Evangeline didn't like Tristan *or* Alice; Nicholas was puzzled that she'd chosen them to be part of her crew. He usually didn't have trouble reading her, but he couldn't imagine what she might be thinking. Tristan, he supposed, would be useful when it came to physically pulling off the heist. But Nicholas couldn't reason out where Alice's involvement came in. Was Alice's mind-reading ability that valuable to this specific Assignment? "You ought to rethink recruiting Tristan. He's like a ticking bomb, Evangeline. Unstable and violent. He'll likely end up dragging us down rather than being of help."

Evangeline sighed and pressed her fingertips to her temple, as though willing herself to be patient. "You know, Tristan said something very similar to me about you just a little earlier. If you two would set aside your differences, you'd understand *why* I selected both of you specifically, looking past your . . . poor relationship."

Poor relationship was putting it lightly. Nicholas furrowed his brow. He was at war with himself. On the one hand, he'd always been happy to listen to Evangeline, as she, like her brother, often proved to be right. On the other, he couldn't see how putting him and Tristan in close proximity could end in anything productive.

"If you're wondering why I've asked for your help," said Evangeline, almost as though she'd read Nicholas's mind, "it's because, after careful evaluation of all possible candidates, I've come to acknowledge your particular set of talents and skills for this task. My late brother"—her voice caught for just a moment, but she pressed on—"left me with enough clues to piece together what I need to do. I've chosen you three to accompany me deep into shaman and faerie territory."

"Shaman and faerie territory?" Nicholas repeated. "But that's . . . no one's bothered the shamans or fae since the treaty was signed." After the turf war ended in the signing of the Treaty of Supernatural Peace, the shamans and fae had each retreated from the human world to their respective territories and had hardly been seen or heard of since. "Why go poking the hornets' nest now?"

"*They* poked *our* nest first, don't you think?" Evangeline snapped. "If Julius's hunch is correct and the fae took our fountainheads, then they, effectively, committed the first act of aggression against us long ago. War, then, would be inevitable, in the eyes of us Descendants."

"Be that as it may, that all happened before the treaty was signed, and . . ." Nicholas shook his head. "I don't like that our fountainheads are still missing, but I don't like this idea either, Evangeline. Trespassing and breaking the treaty is inviting trouble."

"Only if we're caught."

"That's a big *if.* We don't need to take that risk on top of dealing with the oncoming power struggle for Chancellor."

Evangeline shrugged and flicked a piece of lint off her shoulder. She was affecting a nonchalant air, but Nicholas read the tension in her shoulders. Evangeline knew the challenges rising before her, knew the risks of leaving school at this moment to do something as dangerous as trespass on shaman and faerie territory. She would only take on such a risk if it would benefit her massively. There was a connection here, something Nicholas couldn't see yet.

"You're free to turn me down, of course. But I will be proceeding with or without help."

Nicholas liked that idea even less. "Evangeline—"

She raised a hand, and he fell silent. "Do at least consider what I have to say before you leave." She took a deep breath. Alice's eyes darted toward the door, but otherwise she made no indication that she wanted to leave. "If we successfully complete this Assignment, the Circle of Twelve can finally be restored, and we Descendants will have our full power once more."

The Circle of Twelve had been broken for so long that the idea of it being complete seemed like a fool's dream. Nicholas hadn't even allowed himself to entertain any fantasies of what it might be like to be at the height of his powers again—mortal, and yet supplied with endless amounts of magic, the likes of which had been helpful, not destructive. All those decades ago, Nicholas had been gifted with the ability to Heal, and he had been a significant asset to the Descendants. There was a gaping hole in his heart where his Healing powers had once been—a chasm that he had never thought could be filled again, a curse that he had never thought could be broken. For the first time in a long, long time, Nicholas's heart lifted with hope. If Evangeline was right, if this Assignment was the key to restoring the Descendants' former glory, Nicholas could have his old life back. He would never have to worry about the finicky fire within getting the best of him, ever again. Thanks to Evangeline, that dream seemed a little less impossible.

Nicholas's memories of his own actions that day surfaced with a wave of guilt that nearly overpowered him. He had never hoped for the chance to one day redeem himself in the eyes of the other Descendants, and in his own eyes.

"You . . . You know the location of the missing fountainheads?" he asked in a raspy voice.

"It seems Julius had a theory," said Evangeline, her eyes flashing, "and Julius's theories tend to be correct."

She was holding something back, though it wasn't hard for Nicholas to imagine what that could be. He had no doubt that Julius had kept Evangeline in the dark, and that Evangeline would be mightily frustrated about that. "We'll need to head down to the Underworld and find the shamans, get them on our side," she said. "Then we'll need to infiltrate Faerie, where I have reason to suspect the statues are being kept."

Nicholas stared hard into Evangeline's eyes. She was not the type to joke around, especially not about such a serious matter—in fact, he had never, not even once, heard her crack a single joke, in all the time he'd known her. Still, he was paralyzed with uncertainty, with the fear of everything that could go wrong in taking such a massive gamble. "If we're caught, Evangeline . . . if the fae declare hostilities against the Descendants after over a century of peace . . ."

"Of course I understand the risks," she said curtly. "I don't need you to spell out the dangers of this Assignment, Nicholas. I know exactly what I'm getting myself into." Although outwardly she maintained her usual cool, calm demeanor, the volume of her voice steadily rose. "For all of his faults, and as much as I might disagree with his approach, Marcus Niu *does* have one thing right."

Nicholas could hardly believe his ears. "You can't possibly mean that."

"We Descendants have always played it safe—too safe. If we never fight for ourselves, putting our necks on the line, our power and relevance will slowly slip away from us. And I, for one, am tired of standing by, lolling around at the Academy day in and day out. The answer to our problems, the restoration of our glory, is finally at our fingertips—if only we dare, for once, to take that leap of faith."

Evangeline's voice rang with passion and authority. It struck Nicholas, as he stared at her in awe, that she had really been born to reign over an estate, as she carried herself with the grace and elegance of a ruler.

Of course, he'd always thought of her as powerful and capable. When they were kids, Evangeline had stood up to bullies for him again and again. But he had never imagined her acting *this* fearlessly—and passionately. Or perhaps he, like the others, hadn't noticed Evangeline's full potential, with Julius's greatness overshadowing her. Maybe Julius's death had been written in the stars, to allow Evangeline Long to step out of her brother's shadow and into greatness. The thought sent shivers down Nicholas's spine.

"And of course, once we have the missing fountainheads in our possession, we'll be powerful enough to handle the fae, no matter what happens."

The conviction in Evangeline's expression was such that it stirred even Nicholas (who did prefer to "play it safe," as Evangeline had put it). When the Descendants had been at the height of their power, they had been like miniature gods on Earth. Oh, to be so untouchable again . . . Nicholas's throat tightened. As much as he'd tried to squash the desire deep within himself, he, too, craved the return of what had once been. The chance to make up for his faults all those years ago, as best he could.

Evangeline would lead the Descendants to a new age. And Nicholas would do his damnedest to help her.

"The fae," said Alice blankly, breaking the silence. "You want us to go find the shamans and the fae. Aren't they, like . . . sorta evil?"

"They're mischievous, certainly," Nicholas said. Now he was in his element, sharing knowledge. "And powerful. While they haven't declared outward hostility, they haven't really been on the Descendants' side throughout history—take a look, for example, at the building of the transcontinental railroad. That happened almost immediately after the Chinese arrived in the States—the workers labored long and hard hours for little pay, often risking death to finish the job. But instead of stepping in to help, the shamans and the fae turned their backs on all immigrants, including the Descendants."

"So we'll head into Faerie," said Alice, with a false bravado that was only too transparent to Nicholas. Her hands were shaking when she clapped them together. "So what? If they were really that powerful, they wouldn't be in hiding. We don't need to fear them."

Evangeline cocked her head to the side, as though reassessing Alice. "You really are a special human, aren't you," she said softly. It wasn't a question.

Alice flushed.

"The same magic that's within us also flows within you," Evangeline continued. "And what's more is that you have some *extra*-special abilities." Nicholas noticed that her face pinched up as though she'd smelled something foul, but she added, "We'll need you to read the minds of the fae when we eventually breach their territory."

"But I—I'm not sure exactly how my ability works yet," Alice said hesitantly. "I think my . . . my ability, or whatever, works best at school."

"It's not the school that brings out your ability," Evangeline said. "It's being around us, your fellow Descendants. Your father was the same—he drew his power most strongly from being around others. Ruiting Jiang was probably the most powerful human Descendant who ever attended Earthly Branches, and he was wholly unaffected by the curse that had fallen upon the other Descendants. Your powers will come in handy when we've infiltrated the realm of the fae. You'll help us stay one step ahead of the enemy at all times."

Nicholas couldn't read minds, but he could tell by the look on Alice's face that this was making her nervous. Sweat trickled down her neck. Come to think of it, there was sweat running down Nicholas's forehead, too. He prided himself on having a squeaky-clean record. The school would be hard pressed to find a single misstep in his past. The idea that he was about to fling himself into a dangerous heist, all for Evangeline—and, well, for all of the Descendants, but especially for Evangeline—it was almost ludicrous.

Yet Nicholas knew he had to push himself to do this, against all his natural instincts. He would do it, and he would do it again, and again. For Evangeline. For the Descendants.

Evangeline's gaze traveled over Alice and Cecil and then met Nicholas's. Her eyes seemed to burn into his. "And you, Nicholas. You're gifted with deception and disguise. I'll need your talents to help us navigate treacherous territory."

Nicholas nodded. He'd always had a knack for changing his appearance, and it applied to an extent to others' appearances, too.

"Are you both in, then?" Evangeline asked. Her gaze passed from Nicholas to Alice. "You don't have to do this if you don't want to. I won't be upset if you walk through those doors right now." She nodded, indicating the large front doors where they'd entered.

"I'm in," said Nicholas. If he hesitated, he might let his fears and indecision get the best of him. As soon as he said the words, a rush of adrenaline filled his body.

Evangeline's smile widened. He'd really done it now.

"I . . . I'm in, too," came Alice's quiet voice, several beats after Nicholas's.

Now Evangeline was positively beaming. "Excellent. I'll have Cecil prepare a meal for you both. Tristan should be back soon. Once he returns, we head for the Underground."

13
TRISTAN

Tristan had been trained from a young age to kill if necessary for the greater good, but that never made it easier. He, like the other Descendants, just got better at pretending he was okay with what he'd done. With what he was.

Sometimes, late at night when it was impossible to distract himself from the thoughts, Tristan wondered who the real monsters were. One could argue that the supernaturals—who gorged on blood, who turned into frightening creatures, whose beauty could turn mortals mad—were as monstrous as could be.

This summer night at the border of Williamsburg and Bushwick had brought out young professionals in droves, headed for the bars and music venues. To Tristan, though, the sounds of drunken shouting and raucous laughter were muffled, as he slowly, slowly picked his way down a crowded street. More than one elbow dug into him none too gently as passersby moved around him, but none of their swearing or shoving inspired him to move any faster. The air was hot and sticky, hanging with a humidity that normally didn't bother Tristan, but tonight was like a blanket slowly smothering him.

Life. Death. It was all one big cycle, and Tristan, for some reason, was one of the very few exceptions to the rule, for he could not truly die. Nor could he truly live like this. A life in which he was not mortal, but not a god; a life in which every month, he didn't know whether he could successfully control the werewolf within. What kind of life was that?

Tristan closed his eyes, remembering how Ying had looked on the floor of her apartment, the life bleeding out of her. The image would be seared into his brain forevermore. Tristan never forgot those whose lives he'd taken, whether accidentally or because his hand was forced.

Everyone knew the two Niu brothers: Marcus and Max. Alike in so many ways, and yet opposite in others, they complemented each other well and made for a formidable duo when they came together.

Many decades ago, there had been a third brother, the youngest.

Matthew Niu was no doubt the runt of the three. Where Marcus was brawn, Matthew was bone. Where Max was brainy, Matthew was blockish. The natural pecking order of the brotherhood was that Marcus and Max looked after Matthew, bailing their younger brother out of trouble time and time again.

When Shane Ji made fun of Matthew for an unfortunate haircut, Marcus and Max made sure he'd never speak a bad word about Matthew again.

When the Second Opium War brought hordes of British soldiers into the Old Summer Palace, Marcus and Max did their utmost to protect their younger brother from the foreign devils and their advanced foreign weapons.

But they did not expect this: a supernatural curse afflicting all the Descendants. They did not anticipate this: Tristan She, a newly transformed werewolf, losing all control.

When the dust had settled, it revealed this: the broken, dead body of Matthew Niu beneath the werewolf Tristan's claws. Somebody was shaking Tristan and shouting his name, over and over.

"Tristan. Tristan. *Tristan!*"

When Tristan raised his head, dazed, the concerned, bleeding, but no less beautiful face of Evangeline Long came into view, which only served to confuse him more. Evangeline, the girl he'd always liked, who was far too good to notice him—why was she helping him now?

"Are you all right?" Evangeline asked, though it sounded more like a demand. Her face looked . . . different, somehow. Paler. More gaunt. Her front canines protruded sharply, almost like a . . . Tristan didn't let himself finish the thought; it was too absurd. "What happened? Why are you a . . . a—?" Evangeline covered her mouth with her hands, seemingly unable to utter the word.

A monster, Tristan finished for her.

Tristan couldn't even admit to himself what had happened, but his brain had already pieced together the most logical conclusion based on the evidence at the scene. The dead body of Matthew Niu right in front of him, his shirt clawed into bits and pieces, his blood glistening on torn flesh. Tristan's own bloodied claws. It was obvious what had happened here, wasn't it?

"Tristan?" Evangeline's eyes widened as he bent over and retched, vomiting onto the ground.

In the ensuing chaos and confusion, even Tristan himself would not recall the details of what had happened that day. But oh, he would never forget the sight of Matthew's body, when he finally came back to himself. He would never forget the musty iron *smell* of Matthew's blood all over his hands and arms and body. Tristan's memories of that incident had grown hazy, but he would always remember the important details—the fact that he'd become violently ill, vomiting until nothing came out of his mouth except saliva. And the fact that the Nius had advanced on Tristan, intending to deal him a death blow. Tristan, in his blind panic, reached deep within his wells of power; in a matter of life or death, he would not hesitate to use his most fearsome asset, his ability to Strike, in order to protect himself from the two brothers' rage. But rather than finding that familiar pool of power, he grasped at . . . nothing. A terrible, empty nothingness. Tristan, inexplicably, had lost his magic. And he would have lost his life, too, in that instant, if it were not for the Longs, who stepped in and defended him. Evangeline stayed by Tristan's side, drawing her sword as though she meant to protect him, and her older brother swiftly picked his way through the rubble to stand in front of his sister.

"Marcus. Max. We have lost enough lives today," Julius had declared, his back to Tristan. He couldn't believe that Julius, who had never shown any liking for him, was coming to his aid. Julius, too, seemed changed from his usual self. His voice was scratchy, as though he'd screamed himself hoarse. He walked with a slight limp.

A small group of similarly disheveled-looking Descendants had gathered behind Marcus, staring at Tristan with a mixture of shock—and fear. None of them, he noticed, were covered in such a substantial amount of blood, though a few of them had similarly sprouted hair or otherwise appeared . . . quite different. Clearly, whatever was ailing Tristan was also ailing the other Descendants.

"Stand aside, Julius," growled Marcus. There was a steely edge to his voice that Tristan had never heard before, a truly frightening sound. His body was bigger and bulkier than ever, and fur protruded from beneath the cuffs of his sleeves. "That—that *filth* murdered our brother. And after we settle our debt with Tristan right now, Nicholas will be next, for abandoning his duties in the most crucial moment."

When Julius spoke, it was with a calmness that must have been maddening to the raging Niu brothers. "I understand your anger, but this is not the time or the place for it."

"Who put you in charge?" Marcus strode up to Julius and cracked his knuckles.

"My late father was the Chancellor of the High Council. Now that he's gone, the duty falls to me to step in." When Marcus opened his mouth again, no doubt to argue, Julius raised his voice and didn't let him get a word in edgewise. "And you ought to focus on what counts right now, Marcus, rather than squabble with me. Right now, very few Descendants remain; every last member of the High Council died with honor today." Here Julius's voice broke, and his stoic expression cracked to reveal a pain that seemed far too heavy for a young man to bear. "Some terrible curse has befallen those of us Descendants who *do* remain, and we need to all come together or else risk total extinction."

Julius's words fell on deaf ears. The Nius were covered in blood from head to foot, and despite their differences in stature, they had never looked so alike, their faces carved into identical snarls of hatred.

"Get out of the way," Max growled, brandishing his sword at Julius. Max had always been good-looking, but now a change had been wrought in him—he was dazzling, almost too beautiful to look at.

Julius, however, had anticipated the move, and retaliated so quickly that Tristan would have missed it had he blinked. Julius kicked the hilt of the sword out of Max's hands.

Max reddened. "You—"

"I promise that if you challenge me, you will both go down in a very embarrassing and painful manner," Julius declared. It was a mark of how serious everyone knew this threat to be—and how seriously *good* Julius was at combat—that both brothers immediately shut up. "I do not wish to have to fight you two while you are in the throes of grief. Tristan She is one of two remaining living Descendants of the snake bloodline. He must stay alive. If he dies, the chance of the entire bloodline dying rises by fifty percent, and if that happens, the strength of the Descendants will never be the same. That is why I need you *all* to stay alive, to protect one another."

Tristan jerked. He'd only just come to moments ago, and he had not known he was one of the last of his line. "Only . . . two?" he choked out. "Who is the other?"

"Your uncle Hai."

"M-My family," Tristan croaked, speaking up at last. He didn't care that the two Niu brothers directed their ire straight at him, the hatred in their eyes so searing it almost burned him. He didn't care that Evangeline was trying to get him to keep still as he was struggling to get to his feet.

Ma. Ba. His aunts and uncles and cousins. He would never speak to them or hear their voices again. The realization was so swift and horrific that he nearly puked again, even though he'd long since emptied his stomach. He'd lost everything. Even the fountainheads had been stolen.

And who had been responsible for the tragedy today? Which of the Descendants had been on night guard, was supposed to stand watch over the fountainheads, and had abandoned his duties?

A wave of nausea rolled over Tristan as he recalled what Marcus had said.

Nicholas. Nicholas, his friend, his cowardly, timid friend.

Amid the grief, fury rose within Tristan. He had never thought he could feel such rage toward his friend, but grief was driving him mad, and this madness needed an outlet. It needed somewhere to *go.*

"Don't overexert yourself," Evangeline whispered.

Tristan took deep breaths to calm himself down, but the damage was done. He could forgive Nicholas for anything—but this. He could never forgive Nicholas for the deaths of all his loved ones, for the loss of nearly everyone and everything he'd ever held dear.

Max pulled Marcus aside. The two brothers had a whispered but heated conversation several feet away from the others. When they returned, the looks on their faces were no less murderous.

"We will spare Tristan She's life today," Max growled, sounding as though each word were being dragged out of his mouth against his will, "on the condition that he is restrained until he can get himself under control."

Tristan was so dazed, so overwhelmed, that he could not care about his own fate, could not be bothered to fight back against the Nius. After all, he deserved it, didn't he? He was lucky Marcus and Max hadn't killed him on the spot, Julius's words be damned. Tristan had killed their brother, even if he didn't remember it happening, even if he hadn't been able to control his own body. The evidence was right before everyone's eyes.

"I . . . I know it isn't nearly enough, but I'm sorry," Tristan managed. "I can't tell you how sorry I am." He couldn't bring himself to look the Niu brothers in the eye.

In response, Marcus spat at Tristan's feet.

Something wet dropped onto his forehead. He lifted his head with what felt like a gargantuan effort. Evangeline was crying. It was wrong, Tristan thought, that such a pretty, kind girl was comforting him when he'd just taken the life of one of his fellow Descendants in a violent manner. Wrong that Tristan was still alive, when Ma and Ba and everyone else were not. They had been alive only hours before, had cheerily eaten *breakfast* with him earlier that day, without a care in the world.

Tristan had lost everything in less than half a day. His family. His fellow Descendants. Even his own sense of self. He had viciously killed another Descendant, and perhaps the Nius were right; perhaps he ought to die to atone for his crime. Yet Julius had insisted that he be spared—if only because Tristan was the last remaining Descendant of the snake bloodline.

Tristan shrank away from the heated glares of the others. He didn't know what to do, but he turned his head toward Evangeline's shoulder and cried into it. At some point, he and Evangeline ended up holding each other for comfort, two of the few very confused survivors in a world that had seemingly gone mad.

On this day, Tristan's heart cracked nearly in two, breaking to the point where it would take a miracle to heal it again. On this day, he decided it would be better to live a loner than ever to cause such great pain to others again.

That was the first time Tristan had taken a life. And, determined as the remaining Niu brothers were to bide their time until they could return the favor, Tristan would never forget it.

He glanced up at the moon and then closed his eyes. This was the situation as far as he saw it: refuse to help Evangeline, and increase the odds that Marcus Niu would become Chancellor and ruin his life. Cave in to Evangeline's demands, and involve himself in a high-stakes situation where he could potentially hurt more people. His options seemed bleak.

Help . . . your fellow Descendants . . . Tao. Ying's words echoed in Tristan's head. In the end, the shaman had died wishing that he would make a more selfless choice, given the means. That he would help out someone in need. The vial of blood in his hand was hot to the touch, almost like an insistent reminder of Ying's last words.

Tristan opened his eyes and stared down at his hands. The skin on their backs was smooth—too smooth. These couldn't be the hands that had bested countless opponents in combat. These couldn't be the hands that had ended Ying's life moments ago. He squeezed them into fists and released a sigh.

Would there ever be a day when Tristan didn't fear what might come to pass if he couldn't control his werewolf side? Would the Descendants ever be free of this curse? The best chance for that to happen was for Evangeline to successfully pull off this heist; she was so serious about this endeavor that she'd set aside her pride to ask for Tristan's help.

Perhaps the Descendants' only way forward—*Tristan's* only way forward—was to grant Evangeline her wish.

"Fine," Tristan said to no one in particular. "I'll do it. But if anybody gets killed on this Assignment, don't say I didn't warn you."

14
EVANGELINE

An hour had passed, and Tristan still hadn't returned to the mansion. Even though Bushwick was a trek, Tristan was exceptionally fast, and it shouldn't have taken him this long to deal with this business. He couldn't have escaped, either—Evangeline's magical cuffs would have ensured that he'd have no desire to disobey her.

Disappointment made her shoulders sag. What had she expected from Tristan? He'd let her down time and time again in the past. She shouldn't have expected anything different from him this time around. Perhaps in this matter, as with any other, she ought to have taken it into her own hands. Depending on others had left her disappointed more often than not.

Evangeline rubbed her temple to keep a headache at bay. She hadn't revealed this to Tristan, but she *couldn't* keep the cuffs on him for too long, despite her threats, because the cuffs were connected to her body's energy reserves, and it took an enormous amount of energy to wield them. Her strength was being sapped with every passing moment.

However, she could not allow herself to succumb to her exhaustion.

Nicholas and Alice watched her silently. The air in the living room hung with the thick awkwardness of strangers forced into the same space.

"Evangeline, you don't look quite right," Nicholas said brusquely.

"Well, my life did change rather drastically." All in all, recent events had been almost ludicrous in their terribleness, so absurd that Evangeline now needed to squash the manic laughter bubbling inside her. She could hardly think of a less appropriate time to laugh.

"You should take better care of yourself," Nicholas scolded. "I can make you a cup of tea."

"That's kind of you, Nicholas, but I—"

"I'll do it," Cecil interrupted. She was already on her way into the kitchen.

Nicholas paused and then shrugged. He gave Evangeline a tentative smile, which she returned to the best of her ability, though trying to smile in the midst of her grief was nearly impossible. She hated him seeing her at her weakest like this, but if there was anyone who'd seen her at some of her lowest times and had still never swayed in his opinion of her, it was Nicholas.

In the immediate aftermath of the Circle of Twelve's destruction, Nicholas and Evangeline had found each other in the wreckage. Having lost their loved ones, having turned into strange supernatural beings in their new nightmare of a reality, they had been a source of comfort for each other. And nothing about that had changed, even to this day.

"You'll be okay, Evangeline," Nicholas whispered. He pressed his forehead to hers.

"I . . . I know." Of course Evangeline would survive. She had managed to get through her parents' deaths. She had adjusted to vampire life, even if she desperately wished to still be human. But before she could get through to the other side, she would need to ride out this wave of grief, and in the thick of it, it was hard to believe that there *would* be another side.

After a moment, Alice sneezed. The sound jolted Evangeline out of her thoughts.

"Excuse me," Alice mumbled. The girl looked nothing short of pet-rified to be in Evangeline's home, in the presence of the most powerful supernaturals at school. And perhaps she was right to be wary. There was a reason the supernatural and human Descendants took classes on opposite schedules, so as to minimize their contact with one another. The whiff of human blood in such close proximity would have driven a weaker vampire to murder. Evangeline, though, had trained her body and mind to reject the temptation. She couldn't handle a repeat of what happened in that Manhattan subway car all those years ago. Even now, the memory of how many lives she'd taken was enough to evoke nausea.

Now Evangeline felt a tiny stab of sympathy for Alice. She had no idea what she had walked into, and their Assignment hadn't even begun. But what could Evangeline say to Alice? It had been so long since Evangeline had been mortal—she considered that a past lifetime, honestly—and she didn't know what it could be like to be at the bottom of the food chain at Earthly Branches Academy, only to suddenly be lifted up and given what was likely to be the most important Assignment in history.

It must be severely disorienting, to say the least.

Alice was an interesting girl. Although she gave off an overall impres-sion of meekness, she did have her surprising moments, displaying a fiery spirit that the older Descendants lacked. Evangeline would be lying to herself if she didn't admit that a part of her had wanted to recruit Alice just to see if she could coax out more of that unexpected fire. If they were to pull off this heist, they'd need just that.

Thankfully, Cecil saved Evangeline the awkwardness of further small talk by bustling back out of the kitchen with a steaming mug of warm blood ginger tea in one hand and a plate with three blood buns in the other. She placed them on the coffee table at Evangeline's side. "Here, xiǎo jiě."

"Thank you, Cecil," Evangeline said gratefully, nursing the mug of tea. She picked up one of the buns and bit into it. Even though she wasn't particularly hungry at the moment, she'd need her strength for the journey ahead. She couldn't waste a moment being distracted by her stomach. That constant, burdensome hunger for fresh blood was, if anything, further motivation for her to break the curse over the Descendants. She couldn't wait to be cured.

"You really do look quite pale," Cecil whispered. "Paler than usual, I mean."

Evangeline pressed her hands to her cheeks. If Cecil had noticed how pale she had gotten, even though her complexion was nearly white as snow on any day, then that must mean she was really draining her body's energy reserves. But she couldn't admit how much energy it took to use her golden cuffs on Tristan.

"I'm fine." Evangeline waved off Cecil's concern and composed herself. "I . . . I may have given Tristan too much credit, though. I thought he'd have returned by now."

"Historically, you have given Tristan far too much credit," Nicholas fired off immediately.

Whatever animosity Evangeline felt toward her ex-boyfriend, Nicholas had made it clear that he felt that a hundredfold. Cecil, too, gave a savage little nod. Alice said nothing, but her eyes continued to widen as she glanced between the supernaturals. Poor Alice. If Evangeline was in a giving mood later, maybe she'd fill her in.

Evangeline paced on the Moroccan carpet in the living room, trying not to panic just yet. It was too early to conclude that something had gone wrong. Maybe Tristan went the long way around, was purposely dragging this out and making Evangeline sweat. She wouldn't put it past him.

When the doorbell rang, Cecil jumped up and practically sprinted to the door. Then she screamed.

Cecil's reaction confirmed Evangeline's worst fear: that something *had* gone wrong. Evangeline smelled the blood before she saw it, and it wasn't the sweet freshness of human blood. This blood was more pungent, sharper, and it didn't attract the vampire senses as human blood did. It was not the blood of an animal, nor was it that of a Descendant.

Evangeline thought she might have smelled this blood once or twice long ago, but at the moment it escaped her what it could be. Most curious.

As Evangeline rushed over to the door, the answer occurred to her at the same moment she laid eyes on Tristan, who was wild-eyed and shaking, his clothes ripped and stained with blood.

"What happened to you?" Nicholas shouted.

The words slipped out of Evangeline's mouth like an accusation. Tristan's flinch confirmed that she was correct. "You said you'd be back in an hour. Why are your clothes shredded? Why are you covered in blood?" It wasn't concern over *him* that she felt, she told herself; it was concern that already the plan had gone awry.

Tristan turned his wild eyes toward her, and he raised his right hand. In it he clasped a small vial filled with a dark, thick liquid—much darker and thicker than human blood. Evangeline's attention moved to the vial for a moment before returning to Tristan's eyes. The last time she'd seen such a wild glint there, it had been . . . With a sinking feeling in her stomach, she glanced through the huge glass windows above the door. It was a nearly full moon tonight. Instantly Evangeline understood what must have happened here, why Tristan looked so . . . well, *feral.*

"You . . . ," she whispered, but trailed off. Even she wasn't sure what she'd been about to say. After all, wouldn't he hate it if she pried into his private business again, as though they still knew each other as well as they once did?

"I—I have what we need to get into the Underground," Tristan said, in a shaking voice very unlike his usual brusque tones. He glanced away, as though he couldn't bear the sight of what he held in his fingers. "Shaman blood."

After Evangeline removed the cuffs, Tristan took a shower and changed his clothes, and the group made ready to leave the Long mansion. Nobody pressed him with questions about how he'd produced the vial of blood, nor why he'd come back looking like he'd slaughtered a whole houseful of shamans. The answer was obvious. And Evangeline didn't want to know the details. Not yet. First, she needed to see that this mission was a success—that Tristan hadn't done what he had for nothing.

Blood was already on their hands. Now they *had* to succeed.

Cecil helped pack food into a shoulder bag—blood bags for Evangeline, steak for Tristan, and protein bars and trail mix for Nicholas and Alice. When everything was packed up, Nicholas grabbed the bag and clipped it around his shoulder.

"Leave your phones behind," Evangeline ordered. "Phones are traceable, and we don't want anyone somehow figuring out what we're doing or where we're headed."

The others obeyed, Alice most reluctantly, placing their phones in Evangeline's outstretched palms. She put them all in a basket on her coffee table.

"You'll come with us, Cecil," Evangeline said when the vampire began to get teary-eyed.

"I—I will?"

"You'll come with us to the entrance of the Underground," Evangeline explained. "Then I'll have a separate task for you before we enter the shamans' lair."

Cecil deflated again.

Evangeline patted her on the shoulder. "There's something I trust only you to do, Cecil. It's an extremely important part of the Assignment." Tristan snorted, clearly thinking that Evangeline was laying it on thick, but every word was true. She *did* need someone she trusted to stay behind and attend to a task—as well as watch over the Long estate. And the only person who fit that bill was Cecil.

The Long estate had a garage with four cars that Evangeline and Julius took turns driving. Due to the shady nature of the business he conducted at times, and fear of any enemies lurking around waiting for the perfect opening to sabotage them, Julius had had the cars enchanted long ago.

Anyone who came near the cars with less than innocent intentions would find themselves suddenly very distracted by an emergency popping up in their minds, such as having left a boiling pot of water on at home (and, upon actually returning home in a panicked rush, would discover that no such thing had happened at all, which would cause endless head-scratching afterward).

For this heist, Evangeline chose the least conspicuous car, the black Toyota Highlander. Nicholas sat up front with her, after exchanging a heated look with Tristan, who relented—maybe because Evangeline had given him a strange look when he'd tried to sit shotgun. This left Cecil, Alice, and Tristan awkwardly squished together in the back.

For the first minutes, the car was practically silent. This did not last long.

As the car pulled out of the driveway and onto the street, Nicholas said, "Nice night for a heist."

Evangeline groaned.

"What? I'm just saying. It could be raining or something. These are ideal conditions considering that we'll be moving about."

"You can read minds, can't you, Alice?" Tristan piped up. "That's what I've heard."

"Um . . . well, y-yeah," said Alice timidly.

"Tell me what I'm thinking right now," said Tristan. It sounded like a challenge. He was getting some of his usual cockiness back.

"You're thinking of something stupid to ask me."

Evangeline bit her lip to keep from snorting. She glanced in the rear-view mirror, and she could practically see the friendliness vanish from Tristan's expression.

"Listen, I'm trying to be nice, but if you don't—"

"Oh, please, Tristan," interjected Cecil.

Nicholas chimed in, too. "You're over a hundred years older than Alice. Show some maturity, yeah?"

"What about *you*? Haven't noticed you mature a bit in over a century."

Nicholas's back stiffened.

142

"If you don't all stop arguing, I'm going to throw you into a ditch," threatened Evangeline. She shot a glare at Tristan in the rearview mirror. He was staring defiantly at her. "We're almost to the Brooklyn Bridge, okay? Just . . . everyone be quiet."

They obliged and lapsed into silence. Evangeline sincerely hoped that when they were actually on the run for their lives, everyone would be too focused on the task at hand to bicker. Otherwise, she was in for a very long Assignment.

The Brooklyn Bridge appeared in front of them. Even late at night, there were still men and women dressed in everything from suits to street fashion. The East River ferry was docked at the harbor. Despite the late hour, the city was still alive with that uniquely vibrant energy that could be found only in New York City.

The car bumped over something large, jostling its passengers.

"What the hell? Did we run over somebody?" Tristan demanded, rubbing his ear where it had slammed into the door.

"Oops. Went a little too fast," Evangeline said, just a tiny bit gleeful over his distress. The Highlander slowed to a halt at the end of the bridge, where she pulled over onto a side street.

"This is a no-parking zone," Nicholas noted, reading the big yellow sign in front of them.

"Do we care about laws anymore? We're about to stage a heist," Tristan pointed out.

"We're not parking here." Evangeline got out of the car and opened the door.

Cecil stumbled out into the cool night air, looking confused—and even more puzzled when Evangeline placed the car keys in her hand.

"Drive the car up to the Metropolitan Museum of Art and park it there," Evangeline said. "It's going to be our getaway vehicle."

"With our speed, what do we need a getaway vehicle for?" Tristan snorted.

"We're going to be completely exhausted at the end of the Assignment, so it's very unlikely we'll all have enough strength left to travel at top speeds," Evangeline explained patiently. "I'm not going to go through all this trouble just to risk failing the Assignment in the last hour." When Tristan had nothing else to say to that, she turned back to Cecil and continued, "As I was saying, after you park the car, you can go home. I'll leave the care of the estate in your hands."

"But . . . But if I have the car keys, how will you drive the car later?"

"I have a spare set of keys."

"I don't like the sound of this, xiǎo jiě. Using one of the cars as a getaway vehicle? So much can go wrong."

"The Long estate and our cars are well guarded by enchantments in anticipation of exactly this type of scenario, Cecil. You'll be safe at home, so long as you don't go out *looking* for danger."

Cecil shook her head. When she glanced up at Evangeline again, her eyes were glittering with unshed tears. "I'm not worried about me. I'm worried about *you*. I promised—I promised Julius shào yé that I'd protect you."

Evangeline had kept her voice cold and businesslike this entire time, but now her emotionless mask began to crumble, just a little. Oh, Cecil. A small part of Evangeline wished they could embark on this treacherous journey together, but the much bigger part of her wanted to spare Cecil, at least, from the great danger they were heading toward.

Evangeline reached up and stroked Cecil's hair with a fondness that was rarely seen from her. "I know. And I thank you for all your protection over the years. Right now this is the best way you can protect me—by protecting the Long assets. By showing up for the Longs at Earthly Branches, to ensure that our powerful legacy is seen and felt even in my absence." Evangeline read the understanding in Cecil's eyes. If Evangeline couldn't be at school in person, then she needed to plant somebody there in her stead—somebody who was loyal, trustworthy, cunning. Somebody who would be able to counter Marcus's attempts to seize the title of Chancellor for himself before Evangeline could return. "I can entrust this task to no one but you."

Cecil closed her eyes and let out the quietest of sighs. There was no use arguing with Evangeline, for in their decades of close companionship, Cecil had never once won any argument, and she surely would not do so now. She opened her eyes. "All right. But please be careful. Julius would never forgive me if you got hurt."

Evangeline kissed the top of Cecil's head and then clasped their hands together. She swallowed back the lump that formed in her throat. Goodbyes were best kept brief. "I'll be back soon—and I'll have the zodiac fountainheads with me. Take care of yourself, too, will you?"

"I will," said Cecil. She nodded at the others, who'd gotten out of the car to quietly see her off. Then, ducking her head so that her long black hair covered her face, Cecil got into the driver's seat of the black Toyota Highlander.

Evangeline watched in silence as Cecil took off down the street, hoping she was right to be confident in Cecil's safety. The lump in her throat welled again. When the car was out of sight, Evangeline cleared her throat and turned back to the others, who were watching her expectantly. "We need to leave for the Underground," she said. From her pocket she produced the folded-up yellowed paper—Julius's note, which also contained the map of the Underground.

"Where did you get this?" Nicholas took the map first, eyes widening as they scanned its contents.

"Julius. He's kept it safe in preparation for this day, it would seem." Evangeline turned away, her eyes suddenly watering after she'd spoken her late brother's name aloud. She caught Tristan's gaze. He was staring right at her, eyes piercing hers, as though he could see her every thought. She hated how he'd always been able to read her like an open book, able to see past the picture-perfect exterior that she painstakingly crafted.

"What kind of hellish maze is this?" Nicholas grumbled as he consulted the map, glaring at it as though it had caused him great personal offense. "There's no way the shamans don't get lost in their own territory."

"The layout is specifically designed to confuse intruders, I'd imagine," Tristan said. "And I assume this map is incomplete. There must be guards stationed around these tunnels."

"There's a checkpoint marked about halfway between the entrance of the Underground and the prison sector," Evangeline said without glancing at the map. She didn't need to look at it to envision what she was talking about; before setting out on this Assignment, she'd spent hours in Julius's study committing the map to memory just in case something happened to it. "Before we reach that checkpoint, we need to blend in with the shamans—well enough to fool their security. Nicholas, you'll lend us your powers to create that transformation. I'll need four flawless disguises."

Nicholas started with surprise but quickly smoothed over his expression. "Of course."

Evangeline gave him a small, appreciative smile. She knew she was asking a lot of him. Of course, the reward at the end, once they successfully completed their quest, would more than make up for their gargantuan efforts.

"Then, Tristan, you'll be the one to sneak into the cell and release the Scarlet Spy. I trust your slippery thief's hands will be sufficient for this task as well."

"I can't tell if you're complimenting me or not. My assumption is not."

To that, Evangeline only offered a tight grin and a sharpened gaze.

"And what are we supposed to do when we get past the checkpoint?" Tristan asked. "Don't suppose we can just pick up the Scarlet Spy and waltz out of the Underground."

"The Scarlet Spy is locked up in the highest-security cell in the deepest part of the Underground," Evangeline said. "It's guarded with enchantments, the nature of which even Julius didn't seem to know."

"Fun," said Tristan.

"That's why I'm counting on Alice to read the minds of the nearby guards to help us figure out how to get around the enchantments."

"Me?" Alice squeaked.

"Yes, of course you. Did you think I brought you along just to sit here and look pretty? I am counting on your ability to get us in *and* out of the prison sector. You can do that, can't you?"

"M-Most definitely." Alice let out a nervous laugh. Rather than reassuring Evangeline, the response made her less confident than ever in her decision to bring along the human girl.

"Is everyone clear on the plan?" Evangeline asked.

"What's your role, Evangeline?" Tristan asked. It sounded like a challenge.

"*My* role is to make sure the rest of you don't mess up and get us into trouble along the way," Evangeline said crisply. "Now, if that's all, we don't have a moment to waste."

The lights of the city's skyscrapers illuminated the darkened sky. Traffic had slowed. Laughter and chatter floated in the air around them. The waters of the East River glittered under the lights as they headed toward the bottom of the Brooklyn Bridge.

Evangeline's mind began to wander, already jumping several steps ahead in the plan—thinking to when they'd need to infiltrate Faerie. She'd heard stories of the fae, and of the shamans who had fought with them over turf in the early 1900s. Neither the shamans nor the fae were fully justified in their causes, and it was better for the Descendants to stay out of the war, especially as the shamans and fae saw them as lesser beings.

They walked closer to the former location of the Fulton Fish Market, at Beekman and Fulton Streets. The place where Julius had died.

Evangeline fought to keep her expression neutral, to keep her focus only on the mission. Yellow tape surrounded the building, reminding her that this was now the scene of a crime—the scene of Julius's murder.

"You good?"

Evangeline blinked. Despite her best efforts, her thoughts had floated somewhere far away, and she was grateful to be brought back by a familiar voice. Tristan was staring at her, concern in his eyes. "Yeah." The word came out raspy, and Evangeline cleared her throat. "Yeah. I'm good."

They stepped over the yellow tape and drew closer to the abandoned building.

"You're sure this is the entrance?" Alice asked, her voice trembling. "It's sort of . . ."

"It's not glamorous," Nicholas said. "The shamans have never cared much about glamour, though."

Evangeline stepped closer to the wall, trying to find something—anything—that might resemble a door or an entrance.

"Allow me." Tristan walked to her. He held up the vial of shaman blood and carefully uncapped it. Then he dripped it ever so slowly on the wall. A fizzing sound ensued and the wall burned away. Evangeline leapt back in shock. There was a large hole where the wall had stood. An entrance, with no light inside as far as she could see.

"Let's go," said Tristan.

"From now on, we'll all need to take extra care not to be discovered," Evangeline warned. Her solemn eyes met those of each of her comrades.

After a moment's hesitation, Evangeline stepped forward, slightly ahead of Tristan, ignoring the nervous sweat gathering in her palms. This Assignment had been initiated by *Evangeline,* after all. And Evangeline was the prophesized Descendant meant to take back the zodiac fountainheads. Hell would freeze over before she let Tristan take charge of this heist.

The others followed Evangeline into the dark unknown of the Underground.

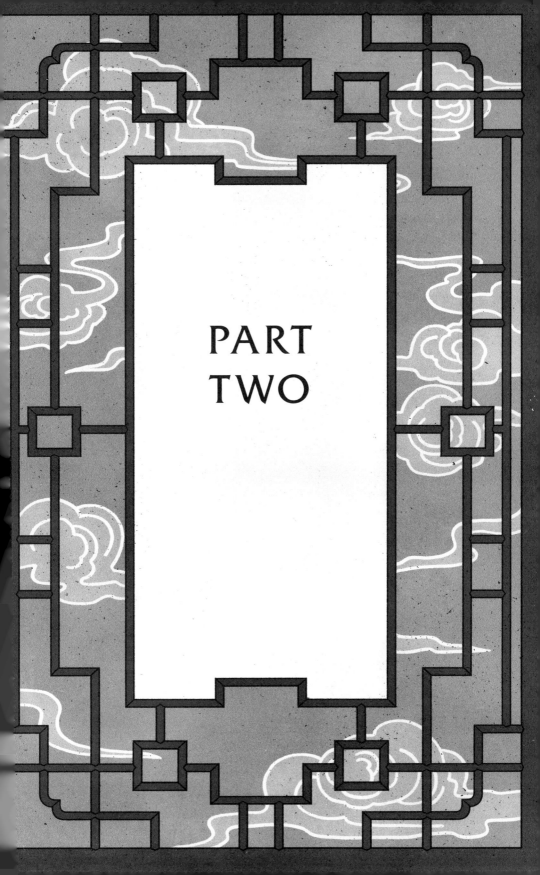

PART
TWO

15
MEANWHILE...

The world over, Manhattan's skyline was famous for its breathtaking sky-scrapers and stunning views. Droves of tourists flocked to see it with their own eyes. Photographers obsessed over capturing its beauty. Songwriters waxed poetic about this concrete jungle of dreams, and filmmakers clamored to shoot their scenes along its most notable streets. Word of the city's splendor had spread even outside the human world—from the deepest pits of the shaman realm to the darkest parts of Faerieland; from the highest reaches of the Heavens to the lowest corners of the Underworld.

Throughout the decades, much about New York City's landscape had changed, but always this remained: the undercurrent of energy thrumming beneath the soles of pedestrians' feet, as though the city were powered by the life of its people. And in many ways, it was. This place breathed with the hopes and dreams of millions, with the promise of something so much bigger and better than itself. The city was its people and the people were their city. Every day, every *hour*, Manhattan embraced newcomers with open arms, fed off the fresh life that helped it keep its youthful energy.

And now one more presence would be added to the mix.

Standing nearly thirteen hundred feet high, the Empire State Building was notable even among the city's skyscrapers. That cloudy night, if one looked up at the right angle at the right time, a large silhouette could be seen very faintly, perched at the base of the building's antenna.

It was not the silhouette of a man, woman, or child. Not the silhouette of any recognizable animal, nor the silhouette of anything that should have belonged on Earth.

This was a creature born from nightmares—a winged beast with teeth sharper than a saber-toothed tiger's, with claws reminiscent of a dragon's. It was something that could have crawled straight out of the belly of the Underworld itself.

When the clouds passed over the moon, a ray of moonlight angled down toward the creature—and revealed it now in the shape of a young woman, sitting on the ledge of the building.

The woman-beast stretched her arms, and the terrifying silhouette stretched along with her. She closed her eyes and inhaled sharply, as though this was the first deep breath of fresh air she'd taken in decades. When her eyes opened again, they were red and distinctly inhuman, like those of a monster.

"Descendants," growled the woman-beast, the word coming out raspy and distorted, as though this was the first time she had spoken in a century. "My lord has summoned me to his side, and I am only the first of many, many more to come. Your days are limited. We rise."

The woman-beast stood on the ledge of the Empire State Building. Stretched out her arms, as though to fly. Leaned forward. And jumped.

If any humans had looked up at that precise moment, they would have witnessed an extraordinary sight: a woman leaping seemingly to her death, only for that woman to warp into a beast with wings midair. She soared around the Empire State Building's antenna—once, twice, thrice—and then dropped down far below, eventually to merge with the throngs of unsuspecting Manhattanites, no less human-looking than the rest.

16
CECIL

Cecil dreaded attending class with Evangeline, Tristan, and Nicholas gone. Human Descendants might occasionally stay home from class due to illness, but supernatural Descendants could not contract human illnesses, and therefore would only miss class if an emergency came up—like an Assignment. With the noticeable absence of such powerful players from Earthly Branches Academy, any Descendant with half a brain would be able to piece together the likeliest explanation. And then, once they did so, they would come pester *Cecil,* as she was the most closely connected to Evangeline.

More than anything, Cecil wished she could accompany her xiǎo jiě on this mission, but Evangeline had been adamant that she stay behind. And Cecil, despite her heart's desires, understood that this was the best decision. Yet it didn't make their separation any easier.

For over a century, ever since Cecil's birth mother had contracted Cecil to the Long family with her dying breath, the two girls had been inseparable. Except now, apparently, on what was quite likely the most important Assignment in the history of the Descendants, Evangeline had cast her aside. How Evangeline could leave her loyal, cunning, and resourceful servant behind and take that timid-looking *human* with her was beyond Cecil. But xiǎo jiě always had her reasons for moving as she did, and Cecil had to trust that Evangeline had left her behind precisely *because* of her resourcefulness.

Not much *was* beyond Cecil's grasp, indeed. She consistently ranked among the top ten students in their classes. The only reason she didn't sweep the top spot across subjects was because she knew to hold back just enough to let Evangeline shine.

Because she'd been helping out Evangeline and the others, Cecil had missed most of her classes for the night, and she returned to Earthly Branches just in time to make her last two classes. She knew it would be an unpleasant evening as soon as she arrived for Supernatural Relations— and found not the scrawny, mousy Elder Gou standing at the head of the classroom but the tall, lithe figure of Max Niu, Marcus Niu's fox spirit younger brother. No, Cecil realized after a moment—the Elder *was* there, but Max had blocked his tiny figure from view. The two were locked in an intense conversation, purposely keeping their voices so low that even with her supernaturally sharp hearing, Cecil couldn't make out their words.

Her stomach plummeted at the sight of Max working his charm on the Elder. He was normally one of the least engaged students in class, yet now he spoke so animatedly with Elder Gou. The reason for this change in behavior was obvious—Marcus had sent his fox spirit younger brother to exercise his powers of persuasion. The Nius were now making their moves out in the open, and they didn't care if Cecil, the Talons, or anyone still loyal to the Longs saw what they were doing. In fact, they seemed to welcome it.

Not only was this whole scene very odd, but there was a new tension in the room. Cecil sensed the stares of her classmates. Normally, she and Evangeline would show up to classes together, and Evangeline's absence was raising many eyebrows. In addition, by now the rumors were swirling, making the Longs' clearest supporters the target of gossip.

What would Evangeline do if she were here? Cecil couldn't see

Evangeline striding up to Max and confronting him right then and there; he wasn't technically doing anything wrong, and causing a scene would only confirm that Evangeline lacked confidence in the Descendants to choose her as the next Chancellor. Cecil swallowed hard. Though she hated to admit it, the best option here was to do nothing at all. Better to patiently bide her time and figure out a plan for quietly gathering support. She gritted her teeth and forced herself to sit down in her usual seat.

"So it begins," murmured a low voice, and the slim figure of Xavier Yang slid into the seat next to Cecil. Xavier, one of Julius's Talons of the House of Sheep, locked eyes with Cecil. She hadn't really spoken to him much before this moment, but now it was as though they had an implicit understanding because of their connections to the Longs. Xavier was popular and well liked. . . . Cecil smiled as a plan began to form in her head.

"Xavier," she said, before she could talk herself out of her spontaneous plan. "Let's get a coffee after school."

"Oh." Xavier raised his eyebrows, looking a little thrown, probably because they'd never really spoken much one-on-one. However, he gathered himself in record time. "Sure."

"Starbucks at six a.m. sharp. Don't be late."

So it began, indeed.

Cecil did her best to sit up straight and proud, as though nothing out of the ordinary were happening. She bounced her leg up and down, itching to be able to *do* something to help Evangeline.

"Good evening, Descendants," Elder Gou addressed the students. Max slouched away with a disgruntled expression on his face. And when he passed by Cecil on his way to the back of the classroom, he stopped to give her a cold sneer.

"Get ready, Cecil. Your precious xiǎo jiě will not be the next in line for Chancellor," he whispered, loudly enough so that everyone around them could hear.

Cecil's fingers curled into fists in her lap. Rather than rise to the bait, she merely glared at Max until he broke eye contact and kept walking toward his desk. Xavier said nothing and gave no indication that he'd even noticed Max's presence—his gaze was glued on the Elder. Cecil needed to give off an equally unbothered air. Even if Max's words had rattled her, she had to keep her poise. Evangeline had trusted Cecil to be her eyes and ears while she was away. And that meant conducting herself with as much as dignity as Evangeline would. She intended to obey her xiǎo jiě to the best of her abilities.

It was like a slow form of torture, trying to get through her last class of the night while fielding curious looks and questions from her peers. More and more rumors began swirling around the student body, speculations about Evangeline's, Tristan's, and Nicholas's absences and what they might mean. The atmosphere was ripe with tension and unease—Cecil could read it in the Descendants' doom-and-gloom expressions, their grim conversations, the foreboding chill in the air. Even if the Descendants didn't know the exact reason why, they intuitively seemed to understand that everything had changed overnight.

"Cecil," called Brian Ji as she tried to leave as soon as possible after her last class. She had to meet Xavier at the Starbucks near campus in fifteen minutes, and there was no way she could be late after telling *him* not to be late. "Cecil, you must know. Where did Evangeline go? And the others?"

Cecil adjusted the collar of her shirt and in an emotionless, even tone said, "Evangeline is attending to important business matters. The Longs have appreciated your loyalty over the years and will appreciate your continued loyalty during this unexpected transition of power."

Brian's expression grew cold and serious. "How many times did you rehearse that statement in the mirror?"

Cecil glared. "Excuse me?"

"We need more than that from you, Cecil. We need information." Frustration brought a hard edge to Brian's words. It was clear he'd been holding in this rant all day and was very glad to finally be able to release it. "All we've heard is that Julius is dead, Evangeline is gone, and High Council meetings are suspended until further notice. Don't you know what Marcus is saying?"

"I learned long ago to tune out whatever comes out of that oaf's mouth."

"Well, you ought to pay attention this once," Delilah Hou interjected, stepping in front of Cecil. Her voice, which had always been unpleasantly shrill, grew higher and more piercing with each word. "He's saying the Wrathlings are behind Julius's murder—that the Elders are hushing it up so as not to cause mass panic. Marcus has promised that he's making the appropriate preparations in the event that the Wrathlings return. What does Evangeline have to say about that? Is she even going to do anything to help?"

Wrathlings? Really? There was no doubt in Cecil's mind that Marcus was spreading baseless rumors to stir up fear among the Descendants and sway them to his side. She lost her patience and snapped, "Evangeline is dealing with very real, present threats, and not fear-mongering around the school."

Rather than shut up the onlookers, this only made them erupt with even louder protests. Cecil took the opportunity to slip out of the crowd and walk away as fast as possible. In her haste, she almost didn't notice before she'd stalked right up to none other than Marcus Niu himself outside the school gymnasium. He was flanked by two High Council members, Travis and Sylvia.

Marcus leered at Cecil.

"I'm not in the mood, Marcus," Cecil started, moving to shove past. "I'm going to be late to a meeting." With all the good it did her, she might as well have spoken to the wall.

Marcus blocked her with his admittedly larger build. Then, strangely, he began counting on his fingers. "One, two, three, four."

Sylvia stayed silent, but her eyes were like laser beams zeroing in on Cecil's expression.

Cecil blinked and then slid her most charming smile onto her face. The muscles in her cheeks hurt. "I'm ever *so* glad you can remember how to count, Marcus, but if you'll kindly let me pass—"

"Evangeline, Nicholas, Tristan, and that painfully plain-looking human girl Alisha."

"Alice," Cecil corrected him automatically.

"Whatever. Four. That's four notable absences today."

"Get to the point," Cecil said through gritted teeth.

But Marcus seemed in no rush to get to his point. He raised his left arm and pressed his palm into the wall above Cecil, blocking her path, as he continued to stare her down. "So Julius Long dies—bless his soul—and his little sister and three other students aren't in school very shortly after. If I'm correct—and I'm so rarely *in*correct—these four will not be in school for a while. They've been excused for a top-secret Assignment, the nature of which Evangeline has not discussed with anyone except . . . you, Cecil."

Cecil scowled. This was exactly what she had feared would come to pass. Marcus clearly had figured out for himself what had happened, considered himself quite clever for doing so, and was only cornering her to confirm his suspicions so he could bolster his own ego. Well, Cecil had never been the type to stroke a man's ego, and she would hardly start now. "Don't you have anything more important to occupy your time?" she said savagely. "I've been told that you're quite spooked by these Wrathlings. Remind me again where they are?"

"It's up to you whether you want to believe the Wrathlings are growing in power or not," Marcus said, "but only a fool would ignore the warning behind the faerie Seer's prophecy. And yes, I know that whatever Evangeline is doing has set off that prophecy, Cecil," he added, interpreting the surprise in her expression correctly. She hadn't expected Marcus, or anyone, to work out for themselves that not only had the others gone out on an Assignment but they had set that long-ago prophecy in motion. "Whatever Evangeline is doing . . . *if greed sows discord, harmony will be in doubt.* If you ask me, harmony has been shattered since Julius was murdered—and as long as we ignore the threat of Wrathlings, things will only grow worse."

Cecil's jaw dropped. "Max," she hissed under her breath. No way had Marcus reached this conclusion on his own; his brother had to be the brains behind the operation.

Travis had remained uncharacteristically quiet this entire time, and Sylvia was avoiding Cecil's eyes. Then it clicked. Cecil hadn't put the pieces together in her head until this moment, but now it was obvious what had happened, why they were flanking Marcus of all people. "You . . ." She glared between Travis and Sylvia accusingly but found, for once, that no words rose to her normally sharp tongue.

"It's time to think more practically about the future of the Descendants," Travis said by way of explanation. There was no guilt or remorse in his eyes, which was all Cecil needed to see to realize that he hadn't been happy with the Long leadership in quite some time; Evangeline's absence was just the precipitating event for him to act on his interests. "I mean no disrespect to Evangeline. I just don't believe in her vision."

"You haven't even given Evangeline a chance. You're making a mistake," Cecil managed to retort, but her words sounded weak even to her own ears. Marcus merely rolled his eyes.

"I don't think I am, Cecil," Travis said softly.

Sylvia spoke before Cecil could get a word in edgewise. "You should be more worried. Julius is dead, and Evangeline is nowhere to be found. You can't possibly expect us to wait around without any guarantee that Evangeline will be back, or when."

"All I can say is that Evangeline will return soon. She'll be back before you know it." Cecil was careful to keep her words devoid of any emotion, empty of the anxiety and uncertainty she was feeling. "I'd like to see anyone *try* to take anything from her." She forced her way past Marcus, Sylvia, and Travis before they could continue their interrogation.

When she'd finally left the school building, she collapsed against a tall oak tree, letting the gravity of the encounter sink in. Evangeline had only been gone for a little while, and *already* she'd lost the loyalty of two prominent High Council members—Sylvia and Travis. Who was to say the rest wouldn't shortly follow suit?

Cecil prayed that her confidence in Evangeline's safe return wasn't just wishful thinking. *Please, for everyone's sake, come back soon, Evangeline.* She was so caught up in her own thoughts, scarcely paying attention to her surroundings, that she nearly walked right into Xavier outside the Starbucks.

"Oh. Hi, Xavier." Cecil summoned a watery smile, hoping she didn't look as awful as she felt. Unfortunately, she must have missed the mark by quite a lot, because Xavier's face took on a sympathetic expression.

"Are you holding up all right?" he asked. "What happened to Julius was sudden and shocking. The two of you were close, I gathered."

Close wasn't exactly the word Cecil would have used to describe it. Nobody really got close to Julius, only as close as he let them, which was at least an arm's length away. Cecil peered closely at Xavier. Although he'd put on a brave smile, his lips were trembling and his eyes were red-rimmed. "You were close enough to Julius, too." The words slipped out of her mouth in a whisper, almost before they'd passed through her mind.

The corner of Xavier's mouth lifted in a half smile, as though he and she shared an understanding. And perhaps they did. That though they grieved Julius's passing, it was like grieving a distant older brother who had never been fully present with them.

"Well, what did you want to talk about?" Xavier asked after they'd gotten their coffees and sat down at an empty table. Although the Starbucks had just opened, it was already filling up with early-morning workers who'd stumbled half asleep into the coffee shop to kick-start their morning. It was noisy enough that Cecil and Xavier didn't need to lower their voices to have a private conversation.

Cecil took a sip of her coffee and immediately winced. Without any blood in it, it tasted like dirt, and it was still too hot. How best to approach this topic delicately? After a few moments of careful deliberation, she gave up. She'd never exactly been delicate, so perhaps it was best to approach this Cecil-style—as straightforwardly as possible.

"Just now I ran into Marcus, and he was with Sylvia and Travis.

They've already thrown in their loyalties with him. We need to gather as much support for Evangeline as possible, and knock Marcus down several pegs," Cecil blurted out. She was speaking too quickly; she made a deliberate effort to slow down her speech. "Evangeline is . . . occupied with an important matter, something that she's had me promise to keep secret. But I've no doubt that once she returns to school, she'll have proof of being the most capable leader for the Descendants."

Xavier's expression showed no surprise. In fact, he didn't even blink, which made Cecil certain that he'd been having the same thoughts. He took a slow sip of his iced latte.

Iced, Cecil thought in frustration. *I should've gotten iced.* Her tongue was still throbbing from the scalding coffee.

"Sylvia and Travis. House of Rabbit and House of Rat. That's a shame. Of course, there's no doubt in my mind that Evangeline is far more suitable for Chancellor than that dunce Marcus," Xavier said. "But you're not here to convince me. You're here because . . ." He raised an eyebrow, clearly waiting for her to fill in the blank.

"Because I need to know that the Talons, at least, are on Evangeline's side. That they'll advocate for her at the school in her absence." Cecil bored her gaze into Xavier's. She needed to drill the message home. The Talons were loyal to Julius, but they hadn't necessarily declared the same undying loyalty to Evangeline, and Evangeline's greatest hope of gaining the Descendants' confidence—until she got those fountainheads—was showing that the Talons would similarly die for her.

After a pause, Xavier leaned back in his chair. "You are interesting, Cecil. Far more interesting than I realized." He studied Cecil as though he was intrigued but couldn't quite tell what to make of her yet. It unnerved her slightly, to feel she was being so thoroughly studied. Of course she'd hid the interesting bits of herself. Cecil knew her place. She was never to outshine Evangeline Long. Even now, she was only making a bolder move, showing more of her true self, to help Evangeline.

"I can't promise you anything," said Xavier at last. "Given the vows we swore to Julius, the Talons *should* be loyal to Evangeline despite our

House loyalties, but with Evangeline departing the Academy so soon after Julius's death without an explanation . . . it doesn't instill confidence, Cecil, you must see that."

She nodded. Of course, if Evangeline had any other choice, she would be at school, but there wasn't any real option. And since Cecil wasn't allowed to reveal the details of Evangeline's absence, the best course of action was to do whatever she could to convince any undecided minds of Evangeline's leadership abilities. "I understand. All we can do is our best."

Xavier stared at her another moment before he smiled. "Very well," he said. "Let's do that, then. We'll do our best to secure Evangeline the spot of Chancellor."

17
ALICE

As soon as the tunnel door closed behind them, Alice began to regret her decision to join this group of supernatural strangers in a mission that was likely to fail. What a way to spend her shortly upcoming seventeenth birthday. Perhaps she'd been too impulsive, too one-track-minded with wanting to find out more about Baba. What would her father's secrets matter if she wound up dead in the process of uncovering them?

The thought of death was so horrifying that Alice had to yank her mind away from that direction. She needed to calm down. She was freaking herself out, overthinking the decision she'd already committed to, and there was no use panicking now; the moment for panic had long passed. Besides, she was in good company, given that the other three Descendants were supernaturals who'd been fighting—and winning—against Wrathlings for over a century. With her mind somewhat calmer, Alice turned her attention to her surroundings.

The Underground appeared to be a cave. It was so dark that she couldn't see more than a few feet in front of her, and she wouldn't have been able to see at all if it weren't for the torches flickering yellow-orange light against the cavern walls.

They'd left the human world far, far behind. Alice had expected the Underground air to smell musty, but instead it smelled . . . pure. And clean. Of course, most places would smell pure compared with the polluted air of New York City, but Alice was certain she'd never inhaled such clean air in her life.

Another difference: the voices. They were faint, as though the speakers were on the other side of the cave wall, but Alice could hear disembodied voices in her mind.

"There's history here." Nicholas ran his fingers along the damp cave wall. "And ancient power."

The Underground was filled floor to ceiling with magic. It hummed in the air; it vibrated deep in Alice's bones; it was so potent that even Alice, who was still relatively new to accepting her powers as a Descendant, could sense that she could be stronger here than aboveground—but on the flip side, if their mission went awry and they offended the shamans, they would be in grave danger.

It was hard to resist the urge to just stop and soak in all this power. Alice's abilities seemed to be coming through sharper than ever. It was difficult to make out what the voices were saying clearly, the thoughts emerging all jumbled. At moments, the words seemed to be coming through well enough for Alice to recognize the language—Cantonese—but then as soon as she started to grasp the shape of them, they would go silent again. In and out and in and out, like a very weak call connection. She might not be close enough to the source to make out the words, but what she *did* know was that there was life nearby. And there was no doubt that the voices belonged to the shamans.

"Don't let your guard down," Evangeline warned as they began to slowly make their way through the cave. "Getting into the Underground was the easy part."

"That was supposed to be *easy?*" Tristan murmured.

Alice glanced over at him. Tristan had been moody since he'd shown up on Evangeline's doorstep covered in blood. Nobody had asked questions or attempted to broach the topic. She didn't know Tristan well enough to have any opinion of him, but now sympathy surged within her. And . . . apprehension. What was Tristan capable of? And what might Alice be forced to do to see through this Assignment?

No matter what the Underground threw at her, Alice would endure it. She could hardly turn back now. And she wanted to emerge from the Assignment victorious. At last, there was hope of learning more about her past, and she wanted answers to the questions about Baba that had haunted her for so many years. This would be her best—and possibly only—chance.

"The shamans are known for their cleverness and trickery. There will be traps ahead," Nicholas said, "the nature of which the shamans have kept top-secret. When the shamans built the Underground, they meant to keep all intruders out. We need to keep our wits about us." When he said this last part, he glanced over at Alice almost instinctively.

If Alice had thought she was out of place before, now that sense had grown so strong that it was nearly impossible to ignore. However, she was no quitter—she never had been—and she would adapt to the circumstances as best she could.

"I'm hearing their voices," she declared. The shamans didn't know they were coming, but Alice could use her powers to predict their every move.

"Already? What are they saying?" Evangeline whipped her head around.

Under the vampire's full attention, Alice shrank away just a little. The more she focused on trying to use her powers, the more her exhaustion grew, and a faint headache was coming on. She'd never tried to use her mind-reading powers for extended periods, but she couldn't imagine doing so would be good for her. "I . . . I can't hear anything clearly right now," she admitted. "We need to get closer."

Evangeline turned away, losing all interest in the conversation, and then continued as though Alice hadn't spoken. "The shamans live parallel to Manhattan's Chinatown," she said to the group at large, though Alice thought it was mostly for her benefit. The cave opened up into four separate tunnels, down which Alice sensed voices growing louder, though she couldn't yet tell in which direction. Evangeline pointed to the corridor second from the right. "Turn right up here." The group obeyed, and at the next fork, Evangeline barked out, "Now left." She made a sharp turn down the left tunnel, and the others followed without question. Alice was amazed that Evangeline could navigate confidently through the twisting, confusing labyrinth of the Underground.

Still, no traps had revealed themselves yet. The anticipation of the unknown was much worse than if the traps had actually materialized in front of them. At least then they would know exactly what dangers they faced. Without that certainty, Alice's imagination was free to run wild—and run wild it did. She'd never seen a shaman before, but she imagined them to be cloaked with magic. How could she defend herself against beings that had been magical long before she was even born?

With each step, Alice's heartbeat grew louder and louder in her chest. Surely the others must be able to hear it echoing throughout the cave.

Evangeline came to a halt in the middle of the tunnel without so much as a warning. "Wait," she muttered. "Perhaps my memory isn't quite . . ." She bowed her head as she pulled Julius's map out of her pocket and consulted it. "We're lost," Evangeline declared after a full minute of staring at the map.

"Lost? How can we be lost? Let me see that." Tristan took the map from Evangeline's hands and held it up to the light.

"I don't know. I was following the map, but then suddenly the tunnels didn't match up to what the map indicated anymore."

"Maybe the map is wrong," Nicholas suggested.

"My brother wouldn't give me a faulty map," Evangeline insisted.

Tristan cleared his throat. "Hate to be the bearer of bad news, but it seems to me like he did just that."

As Evangeline and Tristan argued, Alice's senses began to tingle, until she was on high alert. The voices were still going in and out of her head, but they seemed to grow louder and more urgent. A pounding headache had developed over her right eye, but it was the least of her concerns at the moment. She tried to pin down a direction, but she quickly found she couldn't. First the shamans seemed to be speaking through the wall on her left; seconds later, the wall on her right. It was almost like . . . Alice gasped.

"Did something happen, Alice?" Alice hadn't realized she'd stopped walking until Nicholas's voice brought her back solidly to the moment. Nicholas had paused and was gazing at her with concern.

"The tunnels . . . they're shifting around us," Alice blurted. Her announcement managed to bring Evangeline and Tristan's argument to an abrupt pause.

"What?" Tristan turned around and stared at her in alarm.

"I thought that might be it," Nicholas mused. "The shamans' second line of defense against intruders: mind games. The map might be accurate under perfect conditions, if we don't take any potential enchantments into consideration, and I don't doubt that Julius gave you that map with good intentions, Evangeline."

Evangeline sniffed and faced the other way, pointedly turning her back to Tristan.

"So basically, that map is useless to us now," Tristan groaned. "Excellent. And what are we to do when we run into shamans?" he pressed Evangeline. "Invite them back up aboveground for a drink, I suppose? Have a lovely little chat about trespassing over tea?"

"I think we can do without the smart-aleck commentary, Tristan," Nicholas said tersely.

"One of us has to have a sense of humor, and you seem to have misplaced yours—perhaps up your ass."

"Oh, don't start now," Evangeline snapped, whirling around to glare at the two boys. She strode up to Alice in two swift paces and grabbed her wrist. Alice gasped at the sudden icy, viselike grip. "Can you pinpoint the direction of the voices?"

When she concentrated fully on silencing all other noises, Alice could just barely hear and understand the shamans' words.

Reinforcing defenses . . .

Approach of the Midsummer Celebration . . . preparing the delegation . . .

The Phoenix's command . . .

"Who's the Phoenix?" Alice blurted out.

Evangeline's eyes widened, and she snapped her head around as though she expected to be ambushed at any moment. "The Phoenix? What else did you hear?"

"Something about . . . preparing a delegation. For a Midsummer Celebration?"

It didn't escape Alice's notice that the others exchanged an alarmed look at the mention of this so-called Phoenix. Whoever this figure was, they were powerful and well known, and not to be crossed.

As for the nearby shamans, Alice couldn't make head or tail of what she was hearing, but she knew this much—the voices had grown much sharper and clearer. "On our left. Shamans are fast approaching." By her (very rough) estimation, they had probably minutes—no, *one* minute, if they kept their current pace—before they ran into some shamans, and she highly doubted it would be a pleasant encounter. But surely Evangeline had accounted for the fact that they'd be running into shamans *in shaman territory* and had a plan up her sleeve that she hadn't shared with the others?

Without missing a beat, Evangeline steered the group into a tunnel on the right that had risen seemingly out of nowhere. They hurried down the path, and when Alice chanced a look back, she spotted the flicker of lamplight and dark red robes whipping down another tunnel and out of sight.

Close call. Alice got the feeling that they'd be having a lot of those in the near future.

"Those would be the guards," Evangeline said, sounding completely unperturbed. "I expected we'd begin encountering them earlier than this, to be honest."

Nicholas tensed and shot Evangeline a questioning look, awaiting further command.

Tristan hissed, "Good. I was beginning to grow bored."

Alice's stomach was flipping, but she tried not to let her nerves show on her face. The others didn't appear nearly as bothered, probably thanks to the confidence they'd built up from *decades* of experience navigating dangerous situations.

And Evangeline seemed calmest of all. No doubt she'd concocted a master plan already; Alice only wished that Evangeline had let the others in on the finer details of her grand scheme. Or did everyone else know, and Alice was the only one left out?

Rolling up her sleeves slightly, Evangeline said, "Thank you for the warning, Alice."

Oh. Alice blinked in surprise. There wasn't a moment to relish the thanks, however; those staticky voices entered her head once more. This time, the noise seemed to come from all around—she couldn't really pinpoint a direction. Her heart rate sped up; her palms grew cold and clammy with sweat. Her powers, which had only moments ago gotten them all out of a potential disaster, seemed to be fading on her, and she wasn't sure why. There was no time to question it, either—she needed to react to the situation *now*. They'd reached another fork in the tunnels. Did the voices seem to be coming slightly more from the left, or was that just Alice's wishful thinking?

The others were giving her expectant looks. She couldn't let them down. She didn't want to prove her own fear right—that she wasn't cut out for this Assignment.

"Now we need to turn left," she declared, her voice shaking with uncertainty that she hoped nobody else noticed.

It seemed nobody had, and even Evangeline didn't stop to question Alice. She immediately set out down the left tunnel.

No sooner had Alice finished uttering the instructions than the first pair of shamans rounded the corner, without so much as a warning or a thought for Alice to decipher.

Alice had never seen shamans before, but when they appeared in front of her, she knew exactly what she was looking at. Their eyes were the first part she noticed—blue eyes that danced with the firelight from the torches, that now widened with surprise. One was a man and one was a woman, and both wore their hair away from their faces in braids.

Alice's stomach sank. She'd gambled, and she'd lost—and now, because she didn't fully understand her powers, she'd put everyone in danger.

"I—s-sorry," she squeaked out, but Evangeline and the others seemed far too distracted by the sudden appearance to bother acknowledging her.

"The Jingwei," Nicholas murmured. He appeared to have frozen in place for a moment before he threw a sidelong look at Evangeline, as though deferring to her.

The Jingwei were dressed in long, sweeping high-collared red robes with a golden sash around the middle. Their uniforms almost looked like qí páo, traditional form-fitting dresses, but gender-neutral, and designed for practicality rather than fashion.

Everything happened in quick succession. Neither of the Jingwei had the chance to speak or make a sound before Evangeline lunged at them. Vampires were so much faster than humans that Alice's eyes couldn't follow what happened, but her brain managed to put the pieces together when the two shamans collapsed to the floor, unconscious. For a moment she was stricken with horror, thinking she'd witnessed two murders right before her eyes; but no, their chests were rising and falling with slow, steady breaths. The guards were merely knocked out.

Thank goodness, Alice thought. At least nobody had paid the price for her mistake.

"I'm sorry," she said again. "I don't really know what happened. . . . I—I made the wrong call."

Nicholas gave Alice a sympathetic look, Tristan stared at Evangeline, and Evangeline wasn't looking at any of them.

"It's only natural you'd make mistakes, since you've just started to harness your abilities," Evangeline said after a long moment. Her voice was perfectly devoid of emotion. She might have been reciting an instruction manual. "What's done is done. We keep it moving."

Alice knew, though, that even if she hadn't shown it, Evangeline was disappointed. If she were Evangeline, *she* would be disappointed. Her heart sank, and she wished she could sink right through the floor along with it.

Perhaps everyone would have been better off if Alice had stayed behind at Earthly Branches.

18
NICHOLAS

Back before the Descendants were cursed, back before the Old Summer Palace was pillaged, way back when he was still a young child learning his place in the House of Tiger, Nicholas encountered a guardian angel.

He had first met her months before, when his parents had taken him to greet the Long family. Long shū shu and ā yí were the embodiment of elegance and grace, and they welcomed the Hus into their magnificent garden with open arms. There was a little girl around Nicholas's age who stood in front of her parents, staring at him with unblinking eyes. He'd hidden behind his mother's skirts, too shy to say a word to her. Back then, Nicholas was so timid that he hadn't made any effort to befriend fellow Descendants his age, with one exception: Tristan She, who had practically forced his way into a friendship with Nicholas.

When Nicholas and Evangeline met again—properly—it was at a Lunar New Year banquet at the Long mansion. Although Nicholas had run and hidden on the floor in one of the many guest bedrooms, hoping for privacy to read his book, soon some of the bored older Descendant boys wandered into the room.

"Reading books at a party?" snickered a boy named Weichen. He snatched the book out of Nicholas's hands, and the boys laughed around him. "You're dreadfully boring, aren't you?"

"G-Give it back," Nicholas stuttered, but that only made the boys laugh harder. Tears stung his eyes. What if the boys decided they wanted to do more than just pick on him? What if they were hoping for a fight? Nicholas already knew that he wasn't as physically strong or fast as most of the other young Descendants.

"What are you all doing?" a girl's voice demanded loudly.

The boys all turned around. Nicholas glanced up from his spot on the floor to see that the girl—the Longs' daughter, Evangeline—was standing there in the doorway, her hands on her hips, pigtails shaking along with her head.

Word had already gotten around that Evangeline was one of the best fighters the Descendants had seen in a long time. Weichen laughed again, but this time the sound came out uneasy. "What? Are you his girlfriend or something?" He stared down at Nicholas with a sneer. "You need the protection of your *sweetheart*?"

"She's not my sweetheart," Nicholas mumbled.

"I just hate bullies," Evangeline sniffed.

"What did you just call us?" asked another boy, Tailan Yang, narrowing his eyes.

"Bullies," Evangeline enunciated, as though she thought the boys truly hadn't heard her. "You're bullying him, which makes you bullies."

What happened next, Nicholas would remember for as long as he lived. Evangeline rolled up her sleeves, strode right up to the toughest-looking boy, Weichen, and landed a punch squarely on his eye. Before Weichen could retaliate, Tailan yelled and spun his leg around in a roundhouse kick, but Evangeline had anticipated the move. She ducked, rolled, leapt to her feet, and landed a kick of her own right to Tailan's groin. Both boys were down in less than twenty seconds. The third boy didn't even attempt to fight Evangeline; he just fell to the floor with his arms up in surrender.

"If you tell any of the parents what happened here, everyone will find out that you were all beaten up by a girl," Evangeline threatened. "Now get out of my sight."

The boys couldn't flee the room quickly enough.

Nicholas gazed upon Evangeline in awe as she smoothed her skirt. Not a hair on her head was out of place. She appeared almost angelic in that white skirt, despite what she'd just done.

"Thank you," Nicholas said, remembering his manners. "You didn't have to help me."

Evangeline shrugged. "I know. I didn't do it just to do it."

"What do you mean?"

She picked up Nicholas's book, which Weichen had thrown to the floor in all the chaos. "I know you're very smart. I want you to teach me how to read. There are far too many characters in this language, and I can't keep them all straight."

"You can't read?" Nicholas blurted out. When Evangeline gave him a cold look, he quickly amended, "I can teach you how to read."

The two did not know it then, but that was the start of a friendship that would blossom through the ages—a bond that was destined to be stronger than any force in the universe, including supernatural curses.

Though he'd known on some level that he needed to react quickly, Nicholas had frozen when the Jingwei had rounded the corner. In the aftermath, regret and frustration clouded his emotions. It was always like this with him—he either didn't respond at all, or he snapped and caused great destruction.

The same indecision had cost them all at the Old Summer Palace in 1860. The fiery outbursts had destroyed his relationship with his only brother. In over a century, Nicholas had learned nothing.

"Nicholas?" Evangeline said to him. She gave him a questioning look but didn't press the matter. "Quickly now." She gathered her long, silky black hair into a high ponytail. "Our disguises."

Nicholas had known the command was coming before Evangeline had even parted her lips. He might not possess the ability to read minds, but after decades by her side, he sometimes thought he might know Evangeline better than she knew herself. For example, even in this moment, he could tell that she was putting on an air of confidence to mask her nerves. Her eyes kept darting around the dark tunnels, and tying up her hair was a nervous habit. Evangeline was preparing in case the group was ambushed by more Jingwei before Nicholas could transform them.

However, she needn't have worried. Nicholas was already working his magic before she had even finished calling his name. His body was growing hot with energy, which he channeled into his fingertips.

"If you were going to play your little magic tricks on us, Nicholas, why couldn't you have transformed us much earlier?" Tristan asked, his tone brutish. And it took extraordinary patience for Nicholas not to rise to the bait this time. "Those Jingwei could have raised the alarm just now."

"I can't conjure an adequate transformation without seeing the real thing up close," Nicholas explained through gritted teeth. His magic required enormous imagination and concentration; without one or the other, the process could go quite awry and lead to transformations that were far from . . . ideal. Not that Tristan would understand a process so complex and refined. "Now, if you could please stop badgering me, I'd like to get a move on so the next Jingwei don't—as you put it—*raise the alarm.*"

"Don't let your head swell just because you can do one mediocre party trick—"

Normally Nicholas would let Tristan's snarky comments pass, but his temper was running much shorter than usual, and almost without thinking, driven by the fury and heat that spiked inside him, he snapped, "Is there something you want to say to me, Tristan? It seems you've been holding out on me for a little while now."

"Stop it, both of you," interjected Evangeline furiously, but it was too late. The boys locked eyes, fixing each other with blazing glares.

"Fine, then." Tristan gave a twisted smile. "I would never have chosen you for an Assignment as important as this one, coward that you are."

It was as though Tristan had picked up a drill and rammed it straight into Nicholas's chest and through his heart. "What do you mean by that?" Nicholas managed to spit out. His breaths came in sharp, heavy pants, and his vision slowly turned red. His body trembled.

"If I'd been standing watch over the Circle of Twelve that night—or if it'd been anyone other than *you*—the foreign soldiers could never have destroyed it. I would have died before I let that happen." Tristan's eyes glistened with tears, and the sight was hard for Nicholas to see, as much as he disliked him now. "My family died that day, Nicholas. They died because of *your* cowardice."

Tristan had clearly been holding on to these vicious words for a long, long time. Nicholas wasn't sure who to direct his fury toward: Tristan, who'd managed to cut him where it hurt the most; or himself, because he couldn't really find fault with Tristan's words. Nicholas, after all, had been most friendly with Tristan's family, almost as though they were his own relatives. Whatever blame Tristan assigned to him, it didn't measure up to how much Nicholas blamed himself.

Nicholas *had* failed as the night guard of the Circle of Twelve on that fateful day, the day Tristan's family had been slaughtered, the day the Descendants had lost everything. And Nicholas was certain it would haunt him for eternity, or until he drew his dying breath, whichever came first.

But didn't he deserve to move forward and do his best from now on? Did he have to live each day with the thought that he didn't deserve another chance to be better?

The guilt and anger rose in a tidal wave, and Nicholas's body shook more furiously than ever. A shadow of nine tails could be seen behind

176

him. Tristan stared at Nicholas with a bitter half smile, his eyes issuing a challenge, his hands raised into fists.

Before either boy could say another word, Evangeline stepped between them and pressed a cold palm firmly against each one's chest. "Don't you *dare* move a muscle," she said in a quiet, icy voice that carried more threat than if she'd shouted. "If you disobey me now, I really will do this all on my own—without your help."

Nicholas took a few deep breaths to force himself to calm down. He couldn't fail Evangeline. He couldn't let her take on this dangerous Assignment all by herself. And he knew her well enough to know that she was completely serious.

Tristan, too, backed down, almost seeming to shrink beneath Evangeline's searing glare. Occasionally he did wonder if she had any fondness remaining for him, but the coldness with which she treated him had made it clear—there was no lingering affection there. Whatever spark had once formed between them had *long* been doused.

"Tch," said Tristan, turning away and shrugging.

Now Nicholas turned his focus back to the task at hand, doing his best to ignore Tristan. They weren't done with each other, but this Assignment was more important than a century-old grudge. They could duke it out after they'd successfully stolen back the fountainheads.

Alice would be the first to transform, as she was by far the least equipped for self-defense should they be caught before Nicholas could finish his work. Furthermore, she was a human, and humans were the toughest to transform, as their bodies were more resistant to magic.

"Alice. Come here." Nicholas's command made Alice start. She cast a nervous look at his fingers, which were now encased in a glowing white light. An instant later, he realized how ominous he must appear to this human girl who had never seen transformative magic before. "Don't worry—I won't hurt you."

Evangeline heaved a sigh. "By the gods, Nicholas, you do realize you're only making her more nervous by saying that? Just *do* it already."

Indeed, Alice did not look at all reassured by Nicholas's statement. But there was no more time to waste. Nicholas strode forward and stretched his long, thin fingers toward Alice. He pressed down upon her temples.

"How long will the transformation last?" Alice asked in a remarkably even tone.

"Only as long as necessary."

"And how long is *that*?"

Humans. Always asking so many questions. "You'll return to your normal self when the rest of us do," Nicholas answered.

Alice seemed to have nothing to say to that. She stared at Nicholas, wide-eyed. Again, he couldn't help but wonder why Evangeline had insisted on recruiting a girl so new to the Descendants. Surely there had to be a secret ulterior motive that Evangeline hadn't revealed. It would be just like Evangeline to keep the full extent of her plans to herself.

"This might tickle," Nicholas warned Alice, and then his magic hummed through his body, from his core down the lengths of his arms and into his fingertips.

Alice gasped. She couldn't see what was happening to her, but Nicholas knew she'd be experiencing a strange, warm, tickling sensation that she'd have trouble describing later. Outwardly, her form began to smoke around the edges, until she was covered in a gray haze. Within moments, the smoke had dissipated, revealing a changed Alice.

Tristan whistled. Even that much, coming from the werewolf, was a reluctant nod of approval toward Nicholas's magic.

Nicholas took a step back to admire his handiwork. The transformed Alice wore red robes identical to those on the now-unconscious Jingwei. Her hair appeared much longer and wilder, and her eyes were now red. Her figure had filled out, too. Her face was the most recognizable part of her, but even that had been distorted—her eyebrows were darker and thicker, her nose longer, her cheekbones higher and more pronounced. To anyone who'd only seen Alice in passing before, she would be unrecognizable. To Nicholas, there was still a small resemblance to Alice, but she now appeared as an older, more beautiful Alice. Nicholas was surprised at himself when his heart skipped a beat at the sight of his own magic—no, at the sight of *her*.

"Wh-What is it?" Alice asked tremulously as she glanced first down at herself, then around at the others. She pressed her fingertips into her cheeks. "Did something go wrong?"

"No," Evangeline responded, her cold voice revealing none of what she might be feeling. If she was impressed with this display of magic, she didn't show that, either.

Nicholas made quick work of Evangeline and Tristan, pulling off their transformations within seconds, and finished the job on himself in record time. They all appeared older, wilder, nearly unrecognizable, and most importantly, like shamans. Although the others stared down at their arms in amazement, Tristan glared down at his in revulsion, as though he'd like nothing more than to rip off his own skin.

"I can't wait to get this over with and get out of this ugly disguise," he muttered.

"Oh, I don't think the ugly will go away when my magic wears off," said Nicholas pleasantly.

"Thank you, Nicholas," Evangeline said in a raised voice, sending Tristan an admonishing look, as though to warn him from continuing the fight. Miraculously, he just gritted his teeth and turned away. Evangeline gave Nicholas a tired little smile, and his heart made the tiniest of leaps. No, he wasn't the physically strongest Descendant—far from it—but at least he was skilled in the art of deception, and he was glad to be able to help in any way. Though he hoped he'd be able to prove himself in the physical department as well. He'd spent as much time honing his combat skill at the Academy as any of them, after all.

"And what are we to do about these guards?" Tristan pointed down at the Jingwei still lying by their feet.

Evangeline knelt and dragged the man until he was sitting propped up against the wall. Nicholas was the first to catch on, swiftly doing the same with the woman on the opposite tunnel wall.

"They'll get in trouble for falling asleep on duty, but that's not our problem," Evangeline said, dusting herself off. "Now, onward. We don't have any time to lose."

"So this is where the shamans hide away instead of being useful aboveground," Tristan murmured under his breath, scarcely loud enough for Nicholas to hear even with his supernaturally sharp hearing. Nicholas had no fondness for the shamans, either, but Tristan in particular had an obvious chip on his shoulder when it came to the magical inhabitants of the Underground. "Where's everyone rushing off to, anyway? It's not like there's anywhere to go."

That wasn't entirely true. Although it seemed like they'd spent ages walking through (and getting lost in) the tunnels of the Underground, after a while a clearing opened up in front of them. They saw a bustling village that was the center of shaman life in the Underground. From the snatches of conversation Nicholas could hear from the crowds, the shamans primarily spoke in Cantonese, though he caught bits of Mandarin here and there as well. The Underground reminded him of Manhattan's Chinatown, but for shamans, and the thought brought a small smile to his face.

"Keep your heads down and don't make eye contact," Evangeline hissed as they approached the masses of shamans going in and out of the shops in the village. "We might look the part of Jingwei, but I'm not willing to bet on these disguises holding up if guards see us up close. No offense, Nicholas."

"None taken," Nicholas said swiftly.

Alice said nothing. She'd been fairly quiet this whole time, but especially so since she'd made that mistake, turning them down a tunnel right into the Jingwei. Nicholas could only imagine that she was taking her own misstep hard. He would be.

He didn't know what to say, so he settled for gently patting her on the back. When she glanced up, he said, "You're amazing to have accessed your powers so quickly after enrolling in Earthly Branches, you know? Evangeline chose you for this Assignment for a reason."

Alice gave him a small smile. "Really?"

If Evangeline was listening in, she gave no indication, but Tristan slowed his steps slightly.

"Yeah. We've all had over a century to train for something like this. So don't be so hard on yourself."

"I . . . I'm not," Alice said hastily.

Nicholas wanted to press the matter, because he could tell she still wasn't entirely convinced, but he was interrupted by a harsh whisper from Evangeline.

"Cut the unnecessary chatter," Evangeline warned.

They'd wandered deep into the clearing where the shamans lived. Here, lampposts provided more light than in the tunnels, though there was still so little of it that Nicholas wondered how the shamans could distinguish between the seasons. Small, simple wooden houses were clustered into a little village that reminded Nicholas of the countryside in China. It was easy to pick out the civilian shamans—they were dressed much more casually than the Jingwei, in shirts and trousers and skirts that seemed to be modeled after the fashions of the early nineteenth century. When they passed by, it didn't escape Nicholas's notice that they cast nervous looks at the group and quickened their pace.

A young shaman girl, no older than ten by the looks of her, stepped on Tristan's foot as he walked by.

"Ow!" Tristan winced, pausing to shake out his foot.

An older woman quickly snatched the young girl away by the hand and then bowed her head toward Tristan. "I—I'm so sorry, sir," she stuttered in Cantonese. "My daughter—she's very clumsy and wasn't looking where she was going. We mean no harm."

Nicholas looked up and caught Tristan's eye. Tristan had raised his eyebrows, as though just as thrown by this interaction. Nicholas quickly turned away when it registered that he'd just shared a train of thought with *Tristan,* of all people.

"It's okay—" Tristan started to say, but Evangeline stomped on his *other* foot. "OW!"

Now it was Nicholas's turn to wince. Much as he disliked Tristan, he could empathize—having both of your feet stepped on in quick succession (and one time by your ex) was not fun.

"Get out of our sight," Evangeline said coldly to the mother and daughter.

The pair didn't need to be told twice; hand in hand, they sprinted away without so much as a backward glance.

"What was that for?" Tristan complained with a glare directed at Evangeline.

She brushed invisible dust off her sleeves. "Sorry." Nicholas thought she didn't sound sorry at all. "The Jingwei seem to inspire fear among the civilians. We need to behave as they would behave in order to blend in. That is all."

Tristan rolled his eyes but said nothing more, which was probably for the best. The exchange just then had already drawn looks from passersby; the last thing they needed was for Tristan and Evangeline to get into a full-blown argument and draw even more unwanted attention.

As they made their way, skirting the village, Nicholas thought that some of New York City's unfriendly energy had rubbed off even on its underground shaman occupants. The shamans seemed to be laser-focused on getting from point A to point B without stopping for small talk. This was nothing for Nicholas to complain about, however; it made for easy access to the depths of the Underground—at least, until they arrived at the checkpoint.

"Let me do the speaking in front of the other Jingwei," Evangeline ordered.

It was obvious enough, even without a warning from Evangeline, that they had at last come to the checkpoint to enter the Underground prison.

Several guards stood in a clearing, shoulder to shoulder, legs spread apart, faces set with glowers. Instead of gold sashes around their uniforms, however, they wore silver—a lower rank. That was good. If they were careful, they just might be able to pull this off smoothly.

Nicholas watched as a pair of shamans approached the Jingwei and each produced something from a pocket—a slip of paper. The guards looked the papers over and, appearing satisfied, parted to let the shamans pass. Then they closed the gap between them again.

"How are we going to get past these guards?" Alice whispered.

"Just keep your mouth shut and get in line behind me," said Evangeline. "And Tristan, don't glare so much."

Though he could normally predict Evangeline's movements, this time even Nicholas was mystified as to what sort of plan she might have concocted to slip them past the Jingwei. Surely the guards would require them all to submit a similar piece of paper, and to Nicholas's knowledge, he was not carrying any such shaman-identifying materials with him. Or would they be allowed through merely because they looked like Jingwei? Somehow, Nicholas didn't think so, and he sensed that the first great hurdle of the Assignment was just ahead of them.

Nicholas was no stranger to Assignments or to deception, so it was easy enough to mask his inner doubt as they drew closer to the guards. He composed his expression into one of boredom, as though he regularly passed this checkpoint and this was but another element of his routine. Then he added a touch of suavity: he ran his hand through his hair and smiled at the guard, though this effect was lost on the Jingwei, who didn't seem to care about Nicholas's good looks.

"Identification," grunted the nearest guard when Evangeline strode up to them with a confidence that could have fooled even Nicholas. She kept one hand on her golden sash, no doubt in order to draw attention to the fact that she was supposedly a Jingwei of a higher rank than them. It was working, based on the guards' stares.

Nicholas tried not to let his shock show when Evangeline reached into the sleeve of her robe and produced a slip of paper, exactly as the shamans before her had done. *When* had Evangeline pulled this trick out of her sleeve—literally?

The Jingwei barely glanced at Evangeline's paper before thrusting it back toward her, then suppressed a yawn. "Next," he said.

Next was Nicholas, and Nicholas had not been let in on Evangeline's brilliant plan. He was on the verge of losing his composure; he darted a panicked look at Evangeline out of the corner of his eye.

"These three are with me," Evangeline said, stepping in smoothly. Her voice rang with even more authority than usual, as though the guard were out of his mind to be checking the others. "You can check them one by one, but you're holding us up on an urgent task that was delegated to us by the Phoenix themself. And I doubt the Phoenix will be pleased to hear about that."

Nicholas was careful to keep his expression unchanged as he listened to Evangeline's bold claims, though he was internally screaming. *The Phoenix.* He doubted Evangeline had even met the legendary leader of the shamans, and yet she was dropping the name into conversation so casually, as though they were comrades.

"The Phoenix?" The guard gritted his teeth, and for a moment, Nicholas was certain that he hadn't fallen for Evangeline's bravado, that he didn't believe her at all. Then the Jingwei would frisk them, and they'd surely be found out and thrown into prison—though that could be one way to get closer to the Scarlet Spy. "What sort of task requires you to enter the prison?"

Evangeline summoned a look of such contempt that Nicholas was amazed the Jingwei didn't immediately wither away. "The Phoenix's matters are private business," she said, in such an affronted tone you'd have thought the Jingwei had declared intentions of violence against the Phoenix. "Jingwei Silver Rank would know nothing of the matter, and if you hold us up any longer, I'll have you written up. What was your name again?"

The Jingwei clenched his teeth, but the authority that rang in Evangeline's voice was true—or at least, it would seem true enough to his ears.

"Oh, relax, Old Wu," said the Jingwei beside him. "I told you during your first week that the Jingwei Gold Rank conduct official business on behalf of the Phoenix and therefore are allowed to enter the prison freely. It's much worse to keep the Phoenix waiting."

Old Wu, seeming to decide that his ego was worth less than the possibility of inviting the Phoenix's wrath, gave the group a surly nod and waved them past without another word.

It wasn't until they were out of earshot of the guards that Nicholas felt the tension leave his body. "That was too close," he said sharply, catching up to Evangeline, who was taking long, loping strides toward the prison wall. "You could've mentioned what you were planning to us beforehand, you know."

"There wasn't enough time," Evangeline said in a clipped tone.

"There was plenty. All that time we were in those tunnels—you couldn't have clued us in then?"

Evangeline continued as though he hadn't said anything. "Do you think any of you could have pulled off that act better than me?" Her words were a challenge.

"No," Nicholas admitted. The way Evangeline could lie without even batting an eye, and terrify others even when *she* was the one wandering around dangerous territory, was not normal. One day she would make an imposing Chancellor of the High Council indeed.

Alice said nothing, but she glanced between them with apprehension tightening her face.

Tristan, meanwhile, seemed entirely unworried and was strolling along at a leisurely pace as though they were on a field trip. He was paying so little attention that he stepped on Evangeline's heel and bumped into her.

"Sorry, sorry," he apologized lazily, sending her a charming smile.

Nicholas was pleased to see that Evangeline offered only a stony glare in return. Still, he couldn't help but think that one of these days, Evangeline's tendency to keep others in the dark was going to backfire. He just hoped it wouldn't be during this Assignment.

19
TRISTAN

Just ahead, the tall iron walls of the Underground's prison loomed. The entrance was guarded heavily by shamans wielding identical fiery spears. To any outsider, it would appear to be madness to try to break into this fortress.

Luckily, Tristan thrived on madness. As he thought about what it might be like to break through layers of security and penetrate the shaman prison, his spirits began to lift for the first time since his transformation and the incident with Ying. He almost smiled. Tristan had no love for the shamans, and his blood positively sang with the anticipation of causing chaos in their territory. Even if the pre-heist phase had gone terribly wrong, everything would now go according to his plan. He would make sure of it.

Tristan knew that this segment of Evangeline's plan—physically breaking the Scarlet Spy out of the prison—would be his to lead. Much as he disliked the idea of operating under Evangeline's thumb, it was worth it to feel this surge of adrenaline at the dangerous task before them. And there was no doubt in Tristan's mind that the others *needed* him for this task. Evangeline and Nicholas were both too prim and proper to lead a prison break. In fact, he gathered from Nicholas's unpleasant expression that the idea was downright nauseating to him. Alice, bless her heart, was useful when it came to probing the minds of their enemies, but the girl was unhelpful for practically anything else.

Oh, but a prison break was right up Tristan's alley. The best part was that they'd all be doing things *his* way from now on, even Evangeline. Tristan would savor any opportunity he got to boss her around.

"Tristan," Evangeline called, as though she'd heard what he was thinking.

His shoulders tensed. What was it about hearing his name in her voice that threw him off-balance so? Though he considered the pair of them ancient history already, Tristan doubted anyone would ever both get under his skin *and* set him on fire the way Evangeline did.

"Here. Take Julius's map." Evangeline pressed the yellowed paper flat into Tristan's palm, and he did his best not to react to the skin-on-skin contact that had once been so familiar to him. He might have done his best to erase Evangeline from his mind, but his body clearly hadn't forgotten her yet.

"I . . . right." Tristan stared into Evangeline's eyes for a beat too long, practically forcing himself to turn away.

"We'll follow you, so don't lead us astray." In Evangeline's voice, there was a thinly veiled warning.

It amazed him that even when Evangeline was coming to him for help, she did so in such a demanding, authoritative manner. This was no request for a favor, but rather an order. Under normal circumstances, Tristan would either ignore Evangeline, or be so annoying that she'd regret enlisting his aid.

However, this was no ordinary request. Tristan took a deep breath and tried to summon as much patience as possible. He intended to finish this Assignment, not for Evangeline, but for his people—and for himself.

Nicholas scowled at Tristan. In turn, Tristan flashed the fox spirit his most charming smile, which he knew would grate on Nicholas's nerves.

That in itself raised Tristan's mood considerably. Few things could bring him such an instant serotonin boost, but annoying Nicholas Hu was one of them.

As Tristan started toward the prison doors, every hair on his body stood on end. There was so much magic here. One wrong move, and that magic could bring a quick end to their Assignment.

The thought made his palms sweat with excitement.

It was shamefully easy to enter the prison. The shamans clearly put a lot of trust in their checkpoint security and knew that prisoners who broke out couldn't get far before being caught, so there was no need to heavily layer the security—not near the entrance, anyway.

The walls of the building were covered in grime, and a stench permeated the air. A mixture of old filth and prisoner sweat and something else he couldn't quite place—which was strange, given how his nose could pinpoint just about any scent in the world.

Tristan grimaced and covered his nose as a particularly strong waft entered his nostrils. But real Jingwei would be used to this smell and wouldn't visibly react to it, so he quickly dropped his arms and forced himself to compose a blank expression.

Tristan didn't know exactly where he was headed, but the prison itself seemed straightforward enough to navigate. Evangeline had said that the Scarlet Spy was in the cell that was deepest belowground. That meant they only needed to keep going farther in and the path forward would reveal itself.

They turned a corner toward a staircase that led deeper underground, and a pair of Jingwei stepped forward to block their way.

"Halt. What business have you accessing the high-security cells?" demanded one of the guards.

Tristan glanced down at their belts. Silver. Good. These Jingwei, he could easily bully into getting out of his way. Channeling the same attitude Evangeline had displayed earlier, he composed his face into the most indignant sneer he could muster, as though the guards must be out of their minds to be questioning them; he was rather good at making this particular expression. Then he reached into his sleeve and pulled out the shaman identification paper Evangeline had used earlier, thrusting it under the guard's nose so violently he almost gave the poor shaman a paper cut.

Behind him, Evangeline took a sharp breath, the only indication of her surprise.

"The Phoenix sent us on urgent business to oversee a change of guards," Tristan bluffed, never breaking eye contact with the two Jing-wei. "Surely you understand that holding us up will incur their greatest displeasure."

"Let them pass," the other guard murmured. "Don't be an idiot. You almost got us in trouble last week."

The first guard sneered. He shoved the paper back into Tristan's hands. "Four of you aren't necessary. Two of you can pass. The other two will stay behind."

"We're Jingwei Gold Rank." Evangeline stepped in. "You do realize that, don't you?"

"You heard what I said. No official notice from the Phoenix came to us."

"We *are* the official notice," Tristan returned with such conviction that he nearly believed the lie himself.

"Consider this an extra layer of security. I'm sure the Phoenix would appreciate our vigor." The guard's cold eyes posed a challenge, and his lip curled with the malice of a man who had little authority in his day-to-day life and thus craved any opportunity for a power trip, no matter how insignificant. Though he couldn't risk completely pissing off the Phoenix, he could at least exert his authority to this degree—by making their job slightly harder to pull off. Tristan knew and despised his type.

Tristan darted a glance at Evangeline, but her expression remained impassive. He had no idea what she was thinking. They hadn't discussed what might happen if the four of them were split up. And Evangeline had roped everyone in on this mission for their specific abilities. Would they be able to break the Scarlet Spy out of prison with two of them staying behind?

Then again, right now there were four Descendants against two Jingwei. The odds were in their favor, should they decide to deal with this conflict the hard way (which also happened to be Tristan's preferred method). Tristan shot a look at Evangeline, trying to communicate this with his eyes alone. Unfortunately, he must not have done a very good job, because Evangeline just grimaced at him.

"Well? Have you decided which two will proceed?" the Jingwei snapped.

"Give us a moment to confer," Tristan said as calmly as he could, which was not very calmly. He caught himself cracking his knuckles. What he wouldn't give to be allowed to hand this lug a good thwacking. From deep within, the primal urge of the beast began to stir; this time, he instantly quelled it. The last thing they needed right now was for him to transform and make it quite clear that they were *not* shamans.

Alice stepped forward and pulled on Evangeline's robes. She whispered something quickly that nobody but Evangeline could hear. The guards' beady eyes were glued to the entire exchange.

Evangeline grabbed Tristan by the elbow. "You and I will proceed," Evangeline said, without sparing him so much as a glance.

Tristan started. Somehow, he hadn't anticipated that the four of them might be divided into pairs this way—he with Evangeline, Alice with Nicholas. Though, now that he considered it, this *was* the most logical pairing. Evangeline was the clear leader, and she needed Tristan's help to break the Scarlet Spy out of prison, given that Tristan was the only one who could call in a favor with the shaman. Tristan tried not to think about the *other* times he'd been alone with Evangeline in the past.

Nicholas leaned forward and grabbed Evangeline's hand. Being overbearing, as usual. Tristan rolled his eyes.

"You'll be okay?" Nicholas asked. His eyes searched Evangeline's for just a beat longer than what might feel natural. If Tristan had to guess, he was trying to get an unspoken instruction from her.

"Of course. It's just business as usual. We won't be long," Evangeline said.

"Yes, don't worry so much. It'll give you early wrinkles," Tristan said to Nicholas.

Nicholas did not retort, probably because doing so would raise the Jingwei Silver Ranks' suspicion. However, his lips were pressed into a thin line.

Alice, who was by far the worst of the group at concealing her emotions, bit her lip and shuffled her feet.

The Jingwei waved through Evangeline and Tristan, and the two descended the staircase deeper into the prison of the Underground.

The air grew colder and mustier as they walked. Tristan could no longer tell if the prison's stench had grown weaker down here, or if his nose had simply adjusted to the rancid air. In any case, he no longer had to repress the urge to retch with each breath, for which he was grateful.

Light, cold fingers pressed down on his shoulder once they had descended the stairs far enough that the Jingwei above were out of earshot. His body responded to Evangeline's touch in spite of himself, and he slowed his steps. It had been years since they had touched each other. Years since Evangeline had trusted him enough to let him so close. This time Tristan knew the proximity of their bodies was only due to necessity on her part, not desire.

"What is it?" Tristan asked, glad that his voice remained steady despite what he was feeling inside. The hairs on the back of his neck stood on end as Evangeline's cold breath blew against him.

She murmured, "There's a change of guards in fifteen minutes. Nicholas and Alice will use that window to join us down here."

"How do you know about the change of guards?"

"Alice read the guards' minds."

Of course. That moment right before Evangeline had announced that she and Tristan would proceed. Tristan let out a soft laugh. He had to admit, the human girl was proving far more useful than he'd thought she would be. Perhaps he'd underestimated Alice Jiang. The laugh turned to a wince when Evangeline's sharp nails dug slightly into his shoulder. "Ow! Watch those claws of yours."

Without releasing any pressure, Evangeline hissed, "That stunt you pulled back there. I had no *idea*—I mean, when did you—?"

"—Swipe the paper from you?" Tristan finished, sparing a glance backward to see that Evangeline's face was pinched with annoyance. He smirked. She hated it whenever he put one over on her, and truthfully, he was the only Descendant who had accomplished that in recent memory. "It's the oldest trick in the book. Think carefully, Evangeline."

For once, Evangeline actually listened to him. The skin of her smooth forehead scrunched, and then her lips parted with the dawning of a realization.

It took Tristan a moment to realize that a small, rare smile had crept onto his face. Oh, he was so enjoying this. He didn't often get to speak afterward with the victims of his pranks and thefts, and the realization slowly creeping over Evangeline's face gave him a childish glee. It was extra satisfying to know that he'd put one over on none other than Evangeline Long, who prided herself on being perfect.

"Earlier, right before we ran into those Jingwei, when you bumped into me. I thought you were just being annoying. You *are* annoying," Evangeline seethed.

"You told me to lead us through the prisons, so I am attending to the task," Tristan said loftily.

"That's not—you—"

"And you really should pay more attention to your belongings. You don't even have any pockets, and yet pickpocketing you was like taking candy from a child." Tristan lowered his voice to a gruff whisper. "Careful,

Evangeline. You're so caught up in filling Julius's shoes that you're going to make careless mistakes."

Evangeline pulled back as though he'd slapped her. He'd struck a nerve. But wasn't it true, after all? Evangeline always behaved as though she were chasing Julius's shadow, and somebody so focused on chasing shadows was bound to trip over an unseen obstacle.

"Well—well," she spluttered, "I hardly expected to be pickpocketed by someone who's supposed to be on my team!"

"I *am* on your team. In fact, you're fortunate we're on the same side." Without thinking, Tristan's hand reached for that familiar spot on Evangeline's waist, and he rested it there as he had dozens of times before, pulling her in a little closer. "What if I didn't have your best interests at heart, Evangeline? What if I were secretly a spy?"

"You're too terrible a liar to pull off a stunt like that," she retorted. But she let him draw her nearer.

"Ouch." Evangeline hadn't even hesitated for a moment in her delivery, but instead of wounding Tristan, it only made him smile.

Vampires couldn't blush, but the veins on Evangeline's neck grew more prominent. What did it mean that she didn't immediately pull away from his grip, as he had expected? Right now, she was close enough that he could see her pupils dilate. Now all the reasons they shouldn't be together, the reasons they'd broken up in the first place—they seemed so insignificant.

Back then, Evangeline had caught on to the fact that Tristan was up to something secret, though she hadn't known that he'd been fulfilling requests for the Collector. She'd tailed him to the Lower East Side one night, and when he'd caught her, had confronted him. Although it had nearly torn him to pieces to do so, Tristan had ended things right there. He didn't want to tell Evangeline the truth, didn't want her involved in his messy life. It had been an ugly breakup. But Tristan had thought he'd done the right thing, that he'd done what would have to be done sooner or later.

Now, though, desire for Evangeline clouded his thoughts, and Tristan wasn't so sure he'd made the right decision after all. Even through the shaman disguise, Evangeline's beauty shone so brightly that it was almost painful to look at her, yet he couldn't make himself look away.

"You aren't scared?" he murmured, a last, half-hearted attempt to put space between the two of them. "The full moon . . ."

Rather than speaking, Evangeline responded by closing the distance even further. Dazed, Tristan could focus on nothing but the sight of her heart-shaped red lips as they came closer and—gods, was she going to *kiss* him? His mind went blank. That distinct smell of crisp winter and something so comforting and distinctly *Evangeline* washed over him, and he was suddenly like a parched man desperate for water and couldn't get close enough to her. There had always been this indescribable electricity between the two of them, something that drew them together despite how hard each tried to stay away. Tristan had done his utmost to push Evangeline away even when they were together, terrified that he would end up hurting her, but the temptation now was too overpowering to resist. Perhaps deep down, some small part of him had broken the touch barrier because he wanted to see if that electrifying sensation still existed. Well, he'd gotten his answer, and he wasn't sure if he was regretful or glad. He wasn't sure he could even think straight right now.

Evangeline's lips brushed against Tristan's cheek, and then his ear. He gave an involuntary shudder.

"*You're* very fortunate that you possess useful skills, even if you choose to use them for petty crime. Else I'd make sure you had no future among the Descendants. Did you enjoy being bound by my cuffs a little while ago? I could easily make you obey my every command again if you continue to challenge me." She raised her arms, flashing the golden cuffs.

Before Tristan's mushy brain could come up with an adequate reply, Evangeline pushed his hand off her, turned, and set off down the stairs again, as though nothing had transpired between them.

Now that there was distance between his body and Evangeline's, some of the brain cells returned to Tristan's head. That had been a mistake on his part, fully his, and now he knew *not* to do it again. Allowing Evangeline to turn his world upside down once more could lead to nothing good.

"You haven't been able to get rid of me for decades, and not for lack of trying," he retorted as he raced down the steps after her. "Face it. You're stuck with me. And if you truly had no desire for me to be around, then why did you choose *me* for this Assignment? It's not as though I'm the only thief among the Descendants."

"That's true, but you are the most well connected among . . . certain crowds." It wasn't a compliment, the way Evangeline spoke with obvious distaste.

Though she didn't say it in so many words, Tristan could see it in the tensing of her shoulders and fists. Evangeline was the only one who had suspected Tristan's involvement with the Collector, even though he'd taken great care to ensure there was no proof of it. She'd tried to convince him to turn over a new leaf, and he'd never been able to summon the courage to tell her that he *couldn't* cut ties with the Collector. That connection, among other differences, was one of the reasons they hadn't worked out. The *many reasons,* Tristan had to remind himself, as the shaman version of Evangeline was somehow even more dangerously beautiful than the normal Evangeline, and looking at her for too long was making him dizzy.

He had his secrets. She had hers. They had both put their walls up as high as Mount Everest, and each refused to be the first to bring them down. That was the toxic dynamic that had broken them apart, and it seemed four years had changed very little.

"What are you getting at?" Tristan managed to ask.

"This Assignment is best suited for those who are willing to break the rules to pull it off. Those who are willing to do whatever it takes. And I *need* to pull off this heist, Tristan. No matter what."

It must have cost Evangeline a great deal of pride to admit this to Tristan. He could torture her about that, of course; it would be only too easy, not to mention delightfully fun. However, they were descending the last few steps of the dark stone staircase, on the brink of entering the deepest part of the prison. This was neither the time nor the place for annoying Evangeline any further. He'd have plenty of time to do that later. Right now he intended to set them up for success.

"When you got the shaman blood," Evangeline said, and he heard a quiet, gentle note that hadn't been there before—a note of genuine concern—"did you, perhaps . . . ?"

"I don't want to talk about it," Tristan said gruffly. He turned away. The sight of Evangeline's shining, worried eyes caused an ache in his heart—an unexpected, jarring reminder of something precious that had once existed between them, something that was now broken. Tristan expected Evangeline to keep prying, but instead she fell silent. She knew better than anyone else what kind of beast he was when he turned like that, how much he tried to push back against his natural instincts.

They stepped into the prison, which was damp and dark, lit only by the torchlight flickering along the stone walls. Tristan did not, as he knew Evangeline would, first seek out the target of their breakout. The reason he was so successful in his criminal endeavors, the reason the Collector considered Tristan his most reliable thief, wasn't because Tristan could finish the job every time; it was because on the rare occasions when he *couldn't* finish the job, he could always evade capture. Tristan's ability to slip out of tight situations made him an undeniable asset in any petty crime, and certainly in this Assignment.

First, his eyes swept the ceiling of the prison. The place was far underground, so the only way out was up; and he knew there would be a way out, a crude path of some sort, for the prisoners wouldn't be able to last long down here without a constant supply of fresh air.

And there, above their heads, he spotted it: a rectangular vent in the ceiling. They had a route for escape. Now they just needed the Scarlet Spy.

"You'll be glad you chose me for this task, Ev," Tristan said softly. "Now, come quickly."

20
EVANGELINE

Evangeline followed as Tristan strode forward with confidence, holding up the stolen identification paper for any nearby guards to see. She was careful to keep at least three feet of distance between her and Tristan. After months of not speaking, she had thought she'd scrubbed her system of Tristan for good. She'd been mistaken.

There had been a brief moment back there on the stairs, when Tristan had come into her personal space with the ease of before. She shouldn't have allowed him that close to her again, shouldn't have given in to poisonous temptation and desire. Evangeline was furious with herself. It was such a *human* flaw, which proved she still could fall to mortal weaknesses. She needed to be better, and she would be. Tristan couldn't be allowed to come within arm's length of her again. Not during this Assignment. Not ever.

But Tristan's infuriating words wouldn't stop echoing in her ears. *You're so caught up in filling Julius's shoes that you're going to make careless mistakes.* How *dare* he presume to know what she was "caught up in"?

Yes, maybe she did constantly dwell on how best to lead her little heist crew, and yes, perhaps she'd tried to be more like Julius on more than one occasion. But that didn't mean she would behave carelessly, and in any case, where did Tristan—a thief and criminal, by all accounts—get off lecturing *her* about carelessness?

"Evangeline? You look like you're going to punch the wall in."

Evangeline stopped fuming long enough to fix Tristan with a cold glare. "Focus on the task, please."

He must have sensed that it would be a mistake to push her any further, because he fell silent.

Here, in the deepest part of the prison sector, the cells had been built for maximum security. A tall white pillar stood in the center of the floor. Beams of blue electricity zapped the air between each pair of bars on every cell. Evangeline had no doubt that if she or Tristan tried to touch these bars with their bare hands, they would meet a terrible, painful fate. However, there *had* to be a way for them to bypass the shaman magic that kept the jails locked. After all, the Jingwei were regularly able to access the jail cells, weren't they?

They passed cells of imprisoned shamans who were wearing rags, their hair grown long and wild, dirty hands clasped around the bars as they wailed. In each cell, Evangeline searched for a hint of someone familiar, searched for traces of the Scarlet Spy.

If anyone had told Evangeline that she'd one day be breaking into the prison sector of the Underground to release a shaman spy, she'd have burst out laughing. Evangeline didn't break rules, and certainly not for criminals.

Well, Evangeline was breaking the rules now. And strangely, the thought didn't leave a foul taste in her mouth. This was, after all, for the sake of fulfilling a prophecy about herself. For justice and the greater good.

Surprisingly, only one Jingwei was stationed here amid all the prisoners. Perhaps this was because the prison cells were already guarded by enchantments; Evangeline sensed shaman magic humming in the walls, beneath her feet, in the very molecules of the prison air. The Jingwei were here for show. The real guard was the shaman magic encasing the prisoners. And even Tristan, crafty though he was, would have a job breaking anyone out of here.

Some of the prisoners around them appeared either to be fast asleep or to have resigned themselves so fully to their fate as to be listless. Some, however, were wailing and making a great deal of noise, banging their heads against the wall or scraping the floor with their shoes.

"Who are you?" demanded the Jingwei, regarding Evangeline and Tristan with suspicion as they approached. The guard's hands clutched her spear tightly. There was a golden sash around her waist. This was a *real* Jingwei Gold Rank, which meant the jig was about to be up. "State your title, your superior's name, and your business."

Evangeline opened her mouth, but Tristan beat her to spinning a lie.

"We were sent by the Phoenix to— Oh, you know what, I'm sick of this act," Tristan said. "We're here to break out a prisoner. Get out of our way."

Before the shaman guard could yell for help or even process Tristan's announcement, he stepped forward and swung at the back of her head. She fell unconscious to the floor with thud and a jangling of keys.

Evangeline wrinkled her nose at the guard now spread-eagled at her feet and moved her shoes out of the way. Beneath the robes, the guard wore pants. Evangeline bent over and felt around the guard's pants pocket. There—a set of keys.

"These should help," Evangeline said, rising to her feet and dropping the keys into Tristan's open palm. At the sight of the keys, the prisoners' wails increased in volume. Evangeline glanced around nervously. What if someone took note of the noises and came to check up on the prisoners? And how much time had passed since they'd left Nicholas and Alice at the top of the staircase? Surely their fifteen minutes were almost up. If the guard change happened right now, that would be a problem. "We need to move quickly."

"You remember what the Scarlet Spy looks like, right?" Tristan asked

Evangeline, his eyes flicking from cell to cell with doubt. "They all look rather the same to me—hard to tell under all the hair and dirt."

"I'm sure we'll know." Evangeline wouldn't forget the Scarlet Spy's distinctive appearance. He was so tall, slim, and pale that he was like the shaman version of the Slenderman, and he wore his black hair tied back in a ponytail. His intense stare, too—Evangeline shivered as she remembered the Scarlet Spy's large red eyes, which had always seemed to be able to peer *inside* her.

Evangeline looked from cell to cell, searching for that familiar figure— and there. It took a moment to pick him out of the prisoners, but there he was: somehow even slimmer than ever, his face and hair caked with grime, red eyes duller than before, but still unmistakably the Scarlet Spy. Evangeline yanked on Tristan's robes to pull him back, pointed toward the shaman, and said, "There. That's him."

Tristan's eyes followed Evangeline's finger. He stood completely still for a moment, as though stunned, and then all at once he moved very quickly. He was in front of the shaman in a few long strides.

"Do you remember me, Scarlet Spy?" he asked.

From within the cell, the prisoner slowly raised his head, until Evangeline could see his features clearly in the dim light. Although his face was smudged with dirt, the Scarlet Spy was immediately recognizable, and he appeared not to have aged a day. When he chuckled, his eyes crinkled up in that same warm expression Evangeline remembered. "Haven't heard myself referred to with that title in a while. Now it's all 'you there,' or 'traitor,' or, my personal favorite, 'Surface scum.'" The Scarlet Spy's voice was raspy from lack of use, and he coughed and ducked his head again after speaking. "Of course I remember you, Tristan She, although I must admit I wasn't expecting you to visit me here—though it's kind of you, of course."

"Oh, believe me, it wasn't my idea."

When Tristan cast her a sidelong look, Evangeline walked as close to the prisoner as she dared without touching the crackling bars. "Hello, Scarlet Spy."

The Scarlet Spy raised his head, and their eyes met. There—the familiar intensity of his gaze. He blinked slowly, one, two, three times. Then his eyes lit up and a wan smile spread across his face. "Darling, darling Evangeline Long. What a pleasant surprise. I apologize for not recognizing you at first—you look a little different from what I remembered." He looked her up and down, fixating on the golden sash tied around her robes. "For how long have you been a shaman, and a Jingwei Gold Rank at that?" He sounded quite amused.

Evangeline had forgotten, but now she was forcibly reminded of the Scarlet Spy's inconvenient sense of humor. "This is hardly the time for cracking jokes. We're here to break you out of prison to help us pull off a heist in Faerie. After that, you may roam off as you please."

The Scarlet Spy raised his eyebrows. If he was surprised at all by the mention of a heist or Faerie, he didn't show it. "A most unusual and tempting request. And what if I refuse?"

"Refuse?" Evangeline echoed, as though she'd never heard the word in her life. "You won't refuse. Why would you do that, when in exchange for helping us, you get your freedom back?"

"Why, there are many reasons. Perhaps I've turned over a new leaf and want to live life on the straight and narrow now. Perhaps I enjoy prison. Or perhaps—"

"Oh, please don't insult my intelligence," Evangeline interrupted in a huff. "I've known you as long as any of the Descendants. You've always had a taste for danger, and you won't change for as long as you live."

"You didn't let me finish," said the Scarlet Spy. His face had turned drawn and taut. "There is also, and most notably, the matter of poor shaman-faerie-Descendant relations. Think of the political consequences of my involvement, Evangeline. The consequences of your even *being* here. The Treaty of Supernatural Peace . . . Surely you haven't forgotten."

"I know exactly what I am doing, Scarlet Spy," said Evangeline testily. "Don't tell me you've lost your nerve in prison."

The shaman didn't appear to register her words. He continued to catastrophize aloud. "A criminal shaman infiltrating Faerieland on behalf

201

of the Descendants. The relations among all of our peoples are shaky at best. If I'm caught—if *any* of us are caught—well . . ." He trailed off, but he didn't need to continue. Evangeline could fill in the blanks herself, and she knew the consequences of involving the Scarlet Spy.

If they were caught in Faerie, they could very well be the cause of an all-out war between the supernaturals.

"I've taken this into account," she said firmly. This was no time to waver in her convictions. They would *not* get caught—too much depended on their evading detection. "Julius would have taken all the risks into account, too. This is the only way." This was the only way for the Descendants to stand *their* ground, to take back what rightfully belonged to *them,* and if war was the result of their actions, then so be it.

"Speaking of your brother, how is dear Julius?" The Scarlet Spy furrowed his brow. His tone turned lighter, and there was even a note of fondness in his voice that hadn't been there before. "Why isn't he with you? Surely Julius didn't send his darling little sister on a dangerous Assignment to fetch me on her own. Why, when I was caught and thrown into prison, Julius made it quite clear that I was to face the consequences of my slipup, and he would not risk his neck or even the necks of his underlings to come get me. Lousy friend he is, don't you think?"

It was clear, from the shaman's smirk, that word of Julius Long's passing had not yet traveled far into the Underground—at least, not to its prisoners. The Scarlet Spy honestly believed Julius was alive still, and that he'd sent his little sister to do his dirty work. And oh, if only that were the truth. Evangeline would have given anything for that to be the truth.

She suddenly felt as though there were something large caught in the back of her throat. For a moment, she couldn't respond to the Scarlet Spy. Tristan gave her a sympathetic look, and she turned away. Evangeline never froze under pressure, but now she stood utterly still. She couldn't stand to look at Tristan, to see the pity in his gaze. She hated that he'd seen her so affected by the Scarlet Spy's words—that he'd witnessed her in a moment of weakness.

"What?" asked the shaman, bemused.

"Julius . . . my brother . . . he's dead." The words clawed their way out of Evangeline's throat, emerging with a surprising evenness that she did not feel. She forced herself to lock eyes with the Scarlet Shaman. "He is dead, and his last request was for me to come find you and finish this Assignment."

The Scarlet Spy froze. The cheeky smile slowly slipped off his face. At first, he glanced from Evangeline to Tristan with a questioning look, as though at any moment they would crack their stony expressions and announce that this was all one big, elaborate practical joke. When that didn't happen, the Scarlet Spy slumped back in his cell, his face turning utterly blank.

"Dead? Julius?" he croaked out after a moment. "How . . . Who . . . I mean, how is that even possible? Aren't you vampires supposed to be almost impossible to kill?"

Having to explain her brother's untimely death was the last thing Evangeline needed at this moment. She turned away.

"Never mind that now." Tristan spoke tersely, and gratitude rushed into Evangeline that he could take the reins when it was clear she needed a moment to gather herself. "We can bring you up to speed later. Right now, we need to know how we can get you out of here, and there isn't a moment to lose."

"I . . . well, I am very sorry to hear that Julius has passed. The world has lost an irreplaceable talent. My condolences, Evangeline."

Evangeline waited another beat before turning back around. "Thank you."

Although his red eyes remained misty, the Scarlet Spy hardened his expression. "However, I'm afraid I still have my reservations about joining you both." His voice, too, had mostly recovered from the croakiness of grief. This must be what it was like to have lived for so long as a spy, too accustomed to the whims of death. "Suppose I lose all sense of reason and come with you. I'm essentially trading imprisonment here for a debt to the Longs, aren't I? What's the difference?"

"The difference is that you only need to help me with this Assignment, and then you'll be free to do whatever you like wherever you like. I promise I won't give a damn. Don't even send me a postcard, in fact."

Tristan had been listening to this exchange with an increasingly annoyed expression. He cleared his throat and glanced at Evangeline. She nodded at him. It was time to play their final card. "Remember when I covered your ass that time the Jingwei chased you through the Imperial Gardens? And you swore you'd repay your debt to me one day? Someone once told me that the shamans always pay their debts." Ying was the one who had once told Tristan this, and he felt a pang in his chest at the thought of her.

The Scarlet Spy groaned. "You have quite the memory, Tristan She." It didn't sound like a compliment.

"The better to blackmail with."

"You really played the long game on that one."

"Not at all. You've just been in jail too long for me to bother collecting on your debt until now."

Evangeline had never truly appreciated Tristan's skills and wit until this moment, and suddenly found herself grateful that he was on *her* side, at least for the time being.

Before the shaman could retort, they heard the sounds of raised voices and footsteps clomping aboveground. The change of guards.

Time was up. Evangeline shot Tristan a panicked look; his eyes darted up to the ceiling, back toward the vent.

"We might have to leave him and make a run for it," Tristan murmured to Evangeline.

"No." They were so close; she couldn't give up now, not when the Scarlet Spy was right before her. Otherwise, what was it all for, breaking into the Underground, risking the shaky peace among all the supernaturals?

Julius had been insistent about enlisting this particular shaman's aid. The four of them had broken into the deepest underground prison of the shamans' lair in order to finally encounter the Scarlet Spy. He sat right before their eyes, and she could not trip at the finish line now. Julius wouldn't.

Evangeline came as close to the cell as she dared, staring intensely into the Scarlet Spy's eyes. She hadn't thought she'd need to resort to this: she raised her hands, flashing the golden cuffs. She would make him see reason, even if she had to do so by magical means. "You won't be in debt to the Longs. You'll help Julius help us—a final favor to an old friend—and you'll be handsomely rewarded. I know someone who will be able to disguise you for life so you'll never have to worry about returning to prison."

At that, the shaman perked up.

"I imagine you don't have much money to your name anymore, do you?" Evangeline continued. The footsteps were approaching; she needed to sweeten the deal as much as possible to get the Scarlet Spy's immediate agreement. "You'll receive funds from the Long estate to set up your new life—"

"Hang on," interrupted Tristan. "What about the rest of us?"

Evangeline hit him with her most piercing look, and he fell silent. "Don't be greedy, Tristan."

"Surely the Longs can't afford to throw around money like that for criminal trash?" asked the shaman, raising an eyebrow.

"The Longs will be able to afford that and more if you help me."

The footsteps were growing closer. A door opened, and the voices became clearer as they rang through the prison. The chatter was hard to make out, but Evangeline heard a familiar female voice—Alice's—echoing down the stairs.

"What's the rush?" Alice asked. It sounded as though she was speaking extra loudly for Evangeline's and Tristan's benefit. "I'm sorry, but I'm still so curious about how tough it is to guard these prisoners day in and day out. Can you first show me how you use that *dangerous* weapon of yours?"

One of the Jingwei Silver Ranks responded gruffly, "Oh . . . all right. Stand back." Mercifully, the footsteps paused.

205

Alice was flirting with the guards to buy them some time. And of course it was working like a charm, because men were just *that* simple—didn't matter if they were shaman or human or any other supernatural being in the universe. Evangeline hadn't known that Alice had it in her, but she supposed being thrown into such a high-stakes situation had brought out a different side of her—that fiery spirit that Evangeline had glimpsed back at Earthly Branches Academy. The thought brought a smile to her lips, and she felt an unexpected rush of affection for the human Descendant.

"Hurry," Tristan snapped at Evangeline. "Alice can't delay them for long. If the shaman's not out of the cell in approximately thirty seconds, we're all toast."

"Thirty seconds is a lifetime," Evangeline retorted. Her fingers clenched. Now. She needed to use her cuffs to force the Scarlet Spy into obeying her, unless—

The Scarlet Spy sighed and slowly stood up. At his full height, he towered two heads above Tristan, who was not lacking in the height department himself. "There are two layers to the prison's security," said the shaman. "First, you need to press the blood of a Jingwei into the pillar over there." He pointed toward the tall white pillar in the center of the prison. "That will deactivate the first layer of security, which is barring intruders from touching the prison cell and also preventing shamans from using our magic. After that, it's simple—use the key to unlock this cell."

"More shaman blood," Tristan sighed. "You shamans really like your blood."

"We are a savage species," the Scarlet Spy agreed. "But perhaps the Descendants are, in your own way, just as savage. Very well. We'll risk war, then, to bring back these lost fountainheads of yours. But if it comes to that, we'll need to prepare ourselves for the consequences." There was no trace of humor in the shaman's face, only a chilling gravity that made Evangeline wonder, for the first time, if they were indeed all making a huge mistake.

Evangeline shook her head. This was no time for second-guessing, and in any case, Julius would never second-guess himself. She grabbed the unconscious Jingwei's hand, drew a pocketknife out of her boot, and sliced the blade into his palm. The sharp, pungent smell of shaman blood wafted into her nostrils, and Evangeline imagined feasting upon it for a moment. Luckily, she was still fairly full from the blood buns she'd had right before leaving the estate, and the prospect of drinking shaman blood wasn't anywhere near as tantalizing as drinking the blood of humans. She forced herself to return to her senses.

When blood dribbled out of the cut in the shaman's palm, Evangeline smeared it onto her own palm. Then she ran toward the white pillar and placed her blood-streaked palm against the cool stone.

For a long, horrible moment, nothing happened, except that the footsteps resumed moving down the steps, despite Alice's girlish protests. Tristan was again staring at the vent, his hands clutched into tight fists. Ready to escape through the vent at a moment's notice. Evangeline considered the possibility that her plan could fail. If all went south right now, she had no doubt that she and Tristan would be fast enough to get up to the vent and escape—but what of Alice and Nicholas?

Then, as suddenly as a light being switched off, the crackling beams of blue electricity around the cells simply vanished.

Evangeline grabbed the keys and shoved the first one into the lock of the Scarlet Spy's cell. It didn't work. She cursed and grabbed the next one, praying it would work. This time, there came a miraculous *click.*

Evangeline yanked as hard as she could. The Scarlet Spy's cell door swung open, just as shocked cries came from the foot of the staircase. The Jingwei had arrived.

"I knew there was something fishy about you all," growled Old Wu, who was the first to round the corner, his face flushed. "Who are you? Stop right there!"

"Run!" Tristan bellowed. He leapt up and opened the hatch over the vent.

Evangeline didn't need to bark out any orders to Nicholas and Alice, for which she was grateful; it seemed that, once again, Nicholas had guessed what she had in mind. He immediately whirled and whacked Old Wu over the head. The poor shaman slumped against the wall, unconscious.

"You go first." Evangeline grabbed the Scarlet Spy's hand and hauled him toward Tristan. He was alarmingly light, as though he hadn't eaten a solid meal in ages—more than likely, judging by the state of the prison. Tristan practically scooped up the shaman in one arm. The Scarlet Spy climbed quickly, though, for such a frail-looking thing. Within seconds, his dangling feet had disappeared into the vent.

Nicholas and Alice stood over the two now-unconscious Jingwei, but Evangeline knew the coast wouldn't be clear for long. Thundering steps sounded above. Reinforcements were coming, and by the sound of it, there were quite a lot of them.

Evangeline grabbed Alice by the wrists. Despite the chaos of the moment, the blood pumping in Alice's veins was as loud as thunder in Evangeline's ear, and Evangeline's mouth watered uncontrollably at the irresistible scent of human blood before she forced herself, with an inhuman resolve, to turn away. *Focus,* she ordered herself with every last remaining ounce of strength. If ever there *wasn't* a moment for her to let her weaknesses get the best of her, it was now.

"Up you get," Evangeline said through gritted teeth, and tossed Alice along to Tristan. Alice didn't even have a moment to shriek before Tristan had shoved her safely through the vent. Then Evangeline turned to Nicholas. He shook his head and gestured for her to go up first. "Oh, this isn't the time for chivalry," Evangeline snapped. If somebody was going to get caught here, she wouldn't let it be one of the others she'd roped into taking on this Assignment. A captain went down with their ship—and in Evangeline's case, a leader would not forgo the safety of any member of her crew.

"No, you're going up before me," Tristan said to Evangeline once Nicholas, too, had disappeared above their heads. Tristan grimaced as his eyes darted toward the staircase. Shadows stretched along the dark walls. The reinforcements were moments away from bursting into the prison, and the two of them, powerful though they might be, could not hope to keep a whole squad of Jingwei at bay. "Quickly—there's no time to argue!"

But Evangeline hesitated for a second. Oh, why did Tristan's stubborn streak have to present itself now, of all moments? But he was right. There was no time to argue, and Tristan was too prideful to back down now. And perhaps, deep down, just a tiny bit, Evangeline enjoyed the idea that Tristan was protecting her.

Nicholas extended his hand, and Evangeline grabbed it. She didn't really need help; her reflexes were superb, and her superhuman strength was second to none, so swinging herself up to the hatch was little more than a stretch to her. Then she was inside the vent, a dark, enclosed space where she had to crouch on her hands and knees.

"Stop them!" bellowed a Jingwei's voice down below.

Tristan was even faster than Evangeline, but the shamans were in hot pursuit. Evangeline and Nicholas each took one of his hands and hauled him up. The closest guard made a grab at Tristan's legs, but he swung them up and into the vent in the nick of time. Then, as the Jingwei tried frantically to reach up into the vent, Evangeline slammed the hatch on them.

"How do we lock that door?" Tristan called.

There was nothing to lock it with, and no time to figure out a solution, with the Jingwei prying at the hatch.

"Out of the way." The Scarlet Spy elbowed Nicholas aside. He started to protest, but then flames burst out of the shaman's palms, dancing around the hatch and sealing it shut. Over his shoulder, the shaman shouted, "Get moving! I don't know how long this will last."

The others had crawled a good distance from the vent opening, led by the Scarlet Spy. Evangeline followed them. Her back, neck, and legs were already aching from the awkward crouch. Her body might be unnaturally strong, but it wasn't immune to the normal aches and pains that would bother anyone contorting their body into such an uncomfortable position. After the successful completion of the Assignment, Evangeline promised herself, she would ask Cecil to book her for a nice, long massage at the spa.

Finally, after they'd all crawled a safe distance through the vent and the voices of the Jingwei had faded, Evangeline collapsed backward and took a long, deep breath.

21
CECIL

From the kitchen window, Cecil watched the pink-orange hue of sunrise paint the city skyline as she nursed a hot mug of blood coffee in one hand and a warm blood bāo in the other. She was already dreading the next evening of classes, over twelve hours away. Not even the delicious blood bāo could lift her mood.

Ever since Julius had been pronounced dead, Cecil's whole world had turned upside down. An immense pressure bore down on her, growing heavier with every hour. Her anxiety was at an all-time high.

The sound of Cecil's chewing was the only noise in the silence of the Long estate. The place was so empty in Evangeline's absence that it was beginning to unnerve her. Julius had done his best to replicate the glorious Long mansion in Beijing here in Manhattan, but it had never been more than a shell of a home, a fraction of what once had been.

Cecil closed her eyes, and a rush of sound enveloped her—laughter and chatter from some time long past.

The Longs had once resided in a lively mansion. Back when there were four, and not just the brother and sister. Back when the Descendants lived in such power and splendor, Mr. and Mrs. Long had seen to it that the family had plenty of tutors and servants and business partners and friends constantly going in and out of the house. The Long manor was not just a home, but rather a place of gathering, a central point in the bustling city of Beijing.

Everything changed the day the Old Summer Palace was pillaged. Mr. and Mrs. Long gave up their lives trying to defend their legacy, their country, their loved ones. They had died before the foreigners had even gotten to their mansion.

Distantly, Cecil's mind summoned a faint memory: smoke engulfing the mansion, servants screaming as they were burned alive, soldiers climbing through the wreckage to steal anything they could get their grimy hands on.

Julius Long had just received word that his parents were dead and he was now the most senior Long—and the leader of all the Descendants. Even though he'd been freshly twenty, old enough to have learned most of the family operations but not old enough to have been expected to take over anytime soon, the change in the young shào yé had been immediate.

As the soldiers rushed into the building, Julius turned toward Evangeline and Cecil, grabbed each by the arm in spite of their protests, and shoved them inside his closet.

"Don't move a muscle until I come back for you, no matter what you hear out there" had been his order to them. "Am I understood?"

Evangeline grabbed his wrist. "Let me go with you, dà gē—I'm sure I can Compel the soldiers into stopping—"

With none of his usual gentleness toward his sister, Julius pried her fingers off him. His chest was heaving, and his eyes glittered with a wild light that made him look like a madman. It was the first time Cecil had gazed upon the elder Long sibling and felt her heart lurch with fear. These men, these foreign devils, they were about to be very, very sorry for their actions.

"No. There will be no more Long lives taken today," Julius growled. His eyes flicked toward Cecil, who nearly jumped out of her skin. "I'll

Paralyze every last soldier in my path; they won't even see me coming. See to it that my mèi mei stays out of harm's way, Cecil."

"Yes, shào yé," Cecil whispered, for what else could she say? In the Long household, superiority was dictated by age. She was to obey the eldest Long, always, even if it meant she had to go against Evangeline's wishes.

Then Julius slammed the closet doors shut, enveloping the two of them in darkness. There had been such an unfamiliarly ferocious note in his voice—some inhuman combination of grief and fear and pure unadulterated rage—that neither Evangeline nor Cecil dared to disobey him. Even Evangeline, who never let her brother boss her around, had let him do so just this once. Then came echoes of Julius's bellows of fury, followed by others' shrieks of pain and English curse words.

There was no pity in Cecil's heart for the foreign devils, for they had brought Julius's wrath upon themselves. And though it might not be this day, this year, this decade—one day they would recognize what a grave mistake they had made, to take what did not belong to them. To destroy that which they did not bother to understand. To underestimate the rage and power of the Descendants, and those they protected.

I should be out there fighting with Julius, Cecil thought. *I should be helping him avenge Mr. and Mrs. Long, and all the servants who were murdered here today.*

When Cecil was only two years old, her parents, distant relatives of the Longs, had been killed by Wrathlings. The Longs had found her miraculously alive in the wreckage of her parents' home, wrapped in a little blanket and tucked inside a closet, where her parents had doubtless hidden her as their final act of love. In the aftermath of that tragedy, it was the Longs who had given Cecil the clothes on her back. In exchange for Cecil's helping around the house here and there, the Longs had provided her with a sturdy roof over her head, a warm bed to sleep in every night, and countless meals to fill her belly. Even though Cecil had never developed specific powers like the other Descendants did, owing to the fact that she wasn't a member of their immediate family, the Longs had even given her their family name. If anyone owed the Longs a debt of life, it was Cecil.

Still, she was too frightened to move, and she did not want to disobey the new leader of the Descendants.

"Don't worry," Cecil had whispered to the trembling Evangeline. The two girls hugged each other as their world crashed down around them, holding on to the only sure thing that remained. "If the soldiers find us in here, I'll—I'll protect you." Even then, Cecil had been taking combat lessons and proving her prowess. The Longs had been good to her, and she would do anything to protect one of the only ones who remained alive.

Evangeline had raised her head, her eyes shining with tears—and perhaps a gleam of determination. "Julius and I will protect you, too, Cecil."

Gradually, as Cecil and Evangeline held each other, each listening to the sound of the other's breathing, the terrible noises of carnage faded away. The manor had gone quiet for what could have been minutes or hours—time had ceased to have any meaning in the misery of endless waiting—when at last the closet door slid open. Cecil blinked against the sudden influx of light. There stood the young shào yé, covered from head to foot in dirt and grime, blood smeared across his body from several cuts on his cheeks and arms and legs, a half-crazed expression on his face.

"We need to evacuate the premises at once," Julius declared through gritted teeth.

"What's happened out there?" Evangeline craned her neck to try to see past her brother. "What of the servants? Our friends?"

"Dead." Julius spoke with no emotion, his eyes glazed over.

Evangeline collapsed sideways against the closet door. "Dead . . ."

"I know this is difficult to process, Evangeline, but we have no time to grieve right now. We need to move. The foreign devils carried off five of the zodiac fountainheads. The Circle of Twelve is broken, and it will only be a matter of time before the Descendants begin to feel the effects of—"

Then Evangeline let out a bloodcurdling scream, pawing at her mouth, where her two canine teeth were beginning to protrude like fangs.

Julius's eyes widened in horror, and he stepped forward to touch his sister. "Mèi mei—"

Cecil could hardly register what was happening to Evangeline before a horrible pain, worse than anything she'd ever experienced, began to rip through her entire body.

The sound of an alarm jerked Cecil out of the memory and back into the present. For a moment, she wasn't entirely sure what was going on, but then she remembered. That alarm meant she had sixty seconds to get out of the house if she wanted to make it to the Academy on time for study hall. Cecil didn't usually go to study hall, as it was an optional extra class, but she would rather do that than sit at home with her thoughts racing with worry over Evangeline and the others.

Dusting the crumbs off her hands, she grabbed her book bag and strode out of the mansion. Thanks to her vampire speed, her commute to the school was quick—in moments, she'd traveled from the Long estate onto the overgrown lawn of Earthly Branches Academy, right in front of the building where study hall was to be held.

"Cecil." Xavier greeted Cecil with a somber nod when she sat down next to him. "How are you holding up?"

Ever since their Starbucks meeting, the two had been checking in on each other. Being regarded with such genuine concern from Xavier felt like a warm hug to Cecil after days of anxiety. "I'm . . . hanging in there."

Xavier was now the closest thing Cecil had to a friend at the moment. And, perhaps, the closest thing she had to a friend at all at Earthly Branches Academy. Although Cecil was friendly enough with the other Descendants, she wouldn't consider anyone a *friend*. Most of her attention over the decades had been devoted to serving the Longs. There simply wasn't enough time to forge deep relationships with others.

Besides, the more time Cecil had spent in Evangeline's company, the more she understood that the concept of "friendship" had gotten twisted in the world of the Descendants. Due to the power dynamics among the twelve bloodlines, the Descendants rarely formed friendships without ulterior motives. It was widely known that House of Dragon was the most highly regarded of the twelve, and thus Julius and Evangeline were the most highly regarded among the Descendants. Cecil had found great amusement in watching various families try to cozy up to the Longs over the decades, with varying degrees of success.

Julius had been good at playing the game, but he had ensured loyalty to *himself*, rather than to the Long bloodline. Likely, only the Talons would remain loyal to the Longs no matter what happened from now on. It didn't help that, rather than play the game as her brother had, Evangeline had chosen a path of solitude. Now, too late, Cecil recognized that with Julius gone and Evangeline's rule in question, the House of Dragon was in danger of actually losing power to the House of Ox.

With the absence of the Long siblings, this made Cecil very, very vulnerable.

Cecil was so focused on trying to figure out this conflict that she didn't realize study hall had already ended until someone waved a hand in her face. She blinked. Xavier gazed down at her with concern.

"Oh. Are we done?" Cecil asked. The answer was obvious as she glanced around the nearly empty room.

But before Xavier could reply, a shriek of pain sounded from the halls, followed by loud chatter and laughter. Cecil heard snatches of the conversation outside.

"Stop—I want to go back to my dorm, please—"

"I told you you'd carry my books around for me until the end of my lessons. Was I not clear, human? Or do you need me to *beat* the lesson into you?"

"N-No!"

Cecil rushed out to see what was happening, Xavier hot on her heels. The sight that awaited her was nothing short of sickening.

A small circle of Descendants had gathered. In the middle of the circle,

Thomas Yang from the House of Sheep towered over one of the human Descendants, a girl named Rebecca, who was curled up on the floor.

"Stop! What are you doing?" Cecil shoved her way through the circle of onlookers and put her body between Thomas and Rebecca.

Thomas sneered at her. He'd been cursed into a werewolf, and not one of the better-looking ones. Cecil had always thought of him as a bully in a class below Marcus and Max. At least the Niu brothers weren't complete cowards, preying on those who were clearly weaker than them. "Maybe you hadn't heard, but Marcus is leading the Descendants now, and the rules are changing. Get out of the way."

"Marcus isn't leading anything," Cecil retorted. "You don't want to push me, Thomas. How far apart are our ranks in combat class?"

Silently, Xavier moved to stand next to Cecil. His presence alone was threatening enough; he didn't need to say a word.

Thomas's beady eyes slid from Cecil to Xavier to Rebecca, and back to Cecil. He deflated. Even if he severely underestimated Cecil just because she was a girl, he wouldn't underestimate Xavier, who was a good head taller than him and much more muscular.

"If I hear that you or anyone else is putting hands on the human Descendants, I'll make your life *very* unpleasant very quickly," Cecil growled, cracking her knuckles. She didn't like resorting to threats, but threats were all these bullies seemed to understand. "Now—where can I find Marcus?" If he was indeed giving the green light for the supernatural Descendants to start dunking on the human Descendants, then Cecil needed to put a stop to this fast.

Thomas scowled and pointed toward the dining hall doors, where there was a bit of a ruckus, with students murmuring among themselves.

And when she entered the dining hall, Cecil immediately knew what had set her classmates abuzz.

22
ALICE

In the past few hours, Alice had been forced to repeatedly use her mind-reading powers, let Nicholas change her appearance, and flirt with creepy guards, and all this on top of trying not to collapse from panic over . . . everything.

She'd never felt so stressed. She'd never felt so *alive*.

There hadn't been a moment of peace since Evangeline had summoned her to the Long estate. Alice had never thought of herself as faint of heart until now, but in hindsight, she would have appreciated a more thorough debriefing on what this Assignment would entail. Her heart was ready to burst in her chest, even though they'd narrowly evaded capture by the Jingwei below—for now, at least. If by some miracle Alice survived this Assignment, she feared her heart might give out soon after anyway.

Alice's head ached, and her heart stabbed with a pang of homesickness. She was far away from Earthly Branches Academy and even farther away from home. What would her poor mama think if she knew the types of otherworldly dangers Alice had gotten herself into? Mama, who had hardly been able to let go of Alice long enough for her to attend Earthly Branches Academy? Was the chance of finding out more about Baba worth Alice's life?

To clear her head, Alice sucked in a huge breath—and immediately regretted it. The musty air of the prison assaulted her lungs, and she couldn't contain a hacking cough.

"Are you all right?" Nicholas stared at her with concern.

She nodded, trying to put on a brave expression. "Hard to breathe down here. Or see." Once Alice's eyes had adjusted to the darkness, she could discern the outlines of her comrades. The little bit of light was just enough for her to be able to distinguish one supernatural from another.

That was the second time Nicholas had checked up on her. Did she really appear so delicate as to require his constant observation? Or perhaps he cared for others' well-being more than the average individual. He'd picked up on her disappointment in herself when she'd made that mistake back in the tunnels, too, and had even offered comforting words that helped bolster her confidence. Nicholas was intriguing, Alice decided. She didn't quite know what to make of him.

Mostly so she had an excuse to turn away from Nicholas's concern, Alice assessed the newest member of Evangeline's eclectic crew. The—what had Evangeline called him?—*Scarlet Spy* didn't look as intimidating as Alice had imagined. Sure, he was tall, but his loose skin gave him the appearance of a skinny man who had once been quite a bit larger. No doubt, the shaman's years in prison had worn away any muscle he once possessed. Now he was bony, his figure sunken, like a malnourished giant. Furthermore, he stank. Alice shifted her body as subtly as she could to put some distance between her and the Scarlet Spy. Unfortunately, in the cramped vent, there was no such thing as personal space.

Nicholas and Tristan were regarding the shaman with wariness, and Alice thought they had never been more united than right now. It was a shame they couldn't be on the same page during more crucial moments.

"Everyone, meet the Scarlet Spy," Evangeline said unnecessarily. "Scarlet Spy, meet everyone."

"You can call me Lei," he grunted.

Evangeline raised her eyebrows, the only indication of her surprise. Evidently, she hadn't known the Scarlet Spy's name, either. Though, in all likelihood, it wasn't his *real* name. "Lei is an old friend of the family," Evangeline added without missing a beat. She beamed. "And as he is our only reliable connection who knows his way in and out of Faerie, he is going to lead us into the realm. But first, Lei will show us the way out of the Underground."

The shaman heaved a weary sigh, which made his figure seem to deflate even more. "You've saddled me with quite a tricky job," he said tersely, "given the alarms you must have raised and the layers of security that are being brought down upon us."

"That's why we need the help of an expert criminal such as yourself," Evangeline said brightly.

"Evangeline," Nicholas cut in sharply, still eyeing Lei with distrust, "how are you *sure* that this shaman won't betray us to his people?"

"I have little faith in spies," Tristan added.

Lei sneered at him. "I have little faith in oversized mutts, either, but we'll have to learn how to get through this somehow, won't we?"

Uh-oh. Alice didn't need to be able to read minds to understand that there was already bad tension between these two, which didn't bode well for the rest of the Assignment. Still, she had to admit that Nicholas and Tristan *did* have a point. How could they trust a shaman criminal whom they'd just broken out of prison?

Well, there was one way to uncover somebody's true intentions. Alice closed her eyes for just a moment and concentrated all her efforts on reaching into Lei's mind, but it was like trying to push through a solid wall. There was nothing there for her to read. When she opened her eyes again, Lei was staring at her with a little smile on his face, as though he'd known what she was doing. It was the first time Alice had encountered such strong resistance when trying to enter someone's mind outside of Evangeline's enchanted estate, and she had a feeling it would be far from the last.

"Cut it out, all of you," Evangeline said. "We can trust Lei because he is—was—one of Julius's trusted confidants. And because I promised him his complete freedom at the end of all this. Now, will there be any more stupid questions, or can we get a move on before the Jingwei find us sitting pretty, awaiting capture?"

Though they were clearly unsatisfied with Evangeline's answer, Nicholas and Tristan didn't challenge her. Alice shook her head frantically when Evangeline's sharp gaze fell upon her. She didn't think Evangeline would ever *not* terrify her.

"Quickly, now," Lei said, taking the lead from Evangeline as they crawled forward in the vent, which was now sloping upward. "The vents are built in our favor, because they lead upward. The guards can only catch us from behind, which means they can't corner us on both ends."

This offered little reassurance to Alice, who could hear the Jingwei—both their shouts and their thoughts—growing closer and closer.

Alice's palms and knees were growing sore from dragging herself along, but she knew she couldn't slow down. Even at her fastest, she was just barely keeping up with the supernaturals—and she suspected they were purposely keeping to a more manageable pace for her sake. Alice gritted her teeth. It was yet another reminder of how inept she was compared to the others. Was she truly a Descendant? How could she possibly have thought she could take on this Assignment?

"Do you all smell that?" Nicholas asked.

"I have been doing my utmost to *not* smell anything since we entered this prison shithole," Tristan said, and added, "No offense, Lei."

"None taken," grunted the shaman. "You think I'm operating under some delusion that I'm scented like daisies and sunshine?"

"I smell . . . is that dumplings?" Evangeline asked.

"It's kind of you to try to spare my feelings, Evangeline, but I know I do not smell like dumplings, either."

"Not *you*, Lei. There's a smell coming from deeper in the vent."

Alice certainly couldn't smell whatever it was that the others were smelling—curse these dull human senses of hers—but the mere mention of dumplings made her stomach start rumbling. She had no idea how much time had passed in the Underground, as there wasn't even daylight to mark the passage of time here, but it had been several hours since she'd had her last meal. The adrenaline of sneaking into the Underground and being chased around had distracted her from her body's needs until now, but she was famished.

As the group drew closer to the surface, Alice began to smell it, too—that aroma of fried dumplings and spices that she recognized from somewhere. A bit of light was filtering in from ahead now, so Alice could see more clearly. They were nearing the surface. Thank the gods. She didn't think her hands and legs could take another ten minutes of crawling.

"I see the surface!" Lei shouted. His voice was filled with the amazement and glee of a child. Alice wondered what it must be like for the shaman to have been imprisoned so deep below Earth's surface for years and years, away from daylight or anything that might remind him of the vibrant world above. Alice had only been in the Underground for a matter of hours, and she already missed the world above something fierce.

"Hurry," Evangeline hissed. "The Jingwei are right behind us."

"It's—not—*giving*—" Lei said in frustration.

They'd come to a standstill while Lei rattled the vent hatch above them, and meanwhile the grunts and curses of the guards grew louder and closer. Heart thumping, Alice shot a terrified look back into the darkness. She could see motion behind them. They had maybe a minute or two before they'd be caught here.

Then—"Got it!" With a screeching noise of protest from the hatch, Lei pried it loose. Cool, fresh air filled the tunnel.

Alice darted another look back. The guards were only feet away now, their hands and knees and faces visible. For a moment, the sheer fear of being caught paralyzed her. What would the shamans do to a human who had broken into their prison? Surely their laws didn't apply to humans? But then again, she was in *their* territory now, and nobody would know to come looking for her. They could lock her up in those horrible cells.

Or torture her. Surely the shamans had torture chambers, and whatever shamans found torturous, the effects must be a hundred times worse for a human—

"Alice!" Nicholas grabbed Alice's arm and dragged her forward with superhuman strength, away from the Jingwei, away from her spiraling thoughts. Alice didn't even have the breath to thank him before he used his other hand, reached up to grip the side of the opening, and hauled her up before him.

Alice tumbled out into the crisp morning air, her legs cramping and wobbling as they adjusted to a standing position. Evangeline, Tristan, and Lei were already up there. It took a beat for Alice to register her surroundings, the neon signs with Chinese characters hanging in front of buildings, the colorful paper lanterns that dangled on strings above her head. They'd come out in Chinatown, near the intersection of Mott and Pell. Judging by the sun's position in the sky, it was barely past dawn. Most of the people out at this hour were elderly, and they seemed only mildly interested in the sight of young, dirty people tumbling out of a vent into the streets.

A Jingwei's hand frantically grabbed at Lei's foot, but Lei kicked him. An "Oof!" of pain followed.

"Seal it shut now, quickly!" Evangeline commanded, rushing over to the vent opening. Alice snapped out of it fast enough to dive for the hatch at the same time as Lei, and together, they slammed it over the hole.

"That's not enough!" Alice exclaimed as the Jingwei's fingers gripped the hatch, shaking it. At any moment, they would pry it loose. "It's not going to hold—"

Lei murmured something under his breath that sounded like a chant, and Alice couldn't help but gasp when she glanced over at him. His red eyes were wide open and brighter than ever, as though his pupils were actually filled with fire. A subtle blue light emanated from his palms, which he pressed into the hatch. The same blue light beams that had enclosed the Underground prison cells now wrapped around the vent, crackling with warning.

"Whoa," said Tristan.

"There," Lei panted. He wiped a bead of sweat from his forehead. "That should hold them a little longer, but it won't last forever. We need to get going. Your disguises have worn off, too," he pointed out.

Alice glanced down at her fingers and pressed them into her cheeks, and then looked around her. The shaman was right. Nicholas and Tristan had reverted to normal, which meant she was no longer disguised, either.

"I couldn't keep it up any longer," Nicholas panted, offering a shrug as an apology.

Evangeline was already far ahead of them, waving them into the crowd. Alice made to follow, but she found she couldn't keep up—her legs were weak, and she was parched with thirst, not to mention light-headed with hunger.

"Come on." Nicholas's large, warm hand grabbed hers, gently pulling her along, and her heart skipped a beat at the gesture. She knew it was in his nature to look after anyone, especially a human Descendant whose physical abilities were leagues below the supernaturals'. But Nicholas was treating her as though she belonged among these Descendants who were much older, wiser, and more powerful than her. He shot her a gentle smile, and she swallowed.

This could be bad, Alice thought.

There wasn't much time to think, however, because Nicholas was pulling her into the crowd, on the heels of the others. They dodged vendors selling souvenirs and open baskets of live crabs stacked on the street. Alice glanced back once before her view was obscured by the heads of people moving this way and that. She thought she saw shaman guards emerging into the streets, turning in search of their targets, red robes fluttering in the wind as they moved.

But by then, the Descendants had long since disappeared into the crowd.

23
LEI

As he breathed the air aboveground and took in the sights of Manhattan's Chinatown, Lei did his best not to cry. He'd never thought he'd treasure or miss the mixed smell of fishy markets and spicy meats, but he was so thrilled to be outside in the fresh air that he could have fallen forward onto his knees and kissed the dirty streets. At last, at *long* last, Lei had escaped his dark, filthy Underground cell. He hadn't been sure this day would ever come. Now that it had, a tidal wave of emotions engulfed him.

Even as a small child, Lei had known that he didn't belong in the Underground. It was hard to put his finger on it, but there was always that mildly discomforting, niggling sensation that the Underground was wrong for him, that he was meant for something so much more. The first time Lei took a trip to the Surface confirmed that his gut instinct had been right all along. There was so much open space here, so many cultures and experiences, and Lei's greedy adventurer's heart desired to see it all. Most of the shamans spent the majority of their time in the Underground, and because they did not need sunlight or fresh air as humans did, they were perfectly content to keep to themselves. In fact, many chose not to venture to the Surface at all, given how annoying humans were.

Lei, however, had always been unnaturally fond of humans. Humans were fascinating. Their lives were so short and meaningless, and yet they managed to find purpose in such an ordinary existence. So interesting, too, was the human ability—almost a *need*—to create conflict out of practically nothing. For as long as the shamans and fae had held grudges against each other, they'd never gone head to head in war as often as the humans managed to squabble among themselves.

"Where are we headed?" Lei asked as Evangeline strode through the crowd. With fondness, he spotted the old barbershop he used to frequent, still open and welcoming customers, but he only allowed himself to linger for a moment. Evangeline looked as though she'd personally drag him along by the ears if he held them up. "Back to the Long estate?"

"No. Although the property itself is guarded by enchantments, we'll surely be spotted and ambushed trying to enter the estate. Julius had as many enemies as allies—and I've no doubt that my absence will put nefarious ideas into the heads of the other Descendant families. If the Longs want to remain in power—if *I* want to prove myself worthy of leading in Julius's stead—the best way to show that is to bring back the zodiac fountainheads."

Lei let out a long, low whistle. Impressive. Evangeline was clearly Julius's younger sister. Not only had she planned out how she'd break into the Underground and recruit Lei to her efforts, but she'd simultaneously been thinking about the political implications of her absence back home—and how restoring the long-lost zodiac fountainheads to the families would also prove to any doubters that she was the most capable ruler to fill Julius's shoes. What a frighteningly sharp young woman Evangeline had become in the seven years that Lei had been gone from the Surface. Lei didn't think Evangeline would lead from Julius's shadow. No, she would likely overshadow *him*.

Oh, if only you were still around to witness your little sister's untapped potential, Julius. Lei still hadn't fully registered the fact that Julius Long was

226

dead, actually dead. He ought to be grieving. They'd known each other since Julius was mortal, and Lei suspected he had been one of the closest things Julius had to a friend. He had never imagined his life without Julius in it, and in his darkest days in the Underground prison, he had had delirious dreams of Julius coming to rescue him. It somehow seemed like Julius had to be playing a grand joke on them all, including his sister. Perhaps a particularly outrageous segment that was part of an overall scheme. Julius had so loved to scheme and plot.

But no. Lei knew in his gut that while Julius might have been shady, corrupt, and ruthless in the ways that business and power often caused men to be, his love for Evangeline was true. The Julius Lei knew would never do anything to break his little sister's trust or her heart. If Evangeline said Julius was gone, then it must be the truth.

Lei spoke almost without thinking. "Your brother would be proud of you."

A snort. "More like my brother would be appalled by how long it took me just to break you out of prison. By the way, you could have gone along with things more easily. You did hold us up quite a lot down there."

"I prefer living my life with an element of unpredictability," Lei said brightly.

"Well, you're certainly in the right place for that."

"What's the plan now, Evangeline?" interrupted the unfriendly-looking dark-haired werewolf boy. (What was his name again? Todd? Timothy?) He placed his hand on Evangeline's shoulder. "You *do* have a plan, don't you?"

Lei expected the answer to be a resounding yes, but instead Evangeline went silent for a moment. They bobbed and weaved past a long line of people waiting outside a noodle restaurant.

"The plan right now is to find a place to regroup, Tristan," came Evangeline's reply at last.

"You don't have a plan." Tristan sounded somewhat in disbelief. When Evangeline didn't reply, he continued, "Since when have you ever been caught without at least two different backup plans?"

"Since my dear brother died and saddled me with this impossible heist and hardly anything to go on. Or did Julius happen to give *you* the complete manual for stealing back priceless heirlooms?"

"Say that louder, will you? I don't think all of Chinatown heard you that time."

There was no need to worry about being overheard; the noise around them was far too loud. And in any case, nobody would be as interested in a heist as they were in the best deal on pork buns in the area. In that regard, Chinatown hadn't changed at all from what Lei remembered.

Lei had heard enough of the bickering to have a grasp on the dynamic between Evangeline and Tristan. He had to fight back a grin, as he had no desire to be on the receiving end of Evangeline's death glare next.

"I might be winging it, but I do know what I'm doing," Evangeline said. She made a sharp right turn and led them in front of a bubble tea café. Right next to it, a dingy old staircase led to the floor below, toward a closed door. The space was abandoned, tucked away, and so unremarkable that Lei wouldn't have taken notice of it on his own. "We'll be safe to freely discuss our next steps here."

"And where is *here*?" the silver-haired boy—Nicholas?—asked, sounding apprehensive.

The human girl, Alice, had hardly uttered a word since they'd emerged from the Underground, but Lei noticed that her eyes kept darting in every direction, as though she thought they were still being chased. Likely, they *were* still being chased. Lei doubted the Jingwei would give up so easily. He was a high-profile prisoner, after all.

Tristan moved to open the door, but Evangeline stepped in front of him. "It won't work. The door won't open for anyone but me," she explained.

Lei looked on with curiosity as Evangeline rolled up her sleeves and pressed both of her palms into the wooden surface of the door. Immediately, there came a rumbling noise, and the door began to tremble and glow with a faint white light. Dust puffed up from the motion. Lei coughed and blinked as the particles whooshed into his eyes and nose.

Once his vision cleared, he peered inside at what appeared to be a tiny café that was closed down and abandoned. There were a few round tables with chairs. Behind the seating area were a counter and a small kitchen beyond that.

"This is one of the safe houses the Longs have built over the years," Evangeline explained. Once the last of them, Nicholas, entered the space, Evangeline closed the door and pressed her hands into it once again. This time, the door stopped glowing and resumed its ordinary appearance.

"Did you say . . . safe hous*es*?" Tristan repeated, his back turned to the others as he examined the room. "As in plural? How many are there?"

"A dozen."

"Jesus. Do you Longs expect to be jumped at every corner?"

"Well, the family has had decades to build the houses, so it's not that noteworthy. We have safe houses all over the city, in each borough, and even a few upstate for the occasional excursion gone awry. The Longs and our supporters do have enemies, unfortunately, and we can never be too careful."

Lei had witnessed firsthand—on multiple occasions, in fact—Julius being cornered by people who'd like nothing more than to see his head on a pike. Every time, with the aid of either his Talons or his safe houses or the sheer dumb luck that had always come through for him, Julius had managed to wiggle out of trouble. It was hard to believe that the Long siblings had ever been mortal; they had such a talent for evading death.

"So now that we're *probably* not going to be ambushed and murdered," Tristan said loudly, "please do tell us what you have in mind for the next phase of this plan."

At that, Evangeline gave Lei a pointed look. This had the direct and unfortunate effect of everyone else following Evangeline's gaze and staring at Lei as well.

"What are you all looking at me for? I've been in a cage for seven years. I've just met you all except for Evangeline."

"You're the one who's actually been to Faerie—several times, in fact, if the treason charges are correct," Evangeline said dryly. Ah, that condescending tone. She'd definitely picked that up from Julius. Rather than feeling annoyed, Lei found himself appreciating the glimpses of his old friend that he saw in Evangeline. "We need your help, Lei. We need to know how and when to best access Faerie, and we need to know how to conceal ourselves and navigate it when we're inside."

Lei yawned, because he knew that would set off Evangeline even more. "All those words out of your mouth, and not even a single 'please' among them."

"Don't push your luck. You're the one whose face is plastered on the wanted posters, not us. We could easily give you back to the shamans and let them deal with you."

"Threats," Lei said, nodding in approval. "Julius's teachings, I presume."

Evangeline's glower intensified, and she bared her fangs. Lei refrained from commenting that it was hard for him to take her seriously, as that might make her head explode with anger. She was still the little sister of one of his closest friends, and he doubted he could see her as anything else even if she were made Chancellor. "What happened to that girl you were practically attached at the hip with, by the way? The servant? I'm surprised to see she isn't with you."

Evangeline swallowed hard and looked away. "I asked Cecil to stay behind to attend to affairs at the school."

"Ahh." Of course. The Longs never left any loose ends in their master plans. "And do you think she'll be able to manage?"

Lei hadn't meant to sound as though he was questioning Evangeline's judgment, but she turned back and gave him a cold, defiant stare.

"I believe Cecil will have an *excellent* handle on Earthly Branches affairs."

24
CECIL

Cecil was quickly losing her grasp on the situation at the Academy.

Marcus Niu sat at the high table in the back of the dining hall. This in itself was nothing unusual, except that he didn't sit in his usual spot at the left end of the table. Instead, he chose the seat right in the middle—Julius's usual spot, which should now belong to Evangeline. All eyes were on him as he lounged, putting his feet up on the table and leaning back in the chair. Max was standing right behind his brother, hands folded behind his back, a gloating look on his face.

Cecil's vision nearly went black with anger at the sight of that pigheaded Marcus. How dare he disrespect Julius's memory with this display, when Julius had only been gone for a few days? Fury propelled her legs forward; Cecil was moving rapidly toward Marcus before she'd even thought through what she was doing. That coveted position had belonged to *Julius* for so long, and rightfully should go to Evangeline next.

"Look at that. The Nius have officially declared war," murmured Delilah Hou to her table of eagerly watching friends.

"Can we even call it a war, if Evangeline isn't present to do anything about it?" snickered Brian Ji.

"Oh, don't say that. Evangeline's lackey will surely do something about it."

Cecil shot a cold glare at the occupants of the table. Sure, some of her classmates doubtless thought it was pathetic how she was at Evangeline's beck and call, but Cecil didn't care. Let them say what they liked. Delilah and Brian just stared back at her, their eyes alight with anticipation and bloodlust. They wanted to see Cecil react to their taunts, to Marcus's blatant show of disrespect against the Longs. They wanted a fight. Well, they could forget it. Her usual stare of intimidation wasn't working, and even if she could thwart any of them when it came to academics, that hardly mattered in a situation where a brute like Marcus would overpower her with sheer force alone.

Still, Cecil couldn't back down from Marcus. How could she face her xiǎo jiě if, upon her return, Marcus had taken over Earthly Branches Academy completely unchallenged?

Cecil strode straight up to Marcus, who sneered at her. He'd already rallied a group of Descendants to his side, not unlike the way Julius had gathered his Talons—and speaking of Talons, it seemed a couple of them had already betrayed Julius in death. Kenny Shu and James Gou regarded Cecil's approach with guilty expressions on their faces, and they were the first to break eye contact with her.

Cowards, Cecil thought savagely. *Traitors.* They should at the very least feel the shame of their actions. Besides, she trusted that the karmic justice of the universe would take care of Kenny, James, and any other Talon stupid enough to betray Julius, even in memory. They had sworn vows, after all, and vows were serious among the Descendants. Knowing Julius, he had gone to great lengths to ensure that a painful magical punishment would meet any of his followers who turned their backs on him and the Long family. No, Cecil only needed to concentrate on the biggest, most obnoxious problem at hand.

"A pig sitting on a throne isn't any less of a pig," Cecil said as soon as she'd reached the table. At her words, a chorus of "oohs" rose from the crowd of onlookers.

Marcus seemed so unaffected by the insult that she might as well have complimented him. He let out a sigh and lazily rolled his neck, letting his head rest to one side. "Oh, Cecil, Cecil, Cecil. Aren't you tired of doing the Longs' dirty work for them? Even in their absence, you're forced to bear their public humiliation in their stead, like some common lapdog."

"At least I know what it means to be loyal," Cecil snarled. At that, Kenny and James flinched, and the laughter around Marcus died down. She stepped closer, staring him down. "Need I remind you, Marcus? Centuries ago, the eleven other Descendant bloodlines swore loyalty to the dragon bloodline. The House of Dragon has always led us. Evangeline Long still lives, so this seat should belong to *her.*"

"The words of old fools from centuries ago mean very little in the present day," Marcus growled. Now he leaned forward, eyes flashing, and it took every last ounce of Cecil's willpower not to stumble backward. She could say what she wanted about Marcus's loyalty and class, but even she could not deny that the bastard exuded an aura of power that could easily ensnare those with little will of their own.

"Careful what you say," Cecil warned. "Those are our ancestors of whom you speak."

"And are they here with us in this room? Are they the ones affected by what happens in the here and now?" Marcus spread out his arms. When Cecil didn't respond, his smirk widened. "The Descendants used to be so much more powerful than this. You know it's true. Yet under Julius's lackluster leadership, we have become irrelevant and pathetic."

"As you very well know, we lost our power when the foreigners stole our fountainheads and broke the Circle of Twelve," Cecil said. "Not because of Julius's leadership."

Continuing as though he hadn't heard, Marcus said, "The humans don't know of our existence, of our might. They should worship and revere us. But that will never happen if all we do is stay tucked away at this silly little school." Now he raised his voice and cast his gaze around the room, as though making sure his words were heard all around the dining hall, though there was no need; he'd long since captured the rapt attention of the student body. "And there's not a doubt in my mind that if Evangeline Long were allowed to take over leadership, we would continue to exist in irrelevance. In fact, I suspect she would be even less capable than her dunce of a brother. Recall the warning of the faerie Seer's prophecy: *The key to restoring glory rests with Midsummer's sprout; but if greed sows discord, harmony will be in doubt.* Should Evangeline return, disaster is likely to follow."

"That's *not* what that prophecy means at all," Cecil protested. "If anything, it's *your* greed that will sow discord among us, Marcus. How can you not see that?" A tinge of desperation crept into her voice, in spite of her best efforts to keep it out. It was like being trapped in a nightmare in which only Cecil could see the truth for what it was, and despite her shouting valiantly to try to get everyone else to see reason, they were all too far gone. Indeed, nobody was paying Cecil any mind. Several of the Descendants around them nodded at Marcus.

"So, going by your own logic . . . it would be better if Evangeline didn't return at all, correct?" Marcus said.

"You're putting words into my mouth," Cecil fumed. "How about we talk about the *discord* that *you* are sowing among the Descendants? Ganging up on the human Descendants? Really, Marcus?"

Marcus raised an eyebrow. "I haven't ordered anyone to gang up on the humans."

"Maybe you haven't ordered it directly, but some are taking your beliefs and running with them. We all know you look down on the human Descendants. I won't allow *anyone* to bully them while I'm around."

"Bully? That's a strong word."

"It's apt," Cecil threw back. Marcus's eyes rolled up to the ceiling, but

Cecil wasn't done. If Marcus was goading her to unload her opinion of him, oh, she would do so *gladly*. She only had over a century's worth of pent-up grievances to unleash. "You are a bully. You are far too brash and impulsive to lead the Descendants. Additionally, you are unempathetic and unkind. I will admit that you are charismatic, but as you lack every other trait that *does* make for a good leader, that makes you supremely unfit for the position of Chancellor."

"Oh, don't hold back, my dear Cecil. Please tell me exactly what you think of me," Marcus said sarcastically.

"I warn you now—do not try to oppose Evangeline, Marcus Niu, because you will come to sorely regret it."

"We don't listen to Evangeline anymore, Cecil," growled Brian Ji, who'd been standing in the shadows near Marcus but now stepped forward.

Cecil cocked her head. Brian had always struck her as one of the more spineless Descendants, and he had never even dared to squeak in Evangeline's presence. "I beg your pardon?"

"You still don't get it. You and Evangeline have no say among the Descendants any longer." Brian shook his head solemnly and spoke as though he thought he were doing Cecil a favor with his words. "If I were you, I'd get out of here before things get worse."

"Things get worse?"

Almost as though to illustrate Brian's words, screams erupted from somewhere else in the school—the courtyard, Cecil guessed.

"It's starting." A cold, twisted smile stretched slowly across Marcus's face, and Cecil thought she had never witnessed such a frightening sight in her life. An ice-cold shiver ran down her spine as she realized that nobody, not even one Descendant, had moved a muscle in the dining hall, had spoken up in Evangeline's and Cecil's defense. A terrifying realization took hold.

Brian was right. They were already too late to stop Marcus.

Before Cecil could react, somebody grabbed her arm. "What—?" She turned around, brushing the person off her arm, and found herself face to face with the tall, curly-haired Evelyn Lai, one of Julius's Talons. Evelyn just shook her head at Cecil.

"Leave, Cecil," Marcus said softly. "Unless you'd like to pledge your allegiance to me. I promise I'll be a better leader than Evangeline."

"Never!" Cecil shouted. She cast one last angry look at Marcus, but he'd already turned his attention from her and was conversing with Kenny. So Cecil let Evelyn pull her out of the dining hall, ignoring the stares and whispers from the student body on her way out. With every bit of space she put between Marcus and herself, Cecil calmed down a little more, but her ego grew more bruised with each step as well. Walking away felt like admitting defeat.

Outside, the remainder of the original eight Talons were gathered. Now there were six. Cecil stared from face to determined face, putting to them the names she knew. From left to right, there were Xavier, Stephanie, Megan, Louis, Gina. And, of course, Evelyn.

When the door had closed behind her and it was certain that only Cecil and the Talons occupied these halls, Cecil asked, "What is it?"

The Talons moved in unison. They all got down on their left knee, the knuckles of their right fist pressed down into the concrete—a gesture of absolute obedience that she'd only seen them use with Julius.

Cecil gasped and took a small step backward. Whatever she might have guessed the Talons wanted with her, it wasn't this. Cecil had spent her entire life bowing to others, and she had never expected anyone might bow to *her*. Surely there was some mistake. Perhaps the Talons had gone mad with their grief over Julius's passing. "Wh-What are you doing? Get up!"

"We will follow you, Cecil Long, even if it means leaving the other Descendants for the moment," Evelyn said, and she did not lift her head. "Julius's last orders to us were to remain loyal to the Longs and those in their care. With Evangeline gone, you are the only one we can turn to."

Louis spoke next. "We, the remaining Talons, swore a vow of loyalty to the Longs. We would never turn our backs on them, even if our own blood chose otherwise, and we condemn the heathens who would breach their trust," he said, not bothering to conceal the contempt in his voice. Though he mentioned no names, it was obvious to whom he referred.

"May the traitors burn in Hell," Stephanie growled.

"Your wish is our command, Cecil," said Xavier.

A swell of gratitude rose inside Cecil. She was not typically expressive about what she felt, given that she'd been trained practically from birth to believe that her thoughts and feelings were worth so much less than those of the people she served. Even if Julius and Evangeline had never treated her as such, and never openly condemned any displays of emotion, Cecil had always challenged *herself* to keep that poker face. But now, even for Cecil, it was difficult to contain the rush of emotion, of gratitude and relief. After days of increasing isolation, watching the Long name lose relevance among the Descendants while there was little she could do about it, Cecil allowed the flame of hope to flare inside her once more.

"Thank you. I . . . this is an honor. But please do rise," she managed to choke out.

The Talons obeyed, getting to their feet. That was when something struck Cecil as odd. Everyone at school knew that the Talons had been grieving. They had been wearing white, the color of mourning, every day since Julius's passing, their faces pulled long in identical expressions of misery and gloom. She gave the six Talons the once-over, not caring that a few of them seemed to be uncomfortable under her piercing gaze. *Strange* . . . They still wore their white clothing, but no longer did they appear to be holding back tears. Rather, their faces were tightened with determination and purpose, as though they were soldiers about to charge into battle. These were the Talons Cecil knew—and, inexplicably, they were back.

"What is it?" Cecil asked sharply. "What's happened? Something has changed, and you're keeping me in the dark." She was not used to speaking with such authority, but a sense of power rushed through her as she did so, and then a dangerous, enticing thought rose in her mind. She could quite enjoy being in a position of power if she were allowed to get used to it.

For a moment, the Talons looked at one another.

"You're right. Something *has* changed. We will need to move quickly," said Evelyn. "Moments ago, we received a message indicating that all is not lost. And all is not as it appears to be, Cecil. Because . . ."

Cecil stared at Evelyn in wonder. Evelyn leaned closer and whispered in her ear, and her words changed the game forever.

25
LEI

After sitting in a prison cell for seven years, Lei had grown very, *very* tired of sitting around. However, it seemed that he'd have to endure it a little while longer. The Descendants were cobbling together their plan to infiltrate Faerieland—and if there was one thing Lei could attest to, it was that one needed a detailed, surefire plan of entry and exit before any kind of attempt.

"It feels like too long since we left Earthly Branches Academy," Evangeline said, more to herself than to the others. She bit her lip and crossed her arms over her chest. "Surely Marcus is seizing this chance to take the title of Chancellor for himself."

"Is he, now?" Lei asked. "What do you think are the odds that he'll succeed?"

The others shot him furious looks, and Lei realized he probably shouldn't have sounded so mild about the matter.

"We can't worry too much about what Marcus is doing at the school," Nicholas said gently. "It's out of our hands."

"If I may," Lei said, raising a hand, "I propose that we forgo this school drama for the moment, though I have no doubt that it is very important business. There's a more pressing matter at hand."

"You're both right." Flushing, Evangeline turned away and ran her fingers through her hair. "We can't be bothered by Marcus's hypothetical movements. It doesn't matter if he charms the whole student body—his words won't measure up to my actions. As long as we can pull off this heist, we'll hold the upper hand against Marcus no matter what."

Nicholas reached out to place his hand on Evangeline's arm. She gave him a tight-lipped smile. Alice looked upon the gesture with a slight frown, and Tristan rolled his eyes. Interesting development here. Though no words were exchanged, Lei thought he'd already deciphered the dynamic between these members of Evangeline's crew.

"Lei—your memory of Faerie," Evangeline said, addressing him so suddenly that he started. "How good is it? We'll need a map, or at least a basic sketch of the lay of the land, so we know exactly where we're going. I have a vague idea, but it won't compare to the eyes of someone who's been there."

Lei licked his lips. "You're in luck. My memory is one of the sharpest parts about me. It's one of the main reasons I made such a good spy, you see."

"If you were such a good spy, why did you get caught and thrown into prison?" Tristan murmured.

Lei took a deep breath and counted to ten. For the sake of Evangeline, and the memory of his dear old friend Julius, he would let Tristan's snarky little comment slide, just this once. "Pen and paper, please." Lei held out his hand expectantly but was met with blank stares from the others.

"Who would bring along a pen and paper for a heist?" Tristan said incredulously. "I don't even bring them to class."

"That's nothing to brag about," said Nicholas with a frown. He reached inside his pockets and fished out a sharp pocketknife. "Will this do, Lei?"

Lei was already eyeing the wooden table behind Nicholas. He nodded and took the pocketknife. Then, pressing the tip of the knife into the table's surface, he began to carve the Faerie of his memories, which still haunted his dreams almost every night. The wooden table gave way quite easily beneath the pressure of the knife and Lei's strength.

"So, we're going to have to make our move at the Midsummer Celebration," Lei explained as he began to trace the lands of Faerie onto the table. "It's our best bet for sneaking in, with the distraction of the Celebration going on. There's an entry into Faerie in the Forest of Illusions. . . ."

Within a few minutes, it was done. Lei stood back and admired his handiwork. There it was, spread out in front of him as it had existed in his memory for the past seven years. The Forest of Illusions. The three lower Courts: Dawn, Dusk, Day. The palace of the High Court, across the River of Forgetting. The treasure room, with a back door that led to the Endless Wood.

"Lei?"

He looked up. Evangeline was tilting her head to the side and giving him a strange look. "What?"

"You're trembling."

He glanced down. "Oh." So he was, his fingers shaking as they gripped the knife. He set it down gently and pressed his hands together behind his back. Even now, Lei's body recalled the rush of adrenaline he'd experienced each time he entered Faerie. When the moment had passed and he'd more or less collected himself, he picked up the knife again and stabbed it straight down into the circle he'd drawn to represent the High Court.

"Every year, the High Court displays its finest treasures as centerpieces of the Midsummer Celebration. The five zodiac fountainheads will be a part of that display, per tradition. I've seen it with my own eyes. If the ceremonial arrangements are as I recall, there will be a small window of time—a handful of hours—during which the fountainheads will be brought out of a vault into the treasure room of the palace." He lifted the knife and drew an X at the back of the circle. "In that time, we'll need to break into the room and steal them. Then we'll exit here." Lei carved a line out from the X. "The Endless Wood will lead us back to the human world through the Metropolitan Museum of Art. And then . . ." He trailed off and raised his eyebrows at Evangeline. "How exactly do we plan on hauling five long-lost treasures through the museum and the streets of Manhattan, without attracting all sorts of unwanted attention to ourselves?"

"You'd be surprised," Nicholas muttered. "It won't be the craziest thing anyone sees that day in the city."

"I asked Cecil to drive the car up to the museum already," Evangeline answered swiftly, as though Nicholas hadn't said anything. "It'll be parked and ready for our immediate departure. One of us will likely have to go ahead of the others to bring it around, though. Nicholas?" She held out her left hand, a set of car keys dangling from her fingers.

Without missing a beat, Nicholas nodded and took the keys from Evangeline.

"You really think the heist will be that simple?" Tristan gave Lei an incredulous look. "We just waltz into the Court, grab the things, and then leave?"

"Most heists are actually quite simple smash-and-grab jobs," Nicholas piped up. "I read a book about it once."

Evangeline shook her head, frowning. "We can't 'smash and grab' the High Court. If it were as simple as a matter of lifting the statues, Julius would have taken care of it ages ago. No, it's more complicated than that. There's a prophecy stating that the only one who can take back the zodiac fountainheads is 'Midsummer's sprout' . . . Julius believed that was me, the only Descendant born on Midsummer's Day. I'll go steal the fountainheads on my own."

Evangeline's pronouncement was followed by a long pause. Judging by the mixture of confusion and surprise on the others' faces, this was the first time anyone was hearing about this.

"No, you're not going in alone. It's too dangerous for you to go in and steal the fountainheads by yourself," Tristan said immediately.

"You can't help me with that part of the Assignment," Evangeline fired back. She tilted her chin up, and with a pang, Lei recognized Julius's stubbornness in her pose. "You might be more of a hindrance than a help. And I am perfectly capable of navigating a dangerous situation on my own, thanks."

Nicholas cleared his throat. "I know you like your independence, Evangeline, but you should accept help in such important matters. It's not that we don't believe you're capable of going in alone. We just want to make sure we can protect you as much as possible. If you're caught . . . I don't even want to think of what the Folk would do to you for stealing from them." He shuddered.

"It's hardly stealing if those fountainheads belonged to *us* in the first place," Evangeline fumed.

"On that, we all agree," Nicholas said in a placating tone, "but the fact of the matter is, we'll be trespassing upon their territory, breaking a decades-old treaty, and nicking something they've considered *theirs* for a good while now. We need to cover our asses as much as we can."

To that, Evangeline seemed unable to offer any argument. She fell silent. When she spoke again, it was to change the topic.

"I think . . . I think we've covered all the bases as best we can," she finally said as she stared down at the detailed map, her hands hugging each side of the table. "There's only so much we can try to predict, anyway." She rubbed her brow as though trying to get rid of a headache. When she lifted her head, her eyes were darkened.

While the others' expressions reflected Evangeline's exhaustion, Lei was practically buzzing with the anticipation of stealing precious artifacts from within Faerieland, his palms sweating with excitement. It had been seven years since he'd set foot among the fae. Then, he'd been a spy for them, welcomed into their midst. This time, he'd be returning to move *against* them. If he was caught—if any of them were caught—Lei couldn't even imagine what horrors the fae might inflict on intruders who were set upon stealing from them. His pulse quickened; his mouth dried; his vision blurred. Lei had not felt so very alive in so very long, not since he was caught by the shamans and thrown into prison. For the first time in ages, he was drawing a full breath of air. This was the adrenaline rush that had led him down the twisted path of espionage, and once again it was taking him down a dangerous road. Any fool with half a brain and his wits about him would back out while there was still time. But Lei could not find it in his nature to turn back.

"Let's run through everything once more," Evangeline was saying for the umpteenth time.

A groan from Tristan. "How many times do we have to go over the same exact plan? Aren't you sick of it already?"

"We'll go over the plan as many times as it takes to ensure you don't mess up, Tristan," Evangeline said sharply. Her voice had departed slightly from its usual brisk, businesslike tone; Lei heard a tremor in it, and he wondered if anyone else noticed. She was masking her nerves—and failing. Of course. At present, Evangeline stood to lose the most if they failed in their mission, for the Longs would be sure to fall from power, and what would Evangeline do then? How would she answer to all the people Julius had wronged and offended when he was alive?

"You can make digs about my ability all you want, but it was *your* call to recruit me for your heist, so criticizing me is a mark on *your* judgment," Tristan retorted.

Lei was not the emotional type, but pity rose within him at the sight of Evangeline pacing back and forth on the floor. *Oh, Julius. Are you watching from wherever you are—Hell, most likely? Do you see what your untimely death has done to your poor sister?*

"As I was saying," Evangeline continued, "the Midsummer Celebration is our best shot at infiltrating Faerie—and we can't miss it. We'll take advantage of the influx of guests to slip in and steal the zodiac fountainheads. We'll use every moment until then to hammer out a detailed plan of action, as well as a backup plan."

"It won't be as easy to penetrate Faerie as it was to break me out of the Underground," Lei warned. "Not that that was easy, either, I imagine. We'll need to be thoroughly disguised, and we'll need to constantly keep our wits about us. No eating or drinking in Faerie; that stuff will make the human mind go mad, and though I haven't tested it for myself, I imagine the rest of us supernaturals would suffer a similar fate." He joined Evangeline in pacing around the room as he spoke. Already he was antsy, ready to leave this safe house. Lei had gone from one small, cramped, dusty space to another, and after this Assignment was finished, he'd like never to find himself in one again. It would be a miracle if he didn't develop claustrophobia at the end of all this. "How long do you mean for us to stay hidden in this safe house, Evangeline?"

"It's not safe for us out there," Evangeline said. "In case you hadn't noticed, you're an escaped prisoner from the Underground, and the Jingwei know that you fled somewhere into the city—into Chinatown, specifically. The shamans will most likely have alerted the Descendants by now. And until we've completed this Assignment, I can't show my face around the other Descendants, either."

"I could disguise us," Nicholas offered.

"You should conserve your strength for when we enter Faerie. We'll need perfect disguises then."

Nicholas opened his mouth to retort, but after a moment he seemed to think better of it and instead just turned away. Lei glanced more carefully at the boy. There were alarmingly dark circles under his eyes, and his cheeks were sunken.

The one to break the silence was Tristan, who was peering at Evangeline in concern. "Evangeline . . . is everything all right?"

Evangeline had been staring at Alice a little too intensely to be natural—more specifically, at Alice's neck.

"Is there something on my face?" Alice asked.

Lei studied Evangeline more closely, and he noticed the changes as they happened. Evangeline's pupils widened. The veins in her neck and face grew dark and taut beneath her skin. Fangs protruded from her mouth. Lei had spent enough time around the cursed Descendants, particularly the vampires, to know the warning signs of uncontrollable bloodlust—and he wasted no time in acting. He dove in front of Alice at the same time Tristan grabbed for Evangeline, and not a moment too soon.

Evangeline growled and leapt in Alice's direction, but she was held back by Tristan's grip.

"Get the blood bags, Nicholas!" Tristan shouted. "Lei, help me pin her down."

"Ask me nicely next time, please," Lei said. Normally he'd refuse to be ordered around, but Evangeline looked like she might actually eat Alice—or them—if they wasted any time arguing among themselves. When vampires reached this point of hunger, Lei knew, it was impossible to reason with them until they got enough blood in their system to come back to themselves. Evangeline's eyes had turned fully black, and she was snarling at them like a feral beast. She didn't know them any longer. Before Tristan could react, Evangeline managed to wrench her arm out of his grip, and her fist collided with the side of his head.

"Ow!" Tristan yelled.

The momentary loss of Tristan's strength left too much for Lei to handle. Evangeline practically bowled him over as she charged toward Alice, upending a table in the process.

"Stop—Evangeline—" Lei shouted through gritted teeth, and was relieved when Tristan rushed back into the fray. Slowly, ever so slowly, the two managed to drag Evangeline back, away from the terrified Alice.

It took all of Lei's and Tristan's combined and considerable strength to knock the snarling, kicking Evangeline to the floor. Lei kept one hand on her forehead, pinning her head down so she couldn't bite them. The other hand was busy holding down her arm, keeping her sharp nails far away from his skin so she couldn't scratch him. Tristan grabbed hold of her other arm and both of her legs.

"Quickly, Nicholas!" Lei shouted.

Nicholas had been much slower to react, open shock on his face. He snapped into action at Lei's words, though, and brought the blood bag to Evangeline's face. She gulped several times, drinking until the bag was nearly empty. About a minute later, she went slack beneath Tristan and

Nicholas, all the fight now out of her body. Her pupils slowly shrank, revealing the whites of her eyes once more.

"I . . . What just . . ." Evangeline managed to croak out. She brought a trembling hand up to her mouth and wiped away excess blood. A look of horror slowly dawned on her face. She glanced over at Alice. Poor Alice was partially hidden behind Nicholas, her face so drained of color that she might have been a vampire herself. "I . . . I'm so sorry. I didn't realize I needed blood, I—I must have used up too much energy in the Underground . . ."

"It's all right." Tristan was the first to break the heavy, tense silence. "It's not really your fault."

Lei thought he was speaking for himself, too, not just Evangeline.

"I'm really sorry, Alice." Evangeline could hardly look at the girl, but there was real remorse in her expression. *Remorse. Such an uncommon emotion to spot on a Long's face,* Lei thought. "It won't happen again."

"It's fine," Alice said quickly, but everyone knew she was saying it just to smooth over the situation.

A short, heavy silence filled the room. Evangeline's normally sleek hair was a tangled mess now, and she wouldn't make eye contact with anyone. Lei had never seen her look so low.

"Well, I do think we should all take some time to refuel. I don't suppose there's anything to eat in this safe house, is there?" said Lei, hoping to lighten the mood somewhat.

Tristan glared at him, and Nicholas gave him a side-eye. Perhaps that hadn't worked as well as he imagined it in his head.

"We brought some food," Evangeline offered, sending Nicholas a meaningful look.

Nicholas took off his shoulder pack and rummaged through it, then paused. He raised his head, frowning. "Everything is gone except for your blood bags, Evangeline."

"Everything?" Alice gasped. She'd regained some color in her cheeks; perhaps she, and the others, were ready to move past this incident after all. "Who would have eaten so much in such a short time?"

All eyes turned to Tristan, who, at that precise moment, happened to be unwrapping a protein bar. He stared back at everyone in defiance. "What? I'm *terribly* sorry that I don't have the appetite of a bird, like the rest of you."

Nicholas groaned. "You've been snacking nonstop!"

"And we've been on the run nonstop, so forgive me if my body requires more sustenance than just fumes and vibes—"

"Please don't fight. I can go buy food for everyone," Alice interjected. "I'm the least recognizable one here—I don't think the other Descendants even know who I am. Just tell me what you want."

"It's dangerous," Evangeline warned.

"It'll be more dangerous if we try to infiltrate Faerie without our full strength," Tristan pointed out. There was nothing for Evangeline to say to that, so she just pursed her lips instead. That seemed to settle the matter. "I'll take the meatiest dish you can find, Alice. Preferably a rare steak."

"A rare steak? In Chinatown? Really, Tristan?" Nicholas said.

Tristan rolled his eyes. "But if you can't find that, any beef dish will do. Thanks."

"Get me whatever," Lei chimed in with a wave of his hand. "I'll eat anything." After years of subsisting on little more than stale rice, steamed vegetables, and dry chicken, anything Alice could find in Chinatown would be a massive step up for Lei's diet. He would kill for a pork bun right now.

Alice turned to Nicholas. "And what do you want?"

"I'll just come with you," he said immediately.

Evangeline frowned. Lei could tell that she didn't like the idea of two of them splitting off from the others, but what other choice was there? Lei was famished, and if *he* was this hungry despite the meal he'd had a mere hour before he was broken out of prison, he hated to think of how the others were feeling.

"Fine," Evangeline said at long last. "Make it quick and discreet. And be careful."

26
NICHOLAS

Secretly, Nicholas was glad of an excuse to get out of the safe house. Not only was the place stuffy and dusty, but he also had to put up with Tristan's infuriating presence. It was a shame that they had to leave Evangeline behind, but there wasn't much to be done about that—Evangeline, who even before Julius's death had been famous among the Descendants, was easily the most recognizable of the group. There was still a small chance Nicholas and Alice could be recognized, but it was a risk they would have to take in order to have the strength to finish the Assignment.

As he and Alice stepped into the busy streets, Nicholas threw his hood up over his head. He pulled a pair of sunglasses out of his pocket and tapped Alice on the shoulder. When she turned around, he placed them over her eyes.

"What?" she asked, startled.

"I don't think anyone would recognize you, but we can't be too careful."

Alice nodded, the motion making the shades slip down her nose.

They were at least a size too big for her face and looked nothing short of ridiculous on her, but Nicholas couldn't help but smile. There was something so innocent and endearing about Alice; she reminded him of a newborn lamb. He was afraid that if he didn't look out for her, she'd wander into the jaws of a wolf.

"Has Evangeline done that before?" Alice asked quietly.

Nicholas stopped walking. He closed his eyes. The question brought back a memory he didn't want to recall—the time a starving Evangeline had killed and injured many people in a crowded subway car. It was a memory that had haunted her for so long, and it had haunted him, too. He knew what it was like to have your body betray you, and for it to cost you and everyone around you dearly. "Only once. Evangeline is usually very good about controlling her bloodlust. This Assignment . . . it's really testing all of us. I know Evangeline well, and I know she won't let it happen again." Nicholas quickly added, "But I understand if you'd like to quit and go back to the Academy. Nobody will judge you. You've already been a massive help to us."

For a moment, Alice said nothing. She didn't look at Nicholas; rather, she looked past him, at a new high-rise development in the distance. "I'm not quitting," she said finally. "I knew I was risking my neck when I agreed to join. I'm not doing this Assignment just to help you all out, you know."

"Aren't you?"

Alice turned away and didn't respond to the question, which piqued his curiosity. So there *was* more to this girl than met the eye. Nicholas had been right in his assessment of Alice back at the Long estate; she was indeed a closed-off girl with a hidden fiery spirit, and he, for one, was excited to find out more about what lay underneath.

"Well, if it makes a difference, I'm glad to have you along." Nicholas raised his head and glanced down Canal Street. There were a dumpling place, a noodle house, and a dim sum restaurant. Unless they dared venture beyond this street, the odds of procuring rare steak for Tristan seemed exceptionally low. *Not* that Nicholas felt like trying very hard. He'd seen Tristan eat just about everything under the sun in the school dining hall, and it seemed he never lacked the strength to fight—physically or verbally. Even now, Tristan still had the energy to piss off Nicholas every hour or so; surely he could get by on whatever meal they gave him. And if not, maybe it would be an improvement for the group's morale if Tristan lost the energy to be so annoying.

"Are you okay with dumplings?" Alice asked, and Nicholas sensed she was done talking about the incident with Evangeline. "They should be ready pretty quickly. And we can get beef dumplings for Tristan."

"Yeah, sure, I'll eat whatever," Nicholas replied absently. Aside from the werewolves' preference for bloody, hearty meats, the other supernaturals could get by on little sustenance for sustained periods. That was a distinct advantage they had over the humans—they weren't ruled by their stomachs. Imagine how unstoppable humans would be if they didn't have to pause to eat every few hours.

Nicholas cast a look around at the passersby. The shaman guards appeared to be long gone. Perhaps he was being paranoid. For all anyone knew, the Jingwei were still stuck below the vent hatch, trying to find a way around Lei's magic. He relaxed his stance slightly as Alice opened the door to Chu's Dumpling House.

Nicholas was greeted with the smell of fried food and something spicy, and the sounds of loud chatter in the kitchens and among the patrons. Mercifully, the line for dumplings was short; Nicholas suspected this was because it was late morning, not quite lunchtime yet.

After Alice ordered the food, Nicholas insisted on paying, despite her best attempts to shove his credit card away.

"You didn't have to fight me for the bill," she grumbled as they took their spot waiting near the takeout counter.

"I have decades of experience over you in fighting others for the bill. You're way too green to win over me," Nicholas said with a small grin. He expected that to make Alice laugh. Instead, her expression became a bit sullen, and she averted her gaze to watch the tank of fish near the entrance.

Nicholas's smile slipped off his face. He'd just been trying to cheer her up; why did his words seem to have the opposite effect? Perhaps he wasn't half as charming as he wanted to be. He thought back to what he'd said, wondering if he'd accidentally insulted her. No, he hadn't, he was sure of it. So then *why?* He racked his brains. He seriously didn't think he'd ever understand girls.

"Are you upset?" he blurted out. It was best to be direct.

"No," Alice said quietly, continuing to knit her eyebrows together and look, for all Nicholas could tell, quite upset.

"I would've let you pay the bill if I knew you'd be this upset over it."

"I told you, I'm not upset. I'm just . . . I have a lot on my mind right now. And I'm starving."

Ah. That explained it. It had been so long since Nicholas had possessed such basic human instincts, but he still recalled that any little thing could set him off when he was hangry.

When their number was called, he smoothly grabbed the three bags of food. They were heavier than expected, but nothing he couldn't handle after several decades of strength training. "This should be more than enough."

"At least give me one bag to carry," Alice insisted, holding out her hand.

Before Nicholas could find a way to politely decline, the door dinged, and in swept a group of four men wearing shades. This would not have been a particularly noteworthy event—except that the men, though unfamiliar to Nicholas, gazed upon him and Alice for a moment too long, as though they found *them* familiar.

Instinctively, Nicholas flashed a megawatt smile at the men, but this had practically no effect on them as they advanced.

Time slowed as Nicholas broke down the scene before him, warning bells going off in his head. One of the advantages of being cursed into a fox spirit was that Nicholas's senses were extra sharp, his reflexes superhumanly fast. He noticed things others did not. He noticed, for example, that the man in the front had his left hand in his pocket and was clutching a hidden object—an object that was almost certain to be a weapon. He also observed that these men were wearing black suits on a rather hot day, and based on appearances alone, they did not fit the casual clientele that frequented Chu's Dumpling House. Therefore, Nicholas conjectured that these men had been sent here on a mission that had nothing to do with eating cheap dumplings and everything to do with the people they were staring at—Nicholas and Alice.

No, Nicholas realized, they weren't staring at him. They were completely fixated on Alice alone.

Once, Nicholas had frozen on the spot when he needed to act—and his inaction had cost his people everything. Fear and adrenaline spiked in Nicholas's heart. Hesitation could decide his fate—and Nicholas, at last, was tired of his racing thoughts trapping his body.

"Get the girl," growled the man in the front.

All of this happened within a fraction of a second. And another fraction of a second was all Nicholas needed to respond in kind.

He had no time to overthink or question his abilities.

"Hang on to me," he whispered to Alice, the only warning he had time to give.

First, he dropped one of the bags of dumplings—he hoped it was the beef dumplings; Tristan would have to get along without, what a *shame*—to free up one of his hands. With the freed hand, he grabbed hold of Alice's arm, spinning himself around so that his body was shielding hers. Keeping his balance perfectly centered, he put his left shoe through the handle of the abandoned dumpling bag. He swung his leg up and around, pelting the group of men with fresh dumplings.

With a cry, the man in front threw his arms up to shield his face from the piping-hot dumplings. His suit sleeve shifted to reveal skin, and Nicholas glimpsed familiar black ink that ran down his inner forearm, in the shape of a rat. It only took him another second to register where he'd seen that arm before. Multiple times, in fact, in combat lessons and around the dorms. That arm belonged to Kenny Shu, one of the Descendants and a fellow fox spirit, and one of Julius's Talons.

What the hell's the House of Rat doing here? Nicholas thought. *More importantly, why do they look like they're here to cause trouble?* The House of Rat had always been one of the staunchest allies of the House of Dragon. Nicholas couldn't make out any other Descendants among their would-be attackers, but he had no doubt there were several more with Kenny; for all he knew, they were *all* Descendants. Even if Kenny hadn't meant for any of their identities to be revealed, this was as good as a declaration of treachery and war against the House of Dragon.

Well, Nicholas would have to demonstrate, in the Longs' stead, exactly how the House of Dragon dealt with traitors.

"Hey!" The employee who'd handed them the dumplings began cursing in Mandarin, and a few customers screamed and ducked away.

"What are you *doing?*" Alice cried, but there was no time or breath to waste explaining.

Nicholas leapt into the air and landed a spinning kick on Kenny's head. At the last moment Kenny managed to sidestep and avoid taking the kick full-on, but he still buckled under Nicholas's kick with a groan. Nicholas wasn't given a moment to recover; the three remaining men were charging at him in the blink of an eye. He dove onto his hands, aimed his body at a gap between two of them, and rolled forward in a somersault. The men, who'd built up too much momentum to be able to stop, crashed into one another, their heads colliding with a sickening thud.

More screaming ensued. The remaining patrons scrambled for the door. The indignant owner was shouting in Cantonese. Though most of the man's speech was unintelligible, Nicholas recognized that he was cursing and threatening to call the police. Nicholas imagined trying to explain to Evangeline how their "quick and discreet" trip to get food had turned into being attacked and threatened. Dawdling here for a moment longer was far too dangerous; it was time to make their speedy exit.

Taking advantage of the chaos, Nicholas grabbed Alice's hands and dragged her around the dumpling-covered men and out the exit. They ran through the crowd as fast as they could.

Despite Alice's protests, Nicholas didn't dare slow down until the shouts had long died away. Then he pulled Alice into a back alley behind a local bookstore, where the shadows would give them some extra cover.

Alice opened her mouth, probably to chew him out, but Nicholas placed a finger to his lips and shook his head. She closed her mouth.

Nicholas had been so focused on avoiding the immediate danger that he didn't notice for a moment how close they stood together. His arm was around Alice's shoulder, and her body was pressed against his. He could feel every breath she drew. And though Nicholas didn't like getting close to others, he didn't think he *dis*liked Alice's presence.

The coast seemed to be clear, as Kenny and his henchmen did not come pelting down the streets. In fact, all was relatively quiet around them. The loudest noise was Nicholas's blood thundering in his veins, the sound of his own euphoric thoughts. *I did it. I actually pulled that off.* He'd managed to keep his emotions in control, which meant there had been no risk of fire erupting from his body. His relief was palpable.

He spent a few more moments standing in silence, straining to listen for something, *anything,* to indicate that their attackers were still in hot pursuit. When nothing happened, Nicholas dropped his arm, and he and Alice awkwardly stepped away from each other.

"Do you care to explain yourself now? Wh-Who *were* those people? And why did you throw our dumplings at them?" Alice demanded. She cast a nervous look out into the streets, but there was no sign of the four men.

"I recognized one of them. Kenny Shu."

Alice's eyebrows knit together, as though she was struggling to place the name. "Kenny . . ."

"He's one of Julius's Talons. Or, he *was.*"

"One of the Talons? Shouldn't the Talons be on our side?"

Shouldn't they indeed. "Not necessarily," Nicholas muttered, his thoughts racing a mile a minute. If Kenny and his henchmen had been prepared to attack Nicholas and Alice, when by now it must be common knowledge that they were assisting Evangeline on an Assignment, then that meant the House of Rat was no longer supporting House of Dragon, despite a long history of loyalty. It meant, too, that the Talons could not be counted on to honor their leader's memory in the wake of his death. With each passing moment, Evangeline was actively losing support. And she needed to be informed of this development at once.

Meanwhile, Alice was still bursting with questions. "Why would the Talons be after us?"

"We don't know if it's all of the Talons after us. In fact, I'm willing to bet it's not." Nobody was sure exactly what kind of initiation Julius forced his Talons to undergo, as he'd always insisted on keeping that a mystery, but knowing Julius, there would be a magically enforced clause against betrayal. Kenny was counting his days. "I don't know who was with Kenny or what their goal is, but I know that they're looking for us. For *you,* specifically."

"For me?" Alice's jaw dropped. For a moment, she said nothing else, seemingly at a loss for words. Then: "But . . . why?"

Nicholas's mind raced as he stared at the wide-eyed Alice, trying to make the connection, but he was drawing a blank. Everything he knew about Alice told him she wasn't a threat to . . . anyone, really. In fact, considering that he'd grown up with Descendants who casually engaged in verbal threats and physical harm, Alice was about the least threatening person he'd ever encountered at the school. Nor was she valuable, beyond possessing some intriguing mind-reading abilities. It was just as Alice had said back in the safe house—she was the least conspicuous of the group. Or so everyone believed.

Nicholas narrowed his eyes.

"What are you looking at? Is there something on my face?" Alice raised a hand to her cheek, which had grown flushed. She cast her gaze down, and her curtain of black hair shifted forward, blocking her face from view.

Now Nicholas wasn't sure what to believe. What he *did* know was that

Alice possessed only two remarkable traits: one, the ability to read minds, and two, her relation to Ruiting Jiang, the most powerful human Descendant known to have walked the halls of Earthly Branches Academy.

No, there was something else to this human girl that hadn't yet been uncovered, something so monumental that the House of Rat had gotten involved specifically to target her—likely to abduct her. Judging by the shock in her face, Alice herself had no idea what that might be. If anyone knew anything, it would be Evangeline.

"The safe house," Nicholas said abruptly. "We need to return. Now. And put your shades back on," he added as an afterthought.

Once Alice had done so, Nicholas grabbed her hand once again, holding on even tighter this time. They darted down the streets toward the Longs' safe house, Nicholas keeping his eyes peeled for any sign that they were being tailed. He purposely took a long, winding route through Chinatown back to their destination, to shake off anybody who might be following them. And all the while, his head churned with what he'd learned moments ago.

There must be a secret reason Evangeline had selected Alice for this Assignment, something significant enough that she would overlook her initial dislike of the girl. And now, that reason might have put all of them in grave danger.

27
TRISTAN

Tristan wasn't sure which was more annoying: Lei's snores, which could wake the dead (no wonder his name meant "thunder" in Mandarin), or Evangeline's glower, which would probably melt Tristan's face any second. It was as if that moment they'd shared in the prison sector of the Underground had never happened. In fact, Evangeline was taking every opportunity to throw barbs at him, and it was really, *really* starting to grate on his nerves.

If Evangeline wasn't going to play nice, Tristan wouldn't, either. She clearly believed the worst of him. Why bother trying to change her mind when it was already made up?

"Is there a reason you're staring at me like that?" Tristan asked the question partly because he was curious as to what he'd done wrong *now*, and partly just to provoke Evangeline. The latter was one of his favorite pastimes.

"Staring at you like what?" Evangeline took a slow swig from a blood bag, and Tristan was forced to turn away. Having Evangeline stare at him like that while she was feasting on blood was distinctly unsettling.

"Glaring, really," he said. "Like I've just murdered your puppy."

"If I had a puppy, rest assured it would maul you before you could even think about putting a hand on it," Evangeline retorted. "And I am not *glaring.*"

"Ah, right. That unpleasant look is just your default expression, then."

It seemed Evangeline had bigger concerns on her mind than Tristan's attempts to provoke her into an argument, because she didn't even acknowledge what he'd said. Her forehead was wrinkled in concern, and she'd begun pacing around the small space again. "Nicholas and Alice have been gone for an hour already. It shouldn't take an hour to get food down the street."

"Maybe the lines are long," Tristan suggested. "Or maybe Nicholas lost his nerve about this whole thing and went back home. He's really much more suited for academics."

Evangeline stopped a few feet away from Tristan, her hands on her hips. "*What* is your problem with Nicholas?"

Now it was Tristan's turn to glare. *Nicholas dotes on you, and you don't discourage the behavior, which means you're either secretly madly in love with him or you're leading him on. Either way, it's annoying as hell to watch,* he thought. *You didn't even let* me *dote on you when we were together, and yet you let* him. Not that Tristan would ever say any of this aloud. He wouldn't give Evangeline the satisfaction of knowing how deep his jealousy ran.

"I have absolutely no problem with darling, precious Nicholas," Tristan said, his voice practically dripping with sarcasm. "Nicholas can do no wrong, whereas I can do nothing right, so who am I to judge him?"

Evangeline's brows furrowed. Unless Tristan was mistaken, that was regret that flashed across her face. For a second, he was vindicated; then the moment passed, and he was no more satisfied than before.

"I didn't . . . I never said . . . ," Evangeline muttered, and for once she seemed at a complete loss for words.

Tristan turned away. There was no chance Evangeline didn't know the main reason for the bad blood between him and Nicholas. No, she just wanted Tristan to spell it out, because that was one of Evangeline's many problems that had resulted in their explosive breakup. She could never say aloud exactly what she was implying, and others were meant to interpret her cryptic facial expressions and riddles.

They were slipping into bad habits again. Tristan knew this, but he couldn't help it. It was always like this with Evangeline.

"That's your third blood bag," he said, deciding to change the subject. Evangeline had just finished drinking, and she tossed the empty bag at her feet. "Slow down. We didn't bring along *that* many, you know."

For once, she didn't snap at him with a well-prepared quip. Instead, she wiped her mouth with the back of her hand and stared at the wall.

Evangeline wasn't drinking blood because she was hungry, Tristan realized. She was doing it as though filling up on blood now could somehow make up for what had just happened, in addition to preventing it in the future. She was doing this out of guilt. Tristan knew the feeling all too well. His shoulders slumped. "Everything will get better when we break the curse. I meant what I said earlier, Evangeline. It wasn't your fault. You're doing your best."

Evangeline looked away, but not before Tristan saw that her eyes were shining with tears. He knew that no matter what he said to her, she wouldn't believe it. Evangeline was harder on herself than on anyone else.

They were interrupted by a loud moan from Lei. Tristan glanced over to see that the shaman was sitting up from his awkward sleeping position on the floor. He rubbed his eyes and stretched, yawning. "Would you two care to keep it down, or get a room? Some of us are trying to rest up before we potentially get killed in Faerie."

"Didn't you get enough sleep being locked up for seven years?" Tristan retorted.

Lei flashed Tristan a sardonic smile that didn't reach his eyes. "Oh, you get more charming by the moment. I see why Evangeline hand-selected you for this Assignment."

"Exactly, for the stimulating company," Evangeline deadpanned.

Tristan smirked. If Evangeline was up to bantering with him again, surely that meant her spirits were lifting. "Well, it's not likely you're going to get that from anyone *else* on this cursed—"

The safe house filled with the noise of pounding on the door. All eyes turned toward the front.

"It's us," called a muffled, familiar voice from the other side. "Nicholas and Alice. We're back."

Evangeline strode toward the door. Her hand pressed against it, but she didn't open it. "Prove your identity."

"What?"

"I can't trust that you're not somebody pretending to be Nicholas, so I need you to answer a question only the real Nicholas would know. Where is your birthmark?" she demanded.

"Uh . . ." For a moment, there was no response, but then came Nicholas's quieter voice. "On my left upper thigh."

Evangeline seemed satisfied by this response, because she pressed her palms solidly into the surface of the door, and it opened.

"Left upper thigh," Lei mused, sounding highly entertained by this development. "Now why would you know that, Evangeline?"

Evangeline shot him such a hard look that he turned away and whistled rather than press the matter any further.

Annoyance twinged in Tristan's chest. How *had* Evangeline come to know such private information about Nicholas? Of course, Tristan knew they were close, but he'd had no idea they were *that* close. He gritted his teeth and shook his head to rid himself of the thought. This was not the time or the place to wonder about the relationship between Evangeline and Nicholas. It wasn't his business. It didn't matter.

Nicholas and Alice entered the safe house, both red in the face. Their hair was windswept, too, as though they'd been out for a run. The door closed behind them. While Evangeline sealed it shut again, Nicholas plopped two full bags of food on the table—the one Lei hadn't carved up with his map of Faerie.

"Ah, perfect." Tristan leapt up and made a beeline for the food. Alice was already opening the bags, revealing deliciously steamy dumplings.

Lei let out an audible groan as he stood over the food. "I've never smelled anything so good in my life."

As Alice began serving the dumplings into paper bowls, Tristan sniffed the air and frowned. He smelled pork, vegetables, even shrimp . . . but no beef. "You didn't get any beef dumplings?"

"We did," Nicholas said, avoiding Tristan's eyes, "but, uh . . . sacrifices were made."

"Nicholas threw the beef dumplings at Kenny Shu and some other people who tried to ambush us," Alice blurted out.

"You couldn't have phrased that better?" Nicholas sighed.

This outburst prompted a round of confused questions.

Kenny Shu. Tristan racked his brains. Kenny was one of Julius's diehard Talons. There was no reason for Nicholas to attack Kenny unprovoked, especially given how noncombative Nicholas tended to be.

"Explain," Evangeline said shortly.

After Nicholas and Alice had finished explaining what sounded like a very eventful trip to get food, a horrible, tense silence filled the safe house, broken only by the sound of Lei digging into the dumplings.

Evangeline's face grew redder and redder, and Tristan knew he'd better keep his mouth shut from now on. Evangeline might entertain his quips when she was in a decent mood, but when she was angered like this, teasing her was the same as waving a giant red flag in front of a rampaging bull.

"So the House of Rat has decided to make an enemy out of the House of Dragon, and Kenny has decided to turn his back on Julius's memory," Evangeline seethed. There wasn't much surprise on her face, just cold, frosty disappointment. She had anticipated this development—well, perhaps not *this* specifically, but she had known that the tides of loyalty were shifting. Tristan's heart softened a little. There was no doubt that Evangeline was under a lot of pressure, and even she couldn't keep the little cracks from appearing in her perfect mask.

"So it seems," Nicholas said darkly.

"Well, I'd expect nothing less from the descendants of the *rat*," Lei said with a dismissive wave of his fork. "Julius brought me around his Talons a few times, and I have to say, I never liked the look of that Kenny. Always thought there wasn't much going on upstairs. You're better off without him in the ranks, Evangeline. I wouldn't lose any sleep over this."

Tristan half expected Evangeline to tell Lei off for treating the betrayal of a Talon so lightly, and he was surprised when she nodded in agreement. "If anyone's going to betray Julius—and me—I prefer that they do it early and rambunctiously, like Kenny."

"I don't think he meant to, uh, announce his intentions," said Nicholas. "I think he's just . . . not the sharpest calligraphy pen in the drawer."

"You mean stupid," Lei supplied. He tapped the side of his head. "Like I said—light's on, but nobody's home."

Evangeline pointed accusingly at Nicholas, who stepped back in alarm. "Most importantly—you came here right after that encounter, Nicholas? How can you be sure Kenny and his spineless goons didn't tail you here? You might have put us all in danger."

Nicholas raised his hands defensively. "I made sure to take an erratic route. I don't believe we were followed."

"We didn't see any of them near us," Alice offered.

"Even if you weren't followed, we're no longer safe here—even with the enchantments in place," Tristan interjected. He slid a look toward Evangeline. She was staring down at the table, fists clenched at her sides. He felt he could follow her exact train of thought: If the House of Rat had betrayed the House of Dragon despite decades of support, if Kenny had turned his back on Julius after over a century of steadfast loyalty, then the secret locations of the safe houses were, in all likelihood, no longer secret. However much they'd all had their guards up before, now they needed to raise them even higher.

"Either bring the dumplings along, or finish them now," Evangeline commanded, her head snapping up. There was a sharp, almost manic focus in her eye. "We need to get a move on."

As if on cue, a thumping noise sounded against the door. Everyone in the room froze. Tristan instinctively leapt in front of Evangeline, though he wasn't sure why. She was perfectly capable of protecting herself.

"Evangeline?" came a low voice—Kenny's voice. Kenny was lucky the door to the safe house was between them. Tristan might be a scoundrel in many respects, but he *despised* traitors and their kind. "Come out in peace. We won't hurt you. We just want the human girl."

Tristan was so surprised that he couldn't help but choke. The human girl? Surely they were after Evangeline, not Alice.

"What's her name again?" Tristan heard Kenny hiss at someone. A male voice answered, though too quietly to distinguish the words. "Oh, yes, Alice. Give us Alice, and we'll leave you alone."

Evangeline threw her head back and laughed. The sight was cause for alarm, as Evangeline rarely smiled, almost never laughed, and certainly would do neither because she was actually happy. When Evangeline laughed, it was because some poor fool had pushed her to her wits' end and would come to regret it sorely very soon.

"Oh, Kenny," Evangeline sighed once she was done laughing, caressing the name with her tongue as though he were a lover. "Kenny, Kenny, Kenny. When all this is over, I'm going to take my sweet time killing you."

Tristan stared at the back of Alice's head, bewildered. She stood closer to Nicholas, and he leaned toward her as if in protection. Evangeline bared her fangs but otherwise didn't seem at all thrown that the intruders had asked for Alice and not her. Somewhere, somehow, Tristan had missed a very crucial piece of information.

"I'm sorry, but I'm not following," Tristan said. "What would the other Descendants possibly want with Alice?" What would Kenny want so badly that he'd be willing to betray the Talons for it? Tristan stared at Evangeline hard, as though he might be able to pry the answer out of her with a look alone, but she averted her eyes.

He knew what that meant. Evangeline was hiding something from the rest of them. Something that Kenny somehow knew. Something that the House of Rat was after.

"What do they want with me?" Alice asked. "Should I . . . I don't know, should I go outside and talk to Kenny and them? There's nothing I have that they could possibly want. This all has to be a big misunderstanding."

The incredulous and angry look Evangeline gave her could have made a grown werewolf weep.

"No," Nicholas said firmly at the same time Evangeline responded, "You're not going out, Alice. None of us are."

"Then, please do explain, Evangeline." Tristan didn't bother keeping the frosty edge out of his voice. He was beginning to lose patience. "You asked everyone in this room to put our necks on the line to help you with this Assignment. The least you can do is be transparent with us. It's not fair to anyone, Alice especially, if you're keeping a secret about Alice."

Evangeline whirled on him, eyes turning black with fury, but Tristan held his ground. He was right, and he knew it. How could they protect Alice, protect themselves, if Evangeline was holding back something this important? After a long moment, Evangeline must have sensed that Tristan wouldn't back down and that the others were waiting to hear a proper answer, too. She turned her back to him and crossed her arms over her chest.

"Everyone knows that Alice is the most powerful human Descendant to walk the halls of the Academy since her father," Evangeline said evenly. "Over the years, there have been fewer and fewer new human Descendants joining our ranks, and meanwhile, we lose Descendants—mostly human, but sometimes supernatural—to dangerous Assignments. We supernaturals lost our ability to reproduce when we were cursed into this existence. For a while now, there's been talk of . . . of breeding more powerful human Descendants. Particularly from Marcus and his supporters."

"They want to *breed* me?" Alice shrieked.

Evangeline slowly turned back around, licking her lips in thought. "Well . . . in the crudest of terms . . . yes."

Alice swayed and pressed her palm to her forehead. Nicholas grabbed her arm to steady her.

"For the record, Julius and I have always been against the idea," Evangeline said quickly. "Taking back the stolen fountainheads would rectify the issue without any other drastic measures. Marcus, however . . . Well, let's just say it's in everyone's best interest, especially Alice's, that we ensure he doesn't take the Chancellor's spot by force."

An ominous silence followed. Tristan huffed a short breath. Sure, he had heard rumors about some of the High Council members discussing the possibility of breeding human Descendants, but he hadn't thought those ideas would actually be taken seriously.

After a moment, the pounding on the door resumed.

"The door will hold, won't it?" Tristan asked as the pounding grew louder. He balled his hands into fists. If they were to go down now, he'd take as many enemies as he could with them.

"Of course it'll hold," Evangeline said with the trademark over-confidence of a Long. "Kenny can bash his head against the door all day—hell, he can even come back armed with explosives—and nothing will help him break through. I'm the only one in the world who can unlock it."

"That's good news, isn't it?" Alice perked up, her voice optimistic.

"It's not good news." At Evangeline's sharp response, Alice's tentative smile went out like a light. "Unfortunately, if Kenny has parked his men outside the door, they'll want to wait us out—and we don't have that kind of time to lose if we have any hope of completing the Assignment." Evangeline sounded as though she was thinking out loud. "In fact, the longer they wait out there, the more reinforcements they'll have time to call. Eventually, even if we gave up on the Assignment, we'd have to leave."

"We only have about eight hours until the Midsummer Celebration now." Lei's voice had grown serious, losing all of its usual lightness. "That doesn't count the amount of time we need to regroup in Faerie after we arrive, figure out how exactly we sneak into the High Court. . . . We should get a move on now, actually."

Outside, the pounding continued, as well as the threats. Kenny and his men wouldn't be letting up anytime soon.

"Come," Evangeline hissed, waving the others over. She was already in the kitchen; she'd moved so silently that Tristan hadn't noticed her leaving his side until now. Evangeline pointed behind her. "There's an exit back here."

"Wouldn't Kenny know about it?" Tristan asked.

"No. Julius and I have never told anyone." Evangeline's gaze ran over the members of the crew, and her brow furrowed deeply as she assessed each of them. When she spoke, her instructions were rapid-fire. "Here's what we're going to do. Alice needs to get out first. Nicholas, Tristan—I'm trusting you both to protect her. Lei, you'll bring up the rear with me. I'll be the last, because I need to seal the door shut behind us. We'll regroup at the bottom of the Brooklyn Bridge. Is everyone clear on the plan?"

There wasn't another moment to question Evangeline, and besides, her strict tone indicated that there'd be no use in doing so. They just had to trust that this hasty exit plan would work.

Tristan grabbed Alice's right hand, while Nicholas grabbed her left. Tristan glanced up, met Nicholas's gaze, and nodded, an unspoken agreement passing between them.

"Hold your breath, Alice," Tristan whispered. He didn't give her more than two seconds to follow his instructions before he and Nicholas were racing through the kitchen. Tristan pushed against the wall, and it gave way, spilling them out into the now-evening air of Chinatown. They were on the opposite side of the street—and not a moment too soon.

"Stop them!" Kenny yelled. Footsteps thundered against the pavement, and it became clear that the men with Kenny *must* be supernatural, for they were moving at a superhuman pace.

Tristan glanced behind him. Lei was right on his heels, but Evangeline was still closing the door. She didn't have time to seal it. That much was clear. Kenny was less than a moment away from grabbing Evangeline's arm.

Tristan made a split-second decision. "Take Alice!" he shouted at

Nicholas. He couldn't afford to wait for Nicholas's response. All he could think about was Evangeline, Kenny mere inches away from her. Tristan grabbed Evangeline's arm and yanked her toward him.

"Tristan," she cried, glancing behind wildly. "The door—I haven't—"

"Leave it!"

Evangeline must have recognized that Tristan was right to pull her away at that moment, that there wasn't enough time to seal the safe house door shut, because she allowed herself to be dragged along by him.

Chancing a glance backward, Tristan spotted Kenny and his men splitting off: Kenny and one of them ducking inside the safe house and the two others taking off after the group. There wasn't time to get a better look at what Kenny might be up to, as Tristan and Evangeline accelerated, moving through time and space at breakneck speed.

28
EVANGELINE

Evangeline had been running at full capacity for thirty seconds before an unpleasant realization struck her. She'd all but left the keys in the car ignition for Kenny to steal—in essence, Kenny needed only to pop his head inside the safe house to figure out all of her plans.

Lei's map of Faerie was right on the table in the safe house, in plain view for Kenny and his goons to peruse. There hadn't been a moment to think about covering it up, nor did Evangeline believe they *could* have covered up something like that on a moment's notice, but still, she cursed herself.

Julius would have been able to do it. The thought slipped into her head before she could stop it, and it only upset her further.

From now on, it would be a race against the other Descendants to get to the zodiac fountainheads first. Perhaps the thought would have discouraged a Descendant of weaker mind and spirit, but Evangeline let it fuel her instead. She wasn't perfect, but she'd always performed well under pressure. She had no reason to believe this time would be any different. She would emerge victorious in this Assignment, and when she went back to the Long estate, she would make Kenny, Marcus, and every Descendant who'd doubted her sorely regret that doubt. They *would* respect her as their new Chancellor. And finally, finally, the rest of the Descendants would see her as somebody other than Julius Long's little sister.

Finally, Evangeline would be able to get rid of this terrible curse, too. This curse that had almost caused her to harm Alice. Evangeline wouldn't blame the girl if she never forgave her. Evangeline would bear the guilt of nearly hurting a comrade for quite some time—for falling victim to her weakness, right in front of everyone. She couldn't remember the last time she'd felt so naked and exposed, and all she wanted was to get far away from everyone and everything, even though she knew it would be impossible.

More than anything, Evangeline wished she had her brother back. Julius, who had understood the burden of striving for perfection while bearing the weight of this curse. Her brother was the only one who'd ever fully understood her, and she would never see him again. And today, that knowledge cut that much deeper.

In a burst of adrenaline, Evangeline accelerated even further, her tears blurring everything around her. Running away had never solved her problems before, but just this once, she wished desperately that it would.

Just as she reached the border of Chinatown and the Lower East Side, a hand gripped her shoulder. She quickly wiped away her tears, whirled around, and found herself staring into Tristan's concerned gold-flecked eyes.

"We're not at the bridge yet," she pointed out.

"Slow down. You almost knocked over an innocent old woman just now," Tristan said, jerking his thumb behind him to indicate an elderly lady who'd been crossing the street using a cane. "I don't think we're being followed. And the others stopped."

Evangeline nodded, but she had no intention of letting her guard down. She glanced around them for anyone and anything suspicious. But it was clear, from the expressions of alarm and fright that she received from passersby, that *they* were the most suspicious beings in the vicinity. Pasting a smile onto her face, Evangeline marched toward the base of the Brooklyn Bridge, trying to look as casual as possible.

"Are you okay?" Tristan was examining her without a trace of his usual smirk. Evangeline thought she might actually prefer him with it. Right now, his eyes were searching her face as though he were reading her like a book. If there was anything Evangeline hated, it was the idea that others might be able to grasp her vulnerabilities. There was a reason she kept everyone at arm's length, masking her true thoughts and feelings.

Tristan was the only one she'd started to let in, and what a mistake that had been. For soon after they had begun letting each other draw close, Tristan had begun pulling away, leaving Evangeline feeling so very lonely. Those days, she had wondered time and time again why Tristan didn't care about her enough to let her come near, the way she had wanted him to do. Her self-esteem had slowly eroded in the process, until finally she'd had to break things off. She wouldn't make the same mistake with the same boy twice.

Evangeline turned away and said abruptly, "I've been better." That, she hoped, would be a massive hint to Tristan that she didn't welcome further prying from him.

Tristan was nothing if not obnoxious, however. "I know you're upset about what happened back there with Kenny. Losing the support of the House of Rat is a huge blow."

Evangeline bristled. "How would you know I'm upset?"

"It's obvious."

"It's not *obvious*."

"It is to me."

They stared at each other for a moment, hardly a breath between them, both stubbornly standing their ground, not giving an inch.

"Why do you care?" Evangeline meant for the question to bite and was horrified that it came out as more of a whisper. Part of her wished he'd just throw up his hands in frustration and walk away from her, and part of her was glad he'd stayed.

Tristan's gaze softened, and Evangeline had to force herself not to look away from his golden eyes. She swallowed down the small, secret part of her that didn't *want* to look away. When he finally spoke, the reply came out in a croak. "Of course I care. I always have, and I always will. I just . . . haven't always been good at expressing it." He paused, and Evangeline let out a breath of surprise. "And I'm sorry if I hurt you in the past."

Evangeline pinched herself to make sure this was real, and not a dream. Tristan, admitting his past mistakes? Tristan, *apologizing* to her? What was she supposed to say to this? For years, she and Tristan had been wrapped up in this silly, silent feud, playing an extended round of Who Can Care the Least, and now here he was openly admitting that he'd cared for her all this time.

Tears sprang to Evangeline's eyes. In another lifetime, maybe they would be able to work out their differences.

"I'm sorry, too," she said. Those words had always been so difficult for her to utter. But as she said them aloud to Tristan, an immense weight lifted off her chest.

Time, which had moments ago seemed to be passing by quickly, now had slowed to a standstill. The people bustling about at the foot of the Brooklyn Bridge walked around them. And though Evangeline knew they shouldn't stand here, out in the open, with Kenny and gods knew whoever else after them—she was reluctant to break this moment with Tristan. If she leaned forward just an inch, their bodies would be touching, and oh, gods help her, she didn't think either of them would be able to stop the inevitable from happening next.

Some small, weak part of Evangeline was pleased to see that Tristan had taken notice of her feelings. That there was a part of him that was still watching over her, no matter how much they bickered, no matter how much unpleasantness existed in their history.

Then, before Evangeline could figure out how to reply, Lei, Nicholas, and Alice came running up to them. Time resumed its normal gait, no longer responding to the unpredictable rhythm of Evangeline and Tristan. They shifted apart awkwardly.

"I think we've shaken off any possible tails, but let's get a move on just to be sure," Nicholas was saying. He frowned when he glanced between Tristan and Evangeline. "Oh. Did something happen?"

Evangeline cleared her throat, looking anywhere but at Tristan. "We'll head straight for Faerie." She stared at Lei expectantly.

Lei, on cue, said, "To get there, we'll need to find a Faerie Mound. They pop up at Cherry Hill in Central Park sporadically throughout the day and night."

"Which train are we taking to Central Park?" Alice asked.

Evangeline stared at her and then let out a soft laugh. "Oh, my sweet summer child."

"What?"

"Come along." Evangeline strode up to the human girl and grabbed her hand. Then she crouched down and ordered, "Tristan, help Alice get on my back. We haven't a moment to waste; we need to get to Cherry Hill fast. *Superhumanly* fast."

Alice blinked, and then her lips parted as the message seemed to sink in. All she managed to utter was a quiet, resigned "Not again," before Tristan picked her up and placed her on Evangeline's back. Then, before Alice could even take a breath, Evangeline was yanking her along at vampire speed.

Time and space blurred once more. When she spotted Central Park in her surroundings, tall trees and vibrant flowers framed by skyscrapers in the background, Evangeline returned them to a more normal speed.

"Are you all right?" she asked Alice.

In response, Alice wheezed out, "Yeah. Just . . . doing great."

Well, at least she's still in one piece, Evangeline thought as she gave Alice a once-over. Her face had acquired a slightly alarming tinge of green, but otherwise she looked well enough.

Together, the two stumbled through a patch of flowers none too quietly. Too late, Evangeline realized their little stunt had drawn the attention of a few humans nearby. The onlookers stared and pointed at Evangeline and Alice, no doubt in great interest as to how they'd appeared out of thin air. However, stranger things happened in New York City at every hour of every day, so Evangeline and Alice enjoyed only a few moments of attention before the humans turned their gazes elsewhere. Moments later, the others emerged in the same patch of flowers.

As terrifying as it was to be leaving this world for one that was entirely unknown to her, Evangeline knew that if she slowed her pace even for a second, she might lose her momentum and nerve altogether. So she strode over to the circular mound that was meant to be their portal into Faerie.

"One after the other, then," Evangeline said evenly, turning back to glance at her team. She stepped forward until both feet were planted firmly on the Faerie Mound. She closed her eyes. For a moment, nothing happened. The ground was solid beneath her feet, and there was no indication that she stood on anything besides an ordinary mound of dirt. Her stomach gave an unpleasant lurch as she wondered if something had gone wrong—if they would not be able to enter Faerie after all, would not be allowed to finish the Assignment they'd started. For weeks—no, decades—the Descendants had been hurtling toward this goal, and Evangeline could never forgive herself if she failed them all.

"Evangeline?" Warm fingers landed lightly on her shoulder. She opened her eyes to find Tristan staring at her with concern. "Relax. You're too tense."

Evangeline's lifelong problem, of course, was that she had exactly zero ability to relax. But still, she nodded and tried to release the tension in her shoulders. She was already at this stage, on the cusp of infiltrating Faerie. Panicking now could only increase the likelihood that she'd slip up somewhere, be unable to fulfill the prophecy, and ruin the Descendants' only shot at taking back the fountainheads. So, fighting against her body's instincts, doing the least natural thing in the world . . . Evangeline loosened her limbs, letting all the fight leave her body, and she *relaxed*.

And then the air shifted. Evangeline's stomach dropped again, along with the rest of her body. She was free-falling into the darkness, free-falling into another world.

PART THREE

29
ELSEWHERE...

Deep inside Manhattan's beating heart, past the pulse of pedestrians and drivers waging their never-ending battle for the right of way, there lived the puppet master who orchestrated the ebb and flow of New York City life.

Every New Yorker, born and raised or transplant, liked to believe themselves the main character, the center of the city's orbit. They were dead wrong, each and every last one of them. Only one individual had the power to bend the chaotic city to his whims. The eight million New Yorkers were at the mercy of *his* direction—and his alone.

This puppet master was neither man nor beast. Neither flesh and bone, nor spirit and smoke. Some thought of him as a fallen god. Some spoke of him as a long-forgotten demon. The truth would never be revealed, for those who had come close enough to find out never lived to tell the tale. He rose and fell amid the shadows so seamlessly that he might have been an extension of the darkness itself, ensuring that his targets would not even know what had happened to them by the time he had swallowed them into an eternal slumber. If one wasn't careful, if one crossed the wrong individual, he would rise out of the shadows and claim his next victim.

This was why many spoke of him in tones of hushed fear—the Collector. If he had a proper name once, it had been lost long ago to the ebb and flow of time, just as he had long since left behind any trace of humanity.

To protect the secrecy of his operations, the Collector tied himself to no location. One week, he might be found on the Lower East Side. Next, he might take up residence in the West Village. Rumor had it that he had eyes and ears from the highest corners of Queens to the deepest reaches of Brooklyn, and that he was everywhere and nowhere at once.

This made the Collector very difficult to pin down, even for those he actively employed to do his bidding. Rather than ask his underlings to find him, he had letters sent out to them instead. These letters, of course, were mysteriously untraceable and contained only as much information as the recipient would need to carry out their assigned task. Because he went to great lengths to hide his whereabouts, the Collector could count on one hand the number of times he'd been found when he hadn't explicitly wanted to be. (It had only been once, actually.)

After tonight, that number would have to go up to two.

The Collector had been in the middle of meditating in this week's temporary haunt—a two-bedroom apartment in Astoria—when suddenly he broke his position and slowly, ever so slowly, turned his head to one side. His eyes did not open, and his expression remained serene. He appeared to be listening for something.

"Bo." The Collector broke the silence to address the muscular man who stood on his right. "Yun." Now the man on his left turned at the summons.

Bo and Yun were two formerly homeless urchins who had been on the verge of starvation or prison when they were plucked from their misery by a figure who, in their eyes, was a god. They never could have blended in with society, for there was something frightening about their jagged teeth and yellowed claws that was not quite . . . *human.* It was due to these characteristics, not to mention an unquenchable thirst for blood, that the Collector had hand-chosen Bo and Yun to guard him at all times. This was considered the highest of high honors, as the Collector trusted practically no one. Bo and Yun were not their real names, of course; every individual under the Collector's employment had been given a code name, to be drilled into them with such efficiency as to almost make them forget who they were before their employ. Their lives before this point were irrelevant. Only their service to the Collector mattered.

"A visitor approaches." The Collector spoke evenly, almost pleasantly. This was a frightening development for anyone who knew the Collector, for he was never pleased by anything besides the thought of someone's imminent death. "You will greet them and bring them before me."

It was a mark of how good they were at their occupation that Bo and Yun didn't balk at this unexpected command. For any visitors were expected to schedule appointments with the Collector well in advance, via letter. Unannounced guests were not only not part of protocol—they did not *happen*. If the Collector did not want to be found, he would not be.

Until tonight.

Bo and Yun did nothing to indicate that the Collector's request was anything out of the ordinary. They bowed in obedience and moved as a swift, coordinated unit toward the door. When they returned moments later, the unexpected guest in tow, the Collector was seated behind a large desk that was serving as his office for the week. Nothing in his demeanor suggested that this visitor had been anything but expected.

"Si." The Collector bent forward to acknowledge the visitor before him. And when he leaned into the dim lighting, for a moment, it seemed that the trace of a human man's stern, hardened face could be seen—but that was in all likelihood shadow work, a trick of the light orchestrated by the Collector himself, and in the blink of an eye he had pulled his head back into the shadows. The fleeting glimpse of something human was gone again, consumed by darkness. "You needn't have come out all this way to visit me in person. Responding to my letter would have sufficed."

"This is my response. You're very difficult to track down, by the way,"

Si said. He was distinctly more human-looking than the Collector, but also not quite human. Most of the Collector's underlings were not quite human.

The Collector was used to his presence being regarded with awe, with reverence, with *terror*—not with this casualness, as though they were old friends. He regarded Si with amusement. The slippery underling's sudden visit had caught him off guard, and though the Collector would never show it, of course, he was ever so slightly impressed. Si was not to be underestimated. The Collector had always known this, but moving forward, he needed to act with that knowledge in mind.

"I have been watching you as you attended to your task," the Collector said. "You have been taking your time." There was a note of displeasure in his voice, and he watched as Si's expression twitched. Ah, yes, that familiar flicker of *fear*—delicious.

"This task cannot be rushed," Si explained, his voice strong despite his slightly trembling hands.

"Yet I gave you a deadline, did I not? The hour of action draws nearer, boy." The Collector did not raise his voice, but the underlying threat seeped into his words.

"Everything is going according to plan. I came to see you, though, because . . ." A sigh here, a tensing of the shoulders. Si had been gathering the courage for this moment. "There is something I need in order to pull off the last stage of the plan."

"Oh?" The Collector leaned back in his seat. Although his voice was full of amusement, he was not at all amused. "Something you *need*?"

"Ah . . . rather, something I'd like to request from you, if I may be so bold."

The afterthought of politeness did nothing to move the Collector, who was entirely too used to others granting *his* wishes, and not the other way around. It wasn't a matter of whether he was capable of fulfilling Si's request—there was nothing in this world that the Collector couldn't do, or at least have others do for him. "Have I not already offered you enough in exchange for the successful completion of this task? Do not push your luck, Si." Now the Collector's tone grew raspy with warning. He needed to put pressure on this man, to make it known that he was the one calling the shots.

However, Si did not flinch. Perhaps this was a foolish display of bravery. Or perhaps Si suspected what it was the Collector wanted to hide—that he *needed* the help of somebody as savvy as Si to complete this task for him.

The two stared deep into each other's eyes in a silent challenge. The one who caved first would be submitting to the other, in effect. The Collector would not, could not, let it be him.

I have been alive for longer than millennia, thought the Collector. *I was alive when the gods shaped the mountains and rivers. I was alive when the forces of the universe shaped the* gods. *It is hopeless to challenge me, and even more hopeless to try to win.*

For a long moment, perhaps an hour, perhaps a day, the quiet in the room was such that the grandfather clock ticking in the corner sounded deafening.

At long last, Si looked away. "I didn't mean any disrespect," he finally said, "and I'm sorry if I came across that way. I wouldn't be asking you if I could think of a different method, but I've looked over the details of my plan again and again, and the only solution requires . . . well, magic."

Si was a proud man, and he would never beg, but there was desperation written on his sullen expression. This was the closest he would come to begging, and the knowledge of that caused the Collector to relent just a little. Still, he would not make this easy for his underling; he had a reputation to uphold.

"Magic." The Collector repeated the word slowly as though he'd never heard it before, rolling the syllables on his tongue. "Magic always comes at a cost."

"We can negotiate the finer details—"

"Not a financial cost. Surely you know what I mean, Si."

A brief pause. "Yes. I know."

The Collector sank farther back into the shadows. He said nothing for a long, long time, drawing out the silence—on purpose, most likely. Si stood there for even longer without so much as twitching a muscle, waiting for a response.

"Very well. Tell me what it is that you might like, Si, and I will find something to suit your needs."

Breaking their stony postures for the first time, Bo and Yun exchanged a look. This had been shaping up to be the strangest of nights. It was odd enough that the Collector had been found by one of his underlings. Odder still, the Collector had actually *agreed* to Si's request. They had never heard of their boss agreeing to anything so quickly.

Whatever this task was that the Collector had sent Si to do, it was obviously very, very important. Perhaps it was more important than any task before it.

This, of course, was Si's sign to tread carefully, lest he wander too close to the waiting jaws of a monster. For the higher the stakes climbed, the more likely the shadowy master of Manhattan would soon claim his next victim.

30
ALICE

Falling into another realm was unlike any type of falling Alice had experienced before. It was not like plummeting down a set of stairs, nor was it similar to riding downhill on a roller coaster. It was the feeling of being everything and everywhere all at once, and yet nothing and nowhere at all, and she did not think she would be able to describe this experience properly to anyone later no matter how hard she tried. As she traveled through the in-between that bounded the mortal and Faerie worlds, Alice experienced the strangest sensation of the world shifting around her, not unlike the way she'd felt when being carried along at superhuman speed. This time, however, everything was moving vertically rather than horizontally, and Alice could not tell if time was moving backward or forward. In fact, she couldn't tell if time was still of consequence here at all.

In this dizzying state, Alice entertained the random, unbidden thought that this was what Alice must have felt like falling through Wonderland. And wasn't it fitting, after all, that Mama had given her that name—Alice?

Alice at last landed—miraculously feet-first—on a bed of something soft and ticklish. She'd braced her legs for impact, but no such force came. It was as though somebody had lightly guided her onto a soft surface.

Alice peeked an eye open, then the other eye. Grass. She'd landed in a bed of grass, and the tall green blades were what she'd felt tickling her legs.

At first, she did not notice a huge difference between the nature of Faerie and that of Central Park. But as her vision adjusted from the daylight of the human world to the dimming light of evening here, the differences became more apparent.

In Faerie, the trees grew greener and taller, stretching so high up into the clear blue sky that Alice had to crane her neck and still couldn't see the tops. The flower petals glittered with dew that was so dazzling, it couldn't be anything but magic. The very air was cleaner and crisper than anything she'd smelled before, even visiting the countryside as a child. This was air in its most natural, purest state, completely untouched by anything human, by those careless beings who had slowly but surely polluted and poisoned their own planet.

Alice inhaled deeply, letting the clean air fill her lungs, and was overwhelmed by a feeling of belonging. She'd reached dead end after dead end in her quest to learn more about Baba, about herself. Was it possible that she might find the answers to all her questions here, in Faerie? She took one hesitant step forward, and then two. The grass rustled beneath her feet. With each step, she was more and more overcome by an irresistible pull to walk deeper and deeper into Faerie. And although it was impossible, she couldn't shake off the feeling that she'd been here before, if not in person, then in her dreams.

Alice . . . stolen child . . .

Her dreams. Her strange, frightening, all-too-real dreams.

The whispers grew louder here, and the nameless faces of those who called to Alice became clearer than ever before. She was surrounded by them—those creatures who had beckoned to her even in the mortal world. They were beautiful, sharp-eared faeries, with eyes made of liquid gold and starlight.

Lost child . . . you've finally returned . . .

Slim hands reached for her. They were so close to touching now that Alice felt the air from their movement rush past her. Only now, inches away from them, did she really look into the eyes of these beings, and see that they were alight not with happiness but with a mad, twisted desire.

The male faerie who had taken most prominent form in her dreams now stepped forward, his profile turning sharper than ever before, and in his dark eyes there was a glimmer of greed. He reached out a hand and squeezed her arm in a painfully tight grip.

You will never leave again.

Alice's heart plummeted. She stumbled backward, but they surrounded her on all sides, pressing in.

"Alice—come back," hissed a familiar voice, this one much closer and sharper and more real.

Alice snapped out of her reverie. The faeries and their voices disappeared. She blinked once, twice, three times, and rubbed her eyes just to be sure they were gone. Had that scene just now been a figment of her imagination? It seemed impossible. Alice had never been to Faerieland before now, at least not to her knowledge, and would have no memories of its inhabitants to help her imagine such a sight. There had been such vivid *detail* in their manner of dress, in their timeless and terrifying beauty.

Now an icy-cold hand wrapped around her wrist, yanking her back. Alice turned her head. It was Evangeline, and she eyed Alice with great concern. It was an expression Alice hadn't seen on Evangeline's face before—certainly not directed at *her*—and she wasn't sure whether to be delighted or terrified to have evidently evoked Evangeline's worry.

"What do you think you're doing, wandering off on your own like that? You'll get lost, or eaten—or worse, you'll get us all caught," Evangeline scolded.

Alice winced. The implication that her life was of less consequence than completing the Assignment wasn't lost on her. After all, weren't they all here because, to some degree, they were willing to put their own necks on the line to take back the treasures that were rightfully theirs?

"We need to keep a low profile," Evangeline said, her voice softening slightly, as though she'd recognized that her words had been too harsh. She dragged Alice into a thicket of bushes.

For a moment, the two of them crouched together in a tense, awkward silence. Alice's senses were heightened, and she was very aware of being in close proximity to the vampire Descendant. She did her best to scrunch down and make herself as small as possible.

"I didn't have the chance to say anything before, but the way you distracted the Jingwei back in the Underground was clever." Evangeline spoke so quickly that Alice almost didn't catch what she was saying, and when she did, she wasn't sure she'd heard properly. "You've got some guts, Jiang. I'm glad you agreed to help me with this Assignment."

Alice blinked, at a loss for words. Evangeline had *complimented* her. She'd even said she was glad to have her along. Perhaps when they'd fallen into Faerieland, they'd fallen into a parallel dimension as well. And with Evangeline's compliment, Alice's heart lifted. *You've got some guts.* Alice had never heard herself described that way before, and perhaps, slowly, her time among the Descendants was bringing out a different side of her, a part of her that she'd never known existed.

A beat passed, just a little too long to feel natural, before Alice was able to gather herself enough to form a response to Evangeline's compliment. She cleared her throat. "Oh. I . . . thanks."

"Your father was like that, too. Surprising in the best of ways. It was a disappointment to everyone when he left the Academy to live a normal life."

Finally, there was a lead here, and Alice wasn't about to let it go. "Why did he leave?"

Evangeline stared right into Alice's eyes, and for the first time, Alice glimpsed something deeply heartfelt in the depths of her black eyes. Alice had the sense that Evangeline was about to tell her something monumental—or, at the very least, that she was holding on to such a tidbit of information. Then Evangeline turned away, and the moment was broken.

"I don't know. Descendants have left to pursue ordinary lives for any number of reasons. Leaving the Academy means giving up your magic forever. It is such a tedious, arduous process that very few follow through with it—but your father must have had very good reasons to do so."

Alice did her best not to release an exasperated sigh. Although she'd thought she might finally get somewhere, in the end, Evangeline's answer had hardly been an answer at all—in fact, it left her with more questions than ever. What had motivated Baba to leave the Descendants with such conviction? Was it really just to experience life as an ordinary man? Even after her own brief time with the Descendants so far, Alice couldn't imagine turning her back on them, and she couldn't fathom what had made Baba do just that.

There had to be more to the story, something that maybe Evangeline was holding back. But Alice hesitated before saying more. She didn't want to ruin the fact that Evangeline seemed to be seeing her in a good light.

"I hope you don't regret joining me on this Assignment," Evangeline said after a moment, and there was a fragility, a real vulnerability, that Alice had never heard there before. "I know it's been the most dangerous for you. That's why it's so important that we succeed, you know. We need to break this wretched curse."

Alice looked Evangeline squarely in the eye. "I knew the dangers when I signed up. I wouldn't have come along if I didn't want to."

Evangeline stared at Alice long and hard, and the corners of her lips lifted up. An understanding passed between the two girls. Though they were quite different, at their core, they were similar enough that each could recognize and respect the spirit that burned deep within the other.

Alice glanced upward and marveled at the evening sky—another day gone by—and with a jolt, she remembered that it was her birthday. Seventeen. She was now officially seventeen, and she felt no different than she had at sixteen. For a moment she considered mentioning this, but then she swallowed the words into the pit of her stomach. There were more important matters at hand than her birthday, and she didn't like making a big deal out of the day, anyway. Her only wish for her seventeenth birthday was to finally understand what had happened to Baba.

Then a loud rustling noise interrupted Alice's train of thought.

"Owwww," groaned Lei. "You kicked my head, you idiot mutt!"

"I'm just sorry I didn't kick it harder," came Tristan's cold retort.

Alice glanced downward. It took her a moment to make out the figures that had hidden themselves away in the undergrowth, but she saw that Tristan, Nicholas, and Lei had all made it through to Faerie, too. The boys were hunkered down staring at Alice—Tristan with indifference, Nicholas with confusion, and Lei with curiosity.

"Good of you to join us," Lei said with a half smile, which Alice understood to mean he was teasing her.

"Sorry," she mumbled.

Besides Lei, nobody was smiling, or even close to it. This was the final leg of Evangeline's plan, and tension hung thick in the air. There was no room for error, and certainly no room for Alice to wander off on the trail of imaginary figures and voices.

Although Alice told herself all this, she couldn't shake off the feeling that there was some crucial detail she was overlooking. Had anyone else experienced such a vivid vision of faeries beckoning them?

"We'll head toward the High Court," Lei was saying to the others.

Everyone's focus had returned to the ominous task at hand; Alice would have to wait until later.

"And where is that?" Tristan asked.

Before anyone could answer his question, there came a flurry of movement in their vicinity, the sound of cheerful voices and wheels crunching over fallen leaves. Evangeline motioned for everyone to crouch lower and then pressed a finger to her lips, watching the gravel road that cut through the woods.

Alice's heart was thumping so loudly she thought it must be audible to passersby, and possibly all of Faerie. Another distinct disadvantage of being human, she decided: the loudness of one's breath at the least convenient of moments. Tristan, Nicholas, and Lei still had beating hearts, but they seemed to be much better with breath control. One day, Alice's infernal beating heart would be the death of her.

Through the leaves of the bush, she made out the sight of a silver horse pulling a caravan. The voices grew louder as the vehicle trundled closer along the road.

". . . rather early this year, aren't we, Morfett? We'll arrive at High Court in no more'n two or three hours," a reedy, high-pitched voice was saying.

Someone—Morfett—responded, "Better early than late. The High King has been known to turn away latecomers in past years. And they aren't invited back to the Celebration, either."

"Hmph. Perhaps it would be for the best. The High King grows too comfortable on his throne, and I dislike attending these namby-pamby occasions just for the sake of keeping up the illusion of peace between the Courts."

"Careful with your words. We're not far from High Court territory now. If we're overheard . . ."

The other faerie scoffed but did not continue to argue. Then, a moment later, the voices started up again, only Alice recognized that she was hearing them not out loud, but in her *head*. She didn't have a moment to celebrate the revelation that her powers worked just as well in Faerie. She drew upon all her strength to eavesdrop on the faeries' thoughts.

. . . Have to entertain those Dawn Court rascals in four hours, what a pain. . . .

Will the food be as mediocre as it was last year? At least the wine is always good. . . .

These court musicians I hired last-minute better be worth the obscene fee. . . .

Alice strained her ears, but she could no longer hear what the faeries were thinking, as the caravan was pulling out of sight. However, she'd heard enough. After another minute or so, even the sound of the wheels had disappeared.

"That way," Lei said, pointing in the direction of the caravan, "is the direction of the High Court."

"Well deduced," Tristan said dryly. "Whatever would we do without your magnificent spying abilities?"

Before the two could launch into an argument, Alice blurted out, "The Midsummer Celebration starts in four hours. I read that in the minds of the faeries in that caravan just now—they're from the Dusk Court. And they've brought along a band of musicians from their Court, who are traveling not far behind them."

Evangeline threw Alice an appreciative little smile, and Nicholas patted her on the shoulder. Tentatively, she returned the smile. She was really starting to get the hang of her powers.

"Court musicians," Evangeline mused. Her eyes glinted, and a crafty grin played around her lips. Alice didn't need to possess any supernatural abilities to sense that that look spelled trouble. "Nicholas, I don't suppose you've been keeping your flute skills sharp, have you?"

Nicholas sighed. It was, Alice thought, one of the heaviest sighs she'd ever heard in her life. "I have, but I didn't imagine I'd be putting my musical talents to use on this Assignment."

"That's the fun of it all," Evangeline said brightly. "Right. Court musicians are hardly notable guests; the High King won't even know what they're supposed to look like, and even the Dusk Court won't question them after a glass of wine or two."

"You're not suggesting . . . ," said Tristan, his voice trailing off. His lips thinned. He looked displeased with the direction of the conversation.

"We'll ambush the musicians and disguise ourselves as them as we head into the Celebration. Alice, I've heard you're very good with the violin."

Alice nodded. She suddenly found herself grateful for the torturous years of piano and violin lessons Mama had put her through. Perhaps her musical skills would save her life.

"Aren't we trying to draw as little attention to ourselves as possible?

Masquerading as the court musicians hardly seems to suit that goal," Tristan pointed out.

"The best hiding spot is the one that's in plain sight," said Evangeline.

Maybe she was right, but that didn't make the idea any less terrifying. Evangeline's plan relied on everyone's ability to perform under pressure, while ensuring that no slipups occurred. Alice was fairly certain the others would be fine, but as for her, only time could tell.

"Suppose we go along with this plan to enter the Celebration disguised as musicians," Nicholas mused, his expression thoughtful rather than skeptical. "We'll have to ambush them when they travel down this road, and you mean, of course, for me to alter our features to resemble theirs as much as possible."

Evangeline smiled angelically. "If you would be so kind."

"Then what exactly are you planning to do about the musicians once we've taken their places? Surely you don't mean to kill them. That would raise an alarm for the next Folk who come down this road." Nicholas frowned, as though the thought of murder were a casual inconvenience rather than a horrifying act.

"I'm not opposed to killing as a last resort," Evangeline said, "but the best course of action would be for us to knock them out. Nobody has any objections to that, I presume?" Her cold tone made it clear that she didn't welcome any challenges.

"Once we're inside the Court, we'll split into two groups," Evangeline continued. "Lei and I know the Court better than anyone else, so we'll each lead a group. Nicholas—you'll go with Lei, and the two of you will create a distraction to draw attention away from us."

"I want to go in with you, Evangeline," Nicholas said abruptly, looking not at all happy with her instructions.

"We can't all go into the treasure room. I trust you to operate well without me around," Evangeline said swiftly.

This, Alice observed, was a clever way to handle the situation— although Nicholas still wasn't exactly *thrilled* with the development, he did stand a bit taller, clearly bolstered by Evangeline's expression of faith in him. Alice shook her head, hiding a slight smile. Boys and their egos. Evangeline sure knew what to say.

"Tristan and Alice, you'll sneak into the treasure room with me to find the fountainheads," Evangeline continued. "With luck, the job will take no more than five minutes, and then we'll be on our merry way out of the Court and back to the human world with the fountainheads in hand."

Evangeline laid out the plan so calmly and logically that Alice was almost convinced that it really would be that simple to pull off. However, a million different things could go wrong at each step of the way. And the Folk, Alice knew, were not to be underestimated.

There was little time for Alice to panic, because she started to hear voices again—this time both inside and outside her head.

"They're here," Alice breathed. "The court musicians have arrived."

31
LEI

For seven years, visions of Faerieland had haunted Lei in his dreams, far beyond his reach. Yet now that he'd finally returned to this intoxicating place, where his greatest fears and deepest desires were one and the same, Lei wasn't sure how he felt about being back in Faerie.

A different version of Lei had walked down these dirt roads, flirting with faeries and danger alike. This place appeared largely unchanged—the air as pristine as he remembered; the nature as vibrant—but he returned an older, wiser shaman.

No longer was Lei the brash, rather stupid young hotshot who let his craving for power overshadow his loyalty to the shamans, even if he still liked to act the part. Seven years trapped in a cell had given Lei more than enough time to reflect on the actions that had landed him there. His biggest regret was not that he'd misplaced his loyalty, giving it to the fae rather than the shamans; it was that he'd been careless enough to slip up and get caught. And it had all happened because he'd stepped out of a Long safe house in Midtown to satisfy a ramen craving, of all things, and the worst part was that the ramen wasn't even *good*. That sham of a ramen chef was lucky Lei didn't make a beeline for him as soon as he got out of the Underground.

Though the years had mellowed him somewhat, Lei knew he wasn't likely to completely change his ways. It was said that after a certain age—twenty-five or twenty-six—humans were set, their frontal lobes too fully formed for them to change much. And perhaps in much the same way, Lei was making the same mistakes now as before. After all, hadn't he run away from the Underground, turning himself into a fugitive from the law? He was still a criminal doing criminal things, technically. The only—though rather large—difference was that this time, he was working *against* the fae rather than spying for them. Helping the Descendants take back the zodiac fountainheads and break their curse could only help the shamans in the end, as the two groups had historically been allied; therefore, Lei had turned over a new leaf. At least, that was what he told himself.

Lei certainly didn't feel like he was making a new start as he crouched low, hidden in the shrubbery. All this hunching and crawling about was going to give him bad knees. The unmistakable sounds of a caravan drew nearer and nearer.

"There are six court musicians," Alice murmured to the others. "But there are only five of us. That means that when we take their places, we'll be one short."

"Easy enough to explain away," Evangeline whispered with a dismissive wave of her hand. "Fellow fell ill, was eaten by a troll, and so forth . . ."

"Are there really faerie-eating trolls around here?" Alice glanced around in alarm.

"My dear, you are in Faerieland," Lei said, unable to resist the urge to interject. "You should always assume the worst. In fact, your worst-case scenario is probably actually the best-case scenario."

That caused Alice's already pale face to completely drain of color, and it earned Lei an admonishing look from Nicholas. "Don't frighten her."

"Just telling it like it is." Lei shrugged and turned away. There was no point in sugarcoating the truth when they were all sticking their necks out together, betting that they could pull off this heist while simultaneously avoiding an all-out war. It wasn't his fault if the fragile human girl couldn't handle it. He still couldn't figure out what exactly was so special about Alice that the other Descendants were discussing using her for breeding.

"Everyone, shut up," Tristan growled.

"And arm yourselves," Evangeline added under her breath.

Normally, Lei would balk at being told what to do so rudely, but in this case, he knew making further noise would be a mistake. Evangeline was glaring as though she'd cut any of them if they blew their cover.

The caravan of musicians rumbled along the path until it was about to pass right before them. Lei pressed both hands into the soil beneath his feet, and his fingers wrapped around two palm-sized rocks. He reached for the well of magic deep inside, and in response, his whole body began to heat up and vibrate. It had been so long since Lei had used his magic that he had grown rusty, but muscle memory took over.

Evangeline slowly, slowly began to stand up and shifted into position. "Follow my lead," she said, and then she burst out of the bushes at her full and considerable speed.

Lei possessed extraordinary vision as a shaman, but he thought that if he'd blinked at the moment Evangeline launched herself onto the path, he might have missed her movements entirely. There were no cries from the faeries; either they were reacting too slowly, or Evangeline's movements were far outpacing the sound of their cries. Lei registered all this while he stayed back, aimed the rocks, and flung them toward the faeries with a burst of power; they found their targets, knocking two faeries out at once. Lei charged forward and grabbed the nearest faerie—a young female with long green hair and a shimmering silver dress—and swung the rock down on her forehead.

So much for turning over a new leaf, Lei thought as he caught the now-unconscious faerie in his arms. The entire exchange had happened soundlessly, and he was quite proud that he was no less limber than he'd been before his stint in the Underground prison.

Within seconds, they'd made quick work of the caravan of musicians. The silver horses had stopped in their tracks and whinnied in protest, but otherwise, the entire ambush happened without much noise at all. Nicholas was staring at the faerie faces as though trying to commit them to memory.

"And what do you mean for us to do with these bodies?" Tristan asked, frowning down at the male faerie lying at his feet. "Surely we can't just leave them on the side of the road?"

"No, of course not. Hide them behind the shrubbery," Evangeline ordered. "We don't want other faeries traipsing by and asking questions."

They obeyed, until the six unfortunate court musicians were lying in a heap in the bushes. From the road, their bodies weren't visible at all. As he changed out of his robes into a slightly too-small green tunic that was made out of what felt like leaves, Lei wondered how many faerie bodies had been hidden in this manner. Surely if it had been done once, it had been done a hundred, a thousand, times.

"Nicholas," Evangeline called, and he perked up immediately. "If you can, we'll need those disguises now."

The command had hardly fallen from her lips before Nicholas was placing his hands on the shoulders of the nearest body—Alice. Lei watched in fascination as Nicholas's features scrunched up in concentration and a drop of sweat trailed down his forehead and dripped off the bridge of his nose.

Nicholas stepped back after transforming Alice, and Lei couldn't help the gasp that escaped his lips. Alice still looked *somewhat* like Alice—the general shape of her face and body remained the same—but she appeared younger and beautiful in an ethereal way. Her ears were now sharp rather than rounded, and her nose, too, was longer than before. Her dark brown hair had lightened to a medium-brown shade, and the strands were braided with blades of grass.

Lei brought his hands together. "Bravo, dear boy. Can I be next?"

Nicholas cut him a look that could have wilted a forest. "For that, you can be last."

The smile slipped off Lei's face. Thus far he'd had the impression that Nicholas was one of the nicer beings in Evangeline's little crew, but perhaps he'd misjudged.

One by one, they took turns undergoing their transformations. When at last Nicholas had finished disguising Lei, the shaman extended his hands in front of him and marveled at their pale thinness. When he pressed his fingertips into his cheeks, Lei noticed more prominent cheekbones, and though he couldn't see for himself what he looked like, he imagined that it would be very, very hard for anyone to recognize the shaman underneath.

Evangeline bent over each of the unconscious faeries in turn. When she was done, she walked to the others, wiping an invisible speck of dust off the shimmering silver dress she'd stolen from one of the faerie girls. Somehow, the dress fit her better than its original owner. Then, wordlessly, Evangeline raised her other hand to reveal a small stack of golden papers.

Lei whistled. "Invitations to the Midsummer Celebration." He'd never received one himself and had never expected to. It wasn't like this one was meant for him, either; they'd stolen the invitations.

Evangeline passed one out to each of them, and Lei read his over to find that the faerie he was impersonating was named Ruvin.

"How long will those faeries be knocked out?" Alice asked Evangeline in a hushed tone.

"At least a day or two," Evangeline said. "And when they wake up, their memories will be fuzzy, and they'll likely be wandering around Faerie for a long, long time."

Lei vowed to himself never to upset Evangeline Long.

299

The ride toward the High Court was smooth and quiet. The silver horses, Lei knew, were highly intelligent, and remembered the route without needing a driver. Lei had plenty of time to practice plucking out a decent tune on the instrument he'd been saddled with—a harp. The music of Faerie was mesmerizing, soothing to the soul in a way that could lull lesser beings into a deep, enchanted sleep. It was unlike any music he'd heard before either on the Surface or Underground.

Luckily, Lei had paid enough attention during his many trips to Faerie that he could compose something pleasing to the ear if forced to perform. However, he had his doubts about the others. Tristan was currently blowing such a shrieky, off-pitch tune into his flutelike instrument that Lei feared his eardrums would burst.

"Tristan," Evangeline said calmly while pressing her fingers into her temple, "if you keep up that racket any longer, the faeries really will kill us."

Tristan lowered the flute and scowled. "It was *your* idea to impersonate the court musicians."

"We're not actually meant to play music, are we?" Nicholas asked, sounding concerned.

Evangeline, who was sitting across from him and staring out the window, turned her attention to him. "I suppose not. That will immediately blow our cover." She raised her eyebrow at Tristan, who crossed his arms over his chest and glared in the opposite direction. "We will be long gone by the time the Dusk Court calls for entertainment, I imagine."

"The Midsummer Celebration is the largest celebration throughout the land every year," Lei said. "There will be far too much going on for anyone to notice the Dusk Court musicians disappearing for a bit."

"Is that it?" Alice interrupted. She was pointing past Lei's nose out the window.

Lei didn't need to ask what she meant by "it." In the not-so-far distance, at the end of their long, winding path, a glittering palace emerged above the greenery. The palace of the High Court remained as it was in his memories and dreams, at which Lei was relieved. This Assignment depended heavily upon his recollection of Faerie, and so long as they could count on his memories of this place, they could hope to infiltrate the Court successfully.

Lei's pulse quickened as the caravan drew closer to the palace. Inside, there were bound to be familiar faces. He hadn't directly interacted with the High King—King Gamede—but once upon a time, he'd been good friends with several lords in the Court, and even Prince Titus. *More* than good friends, in Prince Titus's case. Indeed, he had once gotten to know the faerie prince very, very well.

Prince Titus . . . Lei hadn't allowed himself to think about that name in a long, long time, but now that he had unexpectedly found himself back in Faerie, the memories came rushing back as well. Stolen kisses in the prince's private bedchambers . . . secret excursions in the Forest of Illusions . . . Lei shuddered. His cheeks were burning, and he brought his hands up to his face. He was glad of Nicholas's powers, which had transformed him until he was virtually unrecognizable. So long as he was able to contain his own emotions and play the role of a humble court musician, Lei could get through this—assuming he didn't run into Prince Titus. When it came to Titus, all bets were off.

"Are you okay?"

Alice's soft voice broke through Lei's intense concentration, and he blinked. Alice was looking up at him, her eyes wide with concern. For a long moment, he said nothing, his mind freezing. It had been so long since somebody had asked him a question out of genuine concern for his well-being, and it was this unexpected gesture, of all things, that threw him off-balance.

Lei shook his head. "I . . . yes, I'm fine. This place . . . being here . . . it brings back memories." Alice gave him an expectant look, clearly waiting for him to elaborate, but he decided to leave it at that. After the completion of this Assignment, he would take the opportunity to leave behind everything in his past and go somewhere far, far away. In all likelihood, and with any luck, he would never see the Descendants again.

They were almost there now. Caravans were pulling up from all directions. There were the Dawn Court members from the west, whose caravans were woven from vines and fresh dew; Day Court members from the north, whose caravans were made out of branches and grass; Night Court members from the south, whose caravans were crafted from ebony and moonlight.

The noise around them grew louder and louder as they approached the Court. The palace itself was heavily guarded, and given the amount of traffic, it would take them a little while longer to gain entrance into the Celebration.

Evangeline had gone silent for a noticeably long time, save for the tapping of her foot. Perhaps she was nervous. That seemed impossible, but after all, Evangeline was not infallible, and she had more riding on this Assignment than anyone.

Finally, their caravan approached the goblin guards who stood at the hedges in front of the palace's lush garden.

"Act casual," Evangeline said at last, "and leave the talking to me."

32
EVANGELINE

Evangeline thought her head might explode from the effort of thinking so much. The most immediate and pressing matter at hand was, of course, making it safely past the guards. She'd broken down the heist into more manageable steps, as she usually did with any overwhelming task. Now it was much easier to envision the chain of events that needed to happen to achieve her goal. On top of the plan A that she'd shared with her crew, she had a riskier plan B that she'd shared with no one—and she desperately prayed that she wouldn't have to enact plan B.

At the same time, she couldn't shake the feeling that everything was going *too* smoothly. She'd almost expected that the court musicians would overtake the five of them, or at least put up a fight, but the ambush had gone off without a hitch. Of course, there was a good chance she was counting her chickens before they hatched, given that they'd yet to actually enter the palace.

Evangeline hadn't forgotten, either, that Kenny and his goons had tailed them through Chinatown back in the human world. And the most pressing questions . . . *How* had Kenny known the location of the safe house? Why had he come after Alice specifically? It couldn't be that he knew what Evangeline knew about Alice—she hadn't shared that information with anyone. Or was it possible that she wasn't the only one who'd speculated? Kenny had worms for brains, though, so surely it hadn't been his own idea to try to abduct Alice. That meant something even worse—that there was a more powerful player hiding in the wings, giving orders to Kenny and the other traitor Descendants. Marcus Niu? Was he really the type to play such a fine game of strategies? If so, Evangeline had vastly underestimated him, and now the regret was beginning to sink in.

A shiver ran up Evangeline's spine. Perhaps she'd been in her head for too long. She wished Julius were still here; her brother would know what to do, whom to trust.

Trust . . . At the thought, almost unconsciously, Evangeline turned her gaze to Tristan. He was staring up at the ceiling of the caravan, his body slightly trembling, and there was a familiar tight, almost pained expression on his face. It took Evangeline only a moment to place that look. The full moon *was* approaching.

"Tristan, is everything all right?" If he couldn't stop himself from transforming, he'd ruin the entire Assignment.

Tristan jolted, as though Evangeline's words had pulled him out of a reverie. He blinked. When his eyes met hers, they were as gold-flecked as usual, and his body had relaxed. "I'm fine."

Evangeline stared at him hard for just a moment longer before turning away. She'd keep an eye on him, but for now, everything seemed to be in order.

Decades of navigating the society of Descendants as a Long had taught Evangeline how to mask her emotions even from those she held closest. While so many different threads of thoughts competed for attention in her mind, she gave no outward sign that her mind was in turmoil.

Even when two goblin guards called for the caravan to stop and Evangeline pulled back the curtains, her expression revealed none of the nerves she felt inside.

"Invitations," said one of the guards, lazily extending a spindly hand.

One by one, they passed their stolen invitations to the guard. The two goblins put their heads together to pore over the invitations and then to glance back up at the occupants of the caravan to confirm their identities.

The seconds stretched on and on. If Evangeline had still been a living, breathing being, she would have been holding her breath. And though it had been decades since she'd had a heart that pounded, she could almost imagine that empty space beating loudly once again.

"Clear," announced the guards in unison, shoving the invitations back into their hands. Court musicians, after all, were hardly esteemed guests in the eyes of the High Court, merely hired entertainment, and did not need to be treated with much respect.

The curtains swung closed, and the caravan was moving forward once more.

Alice sighed in relief, but nobody else gave any sign that they had relaxed at all. Now came the tricky part. Evangeline thought quickly. They had only moments before the caravan ahead of them—the one belonging to Lord Morfett from the Dusk Court—would stop, and the lord would want to come to this caravan to give orders to his hired musicians. At that point, they would need an excuse to get out of actually performing for the High Court.

"We're going to pretend to be sick," Evangeline announced as she heard raucous laughter and the door slamming on the caravan ahead. This would be easy enough, given that Alice, at least, already was holding her stomach.

There wasn't a moment to go over the plan again before knuckles rapped on the side of the caravan.

"Stand at the attention of your lord, please," came a high, cold voice.

Evangeline tumbled out of the caravan first, clutching her stomach and moaning. The tall, thin male faerie who'd spoken outside the door stumbled back and gave her a wide berth.

"What's the matter with you all?" Lord Morfett himself, a short and squat faerie, had stepped out of his caravan and was gazing down upon what he thought were his hired musicians, all groaning and holding their stomachs. Lei lurched a little too close to him, and the lord backed away as though afraid to catch an airborne illness. "Get away from me!"

"Ate bad mushrooms on the road," gasped Evangeline, grasping the lie out of thin air.

"Need—washroom—" Tristan grunted.

A pale-faced Nicholas grabbed Alice so that she was turned away from Lord Morfett and stroked the back of her head as though trying to ease her sickness, though it was most likely because Alice had the worst acting skills of them by far.

Faeries couldn't lie—Evangeline knew this, of course, and knew that it would only serve their purpose. Lord Morfett might be annoyed, but given that there was no chance his court musicians *wouldn't* be telling the truth, there was little he could do about this unfortunate development except take their word and let them pass.

"Well, this is most unbecoming," the lord snapped irritably. He glanced around, his cheeks turning rosy with embarrassment. Indeed, they were drawing some attention with their act; nearby faeries were beginning to whisper and stare. "T-Take care of your—your *needs,* and then be back here in ten minutes flat. And don't you dare indicate any association with me!" he called to their retreating backs.

This was all going to be a hysterically funny memory in the distant future, but at the moment, it was nothing short of terrifying. Evangeline's body pulsed with adrenaline and fear as she ran through the crowd. She did her best not to look directly at any of the fae. It was hard to look at them straight on, anyway, for they shifted between appearing beautiful or monstrous depending on the perspective of the onlooker. Right now, the faeries appeared to be horrific creatures straight out of a nightmare, all sharp limbs and razor-like teeth. Their laughter, which had sounded light at first, grew louder and more deafening, echoing in her head until she was on the verge of screaming just to drown out the noise. She was forced to pause in the middle of the crowd as her panic spiked, aware of the eyes on her but too petrified to move.

"You're good." A warm hand grabbed her icy-cold one. "Don't over-think it." A golden-eyed faerie was staring at her with concern, and it took Evangeline a moment to register that it was Tristan. He grabbed hold of her hand firmly and tugged her past the onlooking faeries, the confidence in his every stride restoring some of Evangeline's own confidence.

Get it together, Evangeline ordered herself as her panic finally waned. Tristan was right. This was no time to let her fears get the best of her. The others were counting on her. What would they think if she couldn't even make her way through the crowd of faeries without losing her head? With that thought, Evangeline's feet propelled her forward.

Faeries scattered out of the way, grumbling slightly, as Evangeline led the others to a small stone archway at the side of the palace. Though they'd drawn some attention moments ago, there was far too much to marvel at in the garden of the High Court, which was decked out with blooming flowers and lush greenery, and soon the curious faeries had turned their interested gazes elsewhere.

Somehow, Evangeline had made it through. However, there was no time to waste celebrating.

"We'll reconvene out here in fifteen minutes," she said, just loudly enough for the others to hear. "Nicholas, you'll leave before that to get back to the human world and bring the getaway car around. Whether we've got the fountainheads or not, we need to get out of here within fifteen, because we won't be able to keep our covers for much longer than that."

The others nodded. Evangeline stared at Nicholas for a beat longer than the others and then gestured for him to come closer to her. He obeyed with a curious look.

"There is one extra favor I need to ask of you," Evangeline whispered into his ear. Nicholas gave a shiver. Evangeline, of course, recognized the effect she had on Nicholas, knew his loyalty was so true that he would go to the ends of the earth for her, and now she needed to ask for just that.

When Evangeline was done whispering her order to Nicholas, he pulled back. His expression was one of confusion and reluctance. "Evangeline . . ."

Her eyes flashed. It was a warning for him to stop speaking, and he did. "Please. You're the only one I can count on to pull this off. Don't make me remind you what's at stake if we fail."

Nicholas heaved a long-suffering sigh. The sound did give Evangeline a twinge of pity. At the Academy, Nicholas had dutifully done her bidding no matter how much he might question her sometimes, and even though the task at hand now had much higher stakes, somehow their dynamic hadn't changed a bit. Nicholas would pull through for her no matter his personal reservations. He was more reliable than anyone she knew, and he'd been her steady rock throughout the decades.

Evangeline placed a hand on his shoulder and squeezed it, hoping he could feel the extent of her gratitude. "Thank you, Nicholas."

As the others looked on in curiosity, Evangeline allowed herself one extra moment to glance at each of them, memorizing the expressions of her comrades. No matter what happened next, she would always remember this moment, before they attempted the impossible.

"Now, go."

33
ALICE

Fate must be playing a cruel joke on her. Right when she needed to perform at her best, Alice *would* get a bad case of motion sickness from the stupid caravan. She did her best to hide her discomfort and keep it together as she, Evangeline, and Tristan raced toward the palace, but the other two were much too fast, even moving at a somewhat regular pace. Or perhaps Alice was slowing down too much.

Alice wasn't sure exactly what Evangeline intended to use her for—surely Tristan alone would be enough to steal the zodiac fountainheads?—but she desperately wanted to live up to Evangeline's expectations. No, she *needed* to live up to those expectations. Because if she failed now, if they failed now, they'd be failing all of the Descendants. And Alice knew she could not bear such a heavy burden.

With each step she took, the dizziness in her head seemed to grow stronger, along with the irresistible pull she'd felt since the moment she'd stepped into Faerie. It was all like a vivid, horrid dream, Alice decided. She was used to her sleep being plagued by these nightmarish visions, but she'd always been able to wake up and find herself safe and warm in her bed, the details of the dreams slipping away until they could no longer bother her.

Being in Faerieland felt like one of those dreams, only this time no matter how much she pinched herself, she couldn't wake up.

She couldn't be sure she *wasn't* dreaming, but this world and its occupants seemed just a bit too detailed—too *real*—to be a mere product of her overactive imagination. There were the fae, dazzling and glamorous and almost too beautiful to look at. There were stone statues of the Folk, carved with intricate details and positioned around the garden. Flowers bloomed with a vivid splendor the likes of which Alice had never seen. And the *food*—only the finest refreshments had been prepared for the Midsummer Celebration, Alice assumed, and even though her human nose wasn't nearly strong enough to pick up every wondrous scent, she could still smell the intensely fresh berries and cheeses and wine that servants held up on platters. She'd never been able to smell berries this strongly before—earthy and sweet and tantalizing.

Alice's stomach gave a growl, and her mouth began to water. How long had it been since she'd had that rushed meal of dumplings in Chinatown? She watched a goblin servant walk toward her, balancing a large platter of cheese on his hand and bowing low when he reached her.

For just a moment, Alice hesitated. What was it Lei had said about humans eating faerie food? The others seemed to be able to control their appetites fairly well—they were supernaturals who'd had quite some time to practice, after all, and now Alice's human weakness was evident. She was so dizzy and hungry that she couldn't remember Lei's words at all, though she vaguely recalled that he had been giving a warning. Surely something that smelled this delicious couldn't do anything *that* harmful to her body . . . besides, she was already practically in a state of delirium from exhaustion; if she didn't eat something, and very soon, she would be entirely useless to the mission anyway. And it was her birthday, even if nobody else knew it. Didn't she deserve to eat something special on her birthday?

"Thank you," Alice said to the server as she took a slice of cheese.

The goblin stared up at her, his expression startled. She was confused by *his* confusion for a moment, and then it occurred to her that perhaps the servants weren't used to being thanked. Had she blown her cover? Her heart began beating very fast. She glanced toward Evangeline and Tristan, who were several paces away now. She needed to catch up, and she needed to get away before this goblin began to wonder about her. Pushing past a fresh wave of dizziness, she shoved the cheese into her mouth and sped after the others.

Faerie cheese was not like human cheese. That was Alice's first thought as she bit into the slice, flavor like she'd never known bursting into her mouth. Later, she knew, she would have the most difficult time recalling the precise flavor of Faerie cheese, for it was a bold mix of sweet and savory with a spicy kick to it. These flavors should not have complemented each other as they did. Try as she might to come up with a comparison, Alice didn't think any flavors or spices in the human world could stack up to this. And, most pleasantly, the dizziness she had been experiencing was now just about gone, though her head was still not as clear as before.

Nothing bad had happened to her at all. Why had Lei warned them away from the faerie food?

Alice wove her way through the guests with renewed strength. Evangeline and Tristan turned when she caught up to them, seeming to have noticed her lagging behind.

"Now is not the time for dawdling," Evangeline snapped at Alice.

"Sorry, I—" Alice clamped a hand over her mouth before she could say anything further. She was in a particularly truth-telling mood, and her gut instinct told her that the faerie food had something to do with it. But no, Alice definitely shouldn't tell the others that she'd consumed a slice of cheese just now. Evangeline's head might actually explode. At the thought, Alice had to squash the sudden, wildly inappropriate urge to giggle.

Evangeline grabbed Alice's arm in a viselike grip, but strangely, it didn't hurt. Or maybe the sensation of pain was just taking its time to register in her mind and body. Alice wouldn't be surprised to find out that that was yet another difference between the human and faerie worlds.

"When the High King and his procession leave the throne and enter the gardens, I'll give the signal to Nicholas and Lei to set off their distraction," Evangeline muttered in her ear. "Meanwhile, you're to concentrate on reading as many minds as you can. You're my eyes and ears. Any sign that someone has grown suspicious—anything at all—and you inform me at once. Understood?"

Alice bobbed her head up and down, exerting what felt like more effort than usual.

Evangeline's brow creased. For a moment, Alice thought Evangeline had taken notice of her unusual behavior, but all Evangeline did was pat her on the shoulder. "You've done well so far, Alice. We're almost to the finish line."

A warmth spread from the center of Alice's chest throughout her entire body. She could float away on the happiness of receiving Evangeline's praise. Or perhaps she was on the verge of floating away in general. But no, no—she needed to keep herself grounded. She needed to be Evangeline's eyes and ears. *You have one job, Alice. Keep it together,* she scolded herself. With gargantuan effort, she forced her last remaining brain cells to concentrate on the many threads of thoughts surrounding her.

Who does Lord Morfett think he is . . . showing up after acting a fool at the last Celebration?

Is it just me, or do the Night Court lords and ladies look rather malnourished this year? Must be the effects of their drought and downturning economy . . .

While interesting, the thoughts of the nearby faeries raised nothing of concern to Alice. Nothing to indicate that the group was under suspicion or in any danger of being discovered. Evangeline was studying her, so she gave a brief shake of her head to indicate that the coast was clear.

Then Evangeline pinched her nose with her fingers—a signal. The plan was in motion.

34
LEI

There was nothing so awkward as running into your ex-lover while you were wearing a totally new appearance, after you'd spent the past seven years locked away in a prison cell.

Well, technically he wasn't an ex-*lover*. Lei had never dared to try to define the liaison he'd had with Prince Titus back in his days of serving as a spy. Whatever humans thought of as complicated, label-less relationships, the fae were even more confusing with their love. Lei had never been under any illusion that the prince was his and his alone; he'd often see Prince Titus canoodling with male and female faeries alike, and his reputation in the Court was that of a playboy. In fact, part of Lei had wondered if Prince Titus would even remember him after all this time. The only reason he suspected the prince *might* recall him was because he was, as far as he was aware, Titus's one and only shaman lover.

Lei was so taken aback by the sudden appearance of the prince he'd once known so intimately that he nearly ran right into an elf servant carrying a silver tray of green wines. The servant gave a slight scowl but said nothing about Lei's clumsiness.

"Careful," Nicholas muttered. They couldn't afford to be careless in any sense of the word this evening. Nicholas's eyes darted back and forth as though he expected to be attacked at any moment, and there was a line of sweat beaded on his forehead.

"You ought to relax a little," Lei murmured in return. "You're trying so hard not to look suspicious that you look even *more* suspicious."

"How am I supposed to relax with all our necks on the line?"

It was a fair point. And although he was better at concealing his fear than Nicholas, Lei wasn't treating this as a walk in the park, either. Every time he'd entered Faerieland, it had been with a mixture of excitement and terror in his heart. That combination always made for the most *excellent* surge of adrenaline. Lei was addicted to that adrenaline like some were addicted to caffeine.

Nicholas was muttering under his breath, but Lei was no longer paying attention. Instead, his eyes were glued to the tall, broad-shouldered, black-haired prince, who was currently telling a very witty joke to a group of admiring faeries, if the tinny laughter was any indication. Or, most likely, the faeries wanted to butter the prince up.

Prince Titus had come out to the Midsummer Celebration dressed in his finest—a glimmering golden shirt tucked into finely woven black silk pants—and even from a distance, his green eyes were piercing. He was just as Lei remembered him; he hadn't aged a day since they'd last seen each other. The only noticeable difference was that Prince Titus was now favoring his left leg and limping slightly on his right. It was a tiny detail and one that he was trying to hide with some success, but Lei had always noticed the little details about the prince—the mole behind his left ear, the heart-shaped birthmark on the inside of his right wrist. Now Lei wondered how Titus had injured himself.

The prince turned to pick up a glass of wine, and his eyes roved around the crowd and met Lei's.

Quickly, Lei averted his gaze and returned his attention to Nicholas, his heart pounding madly. Perhaps Prince Titus had felt nothing, which seemed impossible and yet quite likely at the same time. After all, seven years had passed. Prince Titus had many, many lovers. Even if, by some miracle, the prince remembered Lei, there was no way he would recognize him in his disguised state.

"Who is that? Someone you used to know?" Nicholas asked sharply.

Lei felt a flush creep onto his cheeks. He couldn't see it for himself, but he imagined they were turning green. "Nothing that concerns you."

"Au contraire, my friend. I believe that anything that might interfere with our mission concerns me. And this—whatever it is—could *definitely* be interfering."

"Nothing will interfere with the mission," Lei said sharply. He kept his back to Prince Titus, doing his best to forget that the faerie from his past was right behind him—within reach—and instead focusing on Evangeline off in the distance.

That was how, when Evangeline began pinching her nose, Lei spotted the signal before Nicholas.

Lei moved in closer and grabbed Nicholas's wrist. "The signal," he whispered, and felt Nicholas's body stiffen.

Now thoughts of Titus and their past had flown out of his head, and all Lei could think about was the Assignment. Lei and Nicholas had only one job, which was to cause a distraction that was disruptive enough to let Evangeline and the others slip into the palace unnoticed. It was imperative that they succeed. If they were all caught now, the consequences would be catastrophic, and even worse, it would be a blemish on Lei's reputation as a slick, capable agent.

Lei thought quickly, taking in a calculated, sweeping glance of the Celebration. The music around them had grown louder, the procession already moving out of the palace. There were any number of ways to divert attention from the three figures heading into the palace. Lei chose the simplest method, which, in his experience, was usually the best.

"If you don't mind." Lei gave a smooth smile to the goblin servant who was passing by carrying a tray piled high with fruits and cheese. Before the servant could do little more than glance at him, Lei grabbed

316

the tray and flung the food in every direction. He made sure to pitch it with his full strength, which he was quite certain could rival a vampire's.

"Really?" Nicholas sighed over the gasps and screams that erupted around them. "This is unrefined, Lei."

"Never claimed to be anything but!"

Despite his grumbling, Nicholas, too, grabbed a plate of food and began pelting passersby with its contents. In moments, faeries had scattered in all directions and the two had been given a wide berth. The procession had paused in confusion and panic. Now that the source of the chaos had been revealed, however, the guards were pointing at Nicholas and Lei.

"Uh-oh," Lei said.

"We need to run now," Nicholas hissed.

The two turned to make a dash for the hedges on the outskirts of the Court, but Lei had only taken a few paces before a tall, imposing figure planted himself in front of the pair.

Prince Titus stared down at Lei, and a sharp, knowing smile played on his lips. His piercing dark green eyes seemed to see right past Lei's disguise. He leaned in close, so close that Lei was hit with a dizzying waft of Titus's all-too-familiar scent—spices, and summer breeze, and something indescribably *him*. . . . Lei's knees were weak before he could even pull his thoughts together. Gods, Lei didn't know how he could ever have thought he'd be able to waltz around before Titus and pretend they had never been anything to each other. This was how things had always been with Titus; Lei would find himself hopelessly, irresistibly drawn into his orbit.

Lei had been wrong, after all. Seven years, and he had learned nothing. Seven years apart hadn't changed their dynamic one bit.

Titus whispered so that only Lei could hear, "Now, I know the shamans weren't invited to the Midsummer Celebration."

35
TRISTAN

Tristan ran into the palace, a half pace behind Evangeline. Behind him, he heard the muddled sounds of chaos as Lei and Nicholas launched their distraction. Before him, there were the silence of a nearly empty throne room, past ivy-covered golden doors, and the sound of Evangeline quickly knocking out the few guards who lingered behind. The guards' unconscious state would soon be noticed; Tristan and Evangeline needed to act as fast as they could.

Tristan particularly wanted to finish up the job as quickly as possible, because the full moon was already high in the sky, and despite the precautions he'd taken, he was beginning to feel the effects on his body. His skin was hot to the touch; his breath came out in sharp pants. These warning signs were all too familiar, and he desperately tried to keep his thoughts on the Assignment, on anything but what was happening to his body. They could be out of Faerie within half an hour—he *needed* to hold on until then. He couldn't let everyone down.

Tristan was amazed by how little resistance they'd met when they raced toward the treasure room, which was the second door on the right, past the throne room. He peeked inside the throne room for a second. There was the golden dais, covered in green vines and white flowers, where Tristan assumed the High King sat; and the smaller stone dais beside it, which could only be meant for the High Queen.

The golden doors to the treasure room had been left open. A lone guard had remained stationed outside while his comrades attended to the chaos beyond, but before he could so much as open his mouth and yell for backup, Tristan grabbed his neck and squeezed down on a pressure point. The guard fell to his knees immediately.

They now had a clear path into the treasure room. No more guards. No visible enchantments protecting any of the treasures. It was nerve-racking how simple the rest of the job seemed. Tristan surmised that perhaps the High King had suspected someone might try to break in and had set a trap. He hadn't realized he'd theorized aloud until Evangeline replied.

"It's the faerie ego," she said. "They have no reason to steal from one another, and furthermore, they believe nobody would *dare* steal from them." She sounded so certain in this that Tristan could only agree.

The treasure room gleamed golden from ceiling to floor. Various pieces of treasure, everything from golden harps to complicated-looking trinkets to bedazzling jewelry, were on display. Any and every form of treasure one could imagine was on show in this room. At the back was another door, just as Lei had said.

But there were no zodiac fountainheads in sight.

The panicked expression on Evangeline's face—a look that Tristan had rarely seen there—made his stomach sink. But surely Evangeline had a backup plan for this nightmare scenario.

"Where are the fountainheads?" Alice whispered.

"They must be here," Evangeline said, though there was a slight quiver in her voice. She sped back and forth around the room, careful not to touch anything as she examined every piece of treasure. "They *must*."

There was no plan B for this situation, Tristan realized with dawning horror. Evangeline had banked on their being able to find the zodiac fountainheads in the treasure room; for where else would they be?

"Lei must have given us false information," Tristan growled. He knew there was a reason he didn't like that shaman, despite their acquaintance over the years. He never should have helped Lei escape the Jingwei. As the temperature in Tristan's body climbed, so did his temper, despite his best efforts to keep himself under control. "That's what we get for trusting a spy."

"Lei wouldn't betray us," Evangeline said immediately. "He has too much to lose. Besides, Julius trusted him."

"Julius this, Julius that." Tristan's frustration was getting the better of him, and he knew he ought to stop talking, but he couldn't keep the words from spilling out. "I told you not to chase his shadow, Evangeline. Julius is dead. You're chasing a dead man—and where do you think that will lead you?"

Evangeline whirled on Tristan, eyes blazing with fury. "Do you really want to do this right now, Tristan? I'm warning you—I'm *not* in the mood, so don't pick any fights with me."

However, Tristan had less sense at this moment than he usually did, and his body *yearned* for a fight, even with Evangeline. Maybe especially with Evangeline.

"Wait—there's a secret door in the ground!" Alice's shouts broke the tension.

The moment was over. Tristan took a few deep breaths and squeezed his hands into fists at his sides. He'd almost lost himself. He'd almost fought *Evangeline.* He steadied his breathing, forcing himself to calm down, the adrenaline slowly draining from his limbs.

Forgetting about Tristan, Evangeline rushed to where Alice was bent over the floor. "There's nothing here."

Alice pressed her fingers down into the floor. In front of her, a white line appeared, tracing the shape of a large square—a door.

Tristan could hardly believe what he was seeing. "Magic? You're

320

capable of magic, and you didn't think to mention this before?" he demanded.

"No! I—I don't know how I did that," Alice said shakily, examining her hands as though she'd never seen them before.

If Evangeline was as mystified as the others, she didn't show it. She lifted the handle of the door as though this had all been part of the plan. And from beneath the door there came a quiet rumbling, and a white stone column slowly rose out of the opening.

On top of the column were five familiar pieces of bronze treasure, slightly larger than a human head.

There was one in the shape of a dog's head; one that bore a resemblance to a rooster; one that could only be a sheep; one that must be a snake; one carved into the magnificent shape of a dragon. The statues bore the signs of wear and age, even though the fae must have cleaned them regularly. Perhaps, away from the source of their power and their people, the fountainheads had lost some of their shine.

Nevertheless, the statues were a sight to behold. All the breath had been knocked out of Tristan's lungs.

Finally, their precious treasures were within reach.

36
EVANGELINE

One hundred sixty-three years, eight months, and eighteen days.

That was the length of time during which the Circle of Twelve had been broken. That was how long it had been since the glory days of the Descendants.

Decades of searching. Over a century of humiliation, of longing. And now, at long last, the five missing zodiac fountainheads were right before them. It seemed impossible; it seemed like it must be a dream. But no dream could be so vivid; no mere vision could evoke such strong emotion from Evangeline that she thought she might choke on it.

"Oh, Julius . . . I wish you could see . . ." A lump lodged in her throat, and she couldn't finish the sentence.

A warm hand reached for hers. She glanced over. Tristan, his eyes brimming with unshed tears, face alight with wonder, was staring at *her* rather than at the statues. He held her hand, and it felt like the most natural intimacy in the world. Evangeline's heart could have burst with gratitude that he, one of the very few who understood the colossal importance of this moment, was here with her. She gave his fingers a light squeeze.

What happened next could only have happened because of the intensity of the moment, because both parties were far away from anything and everything they knew—because, deep down, Evangeline and Tristan had each bottled up their emotions for years, and now they could no longer stop the natural course of the universe. It was not clear who pulled who close, nor did it matter, really.

Tristan's mouth pressed softly against Evangeline's. Uncertain, at first, a question in his lips. When Evangeline responded by leaning into the kiss and lightly resting her hand on his shoulder, Tristan kissed her deeper, harder.

Evangeline had nearly forgotten what it was like to feel such intense desire for another, to be swept up in her own illogical emotions. The kiss seemed to last an eternity. She could have stayed here, in Tristan's embrace, but he was the first to pull away.

"You did it, Ev," said Tristan. "You found the statues."

"*We* did it."

The two stood there for another beat, smiling. Even though so much baggage still weighed on Evangeline and Tristan, even though so much remained unresolved—for the moment, nothing else mattered. They had been there when the fountainheads were stolen; they had been through Hell together, and still somehow found each other in this moment, a moment to remember. They were the first Descendants to lay eyes on the lost fountainheads in well over a century.

An ache, terrible and beautiful and all-encompassing, formed in the pit of Evangeline's stomach. Only one thing was missing from this otherwise perfect moment: Julius's presence. Oh, how Evangeline ached. She wished, more than anything, that her brother could be by her side to behold this magnificent sight. Julius, who never gave up hope in the search for the stolen fountainheads. Julius, who had been with her through everything.

Even Alice, who hadn't even been alive for most of the time the Descendants had mourned the loss of their fountainheads, couldn't keep her eyes dry. "They're . . . they're beautiful," she whispered.

Beautiful was an understatement. But there was no word in the English or Chinese languages—or quite likely, in any language at all—that could capture the gloriousness of the statues before them, the magnitude of this moment.

Now all that was left was for Evangeline to step forward and claim her destiny. She had a prophecy to fulfill.

37
ALICE

Alice was well aware that, unlike most of the other team members, she had no deep-rooted history with nor any personal connection to the zodiac fountainheads. Of course she wanted to help her fellow Descendants pull off this heist; of course she wanted to see the Circle of Twelve restored; of course she wanted history's wrongs to finally be righted. But unlike the others, Alice did not have over a century's worth of aching and longing for justice nestled in her heart.

Yet when she saw the five statues, Alice's reaction was so visceral that it took her by surprise.

Her heart nearly stopped. She sucked in a sharp breath. She had never witnessed a sight so breathtakingly beautiful, and likely never would again.

And as she gazed and gazed at the brilliant zodiac fountainheads, unwilling (and perhaps unable) to turn her eyes away, the strangest sensation enveloped her. She couldn't shake off the most peculiar feeling of déjà vu, the inkling that she had seen these statues before—in another time, another place, another life.

These statues . . . it was an impossible, ludicrous thought, and yet Alice was certain that they *called* to her. Just as she'd somehow sensed that the statues were beneath her feet, that they were trapped beneath a door. She couldn't explain how she had known this with such conviction. She just *knew*, as one knew that the sky was blue.

Almost as if by reflex, she placed one foot in front of the other, moving closer and closer to the shining treasures. Something trickled down her cheeks. Tears. She wiped them away, staring at the wetness on her fingers in wonder.

At last, Alice was no longer lost. She understood why she had been summoned to Earthly Branches Academy, why Evangeline had enlisted her aid for this impossible task. Why, in fact, she had been put on this Earth.

Alice had been born for a specific purpose. And here, now, she was about to fulfill it.

38
TRISTAN

Tristan had, of course, spent considerable time wondering how he might react if he ever laid eyes on the five missing zodiac fountainheads again. He'd imagined himself weeping with gratitude. He'd imagined himself punching the air with joy.

When the moment came at last, Tristan forgot himself. He forgot how desperately he'd been trying to keep his werewolf side at bay. He forgot that they likely had only seconds before the faeries discovered them. All he knew was that this tidal wave of emotion was like nothing he'd experienced before. Longing, mixed with happiness and anger. Sorrow, mixed with vindication and grief.

As the swell of emotions rose within Tristan, so, too, did the beast stir from deep inside. Almost out of instinct, he had reached for Evangeline's hand the moment he saw the fountainheads. He needed something real to ground him. And perhaps, in this remarkable moment, he had finally realized that there was nobody else he'd rather have by his side.

An overwhelming sense of warmth and power emanated from the five statues. Tristan glanced at Evangeline and saw that her eyes were filled with tears, her free hand covering her mouth, and when she met his gaze, he knew they shared the same thought: that with the restoration of these five fountainheads, the former might of the Descendants—and all *their* descendants—would at long last return to them.

He smiled at her, his lips twitching with how unfamiliar the motion felt on his face.

And in the midst of this emotional tornado, one feeling rose above the rest: a hot, burning fury. The wave of anger pulsed through Tristan's body, sweeping him from head to foot, sending his pulse and breathing into overdrive.

Even Tristan himself was taken by surprise by the fierce rage that gripped him. For so long, the Descendants had wondered and waited for a hint, a sign, *anything* at all, to indicate the location of their lost fountainheads. All along, the figures had been tucked away in Faerieland, where the fae had no understanding or appreciation of the treasures they held in their filthy, greedy hands. How *dare* the fae keep the zodiac fountainheads hidden away for so long?

"Tristan?"

Evangeline's sharp voice snapped Tristan back to reality, and he realized he was trembling from head to foot. His vision began to turn from red back to normal. He'd pulled his hand out of Evangeline's without even realizing it. He'd pressed his nails so deeply into his palms that he'd drawn blood—and yet he hardly felt any pain, so all-consuming was his rage.

"The fae will pay," he managed to spit out through gritted teeth. He took a few deep breaths—one, two, three—and exhaled, long and slow.

"I understand your anger—believe me, I do—but we'll be the ones paying if we don't get a move on, Tristan. Besides, we don't know the exact story yet. Perhaps there's more to this than meets the eye."

Tristan didn't know how Evangeline managed to keep such composure, and he didn't know whether he resented her or admired her for it. After all, shouldn't she be just as furious as he was to discover that the fae had been the culprits all along? "I think it's pretty obvious what's happened here," he growled. "Those sneaky bastards thought they'd get their hands on our precious fountainheads and keep them here on display, regardless of how we, the rightful owners, would feel about that loss."

Even now, Evangeline kept a cool head on her shoulders. Her gaze, when she leveled it on Tristan, was full of strength and a shining, burning determination. Somehow, Tristan began to calm down.

"That may well be the case, but we can save our anger for after we find out the truth. We need to focus on the immediate task at hand." She strode up to the statues with her signature measured, businesslike pace. Gone was that moment of overwhelming emotion. Now it was time to keep their feelings in check, to act according to the plan. "We don't have much time," she said, her voice hoarse. It sounded as though she was using all of her remaining resolve to force her plan forward. "Lei and Nicholas have bought us precious moments, but we need to get these fountainheads out of here and meet up with them—now."

"How exactly are we to do that?" Tristan asked. He rolled up his sleeves. Faerie magic encased the statues. There was no doubt in his mind that if they tried to touch the statues with their bare hands, they would find the experience quite unpleasant.

Evangeline was muttering to herself. "*Midsummer's sprout* . . . yes, this has to work."

Before Tristan could cry out or try to stop her, Evangeline reached out to touch the dragon statue. She'd hardly placed a finger upon the bridge of the dragon's nose when she jerked her hand back with a yelp and then shook it in the air, as though she'd been badly burned.

Tristan started forward. "Evangeline—"

"No, it *must* work," Evangeline was murmuring while she clutched her hand in pain. She stared down at her fingers in frustration. "It has to be me. *Midsummer's sprout* . . . even Julius believed that was a reference to . . ."

Something inside Tristan snapped. The zodiac fountainheads were right before them, they had moments to take the statues with them, and there was no *time* for Evangeline to try to figure out the answer on her own. "Can you please explain what's happening, Evangeline? We're past the point of you keeping your plan so secret. We have just moments before we could lose this chance to restore the fountainheads—forever."

"Let us *help* you," Alice added. Though her voice was weak, it seemed that this pleading, at last, got through to Evangeline.

Evangeline turned to face the two. Both of her hands were shaking, and she gazed upon the fountainheads with a wild look in her eye. Tristan had never seen Evangeline so frazzled. This development—her inability to even touch the statues without pain—hadn't been in her calculations, that much was obvious.

"There was a prophecy about the Descendant who would finally be allowed to bring the zodiac fountainheads back," Evangeline said quietly. "The one referred to in the prophecy—*Midsummer's sprout*—Julius thought it was me. *I* thought it was me. I'm the only Descendant born on Midsummer's Day. But . . . I can't touch the statues." Her bottom lip trembled as she finished the sentence, and her face crumpled with an unfamiliar expression. Hopelessness. They'd come so close, but the final step in Evangeline's airtight plan had fallen apart, and she seemed at a loss for what to do.

"Wait." Alice's face had drained of color, turning pale enough to rival the shade of Evangeline's. "Midsummer . . . I was born on Midsummer's Day, too."

The look on Evangeline's face could be described as nothing but pure shock. "You . . . what?"

"June twenty-fourth, 2007."

Evangeline appeared stricken, as though her entire world had turned upside down in an instant. "Why didn't you mention this before?" she demanded.

"I didn't know it would be relevant. And I don't care much for my birthday."

"I . . . well, happy birthday."

Alice blinked. "You too."

"Is this really the moment to be exchanging 'happy birthdays'?"

Tristan burst out. The Assignment was going terribly wrong if *he* had suddenly become the voice of reason.

Both Evangeline and Alice seemed rooted to the spot, but if ever there *wasn't* a moment to be frozen, it was right now, when the fae could burst in on them stealing the fountainheads at any second.

As far as Tristan could see, there was only one way forward. Alice was born on Midsummer's Day, like the subject of the prophecy. Alice was the one who'd somehow, intuitively, located the hidden fountainheads, and accessed them with unknown powers. Tristan didn't know what exactly was going on, but given everything that had transpired before his eyes, he could make an educated guess as to what to do next.

He grabbed Alice by the elbow and moved her until she stood in front of the statues.

"Wh-What is it?" Alice asked, trembling as she stared down at the fountainheads with a mix of wonder and fear in her expression.

"Touch the statue," Tristan commanded.

Evangeline watched with wide, shocked eyes. For once, she had been rendered speechless. A silence fell and time seemed to stop, as if the universe itself were waiting to see what would happen next.

Perhaps it was because Tristan spoke with such conviction and authority that Alice obeyed without further hesitation. She stretched out her fingers. When her fingertips touched the statues, she winced, but she didn't pull away. There was no shout of pain, no yanking her arm back. In fact, when Alice pressed her fingertips into each of the fountainheads, one after the other, they began to shudder and glow.

Amazingly, impossibly, a white light encased the statues, forcing the three Descendants to stumble back and cover their eyes. When at last he'd managed to blink the bright spots out of his eyes, Tristan found himself gazing upon five brilliantly gleaming fountainheads, so polished now that they might have been crafted only moments ago.

"You . . . you really did it, Alice." Evangeline's voice sounded wrong, reedy and high-pitched and choked.

Tristan's first reaction wasn't to look at Alice but to glance over at Evangeline. Her mouth was slightly agape, and there was the strangest expression on her face. One of open devastation.

Having spent the better part of a century in Evangeline's company, Tristan thought he knew exactly what was warring inside her. Relief that they'd overcome an enormous, unexpected obstacle. Embarrassment because she'd been very, very wrong. And envy because the object of the prophecy was Alice, not her.

"Oh," Alice moaned with a small gasp. She teetered in front of the statues.

"Alice?" Tristan took a step toward her, alarmed.

"What's the matter?" Evangeline demanded. She'd snapped out of her initial shock, but her eyes were huge and disbelieving, despite her best efforts to stay in control of the situation. "This isn't the time to be falling apart. We need your help."

"I can't," Alice gasped, swaying. "I—I ate faerie food earlier, and I think it's made me ill," she cried out in a rush.

"You did *what*?" Tristan groaned and smacked his forehead. Just when it seemed they'd figured out how to carry out the rest of the heist, Alice had to tell them this? Evangeline was fuming, her eyes bulging with a mixture of anger and fear, and they were seconds, seconds away from losing everything.

"Sorry, I . . . I didn't mean . . ." Then, before she could finish her sentence, Alice fainted.

39
NICHOLAS

Nicholas had always been unfortunately thickheaded in the romance department. Over the course of the last decade alone, no fewer than half of his classmates had come to him confessing their love, and he could honestly say that he hadn't expected to be asked out by a single one of them. As Evangeline had once put it, he was denser than a rock when it came to matters of the heart. However, even Nicholas thought it was rather obvious that there was history—and quite a lot of it—between Lei and the faerie prince. There was simply no way that two individuals could gaze upon each other with such intensity, with such open longing, and not have shared intimate moments in the past.

Titus leaned in close to whisper something in Lei's ear. Nicholas didn't catch the faerie prince's words, but he had a good idea of what he might have said, given how Lei's eyes bulged out and his cheeks flushed.

"Y-You . . ." Lei stumbled back from Titus, who was gazing at the shaman in disguise with an almost hungry expression.

Nicholas grabbed Lei's arm and pulled him closer. "Do you two . . .

have history?" he muttered. It was a silly question, as the answer was rather obvious.

For a moment, panic spiked within Nicholas, enough to heat up his body. It occurred to him that if there *was* history between Titus and Lei, then Titus must somehow be able to recognize Lei even under the disguise. Their cover was about to be blown. Not only were they trespassers, but they were shaman *and* Descendant trespassers—and the revelation of this secret really could lead to war.

For the love of gods, why hadn't Lei at least warned the others that run-ins with former flings were a possibility? Now they were drawing attention for the *wrong* reason; the partygoers, who seemed to have a radar for drama, were forming a circle around Titus and Lei and gazing on in curiosity.

"What . . . What are you talking about?" Lei asked Titus at long last. The confusion in his voice was well performed. Even Nicholas almost couldn't tell the shaman was bluffing. "I'm a court musician from the Dusk Court."

Titus's lips twitched, as though suppressing a smile. "Really? Where are your instruments?"

While Lei stammered out an answer, Nicholas reconsidered his initial panic. Although this development was unexpected, it could work out in their favor. Prince Titus hadn't immediately sounded the alarm, which meant one of two things. One: he was more concerned with amusing himself than with revealing the identities of the trespassers (good). Or two: he simply didn't care (even better).

Furthermore, any extra drama from this unexpected reunion of prince and ex-fling would help Lei and Nicholas create the most spectacular diversion. Perhaps they could stage a former lovers' spat or something to that effect; it would surely keep the eyes of every onlooker from wandering toward the palace.

Nicholas stared at Lei, hoping to convey this message with his eyeballs, but Lei had eyes only for Prince Titus.

Prince Titus rolled his eyes to the sky, as though he couldn't believe that Lei was still trying to keep up the faerie cover. Then he strode forward and grabbed Lei's wrist. "Come with me."

Lei didn't resist, but he threw a look at Nicholas. Nicholas, however, was less concerned with whatever private matters Titus wanted to discuss with Lei and much more worried that they were losing the interest of the faeries—particularly the guards. As he watched, the guards began to wander back toward their positions outside the palace. This was bad, very bad. The guards only needed to peek inside, and the Assignment would be blown. Nicholas needed to do something extremely drastic and risky—and fast. He considered his limited options and decided there was only one way to ensure that all attention turned toward them. He lunged forward and grabbed hold of the faerie prince's arm.

"What are you—?"

"So sorry to do this, Prince," Nicholas said. Before Titus could react, he yanked his arm so that he was giving the faerie a tight one-armed hug; then he raised his other hand, revealing a sharp knife, which he raised to Titus's throat. This entire exchange took place in a fraction of a second.

Screams and gasps echoed throughout the garden. Nicholas almost felt as though he were having an out-of-body experience. Was he really holding a knife to the prince's throat? Faeries had been beheaded for less, surely? Yet there was no fear in his heart, only—*excitement.* His whole body buzzed with adrenaline. It seemed to Nicholas that he had shot right past the point of fear and reached insanity. If only Evangeline could see him now. Perhaps she'd be shocked. Perhaps she'd shed a tear of pride.

"Are you *mad*?" Lei cried out, looking at Nicholas with horror.

"Most likely," said Nicholas as he fought the nonsensical urge to laugh.

Titus, however, seemed wholly unconcerned. In fact, he was rather slack in Nicholas's grip, as though the knife at his throat were the least interesting thing in the world. "And what is it that you think you are doing?"

"I'm not going to hurt you, but I need you to walk backward with me.

If you do this, you'll get to speak with Lei in private," Nicholas whispered against Titus's skin.

"Very bold plan the two of you have concocted," Titus remarked, as though commenting on the state of the weather. "You're lucky I couldn't give less of a damn about this Celebration. The *dullest* of parties—and my father only puts it on every year in hopes of summoning Midsummer's sprout."

Midsummer's sprout. Something about that phrase nudged at Nicholas, but now was not the time to examine that feeling.

"Very well. I'll entertain you," the prince was saying. He began to slowly walk backward, even putting his hands up in the air. Nicholas thought he was being mocked, but he couldn't be sure.

Lei's pale face popped up right beside Nicholas. "Do you have any idea what you're doing, or have you lost your mind entirely? That is a *faerie prince* you're threatening."

"Just follow me," Nicholas hissed back.

"Go get the High King!" a nearby faerie snapped, and a couple of the guards swiftly moved to obey.

Nicholas's eyes assessed the crowd of onlookers. Although the reactions seemed mixed—some fearful, some shocked, some disturbed—it seemed the overall response was one of amusement. However, he imagined this whole scene was about to get *much* less amusing once the High King arrived.

"Make a run for it," Nicholas hissed. Then, without waiting for Lei or Titus to respond, he turned around, grabbed them each by the arm, and began to sprint toward the Forest of Illusions as fast as he could.

Nicholas had no idea where he was going—the only thought on his mind was that he needed to venture deeper, deeper, and deeper still into the darkest part of the forest.

"I don't think we were chased," Titus called after a moment, sounding not even a little out of breath.

Nicholas stopped and strained his ears to listen. There were strange, animalistic noises coming from deep within the trees, but otherwise he heard no life. However, that didn't mean that the circumstances couldn't change very quickly. Nicholas wasn't going to take chances; it was best to operate under the assumption that they could be found on a moment's notice. Also, since he had just held a knife to Prince Titus's throat before countless eyewitnesses, if he was caught, he would probably be hauled off to whatever equivalent to prison existed in Faerie. Or executed. Neither of those outcomes would aid Evangeline in this heist.

"Now can you explain what we're doing?" Lei demanded. "You held a knife to Prince Titus's *throat,* Nicholas. The High King is going to have our heads—"

"He won't," Nicholas interrupted. He wasn't entirely sure why his conviction was so strong. He wasn't even sure what he was saying, only that his mouth was blabbing out the finer details of his plan almost as fast as he was cobbling them together in his head. "I'm going to take on the appearance of Prince Titus, and I'll return to the Court."

"Hang on," said Titus, frowning. "Did you say . . . you're going to take on my appearance?"

"Yes. You could say it's a little talent of mine."

"Well, I don't doubt you're marvelously talented, given your work on Lei's makeover, but *my* good looks can't be replicated, I'm afraid."

Nicholas just gave Prince Titus a tight little smile. He took a moment to study Titus's face—really *study* it—committing to memory his flawless, pale complexion, every golden ring on his fingers, the exact hunter-green shade of his eyes. Then Nicholas closed his eyes and imagined the looks of Prince Titus imprinted on his skin. A tingling, tickling sensation ran up and down his body. He knew he'd succeeded when Titus let out a small gasp.

"You really . . . This should be illegal," Titus said, though he sounded awestruck rather than angry. "Can you do it again?"

Can you do it again? As though Nicholas were some cheap magician hired to do party tricks, instructed to perform on command. "No, I can't do it again," he said frostily. "You two can stay here and chat as long as you'd like. I imagine there's quite a lot of catching up to do, isn't there?"

Lei grabbed Nicholas's arm. At first, he thought the shaman was going to protest this plan, but instead his eyes searched Nicholas's. His mouth was drawn in a grim line. There was no trace of his usual cheeky grin. "And what about after?"

Nicholas thought quickly. Technically, Evangeline had instructed *him* to leave Faerie ahead of the others to get the getaway vehicle ready. However, if he and Lei were going to separate anyway, and Lei already knew his way around Faerie relatively well . . . Besides, if he was honest with himself, Nicholas loathed the idea of not being by Evangeline's side during the most crucial leg of the plan. He didn't want to be the getaway man.

Sorry, Evangeline. Just this once, I have to disobey you.

Without thinking more about it, Nicholas reached into his pocket, pulled out the car keys, and shoved them into Lei's hand, trying to ignore how Titus was watching with great interest.

"You remember what the car looks like?" Nicholas asked.

Lei nodded. His eyes grew wide, as though he seemed to understand Nicholas's plan. "I'll wait for everyone outside the Met."

"Don't even think about escaping or trying anything funny. The faerie disguise will wear off soon enough; you won't be a free man until I change your appearance permanently, remember? If anything goes wrong, anything at all, I'm going to kill you. Then I'm going to bring you back to life and kill you again for good measure." Nicholas was pleased when Lei let out a nervous laugh.

"The threats just go on and on with you, don't they? I'll be there waiting. Don't worry," Lei promised.

Nicholas shouldn't believe the word of a criminal who'd just spent seven years in prison, but there were a lot of things he ought not to have done over the course of this heist. He simply had to take the shaman at his word.

Nicholas swiftly turned toward Prince Titus next. "What did you mean by what you said earlier? About Midsummer's sprout?"

Titus blinked, clearly taken aback by the unexpected question. "Ah, that. Nothing you'd find useful to your mission."

"Humor me."

The prince gave Nicholas a strange look but nevertheless launched into an explanation. "A relative of mine—one of the High King's grandchildren, someone with mixed Descendant and faerie blood—was prophesized to contain the greatest power of generations. The prophecy referred to the subject as Midsummer's sprout. Every year, Father throws this Midsummer Celebration with the hopes of luring them back home, to no avail. The child would have been born seventeen human years ago." He shrugged. "Not all Seers are legitimate, after all."

Nicholas's brow furrowed. Why couldn't he shake the feeling that he'd heard of Midsummer's sprout before? Not even a moment later, it clicked.

"The prophecy," Nicholas gasped, his eyes wide. He'd heard it for himself over a century ago, when the faerie Seer had delivered it to the High Council. That was so long ago that it had taken him a moment to recall, but now the memory returned to him with sharp clarity. *"The key to restoring glory rests with Midsummer's sprout; but if greed sows discord, harmony will be in doubt,"* Nicholas recited, overcome with the strangest premonition. Evangeline . . . Did she believe herself to be the subject of the prophecy? Was that why she'd gathered everyone to take on this Assignment? But that didn't fall in line with what Titus had revealed just now. "Midsummer's sprout," if Titus was to be believed—and he had no reason to lie about this—was half-faerie, half-mortal, and only about seventeen human years old. . . .

Of course, there was only one Descendant who could possibly fit that criterion.

"Nicholas? You look like you've seen a ghost," Lei said, sounding alarmed.

"I have to go now," Nicholas blurted out. He needed to get this information to Evangeline as fast as he could. They might all have wandered into something more troublesome than they'd realized. "One last thing," he added, pointing at Prince Titus. "You'll keep our identities a secret, of course."

"I find it amusing that you seem to have no regard at all for the fact that I'm a prince," said Titus.

"You'll keep our identities a secret, of course, *Prince* Titus," Nicholas repeated. "Unless you want a political crisis on our hands that would almost certainly lead to all-out war."

The threat in Nicholas's voice must have struck fear into the prince's heart, because he fell silent, the humor wiped clean from his expression.

"I won't say a word," Prince Titus promised. "Faeries can't lie, so you can trust me."

"Well. Thanks." Nicholas cleared his throat, wondering how he could walk away after casually threatening war on the faerie prince. There wasn't a moment to stop and think about how boldly he was behaving, how *un*-Nicholas-like.

He needed to get to Evangeline's side before it was too late.

40
ALICE

Alice was falling again, only this time there seemed to be no end to the falling, no clear destination upon which she could firmly plant her feet. She was conscious enough to be aware that she *wasn't* quite conscious. From some faraway distance, she could feel hands catching her as she fell. She heard voices that seemed to be calling her name across an ocean. However, try as she might, she could not react to their panicked cries. She was no longer in control of her own limbs, and they would not move according to her will. She could not even summon the energy to turn in the direction of the voices; her head was so heavy that it seemed quite possible that she'd never be able to lift it again.

And as her consciousness slipped away from her, the strong hands that caught her transformed into slim, spindly ones—hands belonging to faeries.

"At last," crooned an unfamiliar male voice. "You've returned to us, child."

Alice couldn't move her head, but she could at least open her eyes, though it took all of her strength to flutter open her eyelids. She stared up into the glittering green eyes of a male faerie with long, straight black hair, parted on two sides by a pair of pointed ears. On his neck hung layers and layers of jewelry, some of it fashioned from silver, some from bits of branches and leaves, and some from sharp, jagged *teeth.*

Alice had only glimpsed this figure from afar during the procession of the Midsummer Celebration, but deep down, she knew who it was. Just as she recognized why he'd come for her so clearly now, and why he'd been invading her dreams of late.

"You're the High King," she said simply. She was not sure whether the words were spoken aloud or only in her head. "You . . . you've been appearing in my visions."

"Yes," said the High King. "And you are my precious granddaughter, the long-lost princess of Faerieland, come home at last."

Alice's grandfather stretched his fingers toward hers. The moment they touched, a shock entered her system, jolting up her arms and heading straight to her heart.

"Now, wake up, little one," the High King whispered. "I will see you very, very soon."

Alice jerked out of her subconscious state, back to reality. The High King—her *grandfather,* despite how impossible that seemed—was no longer with her. Tristan was shaking her while Evangeline gazed down in concern, and slowly, Alice recalled what had been happening right before her dream encounter with the High King.

Ah, yes. Alice, Evangeline, and Tristan had been attempting to steal the long-lost magical artifacts. And then right in the middle of that, Alice had inconveniently passed out.

"Are you all right?" Evangeline peered into Alice's eyes. Evangeline had such a demanding way of voicing everything, but Alice was pretty sure that this time, she was actually concerned for Alice's well-being. That still didn't make up for the fact, though, that Evangeline had quite a lot of explaining to do, and fast.

"I . . . I'm good," Alice said. And she was surprised to realize she meant it. No longer was she tired. In fact, the revolutionary knowledge of what had just transpired gave her a burst of energy. Activating the zodiac fountainhead seemed to have triggered something inside her, some secret, buried part of her that was now raring to get out.

And Alice would let it.

"Careful," Tristan said as Alice made to get to her feet, but she did not heed his warning.

She drew herself up to her full height and turned to face Evangeline. "Did you know?" she asked quietly. "I know you've been keeping a secret from all of us this whole time. I've found it odd that Descendants targeted me. Is this the reason? Did you *know* about who I am, Evangeline?"

Evangeline's eyes widened, and her lips parted. But she did not seem confused by the question. "I . . . I did."

At Evangeline's confession, Alice's heart pounded in her chest. Her face turned hot. She was not the type of person who was easily annoyed or angered. In fact, she had always prided herself on being the peacekeeper in any situation, prone to brushing off any personal offenses without retaliation.

This time, however, Evangeline had gone too far. Just when Alice had begun warming up to the cold vampire Descendant, she'd been shown again why trust was a fool's game. Deliberately hiding a secret about Alice from Alice herself was unforgivable. Alice's hands began to shake with emotion as she stared directly into Evangeline's eyes.

Alice opened her mouth, unsure of where to begin. Out tumbled a question, or rather, a factual statement phrased as a question: "I'm one of them, aren't I?"

For a long moment, Evangeline seemed to have no reply. She and Alice stared at each other—for the first time, Alice felt, as equals. Alice had rarely seen Evangeline at a loss for words; she suspected that she could count on one finger the number of times Evangeline had been stunned into silence.

"What do you mean, Alice?" Tristan stood up rather fast. He glanced between Evangeline and Alice, neither of whom seemed like they'd be the first to break the stare.

Alice's mind raced. At first she'd surprised even herself by uttering that question—*I'm one of them, aren't I?*—which had sprung into her head without much rhyme or reason. But no, it was merely that her brain was putting together the pieces of the puzzle as she stood there, and she was coming to a conclusion so shocking that she needed to sit down or she feared her legs would collapse beneath her.

Ruiting Jiang, Alice's father in the human world, had possessed unnatural powers for somebody who was supposed to be purely mortal. He'd passed along these abilities to his daughter. The most obvious explanation was staring her right in the face. Her father had been at least part faerie, and he had stolen away to the mortal world to have a child. *Her.*

And then there were all those odd moments with Mama. Mama was most decidedly mortal, and a very jumpy mortal at that. She'd always behaved as though she expected the two of them to be ambushed at any moment, even though they were hardly well-to-do enough to be the target of any such attack. Or so Alice had thought. Humans might not give a damn about Mama and the faerie child she harbored, but naturally, the *faeries* would.

All these years, Mama had known the truth of Alice's identity, too. Just as Evangeline knew. Who *didn't* know?

But the undeniable proof that Alice wasn't as human as she'd thought was in the powers that had awakened in her in Faerieland. It was Alice who had located the zodiac fountainheads and opened the magically sealed door with just a touch of her hands. It was Alice who could touch the treasures and take them back to where they belonged. She was the one who could push past ancient faerie magic with ease. This was no fluke, and as far as Alice could see, only one logical explanation tied together all these clues.

As heat rose steadily into her cheeks, Alice did her best to keep her rising temper even. Surely Mama had only meant to protect her. But what was Evangeline's excuse for deceiving Alice? Evangeline never made a move that wasn't thoroughly calculated. Why keep Alice in the dark this entire time, unless she sought to use this knowledge to her advantage?

Had Evangeline taken Alice for such a fool? Worse, had she been planning to use Alice as *collateral* during this Assignment?

"You knew," Alice whispered. "All this time, you knew what I was, and *that's* why you selected me for this Assignment. It wasn't because of my stupid mind-reading powers. It wasn't because you think I'm . . . I'm special or worthy." Her voice cracked at the same time as her heart. She could hardly bring herself to finish her venting, but she knew she must. Somebody needed to make Evangeline understand that she couldn't treat people this way, like chess pieces to be moved around without regard for their autonomy. "You selected me because no matter what happens, even if your plan falls apart, you can bargain for safe passage back home with *me.*" Because of course, the faeries would do anything to keep Alice here—including letting the intruders get away with the zodiac fountainheads.

To Evangeline's credit, she received these accusations with hardly more than a blink of an eye. Alice wasn't sure if she admired or loathed her the more for it. "Don't sell yourself short," Evangeline said smoothly. "You're both special and worthy. We've doubtless made it this far only because of your abilities, Alice."

"Oh, don't try to flatter me right now." Alice surprised even herself with the words that erupted from her mouth. She'd never let herself feel hurt and anger like this before, never allowed herself to act upon such strong emotions, and it felt *good.* A small part of her was terrified to let go, but the bigger part was thrilled to finally, finally be set free. "Don't act like you're doing me a favor. My father must have tried to take me away from the Descendants and faeries to give me a shot at having a normal life—and you've ruined any chance of that."

Alice could tell from the confusion on Tristan's face that he, at least, hadn't been in on this rather earth-shattering secret. Most likely, only Evangeline had known. So this was Evangeline's trump card, the weapon she'd guarded so close to her heart—or at least, that hole in her chest where a heart should be.

Brava, Evangeline. You've outdone yourself. "You really are heartless."

345

Alice didn't realize she'd said the words aloud until Evangeline flinched and took a small step backward. Somehow, Alice's words had actually gotten to her, the cold and calculating vampire ice queen.

"I do not feel as humans feel," Evangeline said quietly.

And Alice felt too much. Each part of her—mortal and faerie—was shattering into a million pieces with the pain of betrayal. She thought she might scream. She thought she might break. Although Evangeline had spoken convincingly about how useful Alice's powers were to the Assignment, although Alice had thought that *finally* she'd found her place, in the end, she'd been nothing more than a tool to Evangeline, to be used and discarded once the deed was done.

And to think that, for a brief, stupid moment, Alice had thought that maybe she would no longer be an outsider among the Descendants. Evangeline and the others had never seen her as one of their own—that much was obvious now. Her vision blurred with tears of frustration.

And then the doors to the treasure room burst open.

"I'll ask you to stop there, please," said the High King, in a smooth voice that was completely free of concern, "and step away from what belongs to me."

"What belongs to *you*?" Evangeline's voice trembled slightly, but otherwise, she wasn't backing down in front of the King of Faerie. "These fountainheads belong to the Descendants. It's long past time you returned them to us."

"I was speaking about my granddaughter," the King said, "but given that those fountainheads currently reside in my domain, your argument there is invalid, too." He turned his eyes to Alice, and despite herself, she stumbled back. There was no love there, only a cold recognition.

Alice wasn't sure what to think or how to feel now that she was standing face to face with her grandfather. Mama had told her nothing about her grandparents except that they had died young, before she'd been born. She had never imagined a reunion, and certainly not one of this nature. She had scarcely wrapped her head around the fact that somehow *she* was the subject of this prophecy, that *her* touch had been enough to activate the power of the zodiac fountainheads—and now she needed to process the fact that the grandfather she'd never known was none other than the High King of Faerie.

"My granddaughter stays behind," the High King declared, his eyes never leaving Alice's. Although this should have been the start of a tearful and heartfelt reunion of kin, Alice felt cold inside. Shivers ran down her spine. She'd never imagined her grandparents in detail, but in her mind, a grandfather would appear gentle and soft, not sharp and hard like this faerie king. "You do want to remain here, don't you?"

Evangeline and Tristan moved at the same time, stepping closer toward Alice as though they meant to guard her. Tristan's eyes flashed red, and it was one of the more frightening sights Alice had ever seen; he would not hesitate, she gathered, to spill blood to protect them all.

"I . . ." Alice didn't have an answer for her grandfather, and with each moment that passed, his expression hardened more. It was clear that he'd expected her to offer an enthusiastic yes. But how could she, when all her life she'd only known the mortal realm, when she had a whole *life* back at Earthly Branches Academy, and with Mama? Her head was spinning. Yes, Faerie had called to her in her dreams for years and years. Yes, a part of her was drawn to this place. But she could not make such a monumental decision based on instinct alone.

Then again, perhaps there was no room for her at Earthly Branches Academy; perhaps her presence there didn't matter at all. Else why would Evangeline have viewed her as a pawn, so easily used and then abandoned?

"The fountainheads," Evangeline interjected coldly. "We won't leave without them."

The High King sighed and waved a hand. "Is that all you care about—those silly fountainheads?"

"When the Old Summer Palace was razed and our fountainheads were carried off, we Descendants lost everything," Evangeline said, visibly shaking with rage. "How dare you refer to them as silly? Decades you've held these artifacts in your palace, and not once did you ever appreciate their immeasurable value. To you, these fountainheads might not be worth anything beyond their beauty and monetary value—but to the Descendants, from whom you *stole* them, they are priceless. They mean everything."

"Evangeline," Tristan whispered in a raspy, throaty voice that almost didn't sound like him, "I don't think lecturing is going to get us anywhere."

Something was wrong with Tristan, Alice decided when she glanced at him, and for a moment she forgot the sting of Evangeline's betrayal. His body was trembling. His eyes, which had always been flecked with gold, were now practically shining with the color. A flush steadily climbed up his neck and cheeks. The obvious conclusion struck Alice. Could it be? Was Tristan transforming into a werewolf?

Before Alice could do or say anything, the High King interrupted. "Speak to me with such insolence again, and it will be the last thing you ever do." He tilted his head to one side and studied Evangeline, as though he'd never seen anything or anyone like her before. "We fae like to collect objects of value," he continued, as though he hadn't issued a death threat a moment ago, now speaking in the tone one might use with a toddler. "It is in the nature of our kind."

Evangeline's eyes flashed, and Alice could read from her tightened expression that she was on the verge of saying something extremely harsh. They were in no position to antagonize the High King, however. They were in *his* palace, in *his* land, and here, nobody would help them if conflict actually broke out.

"I think you've said enough," Alice said sharply to Evangeline. Clearly it was unexpected for her to speak up in such a manner, because Evangeline blinked and stared at Alice as though she'd never seen her before.

For a long moment, the room was silent. The High King licked his lips, his eyes glittering. Finally, he said, "You may take the fountainheads and get out of my sight—but only if she stays. My granddaughter, the subject of prophecy, the most powerful child faerie has ever produced . . ." King Gamede's eyes gleamed as he gazed upon Alice, as though she were a pile of gold rather than a being. "So much untapped potential. We will tap it together, child."

Alice stepped backward. The High King's face fell a little, but he quickly resumed his smile after a moment.

"Did you enjoy the food at our celebration earlier, Alice?"

"How did you know I ate the faerie food?" she demanded.

"I see it in your complexion, my dear. Faerie food has brought out the faerie side of you. How do you think you managed to locate and remove these treasures so easily?" the king asked softly. "All the valuables and locked doors in this palace are enchanted to respond only to the touch of royalty. If you stay here—oh, all of Faerieland will be your playground, child."

Alice's blood was pounding in her ears as she registered the meaning of the High King's words. She glanced over at Evangeline, whose expression revealed no surprise. No doubt, Evangeline had already predicted this outcome. No doubt, this was what she *wanted*. They were really going to leave Alice behind in Faerie?

Don't leave me behind. If Alice hadn't had her pride to consider, she would have begged. But she shouldn't have to beg for friendship. She shouldn't have to beg not to be left behind, not to be treated like a sacrificial knight on a chessboard for the sake of Evangeline's checkmate.

Evangeline averted her gaze from Alice's when she nodded at the High King and said, "Deal."

In that moment, Alice's heart could have ripped into shreds.

41
EVANGELINE

Once, half a century ago, a conflict arose between the House of Sheep and the House of Rooster. It was one of those issues that had existed for so long that nobody knew what exactly had started the ember of conflict, the details lost to history. The heads of the houses back then—Vicky Yang and Shane Ji—made it open knowledge that they would kill each other if given the chance. For a long time, Julius avoided interfering. It was a bad look for the Chancellor of the High Council to play favorites among the Descendants.

This time, the houses were squabbling because Shane had made three consecutive public attempts to hurt Vicky, and an undercurrent of fear was beginning to spread around the Academy. Shane, they said, was vicious and unstable, and once he was bored with Vicky, would he move on to another victim? The balance of power, which for so long had been carefully controlled by Julius Long, was shifting. Now somebody else might have the reach to influence the Descendants.

In the midst of the chaos at school, Julius had pulled Evangeline aside to teach her an important lesson.

"Great leaders must be willing to make sacrifices to prove what they stand for," he'd said. *Sacrifice.* This was a word that always seemed to dance on Julius's lips.

Evangeline didn't have a clue what Julius was talking about, but she knew she ought to pay attention. Julius never spoke without intention, and he was a man of his word. Thus, something very important was about to happen.

What happened next, nobody knew for certain. The rumors turned into stories, as they tended to do; and the stories grew legs and traveled wide and far, spiraling far beyond anyone's control.

Rumor had it that the day after he'd taken Evangeline aside, Julius went straight to Shane's dorm room and challenged him to a duel. The evening after, Julius came to class looking the same as usual. Shane, on the other hand, didn't come to class for three more evenings, and when he did, it was on crutches. Just like that, the rumors about Shane's power petered out, and Julius once more rested comfortably at the top of the Earthly Branches Academy food chain. But a small minority of students whispered their dissatisfaction with the violence in Julius's leadership, and they would never like him for as long as he remained in the Chancellor's seat.

As with all of Julius's lessons, Evangeline had taken this one to heart. She knew that when she had taken over for Julius as the leader of the Descendants, there would come a day when she would find herself trapped in a difficult dilemma. There would come a day when she would have to make a choice that would turn her into a hero in some eyes and a villain in others. She was ready to rise to the occasion when it presented itself.

Sacrifice. Now Evangeline would have to sacrifice some of her morals for the greater good; and to enable her sacrifice, others would have to *be* sacrificed. It was the cycle of the cold, cruel world in which they dwelled.

"Deal," Evangeline said to the High King. With that, she knew she could not take back what she'd planned, what she'd said, what she'd done. She couldn't even look at Alice. This was a betrayal, and Evangeline had cemented herself as a villain in Alice's eyes.

And Evangeline would have to be okay with that. Because this was exactly what Julius would have done, had he been in her shoes. When Evangeline returned to the human world with the five zodiac fountainheads safely in tow, she would be a hero in the eyes of so many others. She would command their respect, and she would have their vote of confidence as the next Chancellor. That was all that mattered.

So why, then, did a pang of guilt stab her stomach? *Oh, Julius. Did you ever feel conflicted over the decisions you made to keep yourself in power?* Yet again, Evangeline found herself wishing more than anything that she could consult her brother with all the questions she'd never had the chance to ask.

The High King's dark lips curled into a tight, cruel smile. Evangeline didn't frighten easily, but the sight of it sent cold shivers down her spine. "Good girl."

"Father," interrupted a male faerie's voice, and from behind the High King stepped Prince Titus. The faerie prince strode toward them with no surprise in his expression, as though hosting intruders in the treasure room were a daily occurrence. "If you don't mind, may I have a word with my long-lost niece?"

The High King raised an eyebrow, but he offered no objection. After a moment, he nodded. He stepped aside and gestured for his son to step forward.

Prince Titus's focus was so concentrated on Alice that Evangeline thought Alice must be quite unnerved by its intensity. When he walked by Evangeline, however, the prince sent her a sidelong look that brimmed with *meaning*—so brief that only Evangeline would catch it—as though they were friends sharing a secret. Such a terribly familiar look on a terribly unfamiliar face. Evangeline was mystified. She'd never interacted with Prince Titus before in her life; why would he be gazing at her as though they were in on something together? As Evangeline racked her brains for the most plausible explanation, Titus continued walking toward Alice, until they were standing mere inches away from each other.

The prince stopped dead in his tracks when the High King spoke.

The king's voice was even and casual. Too casual. "What happened to your limp, Titus?"

If Evangeline had had a heart, it would have stopped. Instead, she instantly understood why Titus had given her that look. She didn't know why Nicholas hadn't gone ahead as she'd asked of him, nor did she know why he wasn't with Lei. There wasn't a moment to panic about how the plan had gone awry, either. Evangeline estimated that they had about two seconds before they truly incurred the faerie king's wrath.

Assessing the situation at lightning speed, Evangeline ascertained that there was only one surefire option for everyone to make it out alive with the treasures in tow. She snatched Wrathbringer out of Tristan's hand, grabbed Alice by the back of her clothing, and swung the blade of the sword in front of Alice's neck.

The uproar was instantaneous. Nicholas, disguised as Titus, gave a cry of disgust. The faerie king's eyes narrowed with true fury for the first time.

Only Tristan seemed to see through Evangeline's bluff and, rather than stopping to react, grabbed three of the fountainheads.

"Grab the other fountainheads, Nicholas," Evangeline ordered with a calm that she didn't feel. He must have decided that there wasn't another choice, because even if he was horrified by Evangeline's actions, after a moment he moved to obey. Evangeline didn't meet Nicholas's eyes; she didn't want to see the accusation and outrage there.

"You wouldn't dare harm the Midsummer's sprout," snarled the king.

Evangeline lifted her chin and met his gaze evenly. She let no uncertainty, no weakness, show in her expression. So many already believed her to be made of ice, as cold and unforgiving as the Arctic. Why not let them see what they already wanted to see? Why not have them all believe the worst of her, especially when it suited her own goals?

"There is nothing I wouldn't do for the greater good of the Descendants," Evangeline said quietly. "Surely you understand. Now, you'll let us go without giving chase, or else . . ." She pressed the blade into Alice's neck, drawing a tiny bead of blood. Alice let out a low, terrified moan, yet Evangeline still didn't waver. This demonstration would be key to

Evangeline's image as the future leader of the Descendants. The mere mention of Julius's name had struck fear into his enemies' hearts; Evangeline would make sure that her own name would be enough to command such a response, too.

The faerie king bared his sharp teeth in a sneer.

Then the stalemate was broken, not by the king or by Evangeline but by Tristan. He let out a roar that pulsed through Evangeline's eardrums, and then his body began to transform.

Of course, Evangeline thought hysterically. *It's the Midsummer Celebration. The solstice, and the full moon.*

Before the High King could react, the half-transformed figure of Tristan pounced on him. Fear pulsed through Evangeline's body at the sight—the memory of that full moon four years ago, when Tristan had, during a heated argument, lost control of his body and nearly harmed her—but this time, when he turned toward her, it was concern that blazed in his eyes. In her shock, Evangeline let go of Alice; there was no more need for bluffing now that the scene had been thrown into chaos.

"Sorry," Evangeline murmured to Alice, who had stumbled back from her in fear. "It was a bluff. There was no other way."

But the terror and hurt in Alice's expression told Evangeline that no apology could make up for what had just transpired. And Evangeline would have to make peace with the consequences of her coldhearted actions.

There wasn't a moment to spare. The king had already, with a smooth slice of his sword, sent Tristan slamming into a wall. He would surely retaliate, and when he raised his hands, Evangeline didn't allow herself to think, but only to react. She thrust her cuffs at him, and somehow, miraculously, they bound the High King's wrists in place.

"Hmmm. Shaman magic," said the king mildly as he examined the cuffs with curiosity. His lack of concern was quite alarming; if he didn't fear this crew of Descendants and shaman at all, then that meant he thought they posed no threat.

"You will not speak of what happened here, and you will not come after us if you value the Midsummer sprout's life," Evangeline bellowed at the faerie king, and was rather amazed that the golden cuffs continued to render him immobile. Still, the cuffs didn't stop the High King's expression from curling into one of fury and hatred, and the frightening sight stayed printed on Evangeline's eyelids even after she'd turned away.

She grabbed the dragon fountainhead, which was far lighter in her hands than she'd expected, and sprinted through the back door after everyone else. At the very last moment, she turned and summoned the cuffs; they shot off the High King's wrists toward her, breaking her hold on him.

Evangeline was moving so quickly that she didn't even have time to fear being chased. Lei had told them the path out of here was through the Endless Wood. Faeries gasped and scattered at the sight of her barreling out of the palace. Nearby guards startled and hesitated before giving chase. With what felt like her last burst of superhuman speed, Evangeline disappeared among the trees in the Endless Wood, with Nicholas, Alice, and Tristan on her heels. Tristan appeared to have shaken off his transformation now and was himself again; Evangeline tossed him Wrathbringer, which he smoothly caught.

"What happened back there, Nicholas?" Evangeline asked once she dared to slow enough to speak. "Why are you still here? What about the car?"

"Last-minute change of plans! Lei went ahead to fetch the car!" Nicholas shouted. Now he was the one avoiding Evangeline's eye, as though he couldn't stand to look at her.

"Lei? But—"

"I tried to get here as fast as I could, but it seems I was late. Midsummer's sprout—"

Evangeline looked away. So Nicholas had figured out the truth for himself. That Alice was the subject of the prophecy, and not her. Shame burned through Evangeline's body, from the top of her head to the tips of her toes.

"That stunt you pulled back there was a bluff, wasn't it?" Nicholas's expression was tight. Tristan said nothing, but it was evident he was awaiting Evangeline's answer, too.

"Yes," Evangeline said curtly.

Nicholas nodded, but his face remained just as stiff. In making that split-second decision to pretend to hold Alice hostage back there, Evangeline had evidently cemented a frightening reputation not only with the faerie king but also with her best friend.

And for the first time, she wondered if she had made the right decision.

As though the ground had taken mercy on Evangeline and decided to swallow her up, it shifted beneath her feet, and she pitched forward and down into darkness.

Leaving Faerieland was as abrupt and confusing as entering had been. Evangeline sincerely hoped that after today, she'd never have to make this trip again. After what felt like no time at all and yet far too long, her feet landed on solid ground.

She opened her eyes and blinked against the light. It took a moment to register her surroundings, but as soon as she took in the sight of European faces in paintings along the walls, she knew exactly where they were. The Metropolitan Museum of Art. Good. Despite the hiccup with Nicholas and Lei apparently switching places without notifying her, all was going according to plan. Escape from Faerieland had been easy—almost *too* easy. Evangeline had half expected the faerie king to do his best to capture them, even after she'd threatened Alice's life. There were sure to be consequences later. But for now, all they needed to focus on was getting out of the museum safely.

Evangeline glanced around. Miraculously, Tristan, Alice, and Nicholas had all made it here in one piece. Nicholas's magic had worn off entirely, and everyone looked like their usual selves, albeit more battered and bruised. The five zodiac fountainheads lay at their feet.

"Quiet," Evangeline hissed to the others. Now they only needed to get out of the empty, closed museum. She couldn't believe her luck. She couldn't believe that at long last, they had obtained the five missing fountainheads. For so long she'd schemed and plotted, and Julius for even longer before her, and now Evangeline was on the brink of restoring magic and might to the Descendants. "Everyone, get up. We've done it. Now we just need to get out of here without tripping any alarms." Easier said than done, but if they could navigate the tricky land of faeries, then Evangeline trusted they could pull off this last segment. She prayed that they could get out of the museum without a hitch. They'd been on the run for what felt like ages, and exhaustion was beginning to wear on her.

"You did it, Evangeline," whispered Tristan behind her. "You actually pulled it off. The heist of the century."

"Did you think I wouldn't succeed?" Evangeline rolled her eyes but allowed herself a small smile. This was nice. Sharing an understanding with Tristan was nice. Maybe they'd even have more, once they returned to Earthly Branches Academy and sorted everything out. "*We* pulled this off."

"Ah, ah, ah." A voice, chillingly familiar, echoed in the halls of the empty, silent museum. The hope that had so briefly blossomed in Evangeline's chest was quickly extinguished. "I taught you better than that, didn't I? I told you never to count your chickens before they hatch, mèi mei."

Evangeline stopped cold. It . . . it *couldn't* be. She knew that voice. Knew it better than her own, even. She would recognize it anywhere. There had to be another explanation as to why she'd just heard those words in *that* voice. This was a terrible prank. This was a bad dream.

Tristan, who'd been halfway to his feet, fell back on his butt with a look of complete shock and fear. He didn't bother getting up again. His face slowly drained of color as he looked at whoever was standing behind Evangeline. "You . . . but how can it be *you*?"

Slowly, ever so slowly, Evangeline turned, already knowing what she would see.

It had only been a matter of days since they'd last seen each other, so of course Julius Long remained unchanged in appearance. In fact,

Evangeline thought her older brother looked better than ever, his hair slicked back and his cheeks rosy (not with blood, surely, so she supposed he was wearing blush for dramatic effect and had likely been preparing for this moment for quite some time). Julius had donned a cloak as black as night, which shimmered with his every motion. Surrounding him were six Descendants, also wearing the same cloaks, flanking him on either side. The Talons.

"Death suits you well, dà gē," Evangeline said. She was proud of the evenness of her voice.

The sardonic statement was meant as a barb, but Julius's smile merely widened, and his gold front tooth gleamed in the faint light. "I daresay it does. You've no idea how much good all this free time has done for me. I even took up mah-jongg again. Do you remember when Mama and Baba hired a tutor to give us mah-jongg lessons, Evangeline? They'd be so disappointed if they knew how rusty I've gotten."

Evangeline struggled to reconcile the sight and sound of her brother, rambling on about something as frivolous as mah-jongg lessons, with the headlines that had reduced him to a charred corpse found at the Brooklyn Bridge. Unless Julius had turned himself into a zombie, there was only one conclusion to reach here. Julius Long, for reasons unknown to Evangeline, had let the whole world—let *her*—believe that he was dead. Evangeline sensed the stares of the others drilling into the back of her head, but she didn't have a plan to relay to them yet. She'd thought everything had gone according to her predictions, but this was a wrench that she couldn't have imagined in her wildest dreams. Because why would her allegedly dead brother be standing in front of her, completely *un*dead, looking for all the world as though he was about to stop her from carrying out the Assignment *he'd* delegated to her?

"They found your body charred at the bottom of the Brooklyn Bridge," Evangeline babbled, still in that toneless voice. She wasn't even sure why she was repeating the facts of Julius's "death," only that she needed them both to understand the finality with which she had processed his passing. She needed her brother to feel how deeply she had mourned and grieved.

How she was struggling, now, to process this shocking revelation of deceit and betrayal.

"They found *a* body charred at the bridge," Julius replied tersely. "Do you remember that faerie Seer who prophesized about the return of our lost fountainheads?"

"Yes, but what . . ." It clicked in Evangeline's head. "What exactly did you do to him?"

"Well, let's just say that I evaded his spirited attempts to take my soul, and then found it much more efficient to pretend that his charred-beyond-recognition body was mine. I was surprised by how readily everybody accepted my death, by the way. I half hoped somebody would recognize that that ugly, charred mess couldn't possibly be *me*. Can you imagine what a blow that is to the ego?" He shook his head in obvious disappointment.

"Is there a reason you faked your death?" Tristan growled. "Was it for the pure theatrics?"

Evangeline shot him a sidelong look. Tristan had risen to his feet, seeming to have gotten over the initial shock, and was staring at Julius with a glower of intense dislike. Tristan and Julius had never gotten along in school, and Evangeline sensed that Tristan was waiting for any excuse to jump down her brother's throat. And this was a rather good excuse, she had to admit.

"I would like to know the same thing," Evangeline said. Her brother took a step forward, and Evangeline instinctively took a step back. This was not the Julius she remembered. Perhaps she had never truly known Julius after all, and that was the most frightening thought she'd had in her entire long life. All she knew for sure was that something had broken between them since she'd last seen her older brother—something crucial, something they couldn't get back. Every nerve in her body was vibrating with warning, not affection, as she gazed upon Julius. She had never been so glad of her lack of a beating heart, because it surely would have split in half.

"Three months ago," Julius said quietly, "I was approached by a man of unimaginable power and wealth. A man . . . no, a legend . . . known as the Collector."

It didn't escape Evangeline's notice that Tristan stiffened at that name, but she could do little but note the observation as Julius continued.

"The Collector offered me wealth beyond my wildest dreams, along with lifelong protection and a quiet retirement for the Longs and our descendants, if only I would do him one not-so-simple favor: bring him the five lost zodiac fountainheads. As you can imagine, the reason why the Collector offered such an enormous sum is because the job would be nearly impossible to pull off."

"So you had us do your dirty work for you," Tristan accused.

Julius scoffed. "Well, you're accustomed to that lifestyle already, aren't you, Tristan? Or should I say—*Tao*."

Tristan clenched his jaw, and Evangeline narrowed her eyes. Julius's words had caused the final puzzle piece to click into place in her head. Tristan, who was known to cut class frequently, who had been apprehended for petty theft on more than one occasion, worked for the Collector. For how long had this gone on? Why had Tristan never mentioned it?

"Why not approach us directly, then?" Nicholas asked. He was staring at Julius with barely concealed anger. It was hard to tell with Nicholas, who was usually in careful control of his emotions, but Evangeline had already spotted his giveaway. His fingers were clenching and unclenching at his sides, as though he'd like nothing more than to pummel Julius. "Why go through all the trouble of faking your death and forcing Evangeline to take the lead on this Assignment?"

"Because," Julius said, and now his eyes were boring straight into Evangeline's with an intensity that frightened her, "that damned faerie Seer would have taken my soul in exchange for the prophecy's success. I am not ready to die yet, not now, and perhaps not ever. Besides, I knew my sister needed a kick to take on something as drastic as this Assignment. I knew we would never see eye to eye when it came to the matter of what to *do* with these fountainheads. And because of the prophecy. I knew I wasn't the one described in it, so it needed to be Evangeline to bring back the fountainheads."

"Well, you were wrong on that matter." Evangeline hardly recognized her own voice; it was tight and shrill with anger. "Turns out the prophecy was referring to Alice."

Julius raised an eyebrow. His gaze snapped to Alice, who flinched and shrank away from him. "Oh, really? Ruiting's daughter, is it? Now that's a curveball I didn't see coming. The gods do so enjoy making fools out of us all."

"What do you intend to do, gē?" Evangeline asked. She was growing weary of beating around the bush. "Will you fight us all to get the fountainheads for yourself?"

"That depends."

"On?"

"On whether or not you'll step aside willingly."

Evangeline swallowed her hurt into the pit of her stomach. Later, she could mourn her brother's betrayal, but right now she needed to keep a level head. This wasn't just any Descendant she was going up against—this was Julius, and she could be certain of her victory over any other *except* him.

Desperate, Evangeline made a bid for her brother's conscience one last time. Underneath the tough exterior and callous words, Julius was still her Julius. It had always been the two of them against the world, from the pillaging of the Old Summer Palace to now, and they could get through anything together—even this. Even betrayal.

"I am not your enemy, Julius. I have always been on your side. I am your *sister*." Julius remained quiet and still. Cautiously, she stepped forward, closer to her brother. "Don't you see? All along, the fae have been our true enemy, and now they're watching us go up against each other, while they don't even have to lift a finger. If we fight, we'll be doing their dirty work *for* them. You have to see reason. Let's do the right thing, gē. Let's use these fountainheads to restore the Circle of Twelve. Then we can be human again. We can enjoy human food, and feel deeply, and grow old. . . ."

Julius stared at Evangeline for a long, hard moment. Briefly, his stoic expression wavered, and uncertainty flitted across his face. Hope fluttered in Evangeline's chest. Had she gotten through to him?

Then Julius's expression hardened again. Lines appeared on his face, and now he appeared so much older than twenty—much closer to his true age than ever before. The decades of holding the Descendants together had taken a toll on him. "I have adjusted to immortality and do not wish to return to our old ways. Everything happens for a reason. Perhaps the Circle of Twelve was meant to break and remain broken; it has been decades since we have needed to ward off consistent Wrathling attacks, after all. Perhaps it is time for the Descendants to move forward and start a new chapter."

Evangeline gaped at him. What had happened to the determined older brother who had never given up hope of restoring glory to the Descendants? Who *was* this stranger occupying Julius's body, speaking such vile words out of his mouth? The only explanation she could accept was that Julius had fallen prey to his own greed, to the irresistible pull of money and power. The other explanation—the one Evangeline couldn't accept at this moment—was that Julius had not been her Julius in a very long while. He had deceived her and bided his time, all to betray her at the most crucial last moment.

"You . . . you cannot be serious." It was all Evangeline could croak out.

"You always were so persuasive with your words, Evangeline, but do not waste your breath. My mind is made up. Now, we can do this the easy way, or we can do it the hard way. The result will be the same. I take the fountainheads to the Collector, I keep my life, and I obtain my fortune—*our* fortune if you back down now."

Evangeline clenched her jaw, fuming. Julius spoke as though he'd already won against them, against her. And why shouldn't he? She had never once been able to outwit, outfight, out-anything her brother. There was no reason for him to believe that she could do it now, and that thought only served to infuriate her further.

"Now, see reason, Evangeline. This curse is not so terrible," Julius said. "I quite enjoy immortality, and I daresay I'm not alone. Isn't that why Marcus Niu has so easily swayed the Descendants to his pigheaded cause?"

"How do you know what Marcus has been up to?" Nicholas demanded. "You haven't been in any classes."

"Do you really think I haven't been keeping tabs on Marcus Niu for the past decade or so?" Julius rolled his eyes. "I knew it was a matter of time before that buffoon did something buffoon-like, and I wasn't wrong. Besides, my Talons—the *loyal* ones, at least—never stopped working for me. I have had eyes and ears on the Descendants at all times."

How silly Evangeline felt. How pathetic. With every move she'd made in the wake of Julius's "death," she'd thought she was leaving behind her brother's shadow, carving a name for *herself*. Yet all along, unknown to her, Julius had been one step ahead. Evangeline not only had failed to step out of her brother's shadow but had actually fallen into his trap. She could scream from the frustration.

"And what are you going to do about the inevitable extinction of the Descendants, then?" Evangeline's voice was barely above a whisper, but it grew stronger with every word. "If you go down this path, you'll lose your precious immortality anyway. Unless you actually *do* see eye to eye with Marcus and wish to breed the human Descendants."

"In that matter, as with any form of evolution, the strong will survive," Julius said curtly. "I don't plan ever to die, and I'll go to any lengths for self-preservation. Those who stick with me will surely see eternity, too."

Such a bold claim would have sounded like wishful thinking from anyone else's mouth, but Evangeline had no doubt that Julius would achieve his goal, no matter the cost. She narrowed her eyes. There was nothing more to say.

Tristan moved to stand beside Evangeline, pushing his sleeves up to his elbows. "I've had enough of this chitchat," he snapped. "We're wasting precious time. If you won't get out of our way, Julius, then I won't apologize for what we do to you."

Julius laughed, the sound bouncing off the walls. It was a terrible, mirthless laugh, an awful sound that Evangeline had never heard her brother make before. As chills ran down her spine, she thought that in a way, Julius truly had died at the Brooklyn Bridge.

"Tonight you'll learn," the new Julius said, "that righteousness pays so very little in the end."

He snapped his fingers, and the Talons leapt forward.

42
TRISTAN

Fate worked in funny ways. While in school, Tristan had often prayed for the chance to soundly beat Julius up, but there was never an opportune moment. The insufferable Long had always been surrounded by gaggles of admiring students (many of whom were part of his little gang). Laying a hand on Julius would have earned Tristan retaliation a hundredfold, not to mention the hatred of the entire student body. Not worth it, even to satisfy his itch to see Julius put in his place.

Tristan never expected that the opportunity to finally teach Julius a lesson would present itself in the empty Met, of all places. But he wasn't complaining. He cracked his knuckles and rolled his head from side to side, all the while quickly assessing Julius and his Talons. They all donned the same cloaks, like they were magicians in a traveling circus act. Tristan, in a rare display of restraint, refrained from making a snarky comment. Or rather, there wasn't *time* for him to squeeze in an insult.

Julius snapped his fingers, and his obedient Talons rushed forward, bearing their weapons. It was seven against four, and one of their four was a human Descendant who'd barely learned the basics of combat. This was hardly a fair fight, but they were beyond fair at this point.

Tristan didn't even bother drawing Wrathbringer from his side; he attacked with animal instinct.

The nearest Talon, Louis, came at Tristan, his eyes blazing. He swung two curved knives at Tristan's head, snarling, "This is payback for stealing my watch."

Tristan, fortunately, had predicted that Louis would make a beeline for him, and he easily dodged the attack. He ducked beneath the blades, which whooshed through the air well above his head, and then tackled Louis at the knees. The fox spirit went down with an "Oof!" of surprise, the air knocked out of his lungs. Louis's back had hardly touched the floor before Tristan twisted both knives out of his slackened grip. By the time Louis had raised his head, groaning, both of his own weapons were pointed at his throat.

Tristan shook his head and tsked. "Sloppy, Louis. You're very fortunate you aren't wearing another watch for me to steal. Think I'll keep these fancy blades of yours, though."

Louis bared his teeth, growling. He seemed wholly unconcerned by the knives pressing into his throat. His eyes widened as he stared over Tristan's shoulder, and Tristan reacted to the movement in a split second, spinning around. Sure enough, another Talon—Xavier—had crept up behind him. Tristan swung Louis's knives up just in time to parry as Xavier thrust his sword at him.

"You never were able to defeat me in combat class," Tristan sneered. "Give up now before I hurt you, Xavier."

In response, Xavier spat at Tristan's feet. Well, Tristan had given the Talon a chance. Now he would show no mercy. He threw all his weight behind his knives and drove them forward, pushing Xavier back. To Xavier's credit, he stood his ground well. The two were at a standstill for a few long moments, their faces so close that Tristan could see the beads of sweat forming on Xavier's forehead.

With a burst of strength, Tristan shoved Xavier off-balance. The

Talon stumbled backward and spun around to catch his balance. By then, Tristan was out of range. It wasn't Louis, Xavier, or any of the Talons that Tristan wanted to fight. No, the one he really wanted to see suffer at his hands was Julius Long.

It seemed Evangeline had the same idea. She made quick work of two Talons at once, tucking her body low so that in their attempt to grab her, they collided with each other.

"Behind you, Evangeline!" Tristan shouted just as Louis managed to rise from the floor and sneak up behind her. Louis landed a fist on Evangeline's shoulder, though she immediately grabbed his punching arm and spun him over her knee with unnatural strength. Down Louis went to the floor again, and this time his fall was accompanied by a nasty cracking sound. "That's why you should have stayed down there," Tristan muttered under his breath.

Evangeline didn't appear winded at all from the fight. In fact, not a hair on her head was out of place.

Only two more Talons were still standing—Stephanie and Megan. Both of them rushed at once toward Nicholas, who was standing guard in front of Alice. With a hiss, Megan, a vampire, headed straight for Nicholas's jugular.

Tristan watched this happen as though in slow motion, his horror growing as he recognized that Nicholas wasn't reacting, wasn't moving at all, and if he didn't move in approximately five seconds, he and Alice would be run through with the Talons' swords.

There was only one way to kill a fox spirit, after all, and that was by driving a blade or stake straight through the heart.

Tristan might not like Nicholas much—in fact, he'd hated his guts for a long time, blaming Nicholas for the neglect that had led to the Descendants' downfall. As long as there was *somebody* to blame for the death of his family members and everything else that had gone wrong, Tristan didn't have to shoulder so much emotional burden for the tragedies that had happened that day. He had a target for all the pent-up anger and grief and regret that otherwise had nowhere to go.

But now, in what looked likely to be Nicholas's last moments, Tristan found that he was overcome with remorse for his harsh thoughts toward his former friend. He had likely been unfair, he realized. Over the course of this Assignment, Nicholas had proven that he was more than that one failure back in 1860. Perhaps it was time for Tristan to let go of the past, too. At the very least, he had no desire to see Nicholas killed in such a violent manner. He opened his mouth, and a scream rang out.

"Nicholas!"

43
NICHOLAS

It had happened again.

Hordes of foreign soldiers, wearing red tunics and dark blue trousers and bearing guns, poured through the gates of the Old Summer Palace. They trampled the gardens. They toppled ancient architecture. Nicholas stood alone, completely terrified. He was young, and it was one of his first times serving as the night guard watching over the Circle of Twelve, and now any Descendant's worst nightmare had come to pass—and he could not move.

Nicholas had known that he should act in the face of imminent tragedy—and he hadn't.

In the distance, familiar Descendant faces sped toward the circle of bronze zodiac fountainheads, Mr. and Mrs. Long leading the way.

But Nicholas could see the writing on the wall. The Descendants were outnumbered at least one hundred to one, and nobody was close enough to the Circle of Twelve to defend it—except him. Nicholas froze as he stared death in the face. He wasn't ready to die for this cause. He wasn't. Yet he could see the future clear as day: the Descendants were going to die, all of them, no matter what he did now.

The nearest soldier raised his gun at Nicholas, blue eyes blazing, lips parted in a laugh of malice, and Nicholas was struck with bone-chilling certainty that this monstrous sight was the last he would ever see.

Then someone dragged Nicholas out of harm's way.

"Nicholas!"

"Stay back!" shouted Nicholas's savior, shoving him out of sight behind a huge table. He glanced up and watched Julius Long place both hands on the tablecloth, twist his body into the air, and knock out five soldiers at once.

A terrible, deafening noise rent the air, which Nicholas could only describe as a mixture of metal screeching on metal and Earth itself splitting open. He could hardly bear to watch what happened next, but he couldn't tear his eyes away. The dazzling, beautiful bronze statues—the statues that had for so long been the source of the Descendants' magic; the statues that had protected their people as much as the Descendants had; the statues Nicholas had been meant to defend to his death on this fateful night—

The Circle of Twelve had shattered.

And it was Nicholas's fault.

"Nicholas—watch out!"

A feral scream jolted Nicholas back to the present, over a century after this horrific memory. It was Tristan's scream. Nicholas saw the scene before him as though it were happening in slow motion. Stephanie and Megan speeding toward him and Alice, with their weapons pointed toward them, clearly intending to end their lives. Even though he knew this, even though he'd *thought* he'd gotten over his paralyzing indecision, Nicholas's feet wouldn't move.

You're going to falter and prove yourself to be a coward, just like you did during the Second Opium War, hissed that nagging, negative voice in the back of his head.

The guilt of that day weighed more heavily on Nicholas's chest than ever. For a moment he contemplated finally giving in, accepting blame for the destruction of the Circle of Twelve. Evangeline would fail this Assignment despite coming this close to succeeding—because of him, coward that he was.

At the thought of her name, Nicholas sobered. Evangeline. He *couldn't* fail her. This time, she'd outlined what she was counting on him to do. In his place, Evangeline would know what to do. Evangeline always knew what to do, and even when she didn't, she put on such confident airs that fate still turned in her favor. It was what Nicholas admired most about his best friend. If Evangeline were in his shoes . . .

But Nicholas wasn't Evangeline, and Evangeline couldn't bail him out this time. And if Nicholas failed here, he'd fail Alice, he'd fail Evangeline, and that was all on him.

His temperature rose; his breath came out sharp and hot; the familiar warmth of fire erupting from his body enveloped him . . . only this time, instead of suppressing his powers, Nicholas embraced them.

With a roar, Nicholas charged and tackled both Talons around the knees at once, completely dodging Megan's attempt to bite his neck. Their swords went flying out of their hands. His body was burning hot as it contorted into a taller, more muscular form; flames erupted at the tips of his fingers, and Stephanie and Megan cried under his burning touch. The shadow of nine tails whipping around could be seen against the museum walls. Fire scorched a few of the paintings.

Nicholas forced himself to stay in his own head. He thought of his loyalty to Evangeline; he drew upon his regrets about Dylan; he focused on his fondness for Alice. He conjured any strong, emotional memory that would anchor him in his mind, and somehow, *somehow,* he managed to stay inside his own mind, to feel and control the fire as though it were a natural extension of his own limbs.

Nicholas grabbed the Talons' fallen weapons and pointed them at each of their throats. He was panting hard. He wiped beads of sweat off his forehead. This wasn't the moment to savor victory, however. Julius didn't appear to be bothered by the sight of his fallen brethren, and Nicholas had a bad, bad feeling about it.

"Don't hide behind your Talons like a coward, Julius. Face us yourself!" Evangeline shouted. She beckoned to her brother.

"Much as I wish to, I don't have the time to waste playing this little game with you," Julius said, his tone almost apologetic. He stood alone while his Talons groaned on the floor, his hands behind his back, and he seemed wholly unconcerned with the lack of protection around him. "Urgent matters require my attention."

"Urgent matters? What could be more urgent than this?" Evangeline demanded.

Julius responded not with words but with movement. The next few seconds were a blur. Before Nicholas could process what was happening, Julius had flown out from behind the fallen Talons and landed across the room. Another important detail that registered a second later: Julius had, in the same split second of movement, captured two of the zodiac fountainheads in one arm—the dog and the rooster—along with Alice in the other arm. When had he taken Alice? Curse vampires and their speed. Nicholas's eyes hadn't even registered what happened, and Alice had been taken from right under his nose.

"You—give her back!" Nicholas cried out.

"I suggest you all listen to me now," Julius said pleasantly, holding a knife to Alice's throat, "and little Alice here won't get hurt."

"Let her go, Julius!" Tristan yelled.

Alice's eyes were so wide they practically bulged out of her head, and she was trembling from head to foot. Nicholas pitied her. For the second time in the same hour, the poor girl had been held hostage. Anger surged inside him, too—anger at the Longs. Why did they have to solve everything with intimidation and violence?

"You're more of a coward than I even thought," Evangeline spat. Her words were sharp and vicious enough to leave a scar.

Julius yawned. "So you've mentioned. Can't you come up with more creative insults, mèi mei? I know you're brighter than this."

"Don't you ever call me that again. You are no brother of mine. From now on, you and I are nothing to each other."

At Evangeline's cold pronouncement, Julius merely gave a twisted grin.

Just when Nicholas thought the situation couldn't get worse, a high-pitched alarm began blaring throughout the museum, along with flashing lights. For a moment, the conflict with Julius left the forefront of Nicholas's mind and was replaced by the more immediate possibility of being arrested. "The alarms," he groaned. "Must have been tripped by all the commotion."

Julius tsked and frowned. Clearly, setting off the alarms hadn't been part of his plan. Nicholas estimated they probably had seconds before police flooded the building.

"Let Alice go, Julius. I'm warning you," Evangeline snarled, taking a step toward her brother. She seemed focused only on him, not what was happening around them. "There's no time to argue with me, so don't even try."

"You don't have time, but *I* do." That terrible smile still hadn't left Julius's face. He had yet another ace up his sleeve, some advantage over them—else why would he appear so comfortable and unconcerned?

Nicholas's mind was in overdrive, trying to come up with the best plan of escape; already he could hear the guards shouting over the alarms. There was no more time to deliberate or try to reason with Julius. In the end, as frustrated and agitated as he was by this development, Nicholas could see only one way out.

"Evangeline." He touched her shoulder, and she startled, turning her furious gaze to him. "Listen to me. Now is not the time to handle Julius. We need to leave, before the mortals see too much. Lei is waiting outside with the getaway vehicle."

Evangeline cast a glance at Julius and the Talons, at Alice and the two fountainheads. "But—"

"I know it's far from ideal, but it's our only choice. Unless you have a better idea?"

She didn't. Nicholas could tell from the hopeless expression on her face that for once in her life, no further schemes were forming in her mind. They'd all been trumped, once again, by Julius Long. Begrudgingly, Nicholas had to hand it to Julius this time. Nobody had expected him to fake his death and emerge from beyond the grave to best and betray them.

"We can't give up," Tristan said stubbornly. "Julius has Alice. Gods know what he'll do to her if he takes her with him."

"Julius won't hurt Alice," Evangeline said, although she didn't sound entirely convinced.

Nicholas didn't believe that at all, and his heart twisted when he thought of what Alice might have to endure in Julius's captivity. However, if they didn't escape now, they'd lose everything they'd worked so hard for *and* Alice. "There's nothing we can do." Nicholas's voice cracked, but he forced the words from his mouth. "We need to get out of here. We'll get Alice and the remaining fountainheads back if it's the last thing we do."

"Well, I suppose this is goodbye for now," said Julius as cheerily as though they were old friends parting ways after catching up over a drink. "Await my message. I'll be in touch very soon."

Nicholas spun toward Julius just in time to see him and his Talons turn their cloaks around and vanish into thin air, taking Alice and the two zodiac fountainheads with them.

44
EVANGELINE

No wonder Julius had acted like he didn't care much about the museum guards arriving on the scene. All along, he and his Talons had possessed the ability to disappear whenever they wanted.

"Since when the hell could he do *that*?" Tristan demanded.

Evangeline was stunned. It seemed that Julius and the Talons hadn't chosen to match their outerwear to make a fashion statement; those cloaks were magical. She should have expected no less from Julius, but to be fair, until moments ago she hadn't known he was alive. How much further would she have to push herself to catch him, to overtake him?

The sounds of feet sprinting across a squeaky clean floor rounded the corner, and the first uniformed guard emerged. Immediately he yelled, "The intruders are here!"

"Grab the fountainheads," Evangeline ordered Tristan and Nicholas. "Quickly!" There was no time to relay what it was she intended to do; she assumed Tristan would know, as he infuriatingly knew all of her moves, and Nicholas would be quick to follow.

The three of them grabbed a zodiac fountainhead each, and not a moment too soon. The museum security guards had rounded the corner, and now they were all in plain view.

Evangeline screamed, "Go!" She sprinted and sped up until time and space were a blur, and then used the zodiac fountainhead to smash through the museum window. Her body followed right behind, and she landed lightly on the soft lawn. She'd closed her eyes and used the fountainhead to cover her head before the collision, protecting her face from the shards of glass, but the pain stinging her arms and legs told her that the rest of her body hadn't been so fortunate. Well, no matter. She hadn't fed on as much blood as usual these days, which meant that she wouldn't bleed much; the cuts would be easy enough to patch up later.

The cool night wind whipped against her face as she glanced back around. Tristan was right on her heels, and Nicholas right on his. Behind them, the Met alarms were blaring, and museum guards were standing outside, some of them half-heartedly giving chase. She wondered what tomorrow's papers would say about this incident. They hadn't *stolen* anything from the museum, but they had blown a giant hole into the side of it and caused a fire that scorched paintings, and that was likely to be frowned upon.

Evangeline didn't slow her steps until she'd reached the familiar black car. Ignoring the shocked looks from the passersby on the sidewalk, she yanked open the passenger-side door, jumped in, and slammed it shut just as fast.

Lei whistled. "Looks like we're all criminals now."

"Drive," Evangeline spat out. "As soon as the others get in the car, you need to drive us as fast as you can." She wasn't in the mood for any banter with Lei. The message must have been clear, because he fell silent immediately.

As Nicholas and Tristan climbed into the back seat, Lei glanced in the mirror, and his frown deepened. "Where's Alice?"

"She's not coming," Nicholas said tightly.

"What? Why not?" Lei demanded.

"Can you stop asking so many questions right now, please?" Evangeline's body was beginning to ache and throb where she'd been cut. "Floor it!"

When the museum guards were mere feet away from the vehicle, Lei's foot slammed down on the gas pedal. Evangeline lurched backward as the car tore down the streets of the Upper East Side, tall glass buildings blurring past the windows. She glanced back to stare out at the police cars tailing them, but they were no match for Lei's speed. Soon the closest cars had fallen far behind.

Evangeline sat back in her seat and closed her eyes. Perhaps it was still too early to let down her guard, but the fact that they'd left the museum guards in the dust and were on their way back home—that was surely cause for some celebration.

Lei finally asked, "So what happened back there? Did we lose Alice?"

Evangeline thought she could feel Nicholas's eyes boring into the side of her head. There was no way around it; she needed to explain the situation, even though it left a bad taste in her mouth. *Could* they have done more to help Alice, as Nicholas had suggested?

"Julius took her," Evangeline said in a flat voice.

"Julius? Julius Long, as in your *dead* brother?" Lei choked out.

Oh, right. Lei didn't even know that his old friend Julius was, in fact, still alive. They really did have a lot of explaining to do. "Julius faked his death. It's a long story—I'll explain the details later. The important bit is that he's got the other two zodiac fountainheads."

"And Alice," Nicholas added.

Lei said nothing for a moment, but then he let out a long, low sigh. "Gods . . . I look away for all of thirty minutes . . . ," he muttered, along with a few other words that sounded like Cantonese curses. Then he cleared his throat and raised his voice. "Well, when do we go back for Alice and the fountainheads?"

There was a short silence in the car as all heads turned toward Evangeline. Despite everything, she had pulled off this impossible heist—

mostly—and now they recognized her as their leader. They expected her to be formulating a plan to rescue Alice already. And she was, of course, because until they got Alice back, along with the two other fountainheads, they couldn't consider themselves done with the Assignment. The Circle of Twelve was still broken, and exhausted as she was, Evangeline would not rest until it was restored to its former glory.

Until she had soundly beat Julius Long at his own morbid game, Evangeline would never be satisfied.

She rubbed her shoulder. She was so drained, she thought she might slump over from the sheer weight of responsibility bearing down upon her, but there was still no time to waste. In fact, while they were in the car, headed for the Long estate, was the prime time for planning.

"Julius told us to await his message," Evangeline said after a pause. "I assume that means he's going to hold Alice hostage and exchange her for the remaining fountainheads."

"If he hurts a hair on her head," Nicholas said, "I'll kill him myself."

"We will accept Julius's terms, of course," Evangeline continued.

"What?" Tristan yelped, whirling on her in alarm. "You want us to give in to that bastard?"

"Let me finish, please, Tristan. We will *appear* to accept Julius's terms. However, I have no intention of giving Julius any of the fountainheads, as I'm sure you all don't, either."

"Are you suggesting a double cross?" Tristan's tone had done a complete one-eighty, and now he sounded nothing short of delighted.

"I like the sound of that," Lei said with a whistle.

Evangeline licked her lips. Plotting a heist had been a fun exercise for the body and mind. Planning a revenge that would be her traitorous brother's downfall—well, this classified as positively *delicious*.

"I think a double cross is exactly what my dear brother has coming to him." Evangeline was already scheming, her mind pinning down all the facts she knew about Julius and his Talons to try to pinpoint where they might have gone into hiding. After all, a Long was always thinking at least ten steps ahead of any adversary. She'd just never expected that adversary to be her own brother.

Thanks to Lei's speeding, they were soon pulling into the driveway of the Long estate. There were no lights on in the house, which was a bit odd. Perhaps Cecil was already asleep. Oh, Cecil. Evangeline had missed the girl and couldn't wait to catch her up on everything that had happened.

Evangeline practically leapt out of the car and bounded up the steps to her house. She unlocked and flung open the front door, calling out, "Cecil?" Her voice echoed around the huge estate, but there was no response. No pattering of footsteps, no Cecil bustling into the room. "Cecil?" Evangeline tried again, but her stomach sank. Her intuition was never wrong, and right now it was telling her that Cecil was not here.

"Um . . . Evangeline?" Nicholas sounded tentative.

Evangeline whirled around. He was holding a slip of pink paper toward her. "What is this?" she demanded.

"It was tucked under the welcome mat."

She grabbed the paper out of his hand and unfolded it.

> Marcus Niu was voted Chancellor last night.
> Julius Long is alive. By the time you receive this note, you'll probably know that already.
> My heart is with you, but my duty is to the eldest living Long always; that is what was written in my contract. Julius summoned me and requested my services, so I must go.
> I'm sorry.
>
> —C

Evangeline threw her head back and screamed.

She was too late to stop Marcus. Too late to keep Julius from taking Cecil, too. Cecil, who had always been there for *her* more than Julius. But now that Julius was fighting against Evangeline with his full strength, it meant dealing such low blows to his sister.

Someone was saying Evangeline's name over and over again, the sound coming as though from far off. It took a moment for her to register that Lei, Nicholas, *and* Tristan were calling out her name and shaking her. Evangeline couldn't help it. She couldn't stop herself. All the stress and frustration and hurt had built up to a breaking point, and she couldn't hold in her emotions any longer. She screamed and screamed and screamed.

She had no power at school. No Alice. No Cecil. No Julius. She had failed, too, to bring back all five of the fountainheads. The fae knew what Evangeline and her crew had done; they would surely seek to exact their vengeance in a terrible manner, and the Descendants did not even have the full might of their powers to defend themselves, as she had hoped.

Evangeline was certain she had never sunk so low in her life. She was finally home, but the home that had greeted her would never be the same again.

After what felt like ages, Evangeline's scream finally petered out into a faint wail, and then nothing. For a long moment, there was only silence.

"We'll make Julius pay," Nicholas said coldly.

"Yes," agreed Lei.

"Yes," snarled Tristan.

"Yes," whispered Evangeline. And in the place of that hopelessness, a small ember of rage began to ignite within her. How *dare* Marcus take her position? How dare Julius betray her, his own blood sister, on whom he'd doted for over a century? She wasn't sure how or when, but one day soon, she would make them sorely regret betraying her.

The fae, too, had better not come after Evangeline, for she was certain that her rage alone could give her the strength to take down an army of supernaturals. Her one source of solace was that Lei's identity as a shaman—and not just any shaman, but the Scarlet Spy—had remained a secret, so an all-out war wasn't inevitable . . . yet.

If war was to come, though, Evangeline was prepared to face it. And gods help any foe who dared stand in her warpath. Whatever rage Evangeline experienced now, her adversaries would feel it a hundredfold. That was the price of making an enemy out of her. That was a promise.

And Evangeline Long always, always kept her promises.

45
JULIUS

Julius and his Talons emerged out of thin air onto a subway platform, making the handful of passersby shout in surprise. It was the early hours of the morning. Many of these people seemed to be on their way to work, judging by their business attire and scrubs, or finishing a late night of drinking in the city, judging by their smudged makeup and uneven stride.

Before the humans could do more than indicate their shock at this sudden appearance, Julius and the Talons had already disappeared up the steps of the station, leaving the people below scratching their heads and questioning what had just transpired. Later, they would chalk up this experience to a hallucination that was doubtless the product of long hours and too much wine. After all, this was New York City, and one was expected to accept such strange occurrences as part of the city's charm.

"Quickly, now," Julius hissed, but the order was unnecessary. The Talons were zipping along the streets, the unconscious form of Alice between them. "The Collector won't like to be kept waiting."

Koreatown emerged before them, the streets emptier than usual, given that it was early morning. Julius charged down the streets with purpose in

382

his every stride. Then he made a sharp left, opening the door to a small, narrow hallway between a Korean barbecue restaurant and a bubble tea shop. The Talons were right on his heels, though Xavier and Stephanie had visible trouble squeezing their broad shoulders through the narrow doorway. There were elevators to their left.

"Give me the fountainheads and wait down here for me," Julius ordered, staring at Gina and Louis, who were hauling the dog and rooster fountainheads over their shoulders. "I won't be long." He thought he spotted the twins exchanging a fast, unreadable look before they nodded at him, but perhaps he was being paranoid and it had been nothing at all, a figment of his overactive imagination.

Before Julius could move, Xavier placed a hand on his shoulder.

"Yes?" The word came out more harshly than Julius had intended.

Xavier winced a little, but he didn't back away. "Evangeline was very upset with you."

Julius tensed. Bold of Xavier, to bring up possibly the rawest topic of the moment. The other Talons didn't say a word, but they had stopped whatever they were doing to focus on Julius, as though waiting on pins and needles to hear what he had to say next. Julius chose his next words carefully, speaking around the lump of sadness and remorse that had welled in his throat. "My sister doesn't know what's good for her. She's too . . . idealistic. She's learned a painful lesson, and she'll be stronger for it." He enunciated each word and gave Xavier a hard look, until the poor Talon was forced to avert his gaze. The others avoided Julius's eyes, too. It was clear enough now that the topic of Evangeline was off-limits. He had hurt her, even if it was for her own good, even if it was what needed to be done. Julius did not wish his thoughts to linger on Evangeline any longer than was necessary.

Julius wondered if his Talons could sense his newfound paranoia, his tentativeness in openly trusting them as he had before he'd faked his own death. When he had approached them in secret to let them know he was alive and how he planned to intercept Evangeline's crew to carry out his *own* agenda, he'd anticipated pushback from even his most loyal followers. After all, everyone had been under the impression that if the lost zodiac fountainheads were ever found, they'd be used to restore the Circle of Twelve and break the curse. To instead sell the precious treasures to the Collector would appear to be blasphemy. Yet Julius must have done a better job of instilling loyalty in his followers than he'd realized, because none of them questioned his orders; they'd seemed too preoccupied with relief that he was alive. Xavier had even shed a tear.

With a fountainhead under each arm, Julius hopped into the nearest elevator and used the rooster's beak to press the button for the fifth floor. A short-haired, muscular woman entered the elevator as the doors closed—the only other person in the elevator. Odd. Julius hadn't noticed her nearby. If she found it a strange sight, Julius hauling two long-lost historical artifacts under his arms, she said nothing, staring straight ahead at the closing elevator doors with empty eyes. Stranger still—the woman didn't press any buttons on the elevator, which meant she was going to the same floor as Julius.

This, Julius realized after a beat too long, was another one of the Collector's underlings. A shaman, most likely.

"Hello," he greeted the woman as the rickety old elevator rumbled to a start and slowly crept upward. They were already trapped here together for the short ride up to the Collector; he might as well be polite, awkward as the situation was.

The woman didn't respond, but she shifted away from him ever so slightly. Julius glanced at the elevator wall behind her and nearly dropped the fountainheads from shock.

Her shadow was not that of a woman. It stretched out, much taller and wider than she was, and unless his eyes were playing tricks on him, those were *claws* rather than fingers. The claws of a Wrathling.

Julius flicked his eyes away and back over to the woman. She had shifted again, and now her shadow was too distorted to appear to be anything at all. Had that merely been a trick of the light? The Descendants had always been able to sniff out Wrathlings, and Wrathlings had always been too unintelligent to be able to disguise themselves or move around independently otherwise; though Julius had long suspected the Wrathlings would rise again, there was nothing to indicate that such a thing was already happening—no reports of inexplicably violent murders in the city, no attacks against the Descendants.

Julius shook his head. He *had* grown paranoid, he decided. Perhaps it was an inevitable consequence of leading the Descendants for over a century.

Finally the elevator came to a stop, and the doors opened to reveal a carpeted hallway. The woman stepped out first, and Julius followed.

This floor was glamoured so that mortal eyes would see only an empty office filled with cubicles that clearly hadn't been touched in a while. Julius, of course, could see the floor for what it was—the home of the shadowy lord of the Underground.

The Collector was a huge, hulking figure swathed in darkness. In all of his numerous interactions with the being throughout the centuries, Julius had never seen more of his face than shadows from the black top hat he wore. In fact, Julius had long suspected that the Collector didn't *have* a face, that his body was constructed from the shadows themselves.

The woman had taken her place between the Collector's two bodyguards. She stared right past Julius, as though he weren't even there.

"It took you long enough to return to me, Si." The Collector's voice was a low rumble that might have been the rumblings of Earth's ancient surface itself. As he spoke, a cool draft blew in through the opened window in the back of the dimly lit office. "I was beginning to suspect you'd failed."

"I never fail," said Julius.

"Don't speak so boldly, boy." Only a being as powerful and old as the Collector would dare to refer to Julius as *boy*. "I only see two fountainheads in your hands. Where are the other three?"

Calmly, Julius set the dog and rooster fountainheads on the desk. They thudded down on the wooden surface. "The job isn't finished yet.

I wanted to bring these two fountainheads to you for the time being. I'll soon have the other three fountainheads, too."

For a long moment, the Collector didn't respond, but the air in the room grew steadily colder. Julius shivered, and a bone-deep chill settled in him that had nothing to do with the draft.

"I asked you to bring me the five missing fountainheads." Somehow, the Collector's words were even icier than the air around them. "I did not ask for two installments of two and three."

Julius was not stupid, so he said nothing. He had hoped for the best, but now there was nothing he could say to stave off the Collector's fury. And it was true that even if he'd partially succeeded, he had failed to complete the mission the way he'd promised.

For the third time in his very long life, Julius thought he was looking Death right in the shadowy face. And for the briefest of moments, for the first time, he questioned whether he'd really made the right choice in aligning himself with the Collector—in turning his back on his sister and everything they had once stood for. He told himself that he *had* made the right choice, for he couldn't even consider the alternative. He was doing what was best for the Descendants' future—and a future in which they returned to mortal life, without even the consistent threat of Wrathlings to give them purpose, could never be satisfactory. Julius simply wouldn't accept such a fate.

"How many Talons does a dragon need?" the Collector asked, his voice so calm he might have been asking a playful riddle.

The Talons. No. If Julius had still had a beating heart, it would have stopped.

The Collector's question seemed to be a rhetorical one, because he didn't give Julius any time to respond before continuing. "Six is too many . . . five is an uneven number . . . four is unlucky, but three is yet another uneven number . . ." As he spoke, he counted on his fingers.

Julius waited on tenterhooks for the Collector to finish. He thought he was going to be sick.

"Three," the Collector said at last. "I'll leave you with three, as a suitable reminder of your shortcomings. Three for each of the zodiac fountainheads that have yet to make their way to my collection." The Collector spoke softly, and Julius thought he might be taking pleasure in this. "I'll even let you pick which ones to keep. So, what will it be, Si? Which of your precious Talons get to live? Don't dally and make me lose my patience. Who knows what I might do at that point?"

Julius's mouth went dry. "I . . . ," he rasped. He'd broken his own protocol by showing weakness to the Collector, but he couldn't help it. Against the cruelty of the Collector's punishment, he could no longer keep his tough exterior from cracking.

"I'll give you sixty seconds. If you don't choose by then, I'll take them all from you." The Collector laughed softly.

Julius squeezed his eyes shut, and his vision swam with the faces of his six loyal Talons. Evelyn. Gina. Louis. Megan. Xavier. Stephanie. Decades ago, they had sworn vows to Julius, to the Longs. When Kenny and James had turned traitor, before Julius had even notified them that he was still alive, these six had remained true to his memory. He had trained them at the start, had watched them grow through the decades, had come to consider them as close as family.

And now he needed to choose which three to send to their untimely ends. They were to die for *his* shortcomings. Oh, what a cruel world they lived in—a world that danced to the Collector's tune. Having served as the head of the Descendants for over a century, Julius was used to making impossible decisions. This one ranked up there with the toughest of them.

Julius fluttered his eyes open, his decision made. A leader needed to be able to make difficult decisions on a moment's notice. Julius had always abided by this belief, had instilled it in Evangeline, so he could not question his strength as a leader at the crucial moment, even if it tore him apart inside.

"Leave Gina, Louis, and Xavier." Julius spoke calmly and clearly, and he let no tremors enter his body or voice. "Leave the girl, Alice, too. She's not a Talon. She's our insurance for receiving the three other zodiac fountainheads."

"Very well. Bo. Yun. Jing." The Collector raised a shadowy arm, and the three silent figures at his sides moved toward the door.

"My Talons will put up a good fight," Julius warned. He did not turn toward the guards or give any indication that he'd noticed them. He wanted to at least pretend for a few more moments that all was right, that all six of his Talons were safe and sound.

"*My* underlings will not have any trouble," said the Collector. There was nothing but pure conviction in his voice, and Julius was forced to believe him. "Do not think for a moment that just because I have been lenient with you this time, Si, I will give you another opportunity to fail me in the future. This is your final chance. See to it that the job is finished soon." The very air seemed to crackle with tension at the barely concealed threat in the Collector's voice.

Lenient. Julius hardly considered the murder of three of his Talons to be lenient, but then, the Collector could have taken his and all his Talons' heads for failing to complete the mission. Julius swallowed his grief and pride. He never let anyone see him emotional or weak, and he would not start now. "I understand."

After a few excruciating minutes of silence, the door swung open. Bo, Yun, and Jing returned from their task, perfectly expressionless, as though they had done nothing more notable than going for a stroll. Julius had not heard any noises downstairs—no screaming, no fighting. Nothing to indicate that there was any sort of struggle. Either these floors were completely soundproof, or the deaths of the three unlucky Talons had been quick and painless. He hoped it was the latter. He made a note to say a prayer for each fallen Talon later that evening.

"You'll do well to satisfy me, Julius Long, while betraying the hopes of your people." The Collector's grin, just barely visible in the shadows that swathed his head, stretched to an ominous degree. It was the first time he had referred to Julius by his full name, and Julius sincerely hoped it would be the last. "Oh, you Descendants are an interesting breed indeed . . ."

When Julius turned on his heel and left the office, the Collector's soft laughter followed him long after the elevator doors had closed.

ACKNOWLEDGMENTS

In 2018, I read a *GQ* article titled "The Great Chinese Art Heist," by Alex W. Palmer, about the mysterious disappearances of Chinese art from Western museums. Though Palmer offered speculations about who was behind these daring acts, the truth was that the thieves hadn't been caught. They'd targeted art that primarily British and French soldiers had pilfered from the Old Summer Palace after the Second Opium War; Chinese billionaires then bought up these long-lost art pieces in a grand gesture of patriotism.

After reading this fascinating article, I was overcome with the familiar whole-body tingle of excitement that has preceded every significant piece I've written—the feeling that this intriguing incident would make an outstanding novel, that I could already grasp the shape of the story in my hands. Thus, I began to outline what I hoped would become an epic tale of loss, grief, pride, vengeance, and ancient magic. Six years later, after much reimagining and rewriting, *Zodiac Rising* now sits in your hands.

A million thanks to my incredible agent, Penny Moore, for finding the best publishing home for my books and for keeping up with all the stories I want to tell!

Thank you so much to my brilliant editor, Tricia Lin, for being the perfect partner for the Descendants of the Zodiac series. From our first call about this project, I knew you saw the heart of this story and understood what I set out to do. Your ingenuity helped bring my vision to life! This is without a doubt my most ambitious undertaking to date, and I'm thrilled to have worked on it with you.

Many thanks to all at Random House Children's Books for championing *Zodiac Rising*. To Caroline Abbey, Mallory Loehr, Liz Dresner, Casey Moses, Jen Valero, Barbara Bakowski, Rebecca Vitkus, Tim Terhune, Joey Ho, Kris Kam, Shannon Pender, Katie Halata, Stephania Villar, I offer my eternal gratitude for your enthusiasm and hard work!

I've been blessed with fantastic illustrations for *Zodiac Rising*. Thank you to Deb JJ Lee for the magnificent cover, and thank you to Cathy Kwan for the stunning character portraits.

Thank you to the entire writing community and all the friends I've made within it for always rooting me on. This is my ninth published novel—I can hardly believe it. Special thanks to Aly Eatherly and Eunice Kim for being the earliest readers of *Zodiac Rising*, even before my agent got to see it. Thank you so much to Amélie Wen Zhao, Rebecca Mix, and Francesca Flores for reading and offering such generous blurbs—and for your warm friendship over the years!

Thank you to my friends outside the publishing world for all the wonderful adventures we've had around New York City that helped me craft the vibrant setting of this story. I hope that my love for this chaotic city shines through in these pages and that I've done it justice.

Thank you to my family, in the States and across the ocean.

Last but not least, huge thanks to my readers, both new and returning. I hope to tell many more stories for you in the years to come.